# CALL to ARMS

# THE PALMETTO TRILOGY

CALL TO ARMS

WAR DRUMS

WITH HONOR

# CALL *to* ARMS

# LIVIA HALLAM

*with* JAMES REASONER

CUMBERLAND HOUSE
NASHVILLE, TENNESSEE

CALL TO ARMS
PUBLISHED BY CUMBERLAND HOUSE PUBLISHING, INC.
431 Harding Industrial Drive
Nashville, Tennessee 37211

Cover design by Gore Studio, Inc., Nashville, Tennessee

**Library of Congress Cataloging-in-Publication Data**

Reasoner, J. L.
   Call to arms / Livia Hallam with James Reasoner.
      p.   cm. — (Palmetto trilogy ; bk. 1)
   ISBN-13: 978-1-58182-479-7 (hardcover : alk. paper)
   ISBN-10: 1-58182-479-3 (hardcover : alk. paper)
   1. South Carolina—History—Civil War, 1861–1865—Fiction. I. Title.
PS3618.E25C35 2005
  813'.6—dc22                                                2005022388

Printed in the United States of America

1 2 3 4 5 6 7 8 9 10—10 09 08 07 06 05

*This book is dedicated to the memory of*

MARION REASONER

(1916–2004)

*with the wish that he was still around to read it.*

# CALL *to* ARMS

# PROLOGUE

# The *Star of the West*

JANUARY 9, 1861

THE NIGHT WAS COLD, the rifle on his shoulder was heavy, and the sand of the beach dragged at his feet. Allard Tyler's eyelids drooped as fog wrapped its damp fingers around him. Dawn was not far off. Allard wanted to sit down and go to sleep instead of marching guard duty up and down this beach on Morris Island, facing the main channel that led into Charleston Harbor.

He gave a jaw-cracking yawn. He knew he should have been excited. Rumors abounded in Charleston that the Yankees were going to try to reinforce their meager garrison on Fort Sumter. A Yankee ship was sitting out there on the dark waters at this very moment, Allard told himself, just waiting for the chance to run into the harbor and deliver guns, supplies, and reinforcements to the beleaguered Federals holed up on the man-made island. War fever was in the air.

But that didn't make Allard any less weary. Excitement could prop someone up for only so long.

Footsteps crunched in the sand nearby. That would be Robert Gilmore, fellow sentry, fellow cadet at the Citadel, and best friend. Allard wasn't surprised when he heard Robert's voice ask quietly, "Any signs of trouble?"

"Not a one," Allard replied as he paused. He and Robert weren't supposed to stop walking their assigned sections of the beach, but Allard didn't think it would hurt anything to take a short break.

Robert turned to gaze at the channel. "The *Star of the West* is out there," he said. "I can feel it."

Allard yawned again. "All *I* feel is tired."

The past eight days had been arduous ones for the young men. On New Year's Day, in the Year of Our Lord 1861, Allard, Robert, and nearly fifty other cadets from the Citadel, the South Carolina military academy in Charleston, had boarded a steamer and been transported out here to the sandy, low-lying island. They had brought four cannon with them, 24-pounder siege guns that now pointed out at the channel. Over the next few days, in a cold and miserable winter rain, the cadets had dug out the emplacements, leveled the guns with planks, and filled sandbags to pile up in front of them, adding to the natural protection given to the guns by the island's dunes. They had carried out these duties under the command of Maj. Peter Stevens, the superintendent of the Citadel, and Lt. Nathaniel W. Armstrong, who taught mathematics and military engineering at the military academy.

Allard had to admit that Lieutenant Armstrong had chosen a good site for the battery. The channel passed directly to the east of this long stretch of sandy beach. If the *Star of the West* tried to reach Fort Sumter, it would have to pass right in front of the South Carolina guns.

Maybe the Yankees would turn back, Allard mused as he and Robert swung around and resumed their pacing, this time going away from each other. After all, what was the point? Secession was already a fact. South Carolina had withdrawn from the Union weeks earlier, before Christmas. Surely the Yankees would see that they couldn't—

"Allard! Allard, look out yonder!" Excitement gave the shout a twang that came from Robert's country upbringing.

At the sound of his friend's voice, Allard turned quickly and saw a rocket arching into the sky, casting a red glow against the pale gray of approaching dawn. The flare left a trail of sparks as it rose higher and higher. Before the first rocket reached its apogee, another followed, then another and another. The red glare lit up the channel.

"That's the *General Clinch* firing those rockets!" Allard called as he ran down the beach to join Robert. His rifle was clutched in his hands and held in front of him now, rather than being canted casually over his shoulder. The *General Clinch* was a steamer tasked with the job of patrolling the channel every night, in case the Yankees tried to sneak in.

Robert pointed. "What's that behind it?"

The *General Clinch* was steaming up the channel in a hurry, her crew launching flares as she came. But another ship was behind her, becoming visible now as the fog thinned and the heavens lightened and the rockets burst overhead.

Allard let out a whoop. "The *Star of the West!* It's got to be!"

The crew of the *General Clinch* wouldn't be setting off those alarm flares if the vessel in its wake was friendly. Everybody in Charleston knew about the *Star of the West.* Its mission was one of the worst-kept secrets in the country. An unarmed merchant vessel, it had been chosen by the lame-duck president, James Buchanan, to carry aid to the Federals on Fort Sumter. Buchanan had counted on the ship's merchant status to protect it, even though it was on a military mission.

He was about to find out how wrong he had been.

Allard and Robert whirled around and dashed up the beach toward the gun battery, shouting, "Sergeant of the Guard! Sergeant of the Guard!" as they bounded through the sand. Another sentry joined them, adding his voice to the warning.

The sergeant of the guard was also a Citadel cadet, although a year senior to Allard and Robert. He met them near the guns and demanded a report. The sentries gasped out their news, but Sergeant Smith could see the flares for himself now.

"I'll let the major know," he said, and he loped off toward the abandoned hospital that served as living quarters for the troops on Morris Island.

Robert said, "I'm going to Gun Number One. We'll have the first shot at those Yankee scoundrels."

"I'm with you," Allard said. They hurried to the southernmost of the cannon in hopes that, once they were there, the major wouldn't assign them elsewhere when he arrived on the scene.

In a matter of moments the battery was thronged with cadets and officers as the "long roll" was sounded by the drummers. Major Stevens strode up to Gun Number One; he was trailed by several cadets who would serve as this position's gunnery crew.

Allard and Robert snapped to attention and saluted. Stevens returned the salute, but it was obvious that he was focused on the situation and not necessarily who stood before him.

"They're really trying to come in," he muttered. "I thought even Yankees would have more sense than that."

As the major barked orders, the gunners—including Allard and Robert—prepared the 24-pounder for firing. Stevens sighted in the gun then hastened to the other three emplacements to carry out that chore for them.

The *General Clinch* had passed but still continued to fire flares. The *Star of the West* was only a short distance south of the battery now. Allard looked across the water and saw that the sun was about to edge up over the horizon. Once the vestiges of the fog had burned off, it would be a clear, cool, beautiful day, quite unlike the dreary overcast that had made recent conditions miserable.

A breeze sprang up, and a flapping sound made Allard glance around. A red flag, emblazoned with a silhouette of a palmetto tree, had been run up the flagpole just behind the battery. Allard recalled the ceremony nine days earlier when the ladies of the Vincent family had presented the flag to Major Stevens. The family owned most of Morris Island, and the ladies were proud that the new government of the sovereign nation of South Carolina had chosen this spot to make a stand against the damned meddling Northerners.

The flag had unfurled in the off-shore breeze and now hung there flapping gently. The flag of his homeland, Allard thought, and a tightness filled his chest. The weariness he had felt earlier was gone. He wasn't the least bit sleepy now.

"Steady, lads," Major Stevens urged as he stood once again behind Gun Number One, his hands clasped behind his back, his eyes fixed on the channel. "We'll fire a volley across her bow, and if she doesn't turn back, then what happens next will be on the head of her commander."

Allard's breath seemed to stick in his throat. He looked at Robert and saw the same sort of tense anticipation on his friend's face. This was a momentous occasion, and they were fortunate to be part of it.

Allard wished he held the lanyard attached to the gun's friction trigger, but that duty had fallen to Cadet Tuck Haynsworth. It was enough, he told himself, just to be here, to witness history and to play a role in it, however small.

Stevens climbed the parapet beside the guns so that he could see better. After a moment, he announced, "Commence firing." The command was issued in a firm, level tone. The major didn't shout or impart any histrionics to the order.

Haynsworth tugged the lanyard. The cannon's roar filled the early morning air as the gun rocked back on its carriage. The sound was deafening, or at least it would have been if Allard and the other cadets had not placed bits of cotton in their ears to muffle the blast. They all leaned forward and saw the splash as the heavy ball went into the water in front of the *Star of the West.*

"We just fired on a Federal ship," Robert said in a hushed voice. "What have we done?"

"Fired the first shot in a war, that's what we've done," Allard said as he reached over to slap his friend on the back. "A short, victorious war!"

Guns Number Three and Four belched fire and smoke and thunder. The shot from Number Two actually struck the Union vessel, but the third shot fell harmlessly into the water like the first one, producing a foamy geyser.

"She isn't slowing down, Major!" a cadet called up to Stevens.

"I can see that," the major answered. He hesitated only a heartbeat. "Fire into her, at will."

Allard, Robert, and the rest of the gunners were already swabbing down the cannon barrel and preparing to load another round. Their movements were swift and sure, the result of long hours of practice.

Within moments, the gun was ready to fire again. Tuck Haynsworth yanked the lanyard and sent another ball whistling toward the Federal steamer cutting steadily through the water.

A booming like the sound of distant thunder began to be heard, even through the cotton in the cadets' ears. The batteries at Fort Moultrie, on Sullivan's Island across the channel, were joining in the fight. Clouds of smoke rolled over the water. Allard thought the *Star of the West* was struck several times, but it was difficult to be sure.

"Has that captain lost his mind?" he muttered to himself. "He has to know he can't make it through."

Just then, the small flag that the Yankee ship had been flying was hauled down. Allard caught his breath. Was the captain surrendering?

A larger flag, the brilliant red, white, and blue of the Stars and Stripes, went up the mast of the *Star of the West* in a show of defiance. Allard didn't know whether to be angry or excited. He believed in the Southern cause with his whole heart, but the blood of generations of seagoing men flowed in his veins, and he couldn't help but thrill to the audacity of the ship's commander.

The battery at Cummings Point, at the very tip of Morris Island, joined in the bombardment, too. The *Star of the West* was now taking fire from three directions as it steamed closer and closer to Fort Sumter, the grim gray rock that sat squarely in the entrance to Charleston Harbor.

Robert gripped Allard's arm. "The Yankees have batteries on Sumter," he shouted over the roaring of the guns. "Why aren't they trying to lay down a covering fire?"

Allard had to shake his head. He could only guess why the Yankee commander in the fort, a major named Anderson, wasn't taking a hand in this fight. So far, all the firing had gone one direction, toward the *Star of the West*. If the guns at Fort Sumter opened up in a return of hostilities, this truly would be a war . . .

And it suddenly looked as if that might be about to happen. Major Stevens trained his field glasses on the fort and called, "Everyone down! They've run out one of their guns!"

The cadets manning the battery and the others who had rushed up to watch all dropped to the ground behind the dunes and the heaped-up sandbags, trusting to the barrier to stop any Federal projectiles that might come their way. But after a few minutes in which nothing happened, Stevens ordered them up and back to work. The Yankees weren't going to fight back; that was becoming more obvious by the minute. Allard nodded to himself in satisfaction. Everybody knew the Yankees weren't much when it came to fighting, certainly nothing like Southerners. Everyone in South Carolina had been saying as much for months, if not years.

Robert let out a whoop. "They're turning back!"

It was true. The *Star of the West* had begun to come about. The vessel had suffered numerous hits, but no great damage had been done so far. It was only a matter of time, though, until something worse occurred. Since Fort Sumter was crouched there with its guns mute, like a hulking but defenseless giant, the captain of the ship must have decided that being stubborn was just going to get him killed and his ship sunk.

The enthusiastic fire from the batteries did not cease as the vessel turned and began to retrace its course down the channel. The steamer was struck several more times, but the shots did only minor damage.

The sun was fully up now, casting a reddish gold light over the water, so the cadets on Morris Island saw it plainly when the colors were hauled down on the *Star of the West*. They shouted, threw their caps in the air, and pounded each other on the back.

"Runnin' off like a whipped dog with its tail between its legs!" Robert exulted. He grabbed Allard's hand and pumped it in congratulations. "We gave 'em what for, didn't we? They'll know better'n to come down here and thumb their noses at us again!"

A triumphant grin stretched across Allard's face. His father and the other fire-eaters had been right. The Yankees wouldn't fight. They didn't have the guts for it. With any luck, this morning's action was not only the first shot of the war but the last as well, and the painful separation process begun weeks earlier would finally be over . . .

# PART ONE

And then and thus is the
beginning of the end.

—*Rufus Choate*

# CHAPTER ONE

# Holiday

### DECEMBER 20, 1860

THE SCENT OF THE Christmas tree in the parlor filled Allard Tyler's nostrils as he paused on the stairs and took a deep breath. The smell of the pine mixed with the spicy aromas drifting through the house from the kitchen made a wonderful blend. Allard was glad he had been able to come home for the holiday.

Of course, he hadn't had very far to go. The imposing brick edifice that housed the Citadel was on Marion Square, less than two miles from the home of Malachi Tyler, Allard's father. Despite that proximity, Allard lived at the Citadel with the other cadets while classes were in session.

Footsteps sounded on the stairs behind Allard. "What's wrong?" a voice asked.

Allard turned to see his friend Robert Gilmore coming down the stairs.

"Why are you just standing there?" Robert continued.

"Smell that," Allard said.

"What?"

"Christmas."

"I smell . . ." Robert paused and sniffed the air. "The tree in the parlor . . . apple pie . . . and is that roast goose?"

"It is indeed," Allard said with a laugh. He clapped a hand on

19

Robert's shoulder. "Like I said, the smell of Christmas. Isn't it wonderful? Aren't you glad you decided to spend the holiday here?"

"Certainly," Robert said with a faint smile. "There's nowhere else I'd rather be."

The two young men were an oddly mismatched pair. Allard was tall and slender with thick brown hair that often threatened to fall over his eyes. Robert stood several inches shorter than his friend and had a stocky, muscular build. His sandy hair was tightly curled and cut fairly short to his well-formed head. His eyes were alert and possessed a certain mocking humor, while Allard's expression was more guileless, full of the wonder and joy of youth.

They were almost exactly the same age. Less than a week separated their birthdays in October. They had just turned eighteen this year.

"Is that pie I smell? Coming through! Coming through! Get out of the way, you sluggards!"

Allard and Robert stepped apart so that Robert's younger brother could come down the stairs between them. Allard had invited Robert to spend the holidays with him and his family, since the Gilmores lived a good distance from Charleston, and that meant he had been forced to invite Cam as well. Michael Campbell Gilmore was sixteen and a student at the Arsenal, the military academy in Columbia, the state capital, which served as a preparatory school for the Citadel.

Despite being younger than Allard and Robert, Cam was bigger than either of them, tall and broad-shouldered, with a ready grin and sparkling blue eyes. His enthusiasm always reminded Allard of an overgrown puppy.

Allard reached out to grasp the sleeve of Cam's coat and stop him as the younger boy went past. "Wait a minute," he challenged. "Where are you going?"

"I smell pie," Cam answered, as if that were all the explanation necessary.

"Yes, and we'll be having it after dinner, along with plenty of secessionist talk."

"Why eat pie when you can eat fire instead?" Robert asked dryly.

Malachi Tyler certainly fit the description of a fire-eater. He had inherited a small fortune from his father and turned it into a large one by building one of Charleston's finest shipyards. Vessels that came from the Tyler yards sailed the waters of the seven seas, and their quality was known all over the world.

These days, however, much of Malachi's time was devoted to the secessionist movement. He was a delegate to the convention called by the South Carolina General Assembly for the purpose of passing a secession ordinance. Several days earlier he had gone up to Columbia on the train for the first meeting of the convention, which had turned out to be brief. There was a chance that smallpox was going around in the capital city, so the convention adjourned and the delegates traveled to Charleston to reconvene. There had been a parade on the Citadel Green to welcome them, a parade in which Allard and Robert had taken part as their last duty before being dismissed for the Christmas holiday.

Earlier this very day, the secession ordinance had passed with a roar of thunderous approval from the assembled delegates. Malachi had returned home to give the portentous news to his wife Katherine, his daughter Lucinda, and his son Allard. After dinner he would be returning to Institute Hall for the official signing of the document that would sever ties between South Carolina and the United States forever.

In the meantime there was dinner to get through, and Allard wasn't going to let Cam Gilmore ruin it by bulling his way into the kitchen and gobbling down the pie. There would be other guests for dinner, a get-together in honor of the season that had been planned before anyone knew it would coincide with the dissolution of the Union.

That thought reminded Allard of Diana Pinckston, and his mind began to stray—as it always did when he thought of Diana.

She was a tall girl, but not what one would call willowy. When Diana and Allard were friends as children, it had always been Diana who was taller, bigger, and stronger, who could run faster, wrestle better, and climb trees with a skill equal to or better than that of any boy in Charleston. Her long hair was like flame, and so was her spirit.

As the years had passed, of course, some things had changed. Allard had caught up to Diana in height then surpassed her, although she still didn't have to look up much to meet his eyes. And she had turned from a coltish tomboy into a lovely young woman, a process so subtle and gradual that one day when Allard looked at her, it had come as a shock to him just how beautiful she was.

He saw her often around the Citadel because her father, Stafford Pinckston, was a professor of mathematics and artillery at the academy. Major Pinckston had been Allard's instructor in several classes, and the Tylers and Pinckstons were friends as well, having lived near each other for many years. The Pinckstons were an old, distinguished Charleston family, and if the times had taken a financial toll on them, so that they now lived in genteel poverty in the big old house down the street from the Tyler mansion, everyone was too gracious to mention such a delicate subject.

Stafford Pinckston, his wife Tamara, and their daughter Diana would be at the Tylers' tonight for dinner, along with Everett and Pamela Lockhart and their daughter Jacqueline. The Lockharts were old friends of the family as well and owned a plantation outside of Charleston. They had a second house in the city, where they were spending the holiday since Everett Lockhart, like Malachi Tyler, was a delegate to the secession convention.

Allard looked forward to the evening, not only because he would have a chance to spend time with Diana again, but because he was sure there would be a great deal of political talk among his father, Major Pinckston, and Everett Lockhart. With everything that was going on, how could anyone fail to be interested in such a discussion?

"When are the Lockharts going to get here?" Cam asked as the three young men trooped down the stairs.

"I don't know," Allard replied. "Sometime soon, I suspect."

Cam lowered his voice to a conspiratorial tone. "I believe Jacqueline is smitten with me."

"Don't be an idiot," Robert told him. "She's only laid eyes on you once or twice. You've been up in Columbia at the Arsenal all through the fall."

"I know that." A grin spread across Cam's handsome face. "But how many times does a girl have to see me to fall in love with me?"

Robert muttered something and smacked his brother on the arm with a clenched fist. Cam glared and rubbed the spot but instantly forgot his pain as they entered the parlor. His face lit up again as he greeted Allard's sister. "Hello, Lucinda."

Lucinda was two years older than Cam and looked up from her needlework as she sat in a wing chair beside the fireplace. "Oh," she said coolly. "Hello, Campbell."

"Call me Cam," he told her as he walked over to stand beside her chair.

It was Allard's turn to feel frustrated and impatient with Cam again. Cam followed Lucinda around the house every chance he got, flirting with her. Obviously, he was quite taken with her. Allard supposed she was attractive, with her thick blonde hair and fine figure. Since she was his sister, he never really thought of her in that way. Cam certainly did, though.

But then Cam had a habit of flirting with almost every woman he met, at least the young and attractive ones. And he was utterly convinced that they were equally interested in him.

The problem was that some of them were. Robert had confided to Allard more than once his fear that Cam wouldn't make it through his year at the Arsenal and graduate to the Citadel. Robert worried that his brother would be suspended for gambling—or that some jealous husband or suitor would catch him at just the wrong moment, before he could slip away.

Cam continued talking to Lucinda, who remained politely disinterested. Allard and Robert went on through the parlor and the dining room to the kitchen at the rear of the house, drawn by the aromas. They found Allard's mother there, supervising the cook and the housemaids. Katherine Tyler was a short, middle-aged woman with graying blonde hair. In her face could be seen the remnants of the beauty she had passed on to her daughter.

"Hello, Allard . . . Robert," she greeted them. "What are you boys doing here?"

"Protecting the pie from Cam," Robert said as his brother followed them into the kitchen, evidently tired of being rebuffed by Lucinda.

"Oh, goodness, let the boy have some pie if he wants some." Katherine laughed. "I've never yet seen a growing boy whose appetite could be ruined by a piece of pie. Ellie, get Cam some pie."

"Yes'm," one of the housemaids murmured. She was a young woman with smooth brown skin who had belonged to the Tyler family all her life. About the same age as Allard, they had been friends as children, although neither had ever forgotten the distinction between master and slave. Allard looked away as Ellie cut and placed a slice of apple pie on a plate and served it to Cam Gilmore.

Ellie was pretty enough, especially with a bright red kerchief tied over her hair. More than once Malachi had hinted to Allard that he ought to take Ellie to his bed. "Time you made a man out of yourself," his father had been known to growl around a cigar when he and Allard were alone. "High time. And I reckon that wench can do it for you. She's got good strong legs and a fine bosom. Give you a nice bouncy ride, I'd wager."

Allard supposed that was true enough. The problem was that he had no interest in bedding Ellie. It seemed to him that something like that should be based more on love and respect than on sheer animal lust or a need to "make a man" out of himself.

That was a foolishly romantic concept, of course. But there was nothing he could do about the way he felt. When love entered his mind, he thought of Diana . . . It was a pity she had no idea he felt that way about her.

"This is good, Mrs. Tyler," Cam enthused as he ate the pie. "I'm obliged."

"You're most certainly welcome, Campbell. You boys really should run along now, though, and don't get underfoot here in the kitchen. Why don't you go back out to the parlor and keep Lucinda company?"

"Sure, we can do that." Cam handed the empty plate to Ellie. "Thank you."

She looked a little surprised but bobbed her head in acknowledgment of what he had said. The Gilmores didn't own any slaves, so Cam wasn't in the habit of expecting orders to be carried out and tasks to be performed without any word of thanks to those who did the work.

The three young men left the kitchen and returned to the parlor. Lucinda was still there, but she had put her needlework aside. Most of the time she acted as if Cam's attention annoyed her, but occasionally she returned his flirtations. Now, even though only a few minutes had passed, her mood seemed to have changed. She smiled and said, "Hello again, boys. Cam, if there's dancing tonight after dinner, you'll dance with me, won't you?"

Cam's face lit up in a grin. "Of course I will! It would be my honor, Lucinda."

Robert said, "What about me, Lucinda? Don't you want to dance with me, too?"

Lucinda's smile went away, and she said with ill grace, "I suppose I'll dance with you, Robert."

Allard looked away so Lucinda wouldn't see his grin. He knew perfectly well that his sister and his best friend despised each other, despite any show of politeness they might make. Nothing had ever happened to cause that, as far as Allard knew. It was just a natural antipathy that had sprung up as soon as the two of them had been introduced. Allard supposed he should have been bothered by it, but to tell the truth, he didn't like his sister very much, either. He considered Lucinda to be vain and shallow and usually no better than she had to be.

Putting his left hand on Robert's shoulder and his right on Cam's, Allard suggested, "Let's go outside. The guests will be arriving soon, and we can greet them. Besides, I could use a breath of air."

Cam looked back over his shoulder as Allard steered him toward the front door of the Tyler mansion. "I'll see you later, Lucinda," he called. She smiled brightly at him for a second then glared at Robert.

The three young men stepped outside, under the porte cochere that overhung the drive. It was only late afternoon, but at this time of year the sun set early and it would not be long until nightfall. The lamps on either side of the entranceway were lit, and so were several lanterns that hung in the trees, giving the place a festive look. A groom in black livery stood ready to take care of the horses when visitors arrived.

"The Pinckstons and the Lockharts should be here soon, Parnell," Allard said to the groom, who was short and sturdily built.

"I 'spect they will be, Marse Allard." Parnell hesitated then asked, "Marse Allard, is it true what I been hearin'? The convention done passed that secession ord'nance?"

Allard nodded. "That's right. South Carolina is a sovereign state and, well, a nation of her own now, I suppose. Or at least it will be as soon as the ordinance is signed later tonight."

Parnell frowned and said, "Don't seem fittin' somehow. Carolina been part o' the Union for so many years, and now it just ups an' leaves."

"It wasn't a rash decision," Allard replied, a little irritated by Parnell's evident disapproval. "My God, all we've asked is that the Federal government stay out of things that aren't any of its business. If they can't do that, then it's their own fault we've decided to withdraw from the Union."

"Yes sir, I reckon so. Didn't mean no offense."

Allard shook his head. "Oh, none taken. Don't worry, Parnell. I'm not angry with you." The clatter of wheels on the flagstone-paved drive caught his attention. "Here comes someone now."

Allard stepped forward, a smile once again on his face. He was ready to greet the guests—and he hoped one of them was Diana Pinckston. He hadn't seen her for several days, and it seemed like forever . . .

# CHAPTER TWO

# Guests for Dinner

THE AIR ON THIS December day was chilly, but no chillier than the atmosphere inside the carriage that held Diana Pinckston and her parents.

Diana sat next to her sleek, well-groomed mother, well aware of the angry glances that Tamara Pinckston was giving her husband Stafford. They had argued before leaving the house, but the brief trip had passed in silence since setting out for the Tyler mansion. Diana's parents didn't believe in fighting in front of her—as if she didn't know perfectly well how they felt about each other. She wasn't deaf or blind, after all, and she was seventeen years old, practically a full-grown woman. She was old enough to be married herself.

But who was she going to marry? Allard Tyler? He would never get up the gumption to reveal his true feelings for her, feelings that Diana had been aware of for several years. She liked Allard, she truly did—she might even love him—but he could be the most frustrating boy at times . . .

Stafford Pinckston reached inside his coat and slid a cheroot from his pocket. He was dressed in a sober civilian suit tonight rather than the military uniform he wore while instructing his classes at the Citadel. As he took out a small knife to trim the end, Tamara said, "You're not going to smoke that in here, are you?"

"I thought I would, yes," Stafford said.

"We'll be at the Tylers in a matter of moments. Besides, it's too stuffy in here already to add a cloud of cigar smoke to the air."

Stafford sighed and said, "As you please, my dear." He put the knife and the cheroot away.

"You don't have to take that tone," Tamara said. "It wasn't an unreasonable request."

"Not at all," Stafford said. The tightness of his jaw revealed his anger and resentment, however, despite his apparent cooperation.

Diana looked out the carriage window, her gloved hands clenched together in her lap. Sometimes she wished the two of them would just scream at each other and be done with it. The constant tension in the air between them was enough to drive a person mad. The worst part was that, except for rare occasions, she couldn't remember when her parents had not felt that way about each other.

Tamara Rutherford had had expensive tastes as a young woman. By the time she had married Stafford, the Pinckston family fortune had dwindled to the point that there wasn't much left except the big house. Stafford made enough from his teaching position to support his wife and daughter in a comfortable fashion, but being merely comfortable had never been enough to satisfy Tamara. As Diana had grown older, she had seen that for herself.

Not that her father didn't come in for his share of the blame for the troubles between them. He was an emotionally distant man, caught up in his work, devoted to the study of mathematics. If he had been more willing to see to it that Tamara was happy in other ways, she might not have minded having less money than she thought was proper. Stafford couldn't be bothered to make that effort, however.

Diana wished they hadn't accepted the Tylers' dinner invitation. Seeing how the truly well-to-do lived would just infuriate Tamara that much more, and then she would feel ignored when her husband and Malachi Tyler and Everett Lockhart would spend the entire evening discussing the political situation. There was a lot to discuss, of course, what with the convention passing the ordinance of secession earlier in the day. Tyler and Lockhart were delegates, and of course Diana's father was interested in the situation because of his position at the Citadel. He taught classes in the use of artillery as well as mathematics. Diana had to wonder if her father would soon be instructing his students how to aim and fire those cannon at the Yankees.

The carriage turned in at the driveway of the Tyler estate, passing through the open wrought-iron gates. With a clatter of wheels, it went up the drive and came to a stop under the porte cochere. Diana saw Allard waiting there with Robert and Cam Gilmore.

Allard stepped forward to open the door of the carriage. Cam was right behind him, and he wore an eager smile on his face as he reached up and said, "Let me help you, Mrs. Pinckston."

Tamara took his hand and thanked him. Diana was aware that her mother was still a very attractive woman. Cam Gilmore was aware of it, too. But then Cam panted after every attractive woman he encountered. More than once, when Allard and Robert weren't around, Diana had been forced to tell him firmly to keep his hands to himself.

Allard took Diana's hand as she stepped down from the carriage. "You look lovely, Diana," he said in greeting.

She knew that was true. The dark green gown she wore went very well with her red hair and green eyes and fair skin. When she took off her jacket and shawl, the dress left just enough of her throat and the upper part of her bosom bare so as to be intriguing without being scandalous.

"Thank you, Allard," she murmured. "Are the Lockharts here yet?"

"No, you're the first to arrive. But they should be here soon. We'll be having dinner a bit earlier than normal, since Mr. Lockhart and Father have to get back to the hall for the signing of the ordinance."

"Yes, I want to hear all about that," Stafford Pinckston said as he stepped down to the flagstones. "A momentous day, my boy, a momentous day indeed. If I may be so bold, perhaps the most important day in the history of South Carolina. The sovereign and independent nation of South Carolina, I should say."

"Now that you've been so bold as to say it, Stafford," Tamara Pinckston said, "let's get inside and out of this chill."

Oh, they could go inside, all right, Diana thought—but as long as her parents were around, the chill wasn't going to go away.

JACQUELINE LOCKHART debated with herself whether she ought to tell her parents that Robert Gilmore was going to be at the Tyler mansion this evening. She was reasonably sure her father liked Robert, but her mother was in the habit of referring to him as "that penniless hill country boy."

While it was certainly true that Robert was from the hilly inland country, and while he and his brother Cam had been accepted at the Citadel and the Arsenal, respectively, as State Cadets—meaning that, because of their family's financial situation, they didn't have to pay the tuition that regular cadets paid—the Gilmore family wasn't penniless. According to Robert, they had a thriving farm that supported his parents and three younger siblings.

Of course that paled next to Four Winds, the vast plantation owned by Everett Lockhart. Why, just the house in Charleston that the family used when they were in town was probably worth more than the entire Gilmore place.

But Jacqueline didn't care. All that mattered to her was that she was madly in love with Robert Gilmore.

It hadn't always been that way. They had met in the fall, not long after the Citadel term began, at a dance at the Citadel Green on a beautiful evening when the weather was still warm. On the grass where the cadets marched during their training, instead the gray-uniformed young men moved in graceful circles with the young ladies of Charleston in their arms. The band played not military airs but beautiful waltzes. A table with a punch bowl was set up at one end of the Green, and it was there that Jacqueline had first set eyes on Robert Gilmore.

She didn't know his name then, of course. He was just another cadet with close-cropped, curly hair. Perhaps he stood a little shorter than the other young men. He held a glass of punch in one hand and sipped from it occasionally as he watched Jacqueline talking to Diana Pinckston, Rachel Delacroix, and Jane Marie Humboldt. She had been dancing quite a bit and was winded, so the conversation was an opportunity for her to catch her breath.

Finally his intense regard became too much for her to ignore. She excused herself and strolled over to the cadet who had been watching her so avidly. He must really be taken with her, she told herself.

And that was certainly understandable, since she was quite fetching in a low-cut blue gown. Small and slender, with thick dark hair and a heart-shaped face with a tiny mole on it, she knew she was pretty. More than pretty. Plenty of boys had told her as much, and she believed them.

She hadn't danced with this young man yet, at least not that she recalled. Perhaps she would. It would make the evening memorable for him.

"Hello," she said to him. "I noticed you watching me."

He didn't apologize for staring, as she halfway expected him to do. Instead he took a sip of his punch and said, "I find you fascinating."

"Oh?" She couldn't help but smile. "And what's so fascinating about little ol' me?"

"I was wondering if you were ever going to stop talking. I had to ask myself, too, if you were going to faint from lack of air, since you never seemed to pause to take a breath."

Jacqueline's smile faltered a little. She must have heard him incorrectly. "Did . . . did you just say that I talk too much?"

"Too much is a relative term and implies a value judgment. Practically speaking, however, on a strictly factual basis, I think you talk more than any other human being I've ever encountered."

"Oh . . . you . . . how dare . . . oh!" As it soaked in on her just how insulting he had been, she couldn't do anything but sputter in indignation, and that just made her angrier. She thought about slapping him. Yes, that was exactly what he deserved.

Allard Tyler appeared at the shoulder of the horribly insolent young man. "Jacqueline!" he said. "I see you've met Robert."

She took a deep breath and regained control of her surging emotions. "Yes, I certainly have," she said coolly. "And it was a very enlightening experience."

Robert raised one eyebrow quizzically. "How so?" he asked.

"I didn't think one human being could possibly be so rude. Now I know I was wrong."

Allard opened and closed his mouth and looked shocked. Not Robert. His eyes flashed, but not with anger. Jacqueline would have sworn it was amusement she saw shining there.

"Robert Gilmore," he said, holding out his hand. "At your service."

She took his hand, and he surprised her by bending over and kissing the back of hers.

"I'm . . . not quite sure what's going on here," Allard said as Robert straightened and let go of Jacqueline's hand. "But just in case you haven't been properly introduced . . . Robert, this is Miss Jacqueline Lockhart. Jacqueline, allow me to present my new friend, Cadet Robert Gilmore."

"How do you do?" Jacqueline said stiffly. She wasn't yet ready to forgive Robert Gilmore for his insufferable behavior. He wasn't very handsome, either. That would have made her more inclined to forgiveness. Attractive people deserved more chances than ugly ones.

There was something about him, though, something that made her not want to look away from him . . .

Now, of course, now that she was in love with him, she thought Robert Gilmore was just about the handsomest man on the face of the earth. He had to be. Otherwise she wouldn't be interested in him.

The carriage was almost at the Tylers' house. If Jacqueline was going to tell her parents about Robert, it would have to be soon.

"I'm so looking forward to this," she said.

"Yes, it should be a lovely evening," Priscilla Lockhart replied with a smile. She looked at her husband and continued, "Now, try not to spend the entire evening talking politics, Everett."

Jacqueline's father grunted. "What could be more important to talk about? Secession is the biggest thing to happen to South Carolina since . . . well, since forever!"

"I'm sure that's so, dear, but it's almost Christmas. This should be a festive time."

"Oh, it'll be festive, all right," Everett said. "Wait until the ordinance is officially signed and our ties with the Union are forever severed. *Then* you'll see some festivities, I'll warrant."

"That's not what I meant and you know it."

"Christmas is important, my dear; I take nothing away from the birth of our Savior. But this is secession! This will show that gangling backwoodsman Lincoln he can't tell good Southerners what to do!"

Priscilla rolled her eyes and shook her head. "Please don't start talking about Lincoln." Her resigned tone revealed that she considered her request to be a losing battle.

"It's too big not to talk about. Might as well say that if we find an elephant in the Tylers' parlor, we ought not to mention it."

The comment took Jacqueline by surprise and caused her to give an unladylike snort of laughter. "Please, Father!" she said. "Now every time I step into the Tylers' parlor, I'm going to have to look around for the elephant!"

He grinned at her. Jacqueline's mother just rolled her eyes again.

Jacqueline wondered if the Pinckstons were there yet. She liked Diana, although the girl was impossibly tall and more athletic than was proper for a young lady to be. The two of them had been friends for many years. Diana's mother had been a Rutherford before marrying Stafford Pinckston, and the Rutherfords and the Lockharts moved in the same social circles. It was inevitable that the two girls would be thrown together, and the fact that each was an only child, a definite oddity, brought them even closer. Jacqueline had no idea why the Pinckstons hadn't had any more children, and it would have been impolite to ask. In her mother's case, Priscilla Lockhart's health was simply too fragile for her to go through childbirth again—even though she appeared to be as strapping and healthy as a horse.

The carriage turned in at the drive. As the house slave at the reins brought the team to a stop, the Pinckstons' driver was just moving their carriage out from under the porte cochere. The front door of the mansion was open, and Allard was going inside along with Diana, her parents, and Cam Gilmore, Robert's younger brother. Jacqueline had no use for Cam. He was handsome, there was no denying that, but he was a shameless flirt, and Jacqueline suspected that he was none too intelligent. How he had ever been deemed worthy of acceptance into the Arsenal was more than she could fathom.

Robert hung back when he saw the carriage arriving. He was at the door almost before the vehicle had come to a stop. Swinging it open, he said, "Good evening, Mr. and Mrs. Lockhart." He paused for a heartbeat and added, "Hello, Jacqueline."

"Mr. Gilmore," Priscilla Lockhart said as he helped her out. "I wasn't aware that you were going to be joining us this evening. I'm surprised you didn't go home for the holiday."

"Allard was kind enough to invite Cam and me to spend Christmas with him and his family," Robert said. He was always unfailingly polite to Jacqueline's mother—for what little good it did him.

Jacqueline got out next, and she enjoyed the feeling of Robert's hand taking hers as he helped her down. His grip was strong without being overly firm.

Everett Lockhart climbed out of the carriage and seized Robert's hand as soon as he let go of Jacqueline's. As he pumped Robert's hand, Everett said, "Good to see you, Cadet Gilmore. Won't be cadet much longer, though, will it?"

Robert frowned. "Sir? I'm afraid I don't understand."

"Once the war starts, the cadets will be pressed into active service, I'm sure."

"War!" Jacqueline exclaimed. "Who said anything about a war?"

Her father turned to her. "Darling, it's a foregone conclusion. We've challenged the Yankees, defied their unholy will. They say we've no right to leave the Union, so they're bound to try to drag us kicking and screaming back into it. Sooner or later, that's going to mean war." He clapped a hand on Robert's shoulder. "And that means our fine young men from the Citadel will have a glorious opportunity to put all their training to use and take up arms against the enemy!"

All Jacqueline could do was stare at Robert. She could tell from the solemn expression on his face that he had already realized what secession might mean. But although Jacqueline had heard plenty of war talk, she had never put any stock in it. Had certainly never realized that it could mean Robert would have to go and fight and . . . and perhaps die—

She heard him call her name, heard her mother cry out. And then Jacqueline knew nothing else; she fainted dead away.

# CHAPTER THREE

# The Fire-Eaters

"THE YANKEES WILL NEVER go to war," Stafford Pinckston declared confidently. "They don't have the fortitude for it."

"You mean they don't have the—" Everett Lockhart began before his wife silenced him with a warning look. He shrugged and concluded, "I think they'll back down when they realize we're serious. And after today, they can't fail to realize that."

Sipping his wine, Malachi Tyler observed, "One never knows how a Yankee will react. That's what makes them dangerous."

Pinckston shook his head but didn't say anything.

Malachi carved a piece of roast goose, speared it with his fork, and put it in his mouth. He had been friends with Stafford Pinckston for years, but sometimes the man was an unmitigated fool.

Because he was in the shipbuilding business, Tyler had had much more contact with Yankees than either Pinckston or Lockhart. The Yankees had shipyards of their own, of course, and Malachi knew what fine vessels they made. But ships from the Tyler yards were just as good and sometimes better for certain purposes. More than once, men who owned shipping lines up north had come to Charleston because Malachi could supply them with what they needed. Despite having little use personally for Yankees, their money spent just fine, and Malachi never hesitated to take it.

But he knew how canny they were when it came to business, and he had seen how stubborn they could be, too. He had little doubt they would fight if pushed to it, and they might well regard South Carolina's decision today as just the push they needed. At this very moment, there were probably men meeting somewhere north of the Mason-Dixon Line, figuring manufacturing capacity and manpower of the respective sides and trying to decide if the price of a war would be too high. If they decided it wasn't . . .

Still, knowing all that, earlier today Malachi Tyler had voted with the other delegates to secede from the Union. He was a South Carolinian, born and bred. What else could he do?

Besides, there was always the chance that the Northern resolve would wilt when the time came to take up arms.

Malachi sat at the head of the table, of course. It was covered with a tablecloth of Irish linen. The bone china, the silver cutlery, and the crystal glasses all sparkled in the light from several chandeliers. The table itself was the finest mahogany, as were the chairs. The dining room was large, with a high ceiling that made the voices of the diners echo slightly.

Katherine sat at the far end. Tamara Pinckston was at Malachi's right hand, Priscilla Lockhart to his left. The women's husbands sat beside them. Then came the young people, Diana to her father's right, Jacqueline next to her father. Malachi had noticed the way Allard deftly claimed the chair next to Diana. Likewise, Robert Gilmore had positioned himself next to Jacqueline. The final two chairs were filled by Cam Gilmore, who sat beside his brother, and Lucinda, who was across from Cam.

Malachi glanced at Jacqueline. She still appeared a bit pale, but she had recovered quickly and fairly well from her fainting spell. Malachi wasn't sure what had caused her to pass out; all he knew was that there had been a commotion right after the Lockhart carriage arrived, and then Robert had come into the house with Jacqueline in his arms. The way her head lolled on her shoulders showed that she was out cold.

Robert had placed her on a divan in the parlor, where her mother had chafed her wrists and her father had given her a sip of brandy. Those actions had brought her around. Jacqueline was embarrassed by what had happened and apologized profusely, saying she might be coming down with the grippe. Her mother, along with Katherine and Tamara Pinckston, had fussed over her until dinner was served.

Malachi switched his attention to his son. Allard talked and laughed with Diana, who seemed to enjoy his company. Malachi had never quite understood that. Diana was smart and pretty and ought to be able to do better than Allard Tyler. Malachi felt a twinge of guilt at having such a disloyal thought. Allard was his son, after all, his own flesh and blood. He ought to have a higher opinion of him.

Unfortunately, Allard had never done much to warrant such an opinion. The boy was a dreamer; his head was constantly full of romantic notions. Every time Malachi suggested a reasonable, practical course of action to him—such as following in his father's steps at the shipyard—Allard came up with some reason not to follow Malachi's suggestions.

He never should have told the boy about his grandfather, Malachi reflected now with a shake of his head. If Allard had never learned what sort of man Nicholas Tyler was, he might have turned out differently.

"I think there's been quite enough talk of war," Katherine said, breaking into Malachi's reverie. "I agree with Stafford. It will never come to that."

Stafford nodded and said, "Since we entered freely into the Union, we ought to have the right to leave just as freely. There's nothing in the Constitution to say otherwise."

"Here, here," Everett Lockhart said. "We're in agreement on that, anyway, Stafford."

Malachi pushed his plate away slightly and took his watch from his vest pocket. He checked the hour and closed it with a snap. "There's time for brandy and cigars in the library before we have to return to Institute Hall, Everett. Stafford, you'll join us, of course?"

Stafford downed the last of his wine. "Of course."

Tamara spoke up, saying, "Why don't we all go to Institute Hall later? I'm sure there'll be quite a celebration after the signing of the ordinance, and we should be on hand to witness it."

Malachi saw the fleeting grimace that crossed Stafford's face. He suspected that there was trouble between the Pinckstons, but he never gave the matter much thought. It was none of his business. And Tamara's suggestion was a good one. This was a historic occasion. The families *should* all be in attendance to see it for themselves.

"That's what we'll do," Malachi said. He stood up. "Until then, Stafford and Everett and I will be in the library, if anybody needs us."

The three men strolled out of the spacious dining room. Malachi was glad that dinner was over. Sitting down with the families was all right for a while, but now he needed some plain talk, and there was no room for that with youngsters and womenfolk around.

ALLARD WAITED only a few minutes after his father and Major Pinckston and Everett Lockhart left the table before he stood and said, "Robert and Cam and I are going to step outside for a few minutes and get some fresh air."

"Be sure and put on your jackets," Katherine advised. "There's a chill in the air tonight."

"We'll do that, Mother," Allard promised as he led his friends out of the dining room. That left the three women and the three girls at the table.

Allard, Robert, and Cam went out the rear door of the mansion after putting on their jackets. They strolled through the gardens behind the house until they came to a small shed used by the slaves who cared for the grounds. Allard opened the door, led the way into the shed, and scratched a lucifer into life. He held the flame to the wick of a lamp set on a small table. As he lowered the chimney, the yellow glow of the lamp filled the room and revealed the shovels and hoes and clippers hung on the walls, along with several crates and barrels stored in the shed. Two stools sat beside the table, and as Allard and Robert sat down on them, Cam rolled up a keg of nails that he used as a chair.

Allard reached underneath the table and brought out a bottle of brandy. A small, oilcloth-wrapped package was with it. He unrolled the package and revealed three fine, fat Cuban cigars. He handed one each to Robert and Cam and kept one for himself, clenching it between his teeth as he took out another match. A moment later all three of them were puffing way, filling the air in the little shed with clouds of pungent smoke.

"There's nothing like a fine cigar," Robert commented.

"Unless it's a bottle of good brandy," Cam said. "Open it, Allard."

Allard worked the cork out of the neck of the bottle and then lifted it to his mouth, tipping it up and letting the smooth, fiery liquor flow down his throat. The brandy left a line of warmth behind it and kindled glowing embers to life in his belly.

"Hand it over," Cam said impatiently. "We want to drink, too."

Allard put the cigar back in his mouth and clenched his teeth so that it stood up at a jaunty angle. He passed the brandy to Cam.

"You should have given it to me first," Robert said. "There may not be any left when he gets through with it."

Cam took a long slug of the brandy then lowered the bottle and wiped the back of the hand that held his cigar across his mouth. He jerked his head back as he realized he was about to stick the lit end of the cigar into his eye.

Robert took the bottle away from his brother. "Be careful," he said. "You almost put your eye out. How would we explain that?"

"I don't know," Cam said. "We could probably blame it on Allard, though. He's the one who stole his father's brandy and cigars and hid them here."

"Yes, but it was Robert's idea," Allard pointed out.

Robert took a long drink from the bottle then leaned back on the stool and smiled. "It was a good idea, too," he said. "Unless your father realizes what you've done."

Allard shook his head and laughed. "He's never going to miss one bottle of brandy and three cigars. Besides, he's too busy smoking and drinking with Major Pinckston and Mr. Lockhart to care. They have secession to talk about and whether or not it will lead to war."

Robert passed the bottle back to Allard and asked, "What do you think?"

"About what?"

"About the war," Robert said quietly.

"First of all, there isn't going to be any war."

"Not yet."

"Major Pinckston says the Yankees won't fight."

"What if they do?" Cam asked. "Will we have to fight, too?"

Robert puffed on his cigar for a moment then said, "According to Mr. Lockhart, the cadets from the Citadel will be called on."

Allard shook his head. "I'll believe it when I see it."

Cam took the bottle from Allard and downed another slug. "I wouldn't mind fighting the Yankees," he said. "I hear that one of our boys is worth ten of theirs when it comes to fighting, so I figure I ought to be able to kill a bunch of them."

"You're too young," Robert pointed out. "You're still at the Arsenal."

"I'm sixteen! You think the army won't take sixteen-year-olds? Besides, I'm big for my age."

"Give me that." Robert took the bottle from Cam. "That brandy's muddling your brain."

"If it comes down to war," Allard said slowly, "I'll join the navy."

"South Carolina doesn't have a navy," Cam pointed out.

"If there's a war, South Carolina won't be in it alone," Allard responded. "You know there's already been talk about some of the other southern states seceding and forming a confederacy. If that happens, there'll be a Confederate navy, make no mistake of that. You can't win a war without a navy. We proved that against the British in the War of 1812." Allard drew in a lungful of smoke and blew it out, suppressing a slight cough as he did so. "My grandfather proved that."

Robert frowned. "Your grandfather? I don't think I've heard about him."

"Nicholas Tyler," Allard said proudly. "Black Nick Tyler, they called him. He was a privateer."

"Is that anything like a pirate?" Cam asked eagerly.

Allard nodded. "Very much like a pirate, in fact, only Black Nick had a Letter of Marque from the government that made it legal for him to loot and sink British ships. Where do you think the Tyler fortune came from?"

Robert leaned forward and said with a grin, "Wait a minute. You mean the money that built this mansion and your father's shipyard was *pirate loot?*"

Allard laughed. "That's right."

"Why haven't you mentioned this before now?"

"My father doesn't like for me to talk about it," Allard said with a shrug. "He *hates* to talk about it. When I was young and asked about my grandfather, my parents always told me that he was in the shipping business, too. That was true in its way, of course. He was in the business of capturing ships!"

"How did you find out the truth?"

"I came across some old newspapers in a trunk in the attic. There were stories about him, and when I showed them to my father, he finally admitted it. You know how stodgy my father is, though. He didn't want to admit that he sprang from such a black sheep."

"So your grandfather fought the British," Cam mused, "and the time may come when we'll fight the Yankees."

"If it does, we'll beat them," Allard said.

"No doubt about it," Robert said.

And they passed the brandy around to have another drink on it.

THE FEMALE members of the Tyler, Pinckston, and Lockhart families sat in the parlor in awkward silence. Katherine, Tamara, and Priscilla knew their husbands were in the library drinking and smoking, probably telling obscene jokes about the Yankees, and having a fine old time. It seemed patently unfair that men could do such things while women weren't allowed to, but of course that was the way of the world. Fairness had nothing to do with it.

Diana and Jacqueline were thinking about Allard and Robert, respectively. Lucinda's thoughts were a mystery, hidden behind her carefully bland expression.

Katherine finally broke the silence by asking, "Jacqueline, dear, are you feeling better now? You were so pale when Robert brought you in."

"Yes, I'm fine, Mrs. Tyler, thank you," Jacqueline replied without hesitation. "I apologize again for disrupting your dinner."

Katherine waved a hand. "Oh, there's no need for that. We were just concerned about you."

"Well, I'm all right now," Jacqueline said.

That was a lie, of course. In the back of her mind, fear lurked. Fear there would be a war. Fear Robert would have to fight in it. And fear something would happen to him. At the same time, she felt strangely disloyal to be worrying about her personal happiness at a time like this, on such a momentous day in South Carolina's history. She loved her home, and if South Carolina were to secede from the Union, then she supported that with all her heart. If the Yankees—some would say the damned Yankees, but it wasn't proper for a young lady to even think *that* word—were going to be so stubborn about having their own way and dictating to the rest of the country, then they should expect trouble. Now they were going to get it.

Katherine stood and went to a sideboard that had been polished to a high gleam. She picked up a decanter and asked quietly, "Would you ladies like a bit of sherry?"

"The gentlemen are indulging themselves," Tamara said. "I don't see why we shouldn't."

Priscilla looked less convinced, but after a second she nodded. "All right. Why not?"

"What about us?" Lucinda asked. "Do Diana and Jacqueline and I get some sherry, too?"

"Oh, no," Katherine replied. "That wouldn't be proper at all."

"Why not, Mother?" Lucinda insisted. "All three of us are grown women, whether you want to admit it or not."

"Grown women," Katherine repeated with a laugh. "Why, you're just children!"

Lucinda's chin lifted defiantly. "I'm old enough to hate the Yankees like a man. I wish I was in there with Father and Major Pinckston and Mr. Lockhart, talking about how we'll show the bastards what for if they dare to come down here and try to lord it over us!"

"Lucinda!" Katherine looked shocked and scandalized. "What have I told you about using language like that?"

"Well, the Yankees *are* bastards," Lucinda muttered sullenly. "And the sooner we pepper a few Northern backsides with lead, the better."

"Why, Lucinda," Diana said, "you sound like as big a fire-eater as old Mr. Ruffin himself."

"Edmund Ruffin has the right idea," Lucinda said, referring to the Virginia agriculturist who had published numerous articles in the newspapers and illustrated weeklies defending slavery and the policies of the South. "The Southern states must secede and form our own nation. That's the only way we can prevent the Yankees from keeping us under their domination."

"Oh, not more political talk," Katherine said. "Here, you can have some sherry, Lucinda."

She poured the drink in a short, heavy crystal glass and handed it to her daughter. As Lucinda took the sherry and smiled, Diana wondered if that had been Lucinda's real goal all along.

Katherine turned to Tamara and Priscilla. "Is it all right to give your girls some of this, ladies?" she asked as she held up the decanter.

"You might as well," Tamara said. "Lord knows they'll have to learn to drink sooner or later if they're to put up with the insanity of the men in their lives."

Katherine laughed nervously, as if she were unsure whether Tamara was serious or not. Either way, a few minutes later all of the women had drinks in their hands.

Diana sipped her sherry and wished her mother didn't have to be so bitter.

Jacqueline drank hers and prayed there would be no war to take Robert away from her.

Tamara dulled the pain of her disappointment and dissatisfaction.

Priscilla went along because the others were doing it.

Katherine licked her lips and savored the sherry simply because it made her feel so *good*.

Lucinda stole glances at the other women over the rim of her glass, saw the unhappiness on their faces, and smiled to herself.

ALLARD AND the Gilmore brothers were back inside the mansion a short time later, being careful not to get too close to anyone lest the smells of alcohol and tobacco be detected on them.

Not that there was really much danger of that, Allard thought. His father and Major Pinckston and Mr. Lockhart had been smoking and drinking in the library and weren't likely to notice the smells on anyone else, and when Allard heard his mother laughing even more than usual, he knew she had been in the sherry. Chances were, Mrs. Pinckston and Mrs. Lockhart had had a little nip—or two—as well.

He was surprised, though, when Diana came up to him and he smelled sherry on her breath. She seemed a little giddy.

"Aren't you excited about going to Institute Hall for the signing?" she asked as she leaned close to him.

"Of course. I imagine there'll be quite a celebration afterward."

"And we'll be there to see it and take part in it."

"That's right." he summoned up his courage. "Perhaps you'd like to ride with Robert, Cam, and me? We're taking one of the buggies."

"All right," Diana said without hesitation. "What about Jacqueline and Lucinda?"

"Perhaps we can all crowd in."

The men put on their hats and overcoats while the ladies carefully pinned on their hats and bundled themselves into shawls.

Jacqueline said to her mother, "I'd like to ride in the carriage with Robert and Allard."

Priscilla pursed her lips in evident disapproval. "Unchaperoned? I don't think so, Jacqueline."

"Mother . . ." Jacqueline tried to keep the sigh of exasperation out of her voice. "There won't be anything improper going on. Not tonight of all nights. This is a night to celebrate South Carolina's secession."

"The girl's right, my dear," Everett Lockhart put in, having been close enough to overhear the conversation. "Let the young people go together."

"Very well," Priscilla said, but it was clear that she still didn't care very much for the idea.

The Pinckston and Lockhart carriages were brought around. Malachi and Katherine would ride with the Pinckstons. Better them than her, Diana thought.

Allard found the groom. "Parnell, see to hitching up the buggy."

"Yes suh, Marse Allard. Will you be needin' a driver?"

"No, I'll handle the reins myself."

Parnell frowned. "You sure about that, suh?"

"Just do as I told you," Allard snapped.

Parnell hurried to carry out the order and came back a short time later driving the Tyler buggy with its three seats. The open vehicle would be cold on a December night like this, but there were lap robes to keep the occupants from getting too chilled.

The six climbed into the buggy: Allard and Diana in the front seat, Robert and Jacqueline in the second, and Cam and Lucinda in the rear seat. Lucinda was acting uninterested in Cam again, Allard noticed, but that could change in a moment, depending on her whim.

Parnell handed the reins to Allard and said again, "You sure about this, Marse Allard?"

"Just get out of the way," Allard said. Parnell shrugged and stepped aside. Allard muttered, "Insolent darky," as he flapped the reins and got the horse moving. The buggy rolled down the drive toward the street.

To tell the truth, Allard was neither highly skilled nor very experienced at handling a buggy, but he managed without too much trouble as he followed the carriages toward downtown Charleston. The closer they came to Institute Hall, the more crowded the streets were. Allard grew nervous but tried not to let Diana see it. He didn't want her to think badly of him.

Some people in Charleston were already celebrating. Music and loud talk and laughter filled the air, coming from homes and taverns and hotels. Someone set off a rocket, and it arched up over the harbor, spreading its red glare over the water. A festive mood gripped the entire city, but it was also a mood of anticipation. Big things were about to happen.

The press of people and vehicles in the street finally grew too great for the carriages and the buggy to go any farther. They came to a stop and their occupants climbed out.

"My driver will keep an eye on the carriages," Everett Lockhart said.

"So will mine," Stafford Pinckston added.

With the two slaves to watch over things, Allard didn't worry about leaving the buggy there, too. As everyone started walking toward Institute Hall, which was still a couple of blocks away, he offered his arm to Diana and said, "If you'll allow me, it would be my honor."

She smiled at him and slipped her arm through his. "Thank you, kind sir," she said lightly.

Allard saw that Robert had taken Jacqueline's arm, too, but Lucinda was still ignoring Cam. Cam seemed too caught up in all the excitement to really care. He gazed around wide-eyed at the throngs of people in the street. Bunting had already been hung on the balconies of some of the buildings they passed, and flags flew everywhere.

Not the U.S. flag, however. The Stars and Stripes was nowhere to be seen. Instead, many of the flags were homemade and celebrated South Carolina's secession. Most featured the palmetto tree in some shape or fashion. The color, the noise, the press of people, all were overwhelming and added to the sense that this was history in the making.

Destiny was unfolding on this night, and afterward, nothing would ever be the same.

# CHAPTER FOUR

# Celebration

THE GROUP JOINED THE flow of people into Institute Hall. Malachi Tyler and Everett Lockhart kissed their wives then joined the delegates on the floor while Major Pinckston led the others to the already crowded gallery. With the imposing figure of the major in the lead, they were able to make their way close to the front of the gallery, where they sat to watch the ceremony unfolding below.

There were 169 delegates to the convention milling about and talking until Gen. David F. Jamison called them to order by pounding a gavel on a lectern set on the small stage at the front of the hall until the delegates had taken their seats and an expectant hush settled over the hall. In the gallery, the spectators were equally silent and leaned forward in anticipation.

"You gentlemen know why we're here," Jamison began. "We meet tonight to formally sign the Ordinance of Secession prepared by Chairman Inglis's committee and drafted by Chancellor Wardlaw, which was approved by unanimous voice vote earlier today."

Applause and cheering broke out from some of the spectators and quickly spread throughout the gallery and among the delegates. General Jamison let the raucous demonstration run its course for several minutes before gaveling the assembly to silence again.

The general pointed to a table in the front of the hall where Governor Francis W. Pickens and other high officials of the former state of South Carolina were seated. The Ordinance of Secession had been copied neatly onto official parchment and awaited the signatures of the delegates. It lay on the table in front of Pickens and the other officials.

"One by one, gentlemen, approach and affix your signature to this historic document that establishes once and forever the independence of South Carolina from the United States!"

It was a lengthy process as each of the 169 delegates rose, walked to the table, took up a pen, and scrawled his name on the parchment. Despite the time it took to accomplish this, none of the spectators in the gallery seemed bored. They watched in rapt attention as the signing continued.

Allard felt a surge of pride as his father signed the document. In the past father and son had clashed many times over many different things, but Allard still loved his father and was glad that he was getting to witness Malachi help make history. Diana slipped her hand into his and squeezed. That made Allard feel even better. The touch of her smooth, cool fingers sent thrills of sensation through him. She didn't remove her hand when Malachi sat down, either.

Along the row of seats, Jacqueline felt something of the same pride when it was Everett Lockhart's turn to sign the ordinance. That pride was mixed with anxiety, though. The ceremony meant that South Carolina was one step closer to war—and Robert Gilmore was one step closer to risking his life in that war.

When all the delegates had signed the document, Jamison went to the podium and intoned solemnly, "By rule of law and by the signing of this ordinance, South Carolina is now an independent commonwealth. Our beloved homeland shall be known forevermore as the Republic of South Carolina." He quoted from the ordinance. "The previous union between South Carolina and other states under the name of the United States of America is now *dissolved!*"

With that, the gavel came down like an exclamation point, and

thunderous cheering erupted from the throats of everyone in Institute
Hall as they came to their feet.

Allard had never experienced anything like it. Chills ran through
his body and raised goose bumps on his flesh. His chest was tight with
emotion, and his breath seemed lodged in his throat. The fact that
Diana's hand was still clasped in his made the experience even better.

Suddenly, an impulse overtook him and made him turn toward
her. If he was ever to have the courage he needed, it was here and
now, where men had just made a bold stand against the tyranny of the
North. If his father and all the other men who had signed that ordinance could be so bold, then so could he.

He pulled Diana closer to him, put his left arm around her, and
kissed her.

For a second, she stiffened in surprise, and Allard almost pulled
away, ready to let profuse apologies tumble from his lips. But then
Diana seemed to melt in his embrace, and she returned the kiss with a
pressure of her warm, sweet lips that made Allard's heart pound so
hard it seemed to him the beat of his pulse in his ears was even louder
than the wild celebration filling the hall.

They were hardly the only ones giving in to the moment. Robert
and Jacqueline turned to each other and embraced. Robert saw Mrs.
Lockhart's quick frown of disapproval but ignored it as he leaned in to
kiss Jacqueline. She clung to him almost desperately as their lips met.

All over the gallery, husbands and wives were kissing, and lovers,
too. Cam caught hold of Lucinda's hand, but she put her other hand
on his chest to hold him back. Over the tumult, she said, "I'm three
years older than you!"

"I'm big for my age!" Cam replied, also raising his voice. Lucinda
thought it over for a second then shrugged. She allowed Cam to tug
her into his arms and kiss her. Her hand went behind his neck and
pulled his mouth hard against hers. Her tongue darted against his lips.
Shocked, Cam instinctively parted them so that Lucinda was able to
thrust her tongue into his mouth. She knew good and well that her
behavior was shameless and wanton. She didn't care.

He *was* big for his age, after all.

A few feet away, Maj. Stafford Pinckston looked at his wife. Tamara returned his gaze coolly. Stafford hesitated, seeing no sign of encouragement in her eyes, then with a sigh turned away to look down at the floor of the hall again. All the delegates were on their feet, shaking hands and slapping each other on the back and joining in the general celebration. Stafford applauded and whooped with the other spectators.

Allard finally broke his kiss with Diana. They stared into each other's eyes, and despite the crowd and the noise, for a moment it seemed to both of them as if they were the only ones here. The surroundings faded away until nothing was left but each other.

"Allard," Diana whispered, and even though he couldn't hear her speak his name over the uproar, he knew what she said. Everything that had been between them in the past, the old, easy camaraderie, was gone. All had been transformed into a bond even stronger. The moment their lips had met and their bodies had surged in response to the touch, all was different and could never again be as it once was.

Allard kissed her again.

The cheers were dying down a bit. People could shout at the top of their lungs for only so long. Other sounds took the place of the huzzahs, however. The word had spread quickly from the hall. Church bells rang in the night, filling the cold winter air with their joyous yet solemn pealing. Music sprang up as bands took to the streets. Charleston was a musical town. There were plenty of bands, both formal and informal, and the drummers and pipers who marched through the streets had no shortage of followers as impromptu parades formed behind them. Flags waved and bugles blew. More rockets arched into the air over the harbor. Some carried fireworks that burst in brilliantly colorful displays above the city, sending streamers of red and blue and yellow and green sparks cascading down from the heavens. The captains of some of the ships docked at the piers along the waterfront hurried to their vessels and ordered that the ships' whistles be blown. That shrill keening added to what should have been a discordant cacophony, but somehow all the disparate noises blended into a symphony of freedom and defiance and determination.

The Union was no more. South Carolina, free and independent forever!

And above it all the roar of artillery, as the cannons at the Citadel loosed a barrage of smoke and flame and noise, part of the celebration but also a grim reminder of where all this might lead.

No one thought of that, however, and even if they had, they would have dismissed it immediately.

After all, everyone knew the Yankees wouldn't fight.

THE CELEBRATION spread throughout the city and lasted the entire night and into the next day. Few of the delegates left Institute Hall until quite late, and when they finally did leave, many of them went to hastily organized balls being held in some of Charleston's finest hotels. The group that included the Tylers, the Pinckstons, the Lockharts, and Robert and Cam Gilmore found themselves at one of those balls, drinking champagne and dancing into the wee hours.

Allard kept looking for a chance to be alone with Diana, but there were so many joyous people around that it was difficult. Finally, he seized the opportunity to take her into a deserted corner of the lobby, behind a screen of potted palmetto trees. As soon as they were out of sight of the other partygoers, Diana was in his arms and they were kissing again, locked together in an urgent embrace.

When they finally broke the kiss, she rested her head on his shoulder and said, "Allard, darling Allard. I was afraid this night would never come."

"Secession, you mean?" he asked with a slight frown.

She lifted her head and laughed, then stopped short when she saw the expression on his face. "Oh! You're serious. I thought . . ."

"You thought what?" he prodded when she fell silent.

"Nothing," she said with a shake of her head. "Nothing important."

"No, you started to say something," he insisted. "What was it you thought would never happen, if it wasn't secession?"

She regarded him solemnly and said, "I thought I would never find myself in your arms, which is where I wanted to be, where I was meant to be, all along."

"You mean . . . you mean you've felt like this . . . toward me . . . for a while?"

She laughed. "Of course. Didn't you know?"

He shook his head. "No. No, I didn't." He paused, his frown deepening. Then he said, "Did you know that I've been in love with you for years?"

"Yes, I knew." When she saw the look on his face, she hurriedly added, "But I'm a woman. We know these things. We're . . . we're more aware of them than men are."

"But you never said anything . . ."

"I was waiting for you."

Allard struggled to understand. "Then, if I had never found the courage to kiss you tonight, you would have gone on waiting? You would have kept your feelings to yourself and let me pine away for you?"

"I don't know what I would have done, Allard," Diana said, and the slight edge that crept into her voice was evidence that she was becoming a bit upset, too. "Luckily, we don't have to worry about that. What's done is done and our feelings for each other are out in the open, and that's as it should be."

"As it should be," Allard agreed, "but not as it would have been if things were different."

"We don't know that," she argued.

"I think we do."

She stepped back, looking at him in frustration. "You're thinking too much about this. You should just enjoy it. It's a momentous occasion."

"For South Carolina, perhaps. I'm not so sure about us anymore."
He didn't want to have this argument with Diana, but the fact that she
had been aware of his feelings for her and had done nothing about it
made him wonder if she felt as strongly toward him as he did toward
her. Of course, it wasn't really proper for a young lady to be forward in
situations such as that, he reminded himself, but surely she could
have found *some* way to let him know, to give him even the slightest
sign of encouragement . . .

Instead she had been content to go on acting as if she were willing
to remain just friends with him forever, as it had been when they were
children. But they weren't children anymore. They were grown, or so
close to it that it didn't really matter.

She looked at him and said coldly, "If you feel that way, perhaps
you shouldn't have kissed me."

"Perhaps I shouldn't have."

Diana turned away. "We should get back to the ball. I'm sure our
parents have missed us by now."

"Yes, we should." Allard took her hand as they moved from behind the potted palmettos and made their way across the hotel lobby
toward the ballroom.

But even though she didn't pull away from him, somehow it was
no longer the same.

Inside the ballroom, most of the people were dancing. Robert and
Jacqueline swirled around the room in each other's arms, one of many
couples who filled the floor. On several occasions Jacqueline saw her
mother watching them with disapproval plain to see on her face.
Jacqueline couldn't bring herself to be too angry with Priscilla. She
knew that her mother just wanted the best for her, and Priscilla wasn't
convinced that Robert could give it to her.

Neither was Jacqueline, for that matter. She wasn't sure how she
would react to a life as Robert Gilmore's wife, when she would no
longer be able to afford to buy anything and everything she wanted.
When she no longer rode in fancy carriages or dressed in the most expensive gowns from London and Paris or had slaves waiting to carry

out any order she might give them. It would be quite an adjustment for her, she was sure of that. But she was willing to make those changes in her life, as long as she got to spend the rest of it with Robert.

And, of course, she wouldn't be the only one to change. Surely with her encouragement, Robert would become more ambitious. He might not be content to remain a simple farmer. He was intelligent and could do anything he set his mind to. Everett Lockhart owned not only a plantation but also a sawmill and a cotton gin, as well as having financial interests in several other businesses. He could find a place for Robert in one of them; Jacqueline was sure of that. And one day Robert might even run one of those businesses and be a rich man himself.

But all of that depended on him living through the turmoil that many said was bound to come now that South Carolina had withdrawn from the Union.

"You're frowning," Robert said as they paused in their dancing. "What's wrong? Are you feeling faint again?"

"No," she said quickly, "no, not at all. I suppose I'm just a bit winded from all the dancing. Perhaps we should sit out the next number."

He smiled. "That's what you were doing when we first met, remember?"

She summoned up a smile of her own and tilted her chin up. "How could I forget? That was the night you told me I talked too much."

"And you told me that I was the rudest human being on the face of the earth."

"I didn't say that . . . exactly."

Robert chuckled. "Close enough. And you know what? There was some truth to what we both said. The good thing is that now it doesn't matter, not even a bit."

"No," she agreed. "It doesn't."

She leaned against him, closing her eyes and twining her arms around his neck. Robert shifted his feet a little awkwardly since the orchestra wasn't playing at the moment and yet they were still standing there in each other's arms. No one else in the ballroom seemed to give it a second thought, though.

After a moment, Robert said, "Perhaps if you'd like to sit down, I could get you another glass of champagne."

She nodded, and he thought he felt the dampness of tears on his shoulder where her face had been pressed against him. Carefully, he disengaged her arms from around his neck, took her hand, and led her over to the side of the ballroom where chairs were arranged. He almost stopped when he saw Jacqueline's parents sitting there, but he knew how bad that would look, so he pressed on.

"Jacqueline, dear, are you all right?" Priscilla Lockhart asked anxiously as they came up. "You're not feeling—"

"No, I'm not feeling faint again, Mother. I'm just fine."

"You're rather flushed," her father put in. "Maybe you shouldn't have any more champagne. You're not accustomed to it, you know."

Jacqueline nodded. "Yes, I'm sure that's it." She sank into the chair next to her mother then patted the empty seat on her other side. "Sit with us, Robert."

He hesitated then gave a mental shrug and sat down to Jacqueline's right. It was a bit uncomfortable, of course, with her parents there, too, but he supposed he would have to get used to that if he was going to marry her.

Was he? He realized that was the first time he had seriously contemplated the possibility.

Allard and Diana came over and sat down as well, seeming more stiff and formal than they had been with each other earlier. Allard's parents were still dancing. Katherine Tyler's face was much more flushed than Jacqueline's, but in her case it really did come from all the glasses of champagne she'd had during the ball.

To one side of the room, Maj. Stafford Pinckston stood talking to several well-dressed gentlemen, all of them in animated conversation about secession and the Yankees and the possibility of war. Stafford still maintained that the North would never push things that far—but if they did, they would be sorry, because the South Carolinians could teach them a thing or two about fighting. There were brisk nods of agreement all the way around. Stafford turned his head, glanced toward his wife, and saw that Tamara was sitting by herself. Perhaps he should ask her to dance, he thought fleetingly. But he knew what her answer would be, so he turned back to the men and the continuing discussion of that damned ape Lincoln and his abolitionist allies . . .

All the conversation stopped when the band began to play "Dixie."

The people sitting down came to their feet. No one danced now. They stood and held hands, and some men put their arms around their wives or lovers, and in soft voices that grew stronger as the music continued to play, they sang the words of the song that had come to mean so much to so many.

Beside Robert, Jacqueline began to cry again. He told himself she was moved by the strains of the song. He slipped his arm around her shoulders, and she cried harder.

But she was hardly the only one crying this night. Tears shone in Diana Pinckston's eyes, too, as she reached over to grasp Allard's hand. He didn't pull away. His fingers entwined with hers, and the anger that had been between them a short time earlier seemed foolish now. She was right, he told himself. He did think too much, and now that so much was going on in the world, now that historic events surrounded them, the only thing that was important was that they be honest with each other. Allard knew that he didn't want to let what might be between them slip away.

Husbands and wives held each other and thought of what had been. Young lovers held each other and thought of what might be. And they all thought of how everything had changed this night, how the simple act of seceding from the Union had filled the world with great possibilities—and great dangers.

Nobody thought about Cam Gilmore and Lucinda Tyler, because no one was paying attention to the carriage parked down the street

from the hotel. The driver had wandered off to join with the celebrating throngs, so no one saw the carriage sway slightly on its
thoroughbraces. The cheering, the martial music, the pealing of
church bells, the bursting of fireworks overhead all drowned out the
soft cries that came from within the carriage.

Look away, the song said, and Charleston did. Look away at what
had been.

Look away . . . from what was to come.

# PART TWO

If . . . blood they want, blood they shall have.
. . . For, by the God of our fathers, the soil of
South Carolina *shall be free!*

—*editorial in the* Charleston Mercury,
*January 10, 1861*

# CHAPTER FIVE

# Happy New Year

DECEMBER 31, 1860

C HRISTMAS ITSELF WAS OVERSHADOWED by the uproar in both North and South over South Carolina's separation from the Union. Northern politicians damned the decision while those of the South cheered it. President James Buchanan, who still held the White House and would continue to do so until President-Elect Abraham Lincoln took office in March, fretted and dithered about what to do next—indeed, about whether he should do anything at all.

Near Charleston, Maj. Robert Anderson of the U.S. Army was in command of the Federal troops stationed at Fort Moultrie on Sullivan's Island, east of Charleston Harbor and four miles from the city itself. Sullivan's Island and Morris Island, to the south across the channel, formed the mouth of the busy harbor. There were two other lightly manned garrisons, both in the harbor itself: Castle Pinckney on Shute's Folly Island, very close to the city, and three and a half miles farther out, almost centered in the mouth of the harbor, Fort Sumter, an imposing but unfinished brick edifice built on a man-made island. The army had begun construction of Fort Sumter some years earlier but had never completed it.

Fort Moultrie was in poor repair itself, with large gaps in its defenses where the walls had fallen down, and while its cannon could protect it well enough from an attack launched by sea, its rear was wide open. Although technically on an island, the fort could be reached easily by South Carolinian militia troops, who could march along a peninsula right to the post's back door. Fearing that just such a thing might happen, Major Anderson decided that the wise thing to do was to move his command out of Fort Moultrie.

The only place to go was Fort Sumter. Unfinished it might be, but it still offered a chance for a much stronger defense than either Fort Moultrie or Castle Pinckney. So, on the night of December 26, 1860, under cover of darkness and in absolute secrecy, the Federals took to their boats and rowed across the waters of the harbor to Fort Sumter, taking with them their families and as many supplies and munitions as they could. Left behind at Fort Moultrie were the cannon, which had all been spiked and rendered useless. Anderson had also ordered that the gun carriages be burned, so that the South Carolinians would be unable to get any use out of them.

It didn't take long for observers in Charleston to notice that Fort Sumter was suddenly busy with activity. Southern sympathizers in Washington—some might call them spies—soon became aware of Major Anderson's report to Secretary of War John B. Floyd and the details of the maneuver, and they passed this knowledge on to their contacts in the South. By the time a day had gone by, almost everyone in Charleston was aware of what had happened. They knew as well that Governor Pickens's demand that Anderson return to Fort Moultrie had gone unheeded. In the minds of the South Carolinians, Anderson's move was a direct violation of the "gentleman's agreement" between South Carolina and the United States that Fort Sumter was not to be reinforced.

Pickens acted swiftly in response to Anderson's move to Fort Sumter and refusal to return to Fort Moultrie. The next day, South Carolina troops moved into Fort Moultrie and Castle Pinckney. In addition, the Seventeenth South Carolina Militia Regiment, under the command of Col. John Cunningham, took over the federal arsenal in Charleston, capturing more than twenty thousand muskets in the process. Troops also seized control of other federal buildings in the city, including the customhouse and the post office. In a short time, South Carolina took over every bit of federal property in and around Charleston.

With the very notable exception of Fort Sumter itself . . .

IF THE celebration of Christmas had been muted by events, so was the pending arrival of the new year. But inevitably there were still parties to mark the end of 1860 and the beginning of 1861. It wouldn't be New Year's Eve at the Tyler mansion without such a party.

In the week and a half since the night of secession, Allard had seen Diana several times, but they hadn't been alone together. He hoped that would change tonight. Their brief spat was forgotten. He just wanted to dance with her, hold her in his arms, kiss her again. It was one thing to be in the midst of historical events and recognize them as such; it was quite another to be young and in love.

He was in his room, fixing his collar and tying a silk tie around his neck, when a knock sounded on the door. "Come in," he called.

Robert stepped into the room, followed by Cam. They wore their best suits, as they had on the night of the previous celebration. "Are you about ready to go downstairs?" Robert asked.

Allard nodded as he finished with his tie, giving it a little extra flourish. He wanted to look his best tonight, for Diana.

When he turned around he saw the hangdog expression on Cam's face and said, "What's wrong with you?"

Robert laughed. "He doesn't want to go back to Columbia."

Cam would be returning to the capital the next day to resume his classes at the Arsenal the day after that. He said, "I like it here in Charleston. At Columbia, I won't do anything except go to school."

"That's what we'll be doing, too," Allard pointed out.

"Yes, but there won't be any parties in Columbia. And anyway, you won't just go to class. You're going to get to fight the Yankees."

It was true that the cadets at the Citadel were assumed to be part of the local military, and if there was any action in or around Charleston, they might well be part of it. But no one knew yet if there would actually be any fighting. The politicians were still early in the posturing and blustering stage.

"Your turn will come, little brother," Robert said.

Cam shook his head sadly. "I don't think it will. Even if there is a war, it'll be over with so quickly I'll never get a chance to be part of it."

Allard put a hand on the younger man's shoulder. "Just wait and see what happens. You're wasting time and energy worrying about it. Enjoy the night while you can."

Cam's expression brightened a little. He asked, "You didn't swipe some more brandy and cigars, did you?"

"I'm afraid not," Allard said with a shake of his head. It hadn't even occurred to him. He was too caught up in his thoughts of Diana to have considered such a childish thing as stealing brandy and cigars.

Robert put a hand on Cam's other shoulder. "Come on. The guests are starting to arrive, and the band will be playing soon."

The three young men trooped down the stairs together and walked down the hall to the mansion's ballroom. Katherine Tyler had put a great deal of effort into decorating it. It was one of the most opulent, beautiful ballrooms in the city. Crystal chandeliers sparkled and illuminated the polished hardwood floor for dancing, the tables covered with fine linen, and the ornately carved chairs. The walls were covered in velvet, and thick drapes hung over the windows. Malachi Tyler had once said to Allard, "It looks a little like the fanciest whorehouse in the world . . . but if you ever tell your mother I said that, you'll swiftly find my boot against your backside."

Never having been in a whorehouse, Allard was forced to accept his father's comparison at face value. He liked the ballroom, though. Sure, it was fancy, maybe too fancy, but tonight, it was where Diana could be found, and that was enough to make him think it was the finest place in the world.

She wore a light green gown that was all silk and taffeta, and her red hair was pinned up in an elaborate arrangement of curls. A pendant hung from a necklace around her throat, falling intriguingly close to the dark valley between her breasts. Allard's heart leaped when he saw her, and he left Robert and Cam to cross hurriedly to her.

She held out her hands as he came up to her. Allard caught hold of them. "You . . . you look lovely," he said, knowing the words were inadequate but unable to come up with anything else to describe her.

"You're looking rather handsome yourself, young Mr. Tyler," Diana said with a smile.

"We . . . we should dance."

"The, ah, band isn't playing yet," she pointed out.

"Oh." He laughed. "That was foolish of me, wasn't it? I'm just so overcome by your beauty that I must be hearing music in my head."

"You're a terrible flatterer, Allard."

"I'll have to get better at it, then." Still holding her hands, he leaned closer to her and kissed her lightly on the lips. "Happy New Year."

"Happy New Year," she whispered back.

Allard looked around. "Where are your parents?"

Diana's smile faltered. She said, "Father's here somewhere, no doubt talking to your father and the other men about the Yankees in Fort Sumter. It's all the men can talk about. Mother . . . isn't feeling well. She didn't come tonight."

"Oh. I'm sorry to hear that."

"Allard . . ." Diana's expression was serious now. "What *is* going to happen with Fort Sumter? Will there be an attack on it?"

He had to shake his head. "I honestly don't know. I don't see how we can allow the Federals to continue occupying territory that legally belongs to South Carolina, but nobody really wants to start shooting at them, either. Well, I suppose some people do—"

"My father, for one," Diana put in. "He's an artillerist, so he has great faith in bombardments. He says we could reach Sumter with our batteries from several different directions and blast the fort down to bare rock."

"I have no doubt that we could," Allard agreed.

Diana frowned. "But don't some of the soldiers have their families with them? If we bombard the fort we'll be endangering women and children."

"Major Anderson should have thought of that before he put those women and children in harm's way." Allard shrugged. "But I know what you mean. No one wants to go that far unless we have to. But it may come to that, before the Federals finally come to their senses."

The band that had set up at the far end of the ballroom began to play, launching into a waltz.

Allard smiled again at the sound of the music. "Let's forget about forts and war," he went on. "I've been waiting for over a week to dance with you again. Shall we?"

Diana nodded and said, "Yes. Let's forget . . ."

ROBERT'S EYES searched the room for Jacqueline but didn't find her. He sighed. It seemed that the Lockharts hadn't arrived yet, even though there were quite a few guests already on hand. In no mood for his younger brother's inane chatter, he shook Cam off, saying, "Why don't you go pester Lucinda or something?"

"All right," Cam said, stalking off with his back stiff.

For a moment Robert regretted being so short with his brother. Cam would be returning to the Arsenal the next day, and Robert might not see him again for months. But he was more concerned with seeing Jacqueline, and Cam would just have to understand that.

"Champagne, suh?"

The softly voiced question made Robert turn around. He saw one of the Tyler housemaids standing there, holding a tray of drinks. As he reached out and took one of the glasses, he said, "Thank you."

"You're most welcome, suh." Then, in a quieter, more confidential tone, the girl added, "She ain't here yet."

"Who?" Robert asked with a slight frown.

"Miss Jacqueline. You was just lookin' for her, wasn't you, suh?"

"As a matter of fact . . . yes, I was." Robert's eyes narrowed. "How do you know I was looking for Jacqueline?"

"I don't mean no offense," the maid said quickly. "I just sees things, that's all. I seen the way the two o' you look at each other and talk to each other, and I seen the way Miss Jacqueline's mama look when you do, and I know she wouldn't be lookin' like that if she wasn't unhappy that the two o' you be sweethearts."

The words came out of the maid in a rush. Robert chuckled. "You're Ellie, aren't you?"

"That's right, suh."

"Well, Ellie, you're an observant girl. Jacqueline and I *are* sweethearts, and her mother *doesn't* like it, not even a little bit. That puts us in a mighty bad spot, doesn't it?"

Ellie shook her head. "No suh, not really."

"Oh? How do you figure that?" Robert knew perfectly well that as a young Southern gentleman, he shouldn't be standing here having such a serious conversation with a slave, but he didn't particularly care about that.

"Well, suh," Ellie said, "if'n the two o' you really love each other, then it don't matter all that much what Miss Jacqueline's mama thinks. You and Miss Jacqueline got to do what's right for you."

He nodded slowly. "That makes a lot of sense."

"I know it's mighty forward o' me to be sayin' such things, me bein' just a slave an' all—"

"No, no, that's all right," he assured her. "Good advice is good advice, no matter where it comes from."

Ellie's eyes widened. "Are you sayin' I done give you some good advice, Marse Robert?"

"That's exactly what I'm saying. Thank you." Robert sipped the champagne. "For the drink . . . and for the words of wisdom." He looked across at the entrance to the ballroom and saw Jacqueline coming into the room, along with her parents. With a quick smile at Ellie, he said, "Now, if you'll excuse me . . ." and started toward them.

If he had glanced back, he would have seen the young slave looking amazed that not only had he thanked her, but he had also asked her to excuse him.

"Good evening, sir," Robert greeted Everett Lockhart as he shook the older man's hand. He turned to Priscilla Lockhart and went on, "Good evening, Mrs. Lockhart. You look lovely tonight."

The compliment appeared to surprise Priscilla slightly. "Oh. Thank you, Mr. Gilmore."

That left Jacqueline, and she seemed a bit miffed that he had waited to greet her last. "Jacqueline," he said as he took her hand in a formal manner.

"Seen Malachi?" Everett asked.

Robert nodded. "Yes sir, I believe he's talking with Major Pinckston and some of the other gentlemen."

Everett said, "Thanks," and turned to go in that direction, but his wife stopped him.

"You're not going to go off and eat fire all evening without dancing at least one dance with me first," Priscilla said firmly.

Everett smiled and chuckled. "Of course not, my dear. Shall we?"

As they started out onto the dance floor, he glanced back at Robert and winked. Robert wondered if Everett had stage-managed the whole thing so that Priscilla would willingly give him and Jacqueline a few moments alone together. If so, he was grateful.

"Shall we dance, too?" he asked.

"While my mother is busy, you mean?" She laughed lightly, her annoyance of a moment earlier forgotten. "What's the Latin phrase? Carpe diem? Seize the day."

As he drew her into his arms and they began to move around the dance floor, he said, "I didn't know young Southern ladies studied Latin."

"Young Southern ladies probably study a lot of things you don't have any idea about, Robert Gilmore," Jacqueline said coyly.

As they danced, they swept past one of the servants. Robert caught just a glimpse of her, but he recognized Ellie and saw that she was smiling. He gave her the briefest of nods, and then she was gone as the dancers moved on.

"Who did you just nod at?" Jacqueline asked as she settled comfortably into Robert's arms and into the rhythm of the music.

"What? Oh, no one. Just a friend."

And the oddity of referring to a slave as a friend never entered his mind.

CAM GLARED across the room at his brother as Robert talked to Ellie. Robert couldn't be bothered with his own flesh and blood, but he wasn't too good to spend his time gabbing with some darky house slave. God Almighty, he was actually smiling at her and acting almost like she was white!

He sometimes did the same thing, Cam reminded himself. He supposed he believed in slavery; he was a South Carolinian, after all, and the well-being of the state—now the republic—depended on the cotton crop. Couldn't have a cotton crop without having slaves, now could you? Although his family never owned slaves and didn't grow cotton, for that matter, that didn't mean the peculiar institution wasn't vital to the rest of the state.

He didn't spend a lot of time pondering slavery or states' rights or anything else the politicians liked to talk about. But if there was going to be a war, he wanted to fight in it. Wars were full of glory and adventure. Wars turned boys into men. Cam was tired of being a boy.

Of course, there were certain ways in which he was definitely no longer a boy . . .

A soft hand touched his arm, and a voice whispered in his ear, "There you are!"

Cam turned and saw Lucinda standing there, all fair skin and thick blonde hair and deep blue eyes. She wore a dark blue gown that left her shoulders and the swell of her bosom bare. Cam felt excitement course through him at the sight of her.

"I've been looking for you," he lied. He would have gotten around to it, of course—she was never out of his thoughts for very long these days, not since the night the Secession Ordinance had been signed—but he had been too busy brooding about Robert's treatment of him and his pending return to Columbia and the Arsenal. Now that Lucinda was standing right in front of him, looking more beautiful and exciting than ever, the sight of her chased away all of Cam's other concerns.

"I'm going up to my room," she said in a half-whisper. "Wait about five minutes and then slip out of here and come join me."

Cam frowned. "People are liable to notice that I'm gone."

"In this crowd? I don't think so. The men will be too busy damning the Yankees, and the ladies have to gossip and sip sherry and get quietly drunk, like my mother." The bitterness in Lucinda's voice threatened to make her a bit less lovely, but Cam brushed that aside and looked down the top of her dress at her breasts instead.

"All right," he said, "but if Robert gets mad at me, it's not my fault."

"Don't worry about your brother. He's too busy wooing that little simp of a Lockhart girl to care what you do."

She squeezed his arm and turned away. Cam watched the easy grace with which she moved, the hoop skirt swishing across the hardwood floor. His pulse quickened as he thought about the two of them in that carriage that night. He had no idea to whom the carriage belonged; they had picked it at random because no one was around. The owner had no idea what had transpired there. He probably would have been shocked if he had. Lucinda might look like a well-bred young Charleston belle, but she knew things that she had no right to know, things that would have brought a blush to the face of a harbor trollop.

And since that night she had seized every opportunity to demonstrate those things to Cam. They had been together in several different rooms of the mansion, in the garden, in the shed, in the carriage house. It was all so daring and dangerous, and that made it even more exciting. Cam knew good and well that if Malachi Tyler ever caught them at it, there would be hell to pay. A horsewhip would be involved, and quite possibly a shotgun. Cam didn't care. He was intoxicated, drunk with passion and desire. Best of all, his amorous adventures with Lucinda kept him distracted and prevented him from thinking too much about how he would likely be swept aside and ignored when the war with the Yankees started.

As Cam looked around the ballroom, he saw Robert dancing with Jacqueline Lockhart while Allard was dancing with Diana Pinckston. Neither of them was paying the least bit of attention to him. Judging that five minutes had passed, he began to work his way through the crowd toward the double doors of the ballroom. He slipped out and strode determinedly down a hallway to some rear stairs. It took him only a moment to climb those stairs to the second floor of the mansion, toward Lucinda's bedroom.

"Who is it?" she called when he rapped softly on the door.

"Me," Cam replied. His heart was positively thudding in his chest by now.

"Come in."

He grasped the knob, pushed the door open, and closed it quickly behind him. The room was dim, lit by a single lamp on the night table beside the big four-poster bed.

Lucinda was already in that bed, with the covers pulled up to her chin. Her long blonde hair, loosed now from its pins, spread out around her on the pillow under her head. Cam saw that her beautiful gown with its big skirt had been discarded and lay crumpled on the floor, along with a corset and enough assorted lacy underthings to make him hope that she was nude under those covers.

"Take your clothes off," she whispered.

Eagerly, almost frenziedly, Cam reached for his buttons. He began stripping off his garments but got carried away and forgot his boots. As a result, he had to hop awkwardly, half-naked, while he pulled off first one and then the other. After that, though, things went more quickly, and it wasn't long before he finished undressing. The air in the room was a little chilly, but Cam didn't really notice the coolness. His blood was pumping fast enough to keep him warm.

Lucinda smiled and slowly drew the covers back at a tantalizing pace, gradually revealing more and more bare flesh. "Are you ready to come in here?" she asked in a voice throaty with desire. "I think you are."

"I am," Cam agreed fervently. The covers were all the way back now, and Lucinda lay there naked and inviting, her breasts rising and falling quickly. Cam moved to join her, and she pulled the covers over both of them.

After everything they had done together over the past week and a half, Cam would have thought it impossible that she could still surprise him. But she did, and her actions were bold enough and exciting enough that he didn't think about the war or the Yankees for quite a while, not even once.

ALLARD WAS still dancing with Diana when a heavy hand fell on his shoulder. They stopped, and he looked around to see Maj. Stafford Pinckston standing there, a solemn expression on his beefy face.

"Major," Allard said nervously. He wasn't sure why he reacted that way, unless it was because he had been holding Diana's lithe body in his arms all evening and thinking rather ungentlemanly thoughts about her.

"Cadet Tyler," the major replied.

"Are you cutting in? Would you, uh, like to dance with your daughter?"

Pinckston's stern expression was relieved briefly by a fleeting smile. "As appealing as that prospect is, I'm afraid I'm here on a more serious matter."

"Oh? Nothing to do with Diana, then?" Allard wished he could stop babbling, but the words seemed to come out of their own volition.

"No," the major said. "Do you know where Cadet Gilmore is?"

"He's around here somewhere, I'm sure." Allard looked around the ballroom and spotted Robert on the other side of the floor, dancing with Jacqueline. He nodded in that direction and said, "He's right over there."

"Fetch him, would you, and join me in your father's study? I need to talk to both of you lads."

"Of course." Allard hesitated then asked quickly, "Does this have something to do with the Citadel, sir?"

"Indeed," Major Pinckston replied. He looked serious again, so serious that a tingle of trepidation went through Allard.

"I'll be back later," he told Diana. She nodded. He thought she looked a bit worried, too.

Allard made his way across the room toward Robert and Jacqueline. When he tapped his friend on the shoulder, Robert glanced around and said curtly, "No cutting in."

"I'm afraid I have to," Allard said. "Major Pinckston wants to see us in the study."

Robert and Jacqueline stopped dancing, and Robert frowned at Allard. "Do you know what it's about?"

"No idea other than that it has something to do with the Citadel."

Robert nodded and turned back to Jacqueline. "I'm sorry. I have to go see about this."

"I understand," she said, but she looked and sounded disappointed. Allard hated to take Robert away from her, just as he hated to be away from Diana.

That was the way of the world, though. Duty called and men had to answer, leaving their women behind.

The two young men walked side by side from the ballroom and down a hall toward Malachi Tyler's study. "What about Cam?" Robert asked.

Allard shook his head. "The major didn't say anything about him." His forehead creased in a frown. "Where did Cam get off to, anyway? I don't recall seeing him for a while."

"I'm sure he's around somewhere," Robert said. "Probably getting into something. You know what he's like."

Allard nodded. That was certainly true. Despite his size, Cam was like a big kid.

The study door was closed. Allard knocked on it and heard his father say, "Come in."

When they entered the room, they saw that Malachi Tyler was seated at the big desk while Major Pinckston stood in front of it, hands clasped behind his back. Even though the major wasn't in uniform tonight, something about his bearing prompted both Allard and Robert to come to attention and salute.

"At ease," Pinckston growled as he returned the salute. "I'm glad to see that you recognize this is an official conversation we're about to have, cadets."

"Yes sir," Allard said.

"If I may be so bold, sir," Robert said, "what's this about?"

"It's about the Yankees, which I'm sure comes as no surprise to you," Pinckston replied. "Our observers on shore have been keeping a close eye on Fort Sumter through telescopes and field glasses since Major Anderson and his troops holed up there. We've also gotten word from the men who have been delivering fresh meat and vegetables out there every day. The upshot is this: the Yankees are strengthening their fortifications, mounting guns and the like. Simply put, they're getting ready for a fight."

Malachi Tyler took out a cigar and clenched it unlit between his teeth. "That comes as no surprise, Stafford. What does it have to do with these boys?"

"I'm getting there, Malachi," the major said. "You may have heard that we've set up a facility for manufacturing ammunition in the east wing of the Citadel."

"Yes sir," Allard said. "That's going to cut down on the space available for classes and other instruction, isn't it, sir?"

Pinckston waved off the comment. "You cadets are going to be too busy to worry much about such things for a while."

Allard and Robert glanced at each other. Robert said, "We'll be going on duty, sir?"

Pinckston didn't answer the question directly. Instead, he said, "Tonight, Lieutenant Colonel Branch of the First Regiment, Rifles, received orders. He and his men will be going to Morris Island tomorrow to secure it. It's been decided to build and emplace a battery of cannon near the northern end of the island, where it will command fields of fire on both Fort Sumter and the channel leading to it."

Allard and Robert both nodded. It sounded like a good strategic move to both of them.

"Because of their familiarity with such things," Pinckston went on, "a force of Citadel cadets has been selected to build, maintain, and man that battery." His voice softened slightly. "You lads will be part of that force. Because of my longtime friendship with your father, Allard, I requested that I be allowed to deliver the orders to you and Cadet Gilmore."

"Yes sir," Allard said, but to a certain extent, his response was automatic. A part of his brain had gone numb. Even though he had been expecting something of the sort, now that it was here he felt it like a heavy blow. He and Robert and some of their fellow cadets were going to Morris Island to man those big guns, and that could mean only one thing: sooner or later they would be firing them at the Yankees.

"Thank you, sir," Robert said. "We appreciate that."

Allard glanced over at Robert and could tell that his friend was deeply affected by this news, too. "When we will be going, sir?" he asked.

"First thing tomorrow," Pinckston said.

"So enjoy the rest of the night while you have it," Malachi Tyler advised quietly.

Allard and Robert both nodded, and in the moment of silence that followed, they all heard the sudden ringing of church bells all over Charleston. Malachi took out his watch, flipped it open, and grunted.

"Midnight," he said. He snapped the watch closed. "Happy New Year."

Eighteen sixty was over. Eighteen sixty-one had begun.

And two young men, who at this special moment should have been kissing the young women they loved, were instead contemplating war and all it might bring.

# CHAPTER SIX

# Morris Island

### JANUARY 1, 1861

I F IT GOT MUCH colder, the rain pelting down on Charleston would
have bits of sleet mixed in it. As it was, Allard was wet and
chilled and thoroughly miserable as he trudged up a narrow
gangplank onto a steamer with approximately fifty other cadets. Although he wore a slicker, the rain penetrated to his gray wool uniform
and made it unpleasantly damp. It dripped down his collar and off the
bill of his gray campaign cap.

The hour was not long after dawn. With the thick overcast and
the steady drizzle, the rising of the sun had gone almost unnoticed.
An unrelieved gray hung over the city and the harbor. The sky was almost the same color as the water.

"We picked a good day to go to war, didn't we?" Robert muttered
as he, Allard, and the other cadets milled around the steamer's deck.

"We're not at war yet," Allard pointed out.

Robert shook his head. "It's only a matter of time. With all the
abolitionists yelling at him, even a do-nothing like Buchanan is bound
to send troops and supplies to Sumter. If he doesn't, the Northern
newspapers will have his head on a platter."

"Maybe a compromise will be worked out."

"I wouldn't count on it," Robert said glumly.

In the hurry to get a few hours of sleep and get ready for this assignment, they hadn't had much of a chance to talk until now. Quietly, as they leaned on the railing at the edge of the deck and watched the massive cannons being wrestled up the gangplank, Allard asked, "Have you thought much about what it'll be like in battle?"

Robert shot him a sharp glance. "Are you asking me if I'm scared?"

Allard hated to admit it, even to himself, and he wished Robert hadn't been quite so blunt about it. But he decided there was really no point in denying it.

"That's right."

"I'm not scared now, no. Other than being a little worried we may catch our deaths of the grippe in this terrible weather."

"I'm not talking about now," Allard said. "I'm talking about when the shooting starts."

For a long moment Robert didn't reply. Then he said, "I'm scared of dying. What man, other than a complete fool, wouldn't be? But I'm more frightened that I won't behave properly."

"Of course you will," Allard said, a little surprised by his friend's answer. "You're not a coward."

"No, but I'm just a state cadet." Robert's face hardened in the rain. "Just a poor hill boy who can't afford to pay his own way."

"No one at the Citadel thinks of you like that! We all know you're an excellent cadet, whether you pay the same tuition or not."

"I'm not talking so much about the other cadets, or even the instructors, as I am about . . . other people."

"You can't mean Jacqueline," Allard said. "She thinks the world of you. And I know her father likes you—Oh. You mean her mother."

Robert just shrugged silently.

"Don't let her disapproval bother you," Allard said. "In the end, all that matters is how Jacqueline feels about you . . . and how you feel about yourself."

"What about you?"

Allard didn't hesitate. "I'll be proud to fight at your side, Robert. Anywhere, any time, against any foe."

Robert nodded and clapped a hand on his shoulder. "Thanks. I knew that, but it's good to hear it." He paused then asked, "What about you? Are you scared?"

"I'm so scared I'm half out of my mind," Allard said.

The directness of the reply startled a laugh out of Robert. He slapped his friend on the back and said, "I'm definitely staying right next to you, then, because I know that wherever we are, you'll find the safest place."

Allard laughed, too, but that was just the thing of it, he thought. Sooner or later, they would find themselves in a position where no place was safe.

Both young men fell silent. From the wistful expression on Robert's face, Allard guessed that he was thinking about Jacqueline and how they had parted. He *knew* he was thinking about Diana and the moment they had been forced to say good-bye.

It had been after the tolling of the bells had signaled the end of one year and the beginning of the next. When Allard and Robert had returned to the ballroom from their meeting with Major Pinckston in Malachi Tyler's study, they found Diana and Jacqueline talking together, slightly impatient expressions on their beautiful faces.

"What was that about?" Diana asked as she took Allard's hand.

Allard glanced at Robert and then said to her, "Let's find a place where we can talk privately." He knew his friend would want to have a similar conversation with Jacqueline.

Diana's eyes widened, and Allard thought he saw fear there. "You're leaving, aren't you?" she said.

He steered her toward a corner of the room. Now that the band had already played "Auld Lang Syne" at midnight, the musicians had launched into "Good Night, Ladies," indicating that this would be the last dance. Allard wished he could spend the time with Diana in his arms, gently moving across the dance floor, instead of breaking bad news to her. But he had to be honest with her. He wouldn't taint the newfound closeness between them with false pretenses.

When they were alone in the corner of the ballroom, Allard

turned to Diana and said, "Your father just told Robert and me that we're going to Morris Island tomorrow to set up and man some gun batteries there."

"Then the war has started?"

"Not yet. We don't know what will happen. But obviously it's been decided that if the Federals send reinforcements to Fort Sumter, we're going to stop them."

"And that will mean fighting," Diana said.

Allard nodded slowly. "It certainly could."

She took a deep breath. "We knew this was coming." She sounded like she was trying to convince herself. "As stubborn as those Yankees are, we knew there wouldn't be a compromise."

"Not yet anyway," Allard said. "Once they see how determined we are, things may be different."

Diana shook her head. "I don't think so." She moved closer to him, and he instinctively slipped his arms around her. God, she felt good as she leaned against him! "Allard, I wish you didn't have to go."

"You don't think we're doing the right thing by trying to stop the Yankees?"

She lifted her head so that she could look into his eyes. He was reminded again of how close to the same height they were. "I believe in our cause," she said quietly. "I believe that we have the right to govern ourselves, and that we didn't give that up when we joined the Union. But believing in something . . . knowing it's right . . . doesn't mean you want to see someone you . . . love . . . have to go off and fight for it." Her voice choked as she went on, "It doesn't mean . . . you want them to die for it!"

Allard crushed her against him. "I'm not going to die," he whispered in her ear, trying to sound confident. But even as he did so, he had his own doubts and fears. There was no getting around it—he and Robert and the other cadets were going out to shoot at the Yankees.

Sooner or later the Yankees would shoot back.

Diana clutched at him. "Promise me," she said. "Promise me you won't die. I've only just realized how much I love you. I couldn't bear to lose you now."

"I promise." He tried to make his voice light. "You have my word on it as a Southern gentleman, ma'am."

She gave a short, desperate laugh and held on to him that much tighter, as if she intended to never let go . . .

"How did Jacqueline take the news?" Allard asked as he and Robert stood on the steamer's deck in the rain.

"Not well. She's afraid something's going to happen to me. I tried to tell her that it's not going to be that dangerous. I don't think she believed me, though."

"We don't know that it won't be dangerous," Allard pointed out. "For all we know, the whole Federal navy could show up outside the bar and try to steam past Morris Island with all guns blazing."

Robert laughed and shook his head. "The Yankee navy is too scattered for that. It would take months to get all their ships together. If more than a few try to run up the channel, I'll be surprised."

"So you don't think there'll be a fight?"

"Not now." Robert shrugged. "Not yet. As for the future, . . . who knows?"

That was the problem, Allard thought. No one knew what the future held except God—and He wasn't telling.

MAJ. PETER STEVENS, the superintendent of the Citadel, and Lt. Nathaniel W. Armstrong, professor of mathematics and mechanical philosophy, came aboard the steamer a short time later. Major Stevens would command this expedition to Morris Island himself, leaving the supervision of the Citadel to subordinates for the time being. Stopping the Yankees from reinforcing Fort Sumter was a higher priority than running the military academy. Lieutenant Armstrong, who was an expert on such things, would determine where the battery would be situated and see that the big guns were properly emplaced.

Stevens was a dapper man, clean-shaven except for a narrow mustache waxed to a point on each end. Armstrong had a more serious look about him; his eyes were dark and deep-set, and although he sported the same sort of mustache as the major, the addition of a goatee made the facial adornment seem less flamboyant. Both men were very good at their jobs.

With all the cadets on board, along with the four cannon, the steamer's crew threw off the mooring lines, and the vessel chugged into the harbor a couple of hours after the gray dawn. There was little wind; the drizzle came almost straight down. That meant the harbor wasn't very choppy, so Allard was glad of that. Not for himself—he had grown up around boats, had gotten his sea legs at an early age, and had never lost them. He was glad for Robert and some of the other cadets, though, who hadn't spent as much time on the water. They weren't as likely to get sick during the short ride through the harbor and around Cummings Point to the eastern shore of Morris Island.

Despite the calmness of the harbor, Robert looked a little green by the time the steamer rounded the point. "Will we be there soon?" he asked in a tightly controlled voice.

"Yes, it shouldn't be long," Allard told him. "Of course, that depends on where Major Stevens and Lieutenant Armstrong want to go ashore."

To Allard's surprise, after steaming a mile or so down the shoreline, the boat made a wide turn and headed north again. Robert asked, "Aren't we going to land?"

"I thought we would," Allard replied. "Maybe the officers were just scouting out locations. It might be easier to reach by landing on the other side of the island and cutting across."

Robert let out a groan between tightly clenched teeth. "You mean we've got to ride this boat some more?"

"It looks like it," Allard said.

Sure enough, the steamer rounded the point again and turned south, following the shoreline. It put in where a small creek entered the harbor.

Getting the guns ashore here would be much easier than if the cadets had tried to unload them on the other side of the island, Allard saw immediately. Although Morris Island was low and marshy all over, the ground was more solid here than on the channel side, where sand dunes ran almost all the way down to the water. Wrestling the heavy cannons through that sand would have been quite a chore. On the harbor side, they might still have to put down planks for the gun carriages to roll on, but it would be an easier task.

The cadets and the steamer crew set to work. After carrying their gear on shore, the cadets turned to the job of unloading the guns. That took the rest of the morning and on into the afternoon. They didn't stop for lunch, but no one was very hungry. The young men were all too wet and tired to care about that.

Several carriages rolled up, followed by some wagons and mule teams. A group of well-dressed men and women climbed out of the carriages and huddled under umbrellas. Major Stevens went to meet them. He shook hands with the men and, despite the rain, removed his hat and bowed to the ladies. One of the women handed the major an oilcloth-wrapped package.

Stevens turned to the cadets and ordered stentoriously, "Attention!" The cadets snapped to briskly, and the major continued, "The ladies of the Vincent family, the owners of this island, have done us the great honor of presenting us with a special flag that will fly over our fortifications. This flag, with its depiction of the palmetto tree, represents our beloved homeland of South Carolina and everything good and glorious that it stands for! I want you to show your appreciation for the ladies and their magnificent gesture!"

Cheers rang out from the assembled cadets. They were wet and exhausted and miserable, no doubt about that, but the unpleasant conditions were momentarily forgotten as the emotion of the moment swept over them. These cadets came from all over the state, but the bond between them was strong and unbreakable. They were South Carolinians, they were Citadel cadets, they were Southerners. The Yankees—foolish, arrogant Yankees—stood no chance against them.

Allard and Robert cheered along with the other cadets and waved their caps in the air. When the huzzahs finally died down, Major Stevens shook hands again with the visitors, who then climbed back into their carriages and departed. The wagons, driven by Vincent family slaves, remained behind to help carry the troops and supplies across the island to the eastern shore. The mules were hitched to the gun carriages to pull the heavy cannons. Once everything was ready, the small expedition got underway.

There wasn't room for all the cadets on the wagons. Some had to walk, and Allard and Robert were among that number. The muddy ground sucked at their boots as they tramped along, making the march even more of a struggle than it would have been normally. Water stood in puddles on the ground, and inevitably, some of it seeped into even the best footgear, leaving many with damp socks and cold feet.

Thankfully, the path from the steamer landing to the site Lieutenant Armstrong had decided would be used for the battery wasn't a long one. The wagons and the gun carriages clattered across a wooden bridge over a narrow creek, and the cadets on foot followed. On the other side the clumps of marsh grass became even more sparse. Most of the ground was sand now, gently sloping up to the rolling dunes along the eastern shoreline.

Lieutenant Armstrong strode up to the top of one of the dunes and looked back and forth along the beach. Major Stevens joined him, and the two officers had an animated discussion, waving their arms as they worked out where each of the guns would be placed. The major returned to the cadet column, leaving Armstrong alone on the dune, gazing out to sea as if he were searching through the gray mist for the Yankee navy.

"This will be the location of our battery," Stevens explained, pointing to the dune where the lieutenant stood and then gesturing with his hands to indicate a sweep of slightly lower ground that ran northward for a hundred yards or so before rising to the crest of another dune. "The ground between those two dunes will be dug down and leveled, with the sand being placed in sandbags. Then a plank platform will be constructed for each gun, and a rampart of sandbags will be erected between the dunes. It won't be an easy job, especially in weather like this, but I'm confident that you lads will perform in sterling fashion." The major glanced at the sky. "We still have some daylight left, such as it is. Let's get to work."

Cadet sergeants passed out shovels and burlap bags, and the young men were soon busy. Pairing off, one cadet would scoop a shovelful of wet sand and dump it into the open bag being held by the other cadet. The sand was heavy, and shoveling it quickly wore out the cadets, so they switched off frequently. Allard and Robert worked together, as always. Robert was stronger and had more stamina, so he wound up doing more of the shovel work. Allard felt a little guilty about that, but not enough that he insisted on all things being equal.

Once a sandbag was filled, it was tied shut and stacked to the side. They wouldn't be used until all the ground was lowered and leveled for the gun platforms.

By the time dusk began to settle over the island, it appeared to Allard that the cadets had barely started on the job. When he looked at the ground between the dunes, it looked like the shovels had barely touched it. Getting everything ready for the gun emplacements was going to take several days. He hoped the Yankees waited that long before they tried to slip reinforcements past the island.

Not far away was a squatty brick building that Major Stevens explained had once been a hospital for the families on the island. It was abandoned, but the structure was still in good enough repair that it could serve as quarters for the cadets. The sergeant of the guard detailed several cadets to patrol the beach; they would be relieved later. Guards were also posted to keep watch over the cannons. The rest of the cadets put their shovels in one of the wagons, covered them with canvas, picked up their rifles, and marched to the abandoned hospital.

Three small rooms had been set aside as sleeping quarters. Straw had been spread over the floor and then covered with blankets. It wouldn't make for a very comfortable bed, but after a day of shoveling wet sand, these young men were so tired most of them would have no trouble sleeping.

As they trudged in, Robert glanced through an open doorway into another room and stopped short. He reached out to grasp Allard's arm. "Look in there."

Allard stiffened at the sight of several stacks of long, plain wooden boxes. Their shape was unmistakable.

*Coffins.*

Allard made a quick count and saw that there were thirty boxes. With a hollow laugh, he said, "Not enough for all of us."

"More than enough for some," Robert said.

# CHAPTER SEVEN

# Stalemate

L IKE THE CENTER OF a whirlpool, Fort Sumter was the focal point
for a great deal of activity in and around Charleston over the
next few days. And as with a rock tossed into a pond, the rip-
ples from that activity spread far and wide.

On the man-made rock itself, the Federal troops under Anderson's
command continued to strengthen their defenses and clean up the debris left behind by unfinished construction. In Charleston, angry pro-
testers marched in the streets, demanding that the Yankees be ousted
from property that rightfully belonged to the sovereign republic of
South Carolina. In Washington, Gen. Winfield Scott, hero of the Mexican War who had been affectionately dubbed "Old Fuss and Feath-
ers," blustered that the thing to do was to send well-armed warships
to reinforce Fort Sumter. As the head of the army, Scott's words carried
great weight, but not enough to dislodge President James Buchanan
from the fence he so stubbornly straddled. Behind the scenes Governor Pickens sent envoys to the harbor fort to persuade Anderson to
withdraw his men, but the major refused to budge.

Since the outbreak of hostilities seemed likely, if not inevitable,
the South Carolina militia moved to strengthen its presence around
Charleston and the surrounding area. New militia companies sprang
up overnight as men volunteered to protect their homeland from a

possible Federal invasion. The cadets from the Citadel found themselves in the position of being better trained and more experienced in military matters than most of these fledgling soldiers. So despite their youth, the cadets were pressed into service, drilling the new militia companies and instructing them in artillery and tactics. On Sullivan's Island, at Castle Pinckney, and anywhere else the new militiamen were to be found, some Citadel cadets were there, too, trying to turn the rawest recruits into soldiers.

And on Morris Island, Allard Tyler, Robert Gilmore, and their fellow cadets continued to shovel wet sand into canvas bags as rain drizzled down around them and the waves of the channel pounded the beach fifty yards away.

MALACHI TYLER was in his study, frowning down at the papers spread on the desk in front of him, when a soft footstep made him look up. Thomas, the butler, stood in the doorway. The old slave announced in his deep voice, "Suh, you have a visitor."

Malachi had been so engrossed in the reports from the shipyard that he hadn't heard the bell. "Who is it?" he asked.

"Gen'leman name of Hawkins, he says. Say to tell you that Gov-'nor Pickens sent him."

Malachi's eyes widened in surprise. He couldn't guess why the governor would send anyone to see him. "Show Mr. Hawkins in, of course," he told Thomas.

The butler nodded and went out into the hall, returning a moment later with a tall, lean, well-dressed man. The newcomer had no hat or overcoat, so Malachi assumed that Thomas had already taken them. He was on his feet now and stepped around the desk to offer his hand to the visitor.

"I'm Malachi Tyler."

"Willard Hawkins," the man said as the two shook hands. "I'm an assistant to Governor Pickens. It's a pleasure to meet you, sir."

"Likewise." Malachi gestured at the thickly upholstered chair in front of the desk. "Have a seat, Mr. Hawkins. Would you care for a cigar or maybe a snifter of brandy?" Hospitality, as always, came before business—whatever business it was that brought the governor's assistant here.

Hawkins sat down gracefully and waved a casual hand. "Mighty kind of you to offer, sir, but I'll have to decline—for the moment."

Malachi returned to his seat behind the desk. "I see. Down to business, eh?"

"If you would be so kind."

Malachi gestured for Hawkins to go on.

"Simply put," Hawkins said, "I'm here because of your shipyard."

A chill of apprehension went through Malachi. Was the state going to take over the Tyler yards? In times of emergency—and a pending war against the Union certainly qualified—a state might take desperate actions without much regard for the property rights of its citizens.

Hawkins was smiling, but that didn't have to mean anything. *A man may smile and smile, and be a villain . . .* Malachi recalled the line from Shakespeare, although he couldn't have said which play it was from. The visitor crossed his legs, carefully preserving the sharp crease in his trousers, and continued. "I'm told the finest ships in Charleston Harbor come from your yards, Mr. Tyler."

Malachi nodded curtly. "The finest ones built here, that's true enough. There are some very good ships in the harbor that were built in England and elsewhere, though."

"Well, that's what I meant," Hawkins said. "To put it bluntly, you know ships, and we need your expertise. We're thinking of buying several ships and putting them into the service of South Carolina. Governor Pickens thought you could advise us on which of the vessels might be most suitable for our purposes."

Malachi felt a surge of relief. He wasn't going to lose his shipyard. "That's all?"

Hawkins frowned slightly and asked, "Isn't that enough? I assure you, sir, the governor and everyone in his cabinet and on his staff take this matter very seriously. If war comes, South Carolina will have need of a navy."

"You can't win a war without one," Malachi said. "Our navy is what tipped the balance of power in the War of 1812."

That navy had included, unofficially, his own father. With a scowl, Malachi shoved thoughts of Black Nick Tyler out of his head. The man had been a pirate, nothing more or less, and although Malachi was glad that Nicholas Tyler had fought on the right side in that conflict, he couldn't find anything else admirable about the man.

Hawkins seemingly misinterpreted Malachi's expression, because he went on hastily, "I assure you, sir, we're fully cognizant of the importance of naval power. That's why I'm here this evening. What can you tell me about the *General Clinch?*"

"A smart enough ship, I suppose," Malachi said with a shrug. "A steamer . . . I don't know its tonnage, offhand."

"Well maintained and dependable?"

Malachi shrugged. "As far as I know."

"What about the *James Gray?*"

Malachi took a moment. "A steam tug, not very big, propeller-driven. The *General Clinch,* by the way, is a paddle-wheeler."

"Which sort is better suited for use as a warship?"

"Neither of those ships is that well suited for such use," Malachi said without hesitation. If Hawkins wanted answers, he wasn't going to get them sugarcoated. "For war you want metal ships, or at the very least, ships with metal plating. Ironclads, they're called. The British and French have built one or two." He paused as he saw the pained look that appeared on Hawkins's face. The man wasn't interested in a lecture, and Malachi could guess why. "Of course, that doesn't really matter, because you don't have any ships like that available to you. Isn't that correct?"

"Unfortunately, yes, it is," Hawkins answered.

"In that case, you take what you can get. The *General Clinch* and the *James Gray* are both sound vessels. If you have the opportunity to put both of them into South Carolina's service, I'd say that would be a good move."

"Thank you, Mr. Tyler. That's exactly the sort of practical advice I came here seeking."

Over the next few minutes Hawkins questioned Malachi about several other ships that were moored in Charleston Harbor. Malachi was familiar with most of them and was able to tell the official which ones were suitable for state use and which would be better to avoid.

When he was finished asking about specific ships, Hawkins said, "I know from your service as a delegate to the Secession Convention that the republic can count on your support, Mr. Tyler."

"Of course," Malachi said. "Whatever I can do, South Carolina has only to ask."

"I'm glad to hear that." Hawkins smiled, and Malachi felt a touch of uneasiness again. "You'd be willing, then, to devote the efforts of your shipyard to the production of vessels for the navy of South Carolina or some confederacy of Southern states, if one should come about?"

Malachi had heard a great deal of talk over the past few months about just such a confederacy. South Carolinians were proud, no doubt about that, but they were also practical, and they knew that their defiance of the Federal government would be much more likely to succeed if they had allies. If they were forced to go it alone, the odds against them would be very high.

Either way, though, they would need ships. Especially if Virginia, with its shipyards at Norfolk and the Tredegar Iron Works, remained with the Union. Surely that wouldn't happen, but it was impossible to predict the twists of fate. It could be that Charleston would turn out to be the center of whatever naval power the South could muster.

Those thoughts flashed through Malachi's brain, and he hesitated long enough in answering so that a few concerned creases appeared on Hawkins's forehead. Finally, Malachi said, "Of course, I'd be willing to devote my shipyard to the production of naval vessels for South Carolina. For suitable compensation, needless to say."

Hawkins's jaw tightened. "You would place commerce over devotion to your state, sir?"

"Not at all," Malachi snapped back. "If that was the case I could probably make more money by cooperating with the Yankees. But the materials required to build a ship don't pay for themselves, and you can't expect laborers with families to feed to work for free. Patriotism won't fill up a child's belly. All I ask is a fair price. Otherwise I won't be able to get men to work for me, and then those ships won't get built, will they?"

Hawkins shrugged eloquently. "You make a good point, Mr. Tyler. I'll convey your comments to Governor Pickens, and I'm sure an arrangement satisfactory to all parties can be worked out."

Malachi came to his feet, signaling that this meeting was over. He extended his hand. "I appreciate that, Mr. Hawkins. Please give my best wishes to the governor."

Hawkins stood and took Malachi's hand. Malachi came around the desk and walked with his visitor out of the study and down the hall to the front door of the mansion. With the instinct common to all good servants, Thomas seemed to know that Hawkins was leaving and stood ready with the man's hat and coat. Hawkins put them on and then, with a polite nod, said to Malachi, "I bid you good evening, sir."

"And good evening to you, too, Mr. Hawkins."

Malachi stood there until Thomas had closed the door behind Hawkins. The butler said quietly, "That man strike me as bein' mighty slick, Mr. Malachi."

"He's a politician," Malachi said as if that explained everything, and in many ways it did.

"You gon' do business with him?"

"It appears so. With the state, anyway."

"You do, you keep a mighty close eye on your pocketbook, suh."

Malachi laughed. "Oh, I intend to, Thomas, I assure you. I certainly intend to."

THE RAIN let up from time to time but never stopped for very long. Allard had almost forgotten what it was like to be dry. At night, when the cadets trooped back into the old hospital building, they huddled around a cast-iron stove for warmth. But uniforms soaked from a day of working in the rain never dried completely by morning. Some dampness always remained. That caused a constant chill unless one practically hugged the stove. Freeze or burn, burn or freeze . . . it was a common complaint for soldiers.

So was the sand. It crunched underfoot, it worked its way into socks, it grated in one's eyes, it rasped the nose and throat. No matter how hard the cooks tried to keep it out of the food, every meal carried with it a healthy ration of sand. Allard heard one cadet say that he was surprised a stream of sand didn't come out when he relieved himself.

Discomfort was part of being a real soldier, Allard told himself. Like danger and death, it was a soldier's lot.

Still, he thought as he cleared his throat and spat out the grit, he could do with a little less sand, even if it meant having to deal with a little more danger.

The stretch of ground between the two dunes was just about level now, some five feet below the crest of the dunes. Lieutenant Armstrong had driven stakes in the ground and run strings between them to mark the site of each gun platform. Some of the cadets began laying down the planks that would support the guns and prevent the wheels of their carriages from sinking into the sand. While they were doing that, the rest of the cadets finished leveling the ground in front of the platforms and then began stacking the sandbags to take the place of the sand they had shoveled out.

That seemed rather foolish to Allard, trading sand for more sand, but when he stopped and thought about it he could see the reason. The way the sand was packed into the bags, it made a denser, more solid barrier. The bags were stacked in place like bricks in a wall, each level offset by half the length of a bag from the level beneath it. As the fortification began to grow taller, it took on the look of a wall, too.

The gun carriages were brought up and wheeled into position as soon as the platforms were ready. They were to be placed in barbette, meaning that their barrels would extend over the top of the sandbag barrier rather than through embrasures or gunports. The cannons had to be in position so that the cadets would know how high to stack the sandbags.

Allard was sore and tired from the days of hard work, but despite that he felt a thrill as he saw the battery shaping up. His comrades and he had done a good job under harsh conditions.

On the evening of January 5 Allard and Robert spotted two steamers patrolling the mouth of the harbor. Fearing at first they were Yankee vessels, the cadets hurried to find the sergeant of the guard. Sergeant Smith explained, "No, they're ours. I heard about them from Major Stevens. One of them is the *General Clinch;* the other is the *Aid.* That's part of the South Carolina navy you're looking at, boys. They'll be on guard out there in the channel every night in case the Yankees try to slip a ship past us."

As he walked his post later, Allard looked at the ships and wished he was on one of them rather than trudging up and down the desolate beach on sentry duty. The sea had always exerted a powerful influence on him. As far back as he could remember, whenever he stood on shore and looked out at the water, he felt it tugging at him, calling to him like the song of a siren. He supposed that was because he had some of old Black Nick's blood in his veins. Nicholas Tyler had been a seagoing man all his life.

It was strange the way some things seemed to skip a generation. Malachi Tyler built ships and worked with ships—he understood instinctively what made a vessel good—and yet he had none of that desire to spend his days and nights tossed about on the foamy brine or the briny foam, whichever it was. He was content to stay in his shipyard office and never get any closer to the water than that. Allard had had to face that realization a long time ago—his father was a landlubber.

Wagons came out regularly from Charleston with food and other supplies and newspapers. On January 7 the Charleston *Mercury,* owned by the noted fire-eater and secessionist Robert Barnwell Rhett, reported angrily that, on President Buchanan's orders, the merchant vessel *Star of the West* had set out from New York with supplies, ammunition, and reinforcements for Fort Sumter.

Although the Yankees had tried to keep the ship's sailing and its mission secret, that proved to be impossible in gossip-ridden Washington and New York. The *Mercury* reported that Secretary of the Interior Jacob Thompson had resigned from the president's cabinet. It didn't take much deductive skill to realize that Thompson, from Mississippi, must have passed along the news about the *Star of the West,* probably as soon as he resigned, perhaps even before.

No matter what the source, the news was common knowledge, and as Allard listened to the buzzing talk among the cadets, he realized that it also explained why they had heard three cannon blasts earlier that morning from Charleston, the sounds faint with distance. They had been warning shots, alerting all the troops of impending trouble.

"How long will it take that Yankee ship to get here?" Robert asked, knowing that Allard was much more well versed in nautical matters than he.

Allard thought about the question and shrugged. "Three to four days, depending on how bad the weather is."

"They sailed on the fifth," Robert mused. "This is the seventh. That means . . . they'll be here tomorrow or the next day?"

"More than likely," Allard said.

He wasn't sure if he was scared or excited by the prospect of the Yankees trying to force their way into Charleston Harbor. A little of both, probably, he decided. The newspaper hadn't mentioned if the *Star of the West* was armed. As a merchant ship, there was a possibility she didn't carry any guns. Even if she did, there would be only a few cannon. The ship wouldn't be able to put up much of a fight.

It took only one cannonball to kill a man, though. Even if that was the only shot fired, anybody unlucky enough to be hit by it would be just as dead as if he'd been caught in a bombardment.

Allard tried not to think about the fact that the cadets might soon be shooting at the Yankees—and the Yankees might be shooting at them. He occupied his thoughts instead with visions of Diana. That was maddening in a way, because it made him miss her even more. He longed to hold her in his arms again, to press his lips to hers and taste the sweet warmth of her mouth. He had spent so much time being her friend and then falling in love with her, and then circumstances had forced them apart so soon after he had declared his love and found that it was returned. It was unfair . . . but at least it took his mind off the miserable weather and the drudgery and the ever-present lurking fear.

January 8 passed without any further news of the *Star of the West.* The rotation of guard duty found both Allard and Robert pacing along the sandy beach before dawn on January 9. At least the rain had finally stopped, although the air was still damp with a clinging fog. Allard's route brought him close to Robert, and the two young men exchanged a few words before turning to retrace their steps.

Suddenly a red warning rocket arced into the sky from the *General Clinch,* lighting the predawn darkness with its garish glare—and changing everything . . .

# CHAPTER EIGHT

# Homecoming

ALLARD'S OPTIMISTIC MOOD DID not last long after the *Star of the West* was turned back by the cannon fire from Morris Island and Fort Moultrie. The newspapers brought out to the battery the next day were full of fire-eating, smoke-spewing editorials, of course. The citizens of Charleston were justifiably proud of their boys who had sent the Yankees packing. Congratulations on their stand also poured in from other Southern states. Given South Carolina's successful defiance of the Union, it seemed likely that more and more states would secede. That process began on the same day, in fact, as the firing on the *Star of the West*. Mississippi's legislature passed a secession ordinance. The proposed Confederacy was on the verge of becoming a reality.

And yet amid all the celebration in the newspapers and in the streets of Charleston, there were dark hints of more trouble to come. Major Anderson sent a messenger from Fort Sumter to Governor Pickens, protesting in the strongest possible language the firing on the unarmed merchant vessel. Anderson demanded that Pickens disavow the action. Pickens's refusal to do so was curt and unequivocal.

The politicians in Washington were also in full cry over the incident and stirred up war talk just as surely as did their Southern cousins. As Robert and Allard stood behind the wall of sandbags the next day, Robert said, "What do you reckon the Yankees will try next? Or do you still think they've had enough and will give up?"

"I wish that were the case," Allard said, "but I'm afraid it won't be. Mississippi's gone out now, and there's talk that Florida and Alabama will do the same in the next day or two. The Yankees won't just sit by and let state after state secede."

"How are they going to stop it?"

"By striking at us, here where it all began," Allard said gloomily. "I won't be a bit surprised if they try to land troops, maybe right away."

Robert rubbed his chin, where he had started to grow a beard. "Hand-to-hand fighting, eh?"

"It might come to that."

"You know there aren't enough of us out here to stop them if they land a shipload of troops."

Allard nodded. "I know."

There were approximately seventy cadets on Morris Island. If the Yankees launched an invasion, this was the perfect spot for it. And if that happened, the cadets would surely be overrun. Allard worried that he would be killed or taken prisoner, that he might never see Diana again . . .

That was why the news of reinforcements later that day was especially welcome. Some of the cadets who had been on the island since New Year's Day were being relieved and sent back to Charleston. Allard could only hope that his name and Robert's would be among those called when it came time to leave.

As luck would have it several days later, they were. Several dozen cadets, including Allard and Robert, were gathered by Major Stevens, who told them, "Don't think that just because you're going back to Charleston that your part in all this is over, gentlemen. In thanks for your sterling service, you'll be granted two days' leave, but then you'll be returning to your studies at the Citadel."

The cadets were too well drilled to show any outward reaction, but Allard sensed a certain disappointment sweep through the group. Although all of them were pleased with the prospect of a little time off, they weren't as happy with the idea of concentrating on academics again. After all, they had seen the flash and heard the roar of cannon, had smelled the acrid tang of powder burned in an attack on their enemies. It wouldn't be easy to go back to a dull classroom and study in theory the things they had experienced in practice.

Stevens went on, "Not only that, but your service will be required in the training and drilling of the military units now stationed in Charleston." The major smiled. "I don't have to tell you boys that you're now the seasoned veterans that South Carolina is counting on to mold its forces into a real army. It's a large responsibility, but I've assured Governor Pickens that you're up to it."

That brought a cheer from the young men.

Soon after, the departing cadets began their march across Morris Island. They tramped across the bridge spanning the stream that Allard now knew was called Light House Creek. Marching right along with them was a tall, stern-faced man in his sixties who sported long white hair and wore the uniform of the Palmetto Guard, one of the militia companies. He was Edmund Ruffin, the noted Secessionist and firebrand from Virginia who had come to South Carolina after his home state's refusal to secede immediately after South Carolina had done so in December. Ruffin had traveled to Morris Island to visit the cadet battery as a guest of Major Stevens, and now he was returning to Charleston.

Allard and Robert were close enough to hear Ruffin's conversation with the major. The old man's fiery condemnations of the Yankees and his confident predictions of victory for South Carolina and the other Southern states courageous enough to join her in secession were enough to stir the blood of the cadets. They marched with some extra pride and vigor until they reached the inlet where the steamer that would take them back to Charleston was moored.

Only a few replacements were going out to the battery, Allard noted. The complement of cadets on Morris Island was being reduced. Surely, he told himself, that had to be a sign that war was not as imminent as he had thought.

Charleston was still in a festive mood, as if the holiday season had never ended. Christmas and New Year's might be over, but the celebration of secession was still going strong. Bunting hung on the front of most of the buildings in the downtown district, and flags of various colors and designs were displayed at nearly every business and residence in the city. Brass bands blared day and night, and the streets were filled with the tramping of feet as militia units paraded and drilled, sometimes joined impulsively by civilians. Some of the hilarity seemed to Allard to have a note of hysteria in it, and he wondered as Robert and he made their way to the Tyler mansion just how long Charleston could sustain this state of martial enthusiasm.

When Allard tugged on the bell pull, the door of the mansion was opened not by Thomas but rather by the young housemaid Ellie. Her face lit up with a smile when she saw them, and she exclaimed, "Marse Robert! You're back!"

Allard frowned slightly. Why would Ellie greet Robert with such obvious pleasure, when *he* was the son of her owner, not Robert? But then it occurred to him that perhaps that was the reason. Slaves were often resentful of their owners and the owner's family.

At any rate, Ellie turned to him, still smiling, and went on, "It's mighty good to see you, too, Marse Allard. Ever'body done been missin' you."

She stepped back to let them into the house. Thomas came down the hall toward the foyer, his steps slowed by his age, but there was youthful enthusiasm in his voice as he saw who had rung the bell. "Lawsy, it's good to see you two young gen'lemen. We didn't know you was comin' home today. Is you home to stay?"

"For now," Allard said. "We'll be going back to the Citadel in a couple of days, but we'll still be here in Charleston."

"That's wonderful, jus' wonderful. Go on down to the parlor, Marse Allard, and see your mama and your sister. They be in there, I think."

"My father's at the shipyard?" Allard asked.

"Yes suh, I 'spose so. He ain't here. I don't know where else he'd be."

Allard started toward the parlor then stopped to ask Thomas, "Have you seen Miss Pinckston since I've been gone?"

The old man shook his head. "No suh, I ain't. She ain't been over here. I'm sure she's fine, though, else I'd've heard somethin' about it."

Allard nodded and went on down the hall. Behind him, he heard Robert ask, "I don't suppose Miss Lockhart has been around either?"

"No suh, she ain't. I 'spect she an' her folks done gone back out to they plantation."

"Yes, I imagine so," Robert said.

Allard paused again and looked back, motioning to his friend. "Come on, Robert. I'm sure Mother and Lucinda will want to see you, too."

That might not be completely true in Lucinda's case, but it would be in Katherine's. She had come to look on Robert almost like a son.

Robert followed Allard toward the parlor, leaving Thomas and Ellie in the foyer. The old man leaned close to Ellie and hissed, "Girl, you done lost your mind?"

"What are you talkin' 'bout?" she asked defensively.

Thomas jabbed a finger toward the door of the parlor, where the two young men had gone. "I'm talkin' about the way you was lookin' at Marse Robert. You think he's so blind he ain't gonna notice you makin' cow eyes at him?"

"I never done that!"

"The hell you didn't!" Thomas moved even closer, and his voice was little more than a whisper as he went on. "Listen, I seen gals like you get it in they heads that they smitten with some white boy. They get so they forget he's one o' the masters an' she ain't nothin' but a slave. Just a damned ol' darky slave. Think that jus' cause he might smile at her ever' now an' then that he's forgot she's a slave, too. But it ain't never that way. *Not never.*"

"You got it all wrong," Ellie protested. "I . . . I don't feel nothin' like that for Marse Robert. I'se jus' friendly to him 'cause he's nice to me. He smiles at me and he don't order me around, and I reckon there's times when he don't act like he thinks o' me as a slave. But that's just 'cause his family don't own no slaves and he ain't that used to bein' around 'em. I know that. I know it don't mean nothin'.' "

Thomas glowered at her for a long moment before he finally gave her a grudging nod. "You best remember that," he said. "I seen plenty o' gals who thought that if they could get the master to take 'em into his bed ever' now an' then, things'd be a lot better for 'em. But that ain't the way it worked out. It never brought 'em nothin' but grief."

Ellie stared down at the polished hardwood floor, obviously embarrassed and uncomfortable. "I never thought that," she said.

Thomas just snorted, shook his head, and turned to walk off. He hoped Ellie was telling the truth. Marse Robert was a nice enough young fella, but he was still white. Ellie would do well to remember that.

Inside the parlor, Katherine Tyler jumped up from the chair where she had been knitting and rushed forward with a huge smile on her face to throw her arms around her son. "Oh, Allard!" she said with a joyous laugh. "Why didn't you let us know you were coming home?"

"I didn't know myself until today, when they told us to line up and march away from that battery," he explained. "There wasn't any chance to let you know."

"Well, you're here now, and that's all that matters." She gripped his arms and took a step back. "Let me look at you. My lands, are you growing a beard?"

"Not really," Allard said with a grin. "I've just been too busy to shave regularly."

"I'm the one who's growing a beard," Robert put in. "How do you think it looks, Mrs. Tyler?"

"Why, I think it looks wonderful." Katherine gave him a big hug, too. "It's good to see you, Robert." She turned her head toward her daughter. "Lucinda, come say hello to your brother and Robert."

"I can tell them hello from here," Lucinda said without getting up from the divan where she sat, an open book in her lap. Her voice was cool as she went on, "Hello, Allard. Hello, Robert."

"Lucinda." Allard went over and sat down next to her. "Did you miss us?" he asked slyly, knowing full well what her honest answer would be.

"Of course," she lied. "Did you have a good time out there shooting at that Yankee boat?"

"You have to tell us all about it," Katherine said before Allard could reply. "The newspapers have been full of little else except the way our gallant Citadel cadets turned back the *Star of the West*." She still didn't let him speak. Instead she picked a small bell from one of the tables and rang it, at the same time calling, "Thomas! Thomas!"

The butler came in a few moments later, saying, "Yes'm, what can I do for you?"

"Send a messenger to the shipyards right away to inform Master Malachi that his son has returned home."

Allard said quickly, "Mother, you don't have to take Father away from his work—"

"Nonsense! He'd want to know as soon as possible."

Allard shrugged acceptance. To tell the truth, he wanted to talk to his father, although he preferred that the conversation be in private. He'd had a great deal on his mind lately, what with the possibility of war looming over their heads, and he had made some decisions about what he wanted to do in the event that an armed conflict actually broke out. He needed to talk about those things with Malachi.

But that could wait, though. Now he said to Katherine, "Mother, have you seen Diana recently?"

"No, not since New Year's Eve." Her face lit up all over again as an idea occurred to her. "But I'll see to it that she comes to the party." She looked over at Robert. "And Jacqueline Lockhart, too, if it's possible."

"Party?" Allard repeated with a frown. "What party?"

"Why, the one we're going to have to celebrate the fact that you and Robert have returned safely from the war."

"What war?" Robert asked. "It was one ship, and I don't think it even had any guns."

Katherine waved a hand. "Oh, that doesn't matter. What's important is the party!"

If it meant that he'd have a chance to see Diana again, Allard wasn't going to argue with that.

MALACHI TYLER came home early from his office, summoned by the messenger sent by Thomas. When he found Allard he gripped his hand hard then threw his arms around his son and pummeled his back. It was an unusual demonstration of emotion from Malachi, and afterward he seemed a little uncomfortable.

He shook hands with Robert as well. "Good job you lads did out there," he said. "Although I must admit, it pains me a bit to think of someone shooting at a ship, even a Yankee ship."

"They had it coming," Allard said. "They were warned not to reinforce Fort Sumter."

Malachi nodded. "True enough."

"Allard and Robert are going to tell us all about it at dinner," Katherine said.

"That's fine." Malachi leaned toward the two young men and added with a wink, "And afterward, over brandy, you can tell me what *really* happened out there."

Allard hoped his father wasn't going to be disappointed. There weren't any exciting details—or any unexciting details, for that matter—that were not suitable for the dinner table. It had been a simple affair, really. The *Star of the West* had steamed up the channel, taken fire, and turned away. Fairly thrilling at the time, because no one had known what was going to happen. The Yankee ship could have been armed, and the fort's guns could have opened fire and made a real fight of it. But that had not happened, and in hindsight the whole thing was pretty cut-and-dried.

Yet Allard was glad his father wanted to discuss the matter over brandy. That was a sign Malachi was accepting him as a grownup. And that would be a good time as well to discuss his future.

During dinner, Katherine asked dozens of questions about Allard's and Robert's experiences on Morris Island, and the two young men did their best to answer truthfully. Katherine was also bubbling over with plans for the party the next night. It would be a small, informal affair, she said. Only fifty or sixty of Charleston's best people.

Lucinda was quiet, asking only, "Will Cam be coming for this party?"

"Oh, I don't think so, dear," Katherine answered. "He's all the way up in Columbia at the Arsenal. There wouldn't be time to get in touch with him and have him get down here by tomorrow night. Besides, he has his studies."

"Why would you care whether or not Cam was here?" Robert asked.

"I just happened to think of him," Lucinda replied in surly tones. "I don't care whether he's here or not. He's your brother, not mine."

She asked to be excused a short time later and went up to her room. With dinner over, Malachi headed for his study, motioning for Allard and Robert to follow him.

When the door was firmly closed behind them, Malachi went to the sideboard and poured brandy into three glasses. He handed the drinks to Allard and Robert and then lifted his own. "To South Carolina," he said.

"To South Carolina," they echoed as they clinked their glasses against his.

"Now," Malachi said after he had propped a hip on the corner of his desk, "tell me what really happened out there."

"You've pretty much heard all of it already," Allard said.

"Except the part about the whiskey," Robert put in.

Malachi's eyebrows rose toward his mostly bald scalp. "Whiskey?"

"Oh, yes," Allard said. "I had forgotten about that."

"One of the boys managed to smuggle in a few jugs of whiskey," Robert said. "I'm still not sure how he did it. But he had them, so we hid them under the straw used as bedding in the old hospital building. We had to be careful where we stepped, because we didn't want to break any of the jugs."

"That would have been a waste of good whiskey," Malachi said with a smile.

"Not to mention the fact that Major Stevens or Lieutenant Armstrong probably would have smelled it, and then we would have been in quite a bit of trouble."

Malachi's face turned stern. "I don't want you boys to think that I condone smuggling whiskey into a military encampment . . . but I'm sure this is hardly the first time such a thing has been done."

"No sir. The problem was that last night we still had some of it left—"

"And we didn't want to waste it," Allard added. "So since we knew there was a chance we'd be leaving the island today, we decided we had better drink it."

Malachi chuckled. "I'll bet some of the boys had big heads this morning, eh?"

"Some of them," Robert agreed. "I was all right, though."

"And so was I," Allard added.

"Of course you were," Malachi told his son. "You're a Tyler. You can hold your liquor." He looked at Robert. "And I'm sure the Gilmores can, too."

"Yes sir." Robert downed the last of the brandy in his glass. "And to that end . . ."

Malachi laughed and reached for the decanter on the desk. "You require a refill, eh? Here you go, my boy."

It bothered Allard a little to hear his father refer to Robert as "my boy," but he knew Malachi didn't mean anything by it. Allard had never doubted his father's love for him. But it was certainly true that Malachi didn't always understand him, and he was afraid that might be the case this evening.

No point in postponing the inevitable, he told himself. It might have been better if he and his father had been alone, but perhaps Robert's presence would mean that Malachi wouldn't get as angry when he heard what Allard had to say.

"Father," he began, "I've been thinking—"

Malachi chuckled. "That's a dangerous thing for a young man to do."

"Yes, but there was plenty of time to do a lot of it out there on the island."

Robert put in, "It really was pretty boring most of the time."

"Anyway," Allard went on, hoping he wouldn't be interrupted again, "I've been thinking about what I'm going to do if there's a war with the Yankees."

Malachi looked blankly at him. "What do you mean? You're a student at the Citadel. I assume you'll continue your studies and perhaps be assigned some additional duties, like the one that took you to Morris Island. I wouldn't be surprised if the cadets wound up serving as a sort of home guard—"

"You don't understand," Allard cut into his father's words. "If war is declared, I intend to resign from the Citadel."

# CHAPTER NINE

# Plans for
# the Future

I N THE SILENCE THAT followed Allard's declaration, both Robert and
Malachi stared at him in surprise and confusion. After a moment, Robert said, "You never told me anything about that."

Before Allard could respond, Malachi said, "What in blazes do you
mean you're going to resign from the Citadel? Do you realize how
much it cost to get you in there?"

Allard saw Robert's jaw tighten and knew his friend was sensitive
about his own status as a nonpaying state cadet. At the moment,
though, he wasn't really worried about his friend's feelings. He had
reached an important decision, and he hoped his father would let him
explain it.

"I know you've spent a great deal of money," he said, "and I do appreciate that. But if it comes to a war, I believe there are more important things for me to do than sit in a classroom. Or drilling and
parading as a member of the home guard, for that matter."

Malachi's stern glare lasted a few seconds longer then began to
fade. "Wait a minute," he said. "I think I'm starting to see what you're
talking about, Allard."

Allard blew out a sigh of relief. That had gone easier than he expected. "Thank you, sir. I hoped you'd understand."

"You want to resign from the Citadel so you can work with me at the shipyard." Malachi stepped over to Allard and clapped a hand on his shoulder. "You don't know how glad I am to hear you say that, son. I assumed all along, of course, that eventually you'd come into the business with me, but if a war speeds things up . . . well, you know what they say about a silver lining in every cloud."

Allard stared at his father for an instant and finally said, "You don't understand."

"What do I not understand? You just want to do what I planned all along for you."

"But I don't! I never said that. If there's a war and I resign from the Citadel, I'm not going to work at the shipyard."

Malachi's frown came back, darker than ever. "Then what *are* you planning on doing?"

"I plan to join the Confederate navy. I'm sure one will have been formed. There has to be if we're to have any hope of winning a war against the North."

Malachi stared at Allard, seemingly thunderstruck. He struggled to speak and at last was able to choke out, "Join the navy?" His voice rose in anger. "Why in God's name would you want to do *that*?"

"You build ships," Allard pointed out instead of answering directly. "Why would you object to my serving on one?"

"Building ships isn't the same as sailing on the damned things!" Malachi began to pace back and forth, his quick, stiff steps a good indication of his emotional state. "I know what it is," he said. "This is about your grandfather, isn't it?"

"Black Nick served in the War of 1812—"

"Don't use that name!" Malachi made a sharp motion with his hand. "My father had a perfectly good name. Nicholas Tyler. A name to command respect . . . until he sullied it by becoming a pirate!"

"He was a privateer," Allard objected.

"It's the same thing." Scorn dripped from Malachi's voice.

"No," Allard insisted. "It's not the same thing at all. My grandfather fought the British and helped defeat them. He served his country. He *was* honorable, Father, whether you want to believe that or not!"

"Bah!" Malachi turned away with a shake of his head. "There's no reasoning with a young fool. Suffice to say, if that's what you have in mind, Allard, I forbid you to resign from the Citadel. If war breaks out, you can continue your studies or you can come to work with me. Those are your options."

Allard lifted his chin in defiance, determined not to let his father see how shaken he was. Malachi had always gotten his way, but not this time, Allard vowed. Not this time.

"How are you going to stop me?"

"You're not of age. You'd have to have my permission to enlist, and I won't give it. It's as simple as that."

"Do you really think that if it comes down to a war with the Yankees, the military will be that particular? Or will they accept any man who's old enough and able-bodied enough to lift a weapon?"

Robert had been silent while father and son argued, but now he ventured, "Allard has a point, Mr. Tyler. In times of war the rules are often relaxed."

"Stay out of this," Malachi snapped at him. "You're a guest in this house, not a member of the family."

Robert caught his breath. "Of course, sir," he said tightly. "My apologies."

Allard knew from the look in Robert's eyes that his father's words had stung. The anger he felt at that just made Allard all the more determined. "You know that if war comes, the Yankees will try to blockade our coasts and curtail our commerce with England. They'll attack our seaports and invade our rivers. Cutting us off from the sea will starve us, and taking over our waterways will strangle us. The only way to stop that from happening is to have a navy that's every bit the equal of theirs. You know I'm right, Father. You've studied the history of naval power, too."

"Whether you're right or not doesn't have anything to do with whether you join the navy," Malachi said. "Yes, if a Confederacy of Southern states comes about, we'll need ships. I've already been working toward that end with Governor Pickens."

That news took Allard by surprise. "You have?"

"Damn right," Malachi said. "From now on, the efforts of the Tyler Shipyard will be directed toward supplying the naval needs of South Carolina and the Confederacy, too, if that's how things wind up. So you see, I'm as firm a believer in the importance of such things as you are."

"I . . . didn't know." Allard thought for a moment and then took a deep breath. "But it doesn't change anything. I'm glad you're going to build ships to fight the Yankees. But I still intend to be on one of them."

Malachi threw both hands in the air and shouted, "I forbid it!"

"Forbid all you want to," Allard said, trying to keep his voice from trembling in the face of his father's wrath. "I'm going to do it."

"You do and I'll—"

Whatever threat Malachi was going to make went unstated as the door of the study opened and Katherine Tyler stepped into the room. "My Lord, what's going on in here? Malachi, why are you shouting?"

Malachi thrust a finger at Allard. "Do you know what this son of yours just said?"

"No, but I'm sure it didn't warrant shouting like some sort of fish-monger! Land's sake, Malachi, he's just a boy."

"That's right, and he's going to do what I tell him to do."

"Not exactly—" Allard said.

His mother turned toward him and fluttered her hands. "Hush now, Allard. You know how your father is when he gets like this, all red-faced and apoplectic."

"I am *not* apoplectic!" Malachi objected.

"Why don't we all calm down?" Katherine said.

"But, Katherine, he said that if there's a war—"

"Well, maybe there won't be." She laughed nervously. "Who knows, maybe the Yankees will see the light of reason and agree to let us live our lives the way we see fit. After all, it's only right that they do so."

"And maybe pigs will grow wings and fly," Malachi muttered.

Allard was in agreement with his father on that much, at least—
the Yankees weren't going to back down. There might still be some
hope of a compromise, but it was slipping away as more and more
states seceded. By now five or six or maybe even seven had left the
Union, one right after the other. It was all happening so fast that
Allard had lost count.

"If there's no war, then there's no need to argue," Katherine insisted. "Let's just wait and see what happens."

Malachi frowned and grimaced and cleared his throat, but finally
he said, "I suppose we could do that." He added, "I don't like being
talked to like that by my own son, though! A child is supposed to
honor his father, not defy him."

"That's fine when a child is young, dear, but sooner or later they
all grow up and have minds of their own."

"Doesn't matter," Malachi said. "The Good Book doesn't say anything about honoring your father and mother until you get to a certain age, now does it?"

"Maybe you should remember to honor your own father," Allard
said.

Malachi turned sharply toward him, clenching a fist as he did so.
For a second Allard believed his father was going to take a punch at
him. Malachi had threatened to kick his rear end all the way from
Charleston to Columbia on many occasions, but he had never really
done such a thing, of course.

Katherine moved swiftly between them. "Allard, get out of here,"
she directed.

"But, Mother—"

"Just go. Please, Allard."

"Well . . . all right." He paused on the way out of the study. "But
he's wrong about this."

"Oh, fiddle!" his mother said. "I don't care who's right or wrong.
Just go on and let your father calm down."

Allard shrugged and went out, followed by Robert, who closed the
study door behind them. As they walked down the hall, Robert asked

quietly, "Why have you never said anything to me about this plan to join the navy?"

Allard gave a hollow laugh. "I was afraid you'd try to talk me out of it. So I didn't say anything until I had made up my mind."

"Well, I'm not surprised you want to leave the Citadel and fight Yankees. To tell you the truth, I was sort of planning to do the same thing myself."

Allard stopped and turned toward his best friend. "You want to join the navy?"

"Good Lord, no! I got sick as a dog just steaming over to Morris Island. I'm a hill-country boy, Allard. I'm not at home out on the water and never will be."

Allard looked confused. "But I thought you just said you plan to leave the Citadel—"

"If war breaks out, that's exactly what I'm going to do. But then I'm going to join the army and put all that training to good use."

"The army?" Allard stared at his friend. "You really want to tramp around in the mud and the rain and the cold like we've been doing for the past week and a half out on that island?"

"Doesn't it rain at sea?"

"Well, of course it does, but it's not the same. There's no mud—"

"But boats sink."

"What about hand-to-hand fighting? Can you shoot a man or put a bayonet into his belly when he's looking at you from six inches away, even if he *is* a Yankee?"

"Dead is dead, no matter how far away the man who kills you is. If you sink a Yankee ship, won't most of the men on it drown? Is that a better way to die?"

The two young men stood glaring at each other, neither of them able to answer the other's questions.

That was when Katherine came out of the study and closed the door quietly behind her. She came down the hall toward them and said to Allard, "Your father has settled down some. Whatever in the world did you say to him to get him so upset?"

"I told him that if there's a war, I plan to resign from the Citadel and join the Confederate navy."

"Oh, my." Katherine laughed again, but she didn't sound amused. "I don't think that's a good idea at all."

"It was good enough for Black Nick," Allard said.

Katherine put a hand to her breast. "Lord have mercy! You didn't bring up your grandfather, did you? No wonder your father like to had a fit."

"I was just trying to explain—"

Katherine bustled on down the hall. "We'll talk about this later, Allard. Right now I have to figure out everything that has to be done before tomorrow night. I want this to be a good party, you know."

"Of course, Mother," Allard said, knowing the futility of continuing the discussion with Katherine. Her head was full of party details now. There was no room for anything else, like the impending war with the Yankees and the part her only son would play in it.

"I'll never understand you, Allard," Robert said. "I thought I did, but I reckon I don't."

"What's so hard to understand? I want some excitement, some glory. I'll have the rest of my life to sit in an office at the shipyard."

"*If* you don't go down with the ship."

"That's a risk I'll just have to run, I suppose."

Robert smiled faintly. "If it's a risk you want . . . wait until you tell Diana about your plans."

Allard's eyes widened. Robert was right: he hadn't really thought about what Diana would say when he told her. He hadn't even figured out how he was going to break the news to her.

But the one thing he could count on was that she would understand. She loved him, didn't she?

"ALLARD, HOW . . . how could you?"

He looked at Diana, flabbergasted by her response. He had just explained his plans, and the look on her face had grown more horrified as he went along. He was stumbling over his words as he tried desperately to think of some way to make her see what he was feeling.

They sat on a divan in the parlor of the Pinckston house, the day after Allard's return to Charleston. He had come to visit before the party that night, because he didn't want to try to tell her what he was going to do while there were so many people around. Maybe that had been a mistake. Diana might not have been so angry if they had been in the middle of a crowd.

"You have to understand," he said, "this is something I have to do—"

"You have to go off and get yourself killed?" Diana's hands knotted together in her lap.

"I'm not going to get myself killed. I'll be fine—"

"How can you be sure of that?"

"How can anyone be sure of anything?" he said. "A man can be run over by a wagon while he's walking down the street. Just getting up in the morning is dangerous."

She gave a ladylike snort of disagreement. "It's not the same thing, and you know it."

"I'm sorry, Diana. I thought you of all people would know what I was talking about. After all, your father is an officer. He fought in the Mexican War. You've been raised in a military family."

A look of indecision crossed her face. "I . . . I know what you're saying is true, Allard. And I'm proud of you for wanting to protect our homeland from those . . . those Yankee devils." She caught hold of his right hand with both of her hands. "But I couldn't stand it if anything happened to you. I simply couldn't."

"Like I said, I'm sure I'll be fine—"

She leaned toward him. "Hold me. Convince me of that. I beg you, Allard, convince me."

He put his arms around her and drew her close to him. His heart pounded heavily in his chest as he felt the soft warmth of her body pressed to his. The clean fragrance of her hair filled his senses.

Maybe he *had* been wrong to think about leaving Charleston . . .

*No.* He couldn't allow what he felt for Diana to distract him from the realities of the situation. Major Anderson and the rest of the Yankee garrison were still sitting out there on Fort Sumter, thumbing their noses at the good people of South Carolina. Such high-handed behavior could not be tolerated. And it would only get worse as time passed. Every day the Yankees occupied the fort that didn't belong to them, the more daring and arrogant they became. Allard was sure of it. Hadn't they tried to slip the *Star of the West* up the channel even though they had been warned not to do so?

A few glimmers of hope remained. Newspaper stories that filtered down from the North revealed that President Buchanan had had a change of heart at the last minute and tried to recall the *Star of the West*. He had been too late, though, and the merchant ship had sailed ahead on its ill-fated mission, unaware of Buchanan's decision.

Soon, though, in a little over a month, in fact, they wouldn't have the dithering Buchanan to deal with anymore. Abraham Lincoln was going to take office, and the president-elect was a sworn enemy of slavery and the South, despite his recent comments about seeking a peaceful solution to the problem. Lincoln had been elected to put an end to slavery and implement the economic subjugation of the South before Southern ties to England and other foreign nations grew too strong. The rich Northern factory owners could not stand the idea of the Southern states becoming less dependent on them. They didn't care a whit about slavery; that was just a convenient issue for them to hang their hats on, something they could use to stir up the public while they pursued their real agenda—economic dominance of the country. It was sickening the way they had turned what might have been genuinely noble sentiments to their own benefit. The Yankees who cried the loudest about abolition thought they were really trying to free the slaves. They had no idea they were just puppets, their strings being pulled by men whose only ambition was to amass wealth . . .

Allard gave a little shake of his head to force out those thoughts. He had heard his father espousing those theories in the past, and on this subject he agreed with Malachi. But that did not change anything. No matter the motivations of either side, in the end it came down to the fact that a man's homeland had to be defended, if need be, to the last breath and the last drop of blood. Honor demanded it.

He leaned back, and Diana straightened. He saw tears shining in her eyes and felt his heart go out to her. Why did war have to be so damned *difficult?*

"You'll come to my mother's party tonight, won't you?"

"Of course." Diana summoned up a smile. "How could I not be there to welcome home the man I love?"

Allard wasn't quite sure he was a man yet, but it did him good to hear Diana say it. He leaned forward and kissed her forehead. "Thank you," he murmured.

They sat together and talked for a few more minutes, and after another quick kiss, Allard took his leave. Diana walked with him to the front door of the Pinckston house and smiled at him as he went down the walk to the street.

When she closed the door and turned away from it, she found her mother waiting on the other side of the shadowy foyer, a silent wraith in the gloom. Not so gloomy, though, that Diana couldn't see the glass in Tamara's hand.

"He'll disappoint you, you know. They always do."

"I'm not you, Mother," Diana said coldly. "I haven't forgotten how to love."

Tamara began to laugh. "I haven't forgotten, you little fool. I remember all too well." She tossed the sherry down her throat then licked her lips and asked rhetorically, "Why do you think I drink?"

# CHAPTER TEN

# The Arsenal

"I BELIEVE THAT'S A full house, gentlemen, and the pot is mine." Cam Gilmore laid his cards down on the blanket spread in the common area between the rows of bunks. He chuckled as he leaned forward to draw in the pile of coins and bills and promissory notes that made up the pot. Cam didn't like taking the notes, but a fellow almost had to. Honor and all that. Couldn't act like he didn't trust his fellow cadets—even though he knew some of them would never pay him what they owed.

One of the other young men reached out to grab Cam's wrist. "Wait just a minute!" he said. "You have jacks and sevens. Three jacks, to be precise. But two of them have already been played!"

Cam frowned at the other cadet, Lucius Barlow. "That's impossible. You can see for yourself that there are three jacks right there, in the hand I just played."

Barlow reached for the pile of discards. "Let's just see if the fifth one isn't already in here."

This time it was Cam's hand that shot forward to grasp the other's wrist. "Let's not," he said coldly. "I do believe you're calling me a cheat. You're accusing a fellow cadet of being less than honorable. Is that really what you want to do, Barlow?"

Barlow was a slender, pale-faced young man with dark red hair, well built for his age but smaller than Cam. He grimaced as he hesitated. Then he said, "I make no such accusation."

Cam let go of Barlow's wrist. "I thought maybe you didn't."

"But an honorable man would turn over those discards himself, just to prove his honesty," Barlow said slyly.

Cam's face flushed with anger. That was a neat trick. Now Cam had no choice. "All right," he said as he began to turn over the discards. "If that's the way you want it."

Barlow leaned forward eagerly, as did the half-dozen other cadets gathered around the blanket, their faces somewhat ghostly in the dim light of the single candle that illuminated the game. Ever since they had come to the Arsenal the previous fall, Cam Gilmore had always been the big winner in these poker games. Maybe some of the others thought he was a cheat, too; Cam didn't know about that. But Barlow was the first one who had said anything.

Cam picked up several of the cards at once, turned them over, and spread them out on the blanket so everybody could see them. He did that again and again until all the cards from the discard pile were face up. Barlow plucked up the jack of diamonds and said, "There's one of them. The jack of clubs is here somewhere, too."

Cam tapped his finger on one of the cards in the hand he had just laid down. "Yes, it's right there," he said. "Honestly dealt and played."

"No, it's got to be here," Barlow muttered as he began pawing through the discards. "I know it is. I'm sure I had it in one of the hands I threw away earlier."

"You're confused. You threw away the jack of diamonds."

Barlow shook his head. "No, it was a club . . ." His pawing at the cards became more frantic. "It's here, I know it is!"

"I don't see it, Lucius," one of the other cadets said.

"But it has to be!"

Again Cam tapped the jack of clubs that lay before him with the rest of the full house.

Barlow's head jerked up. His lips were drawn back from his teeth. "He . . . he's done something with it! Damn it, we should search him—"

"That's enough," another cadet said coldly. "There's no extra jack, Barlow. You were mistaken, and you might as well admit it."

"No! Search him—"

"You've insulted a fellow cadet's honor enough for one night. Let it go."

Cam drew the pot in. "Under the circumstances, I don't think I feel like playing anymore. That's enough for tonight." He looked stonily at his accuser. "I won't forget this, Barlow."

"Neither will I," Barlow said as his face contorted into a snarl. "Neither will I," he repeated.

Cam gathered up his winnings. The cards belonged to one of the other cadets. He never played with a deck that belonged to him.

Cam piled into his bunk after putting the money and notes in the locker at the foot of his bed. Someone blew out the candle, plunging the barracks into darkness. It was late, long past the time when these young men were supposed to be asleep.

When the snores from the other bunks around him told Cam that the rest of the cadets were asleep, he carefully eased the extra jack of clubs out of the sleeve of his long underwear. It was identical to the one from the deck they had been using. Palming it and slipping it up his sleeve as he picked it up from the discards in full view of the other cadets was one of the slickest tricks he had ever pulled. The long hours of practice with his nimble fingers had saved him from some unpleasant consequences—a thrashing at the very least; at worst, being reported to the head of the Arsenal and forced to resign from the academy.

A smile stretched across his face. He wanted to laugh out loud, but of course he couldn't. And he would have to pretend to be angry and offended by Barlow's accusation for the next few days, as if he were truly the one who had been wronged.

He had come close to being caught tonight, but as usual, he had gotten away with it. And as usual, the thrill that had gone through him was incomparable. There was nothing like danger to give life the spice it needed to be really enjoyable. If there was no chance of being caught, then what was the point in doing anything? Like all those times in Charleston with Lucinda Tyler . . .

Cam went to sleep with the smile still on his face.

THE ARSENAL had begun its existence as a real arsenal, a storage facility for guns and ammunition belonging to the state of South Carolina. It was still used partially for that purpose. Two magazines of ammunition stood adjacent to the square in front of the buildings where the cadets were housed and educated in all things military, historical, and classical. Originally two separate structures standing on Arsenal Hill in Columbia, the buildings had been joined by a connecting third wing. Another building nearby served as officers' quarters.

The bill passed by the South Carolina General Assembly that created the Citadel and the Arsenal stated that the cadets in both academies would serve as guards for the munitions stored there while at the same time receiving the finest military education possible. Although it was not required that, upon graduation, the cadets would serve in the U.S. army, most of them did, and members of some of the early classes served with distinction during the Mexican War in the late forties and on the American frontier during the 1850s. Personal honor was paramount; nothing was more important to the Citadel cadets, and that feeling extended to their younger brethren at the Arsenal.

Because of that, Cam Gilmore sometimes wondered just what in blazes he was doing there.

It wasn't that he was totally *dishonorable*, of course. When he gave his word to someone, he kept it—usually. True, he cheated at cards sometimes, but if his fellow cadets who had lost money to him were to ask for it back, he would have given it to them—probably. He was more interested in the excitement of getting away with something than he was in the winnings themselves.

And when it came to women and girls, he never slept with one who hadn't suggested it first—like Lucinda, who had taken his hand

and dragged him into that carriage and then practically ravished him. That was the way he remembered it, anyway. She had bit his lip and cursed him and warned him that what they were doing didn't really mean anything, not a damned thing, and then she had moaned and clutched at him and somewhere in there—he was almost sure of it, although his memory was a little fuzzy on the matter—she had gasped out that she loved him.

They usually did, sooner or later.

Cam firmly believed that he had a special talent for pleasing women. From the very first time he had been initiated into the pleasures of the flesh by Susannah Milligan, who lived on the farm next to the Gilmore place and was four years older than him, none of the women he had been with had ever complained. Most of them had complimented him on his skill and endurance. It came naturally to him.

Of course, folks weren't supposed to fornicate outside of marriage. Cam knew that. He had heard Reverend Culhane bellow about it enough during church services.

He had also heard Reverend Culhane's daughter Judith cry out beneath him and tell him that he was just the most darling boy there ever was, and Cam figured it would be a sin to disbelieve her. Anyway, it felt so good and brought so much happiness to the gals who invited him into their beds, so even if it *was* a sin, Cam hoped it was sort of low down on the list and wouldn't cause him to wind up burning in the pits of Hades. That wouldn't be good at all.

A FEW nights after the card game, he was about to doze off when Eleanora Massie, the wife of Lt. Albert Massie, instructor of moral philosophy at the Arsenal, punched him lightly on the shoulder and hissed, "Cam, you've got to get up. Al will be home soon, and if he finds you here, he'll take his saber to you, sure enough."

Cam groaned and rolled over. He was tired. Mrs. Massie had been especially demanding tonight. She had worn him out until he felt limp all over. In the back of his brain, though, he knew she was right. He was risking his life if he overstayed his welcome here.

Lieutenant Massie and his overeager wife lived in a small cottage on Richmond Street, less than a block from the Arsenal. Unmarried officers lived in the quarters on the Arsenal grounds, but those with families had homes nearby. Earlier this evening, moving with the adroitness of a wild Indian in the dark, Cam had slipped out of the barracks and made his way here, responding to a note that Eleanora had sent him that afternoon. The lieutenant was going to be away, probably until nine or ten o'clock that night, and she wanted Cam to visit her if he possibly could.

Cam wasn't going to turn down that invitation, that was for darned sure.

She had greeted him with open arms, wearing a flimsy getup with all kinds of lace on it. Her blonde hair hung in tight ringlets on either side of her face, and he could see her plump, pink body in places through the flimsy garment she wore. She crushed her mouth to his, clutched at his muscular arms, and pretty much dragged him to bed.

Now, still a little groggy from lovemaking, he sat up and swung his legs out from under the covers. The wooden floor was cold on his bare feet as he stood and reached for his clothes.

That was when a door opened and closed somewhere in the front of the cottage.

Mrs. Massie gasped in horror, leaped out of bed, and grabbed Cam's arm. "That's Al!" she whispered frantically. "You've got to get out of here!"

Cam had once heard Robert and Allard discussing a play they had seen in Charleston, written by some French fella, that was about folks running in and out of bedrooms and nearly getting caught in the wrong place at the wrong time. They shouldn't have gone to see such a production, since it was really for adults, but they had gotten in somehow and then talked a lot about it later. That was the first thing Cam thought of when Eleanora pitched a fit for him to get out. It was like he had wandered into some French play.

Lieutenant Massie wouldn't be playacting, though, when he took his saber and started slashing at Cam with it. Cam knew that, so he yanked his trousers on, grabbed his shirt and coat and boots, and went headfirst out the window that Eleanora hastily opened. That probably wasn't the best idea he'd ever had, since he banged his head on the ground when he landed and had to lie there for a few minutes while the world spun around and tried to throw him off. He had knocked himself silly.

But he was still able to hear and understand Lieutenant Massie when he said, "For God's sake, Eleanora, what's that window doing open? It's cold out there tonight."

"I know, darling. I just felt like I needed a breath of fresh air."

"Better be careful. You'll catch your death."

"I'll close it now," she said, and the window began to rasp down in its frame. Cam heard her say, "Come on to bed now. I've been waiting for you . . ." and then the window slammed shut and he couldn't hear anything else.

His wits returned to him enough so that he was able to roll over, push himself onto hands and knees and crawl away through the thick shadows next to the cottage.

By the time he got back to the Arsenal, he was fully dressed again and had all his wits about him. He was confident that he could sneak back inside without anyone knowing about it. He had done that dozens of times in the past.

Tonight was different, though. Tonight his luck was decidedly mixed, instead of being all good as it usually was. As he cut across the edge of the square in front of the buildings, several dark shapes suddenly loomed up in front of him.

"There he is!" a familiar voice said in a triumphant half-whisper. "I knew he'd come skulking back in sooner or later."

"Barlow!" Cam said. "What are you doing out here?"

"Waiting for you, you damned cheater. I've been watching you ever since the card game, and I saw you sneak out earlier tonight."

A tingle of apprehension went through Cam as Barlow and the cadets with him began to advance, spreading out so that they formed a half-circle as they moved in. "Look, Barlow," Cam said, "I showed you that I didn't cheat. I proved it."

"You didn't prove anything except what a slick scoundrel you are. And now you're going to pay for it."

"I'm nearly twice your size. It wouldn't be honorable to fight you."

"That's all right. I have friends enough to even the odds."

"That's not even! There are five of you. This isn't fair."

"Yes, there are five of us," Barlow said. "One for every jack in that deck of cards."

Cam was nothing if not practical. They weren't going to let him go. Barlow wouldn't stand for that. He was in the center, with two cadets to either side of him, and there were several feet between each of the cadets. Barlow was the smallest of the bunch, therefore the weakest link.

With no warning, Cam lunged forward, driving straight at Barlow and swinging a punch with all his strength behind it.

Barlow had no chance to get out of the way. Cam's fist crashed into his jaw and knocked him back a good five feet. As he collapsed, Cam hurdled over him and landed running. He knew there was no refuge for him in the buildings. He didn't want to be discovered outside of his quarters at night. So he turned and cut straight across the square, hoping to outdistance the friends of the fallen Barlow who pounded after him.

Cadets walked sentry duty around the Arsenal all night. Slipping past the guards wouldn't have posed much of a chore for Cam if all had gone as planned, but it was hard for the sentries to miss a whole procession of runners thundering across the square. Someone yelled, "Halt! Halt! Who goes there?" An itchy trigger finger contracted, and a musket roared. Ever since abolitionists led by John Brown had stormed the federal arsenal at Harpers Ferry, Virginia, a year and a half earlier, most soldiers who stood guard over munitions storehouses sometimes felt a little nervous, and that definitely included cadets. John Brown's body might be a-molderin' in the grave now, but that didn't mean such things could never happen again.

So as the uproar continued to grow, Cam decided that his best bet would be to reach the far side of the square, circle around the buildings, and join the crowd of cadets who would soon be rushing out to see what all the commotion was about.

First, though, he had to get away from the ones who were chasing him.

He had always been the fastest runner in his family, swifter than Robert or any of his other brothers or sisters. Tonight he wasn't swift enough. One of his pursuers launched himself into the air in a flying tackle and slammed into Cam's legs from behind. With a grunt of dismay, Cam went down, landing hard on the ground and rolling over a couple of times.

He kicked out as hands grabbed at him and felt the satisfaction of his boot landing solidly on flesh. At the same time, a heavy weight came crashing down on top of him, knocking the air out of his lungs. He gasped for breath, but before he could draw any into his body, strong fingers clamped around his throat, shutting it off.

This was bad. Cam knew he couldn't last very long like this. He lifted his right leg high and managed to get it across the throat of the cadet choking him. Cam lunged up off the ground, thrusting back with his leg as hard as he could. His attacker was thrown off and had to let go.

Cam rolled over, slapped his hands against the ground, and surged to his feet. He dragged air into his lungs. It rasped in his now-sore throat. A fist pounded into his ribs from the right side. He brought his elbow up and jabbed with it. The point of the elbow hit something soft. Somebody's throat, to judge by the gagging sounds. Cam reached out, grabbed an arm, and whirled, pulling his attacker against him. As he bent from the waist, he hauled harder on the cadet's arm. With a yell, the young man flipped over Cam's hip and went flying through the air.

All that rasslin' and bare-knucks, no-holds-barred scuffling he had done growing up in the hills came in handy now. He caught a glimpse of a lantern bobbing in the air as guards ran toward the fight, but he couldn't worry about that now. The other three were all around him, slugging wildly at him. He ducked some of the blows, parried others, and struck back with a wicked speed. His fists scraped the sides of heads, smacked into jaws, jabbed at noses, and sunk in bellies. He twisted and turned and seemed to be everywhere at once. One time back home, Jupe Monroe and Jupe's two brothers had caught Cam in a blackberry thicket and tried to pound the stuffing out of him. Cam wound up tossing all three of them in the blackberry plants, so that they came out looking like they'd run into a wildcat. This fight was just more of the same, Cam battling for his hide against heavy odds. He might get thrashed in the end, but Lord, it felt good every time one of his punches landed solidly.

The yelling was close by now. Suddenly Cam's attackers broke off their assault and ran. Cam would have tried to get away, too, but his muscles betrayed him, going weak and limp and dropping him to his knees. The sentries, accompanied by an officer, stomped up to him and played the light from their lanterns over him. Cam saw several muskets pointing at him. He grinned and said, "Don't shoot, boys. I never been north of the Mason-Dixon Line in my life. Long live South Carolina!"

"Gilmore," the officer said in disgust. "I should have known you'd be involved in this. What are you doin' out here? Aren't you supposed to be in your bunk?"

"Yes sir, but I saw Cadet Barlow sneaking out and went after him to tell him to come back." Cam didn't know where the lie came from or whether it would be believed, but he said it anyway. He pointed and went on, "Barlow's right over there. He and his friends jumped me when I challenged them, and I had to knock him out."

The officer grunted. "You were just tryin' to keep Barlow out of trouble, is that right?"

"Yes sir."

"Even though you knew you were breaking the rules, too?"

"Well, sir, I, uh, put a fellow cadet's welfare above my own."

"Gilmore, you're the biggest liar I've ever seen. I don't care what you were doin'. You're gonna be pullin' extra duty for a month, you hear me?"

"Yes sir." Cam added, "What about Cadet Barlow, sir?"

"Oh, he'll be punished, same as you. I reckon if I was to ask him, he'd lie about what he was doin' out here. So I won't waste my time." The officer spoke to the guards. "Get both of 'em on their feet."

One of the guards said, "Lieutenant, there's another one over here. Looks like he got the wind knocked out of him."

"Get him up, too. Hope you boys didn't plan on gettin' any more sleep tonight. You're gonna be in the kitchen, scrubbin' down every pot and pan in there."

"Aren't they already clean, sir?" Cam asked.

"That don't matter. You're gonna scrub 'em anyway. Get movin'."

As Cam, a groggy Lucius Barlow, and Barlow's friend all marched toward the buildings, the officer fell in step beside Cam and touched his arm so that they hung back behind the others. The lieutenant asked quietly, "How many of 'em jumped you, Gilmore?"

"Five, sir," Cam answered, equally quietly.

"And you did more'n hold your own against 'em, didn't you?"

"Yes sir, I reckon I did," Cam said proudly.

"You're just a fightin' fool, Cadet Gilmore. One of these days, probably before too much longer, South Carolina's gonna have need of young men like you. We're gonna need all the fightin' fools we can find to kill Yankees."

"When the time comes, I'll be ready, sir," Cam said.

"Yes," the officer said slowly, "I do believe you will."

# PART THREE

All we ask is to be let alone.

—*Jefferson Davis, inaugural address, Montgomery, Alabama, February 18, 1861*

# CHAPTER ELEVEN

# A New Nation, an Old Problem

B Y THE END OF January the General Assembly of South Carolina had passed a new bill establishing a battalion of state cadets at both the Citadel and the Academy, formally making the cadets part of the military organization of the state and putting them on equal footing with the militia and all other military units being formed. Not only that, but all graduates of the Citadel were now eligible for an immediate officer's commission.

That was all well and good, but it didn't affect the plans of Allard Tyler and Robert Gilmore. Both young men were still determined to resign in the event of war and enlist to get into the fighting as quickly as possible.

As the days wore on, the war that most people already considered inevitable became even more so. Southern states continued to secede—Mississippi, Florida, Alabama, Georgia, and Louisiana all joined South Carolina in leaving the Union. It was a speedy process but not an easy one. Shouts of debate rang out in the state houses as the legislatures and assemblies decided on their course of action. A few voices counseled patience and reason, but they were drowned out by those calling for separation.

In February, representatives from the six seceded states gathered in Montgomery, Alabama, and formed the much-anticipated Confederate

States of America. Former Senator and Secretary of War Jefferson Davis was selected to be the president of the newly established nation—a nation whose very right to exist was still being hotly debated elsewhere.

In the South, though, there was no doubt. The Confederacy was real. It quickly garnered another member when Texas was admitted on March 5, 1861, only one day after Abraham Lincoln had taken office as the president of the United States. In Lincoln's inaugural address, he spoke of welcoming the Southern states back into the Union if they chose to return. He made it clear, however, that there would be no concessions to them. Lincoln stated as well that Federal forces would continue to occupy—and defend—any installations they held in Confederate territory. No one made any mistake about that. Lincoln was talking about Fort Sumter. Throughout the South, his speech was regarded as one more example of high-handed Yankee arrogance.

Later in the month, however, rumors circulated that Major Anderson's troops were to be evacuated from Fort Sumter. Behind the scenes in Washington, some of Lincoln's advisers were becoming aware of the military realities of the situation. While there was plenty of ammunition inside the fort, the same could not be said of food. At first meat and vegetables had been delivered daily from Charleston, but that commerce had dwindled to almost nothing. Within another month or so provisions would run very low. The families of the soldiers had already left the fort; it began to seem a foregone conclusion that the troops themselves would soon follow. Once again the threat of war faded slightly.

But it didn't go away, because despite everything, the Federals continued to occupy Fort Sumter. Gen. P. G. T. Beauregard, formerly for a short time the superintendent of the U.S. Military Academy at West Point but now a brigadier general in the newly formed Confederate army, arrived in Charleston to take command of the forces assembled in the city. It was the dapper Creole's job to mold the haphazard collection of militias and state regiments into an army, and Beauregard set about doing so with no delay.

Allard and Robert were among the cadets who paraded on the square in front of the Citadel as the watchful eyes of General Beauregard observed them from a reviewing stand packed with dignitaries, among them the firebrand Edmund Ruffin, who was now a frequent visitor to the Citadel. In addition, the streets around the square were thronged with thousands of spectators. From the windows of buildings overlooking the square, more onlookers waved flags and cheered. It was a thrilling spectacle, and Allard felt a tingle of pride that he was part of it. His resolve to join the navy had not wavered, but he was glad that he was part of this magnificent group of cadets.

For the past few weeks Allard and Robert had spent most of their time drilling and training recruits. Every open space in Charleston became a parade ground as raw troops continued to pour into the city. Cannon were wheeled into position everywhere they could be pointed at the harbor and the grim gray fortress at the mouth of it. Off Sullivan's Island, not far from the now Confederate-occupied Fort Moultrie, a floating battery was built. Mounted upon it were four cannon, two 42-pounders and a pair of 32-pounders. The use of artillery had never been one of Allard's strong points in his studies, but he wished he could be stationed on that floating battery. He had been on hand for the firing on the *Star of the West,* and he suspected that the next historic blow, if indeed it occurred, might well come from the floating battery.

In the meantime there were other things going on, such as the annual cadet ball, scheduled for April 5. The ball was in honor of the Citadel's twenty-five graduating seniors, who would take part in commencement exercises on April 9. Another year of peace, and Allard and Robert would have graduated. Neither of them truly believed that they would be granted that year's grace, however.

Graduating or not, all the cadets—and their ladies—attended the cadet ball. Diana arrived with her father but quickly made her way to Allard's side. He was in full-dress uniform tonight, as were the other cadets, and looked splendid in the gray jacket with brass buttons, gray trousers with a black stripe tracing the outside seam, gray vest, and

139

boiled white shirt. A black-silk bow tie was around his throat. His black shoes were polished to a brilliant sheen. He looked dashing, and he knew it.

Diana looked better, though, with her thick red hair piled high in an elaborate arrangement of curls. She wore a pale green gown, tightly cinched at the waist and flaring out into an impressive hoop skirt. The neckline was cut low so that the pale upper swells of her breasts took Allard's breath away. He forced himself not to stare.

The band played a merry waltz. Allard took Diana's hand and smiled at her. "May I have this dance, Miss Pinckston?"

She smiled back at him. "You may, Cadet Tyler."

It was amazing what the human mind could ignore when it wanted to, Allard thought as he whirled her into the intricate steps of the dance. The future was a forbidden subject to them these days, at least when they were together. At those times, they lived solely in the moment, as if there would never be a reckoning between North and South. They hadn't discussed it, and it hadn't been a conscious decision on their part. It was something they fell into, a way of avoiding worry and pain.

Elsewhere in the ballroom, Robert danced with Jacqueline Lockhart. She chattered about the decorations and about the gowns worn by the other ladies, and once she tightened her hand on Robert's and asked in a low, urgent voice, "My God, Robert, is that General Beauregard?"

Robert looked around and saw the handsome Louisianan surrounded by the elegantly dressed ladies of Charleston. Several of the women took scarves and corsages they had worn to the ball and pressed them on the general, who had no option but to accept the tokens graciously. Clearly, Beauregard was already a favorite, at least with one segment of Charleston's population.

"That's him, all right," he replied to Jacqueline.

She slipped out of his arms. "I want to go see him and welcome him to the city."

"I think he's already being welcomed," Robert said dryly, but

Jacqueline was already making her way through the crowd toward the general. Robert sighed and followed her. At least he would be on hand to reclaim her once she tired of her hero worship—if, in fact, she did.

On the far side of the room, Stafford Pinckston stood with Major Stevens, Lieutenant Armstrong, and other officers and instructors from the Citadel. Malachi Tyler and Everett Lockhart approached the group, shook hands all around, and then Malachi said quietly, with a concerned frown, "Is there any truth to the rumors we've been hearing about a slave revolt?"

Stafford said, "There's been wild talk of such a thing for months, Malachi. What makes you think they're any more credible now than they've ever been?"

"I'm not so sure it's wild talk," Everett Lockhart put in sharply. "My overseers at Four Winds report that the field hands are more surly and difficult to work with than ever."

"Things are different on a plantation than they are in the city," Stafford said with a shrug. "You've got a lot more slaves out there in the country than we do here in town."

"So you're saying that we have more to worry about?"

"I don't think there'll be an uprising. Even field hands are smart enough to know that wouldn't get them anything except a load of buckshot or a hang rope." Stafford turned to Malachi. "Have you heard anything from your slaves?"

The Tyler family owned only a few house slaves. Malachi shook his head and said, "Thomas mentioned the other day that some of the maids think that Lincoln is going to come down here personally and set them free. They've talked about how they're going to sing and dance when Abe gets here. But that's all."

"Well, then, there you are. Let them have their dreams. We all know that's never going to happen. It'll be a cold day in hell before Abraham Lincoln ever sets foot in Charleston."

With a frown, Everett said, "That still doesn't answer my question, Stafford."

"Your overseers are well armed, aren't they?"

"Of course."

"Tell them to be watchful. And if you hear too much talk from the darkies . . ." Stafford shrugged again. "Whipping the most talkative ones usually shuts them up, or so I've heard."

Everett nodded. He had never liked having his slaves whipped. The better the treatment, the better the worker, that was his theory. As Stafford said, though, sometimes a lashing was necessary.

Many of the ladies were still clustered around General Beauregard, but not Tamara Pinckston or Priscilla Lockhart. As they stood together, watching, Priscilla commented, "That's rather a vulgar display, isn't it?"

"The general is a handsome man, and he's come to deliver us from the evil Yankees," Tamara said. "It's only natural for the ladies to admire him."

"I admire him, but I'm not going to flutter around him like . . . like . . . like . . ."

"Like your daughter is doing?" Tamara said.

It was true—Jacqueline had joined the throng of belles as they took turns laughing gaily and lightly touching the sleeve of the general's jacket. Her mother watched for a moment then said, "Jacqueline is young and impressionable. Otherwise she never would have become so smitten with that Gilmore boy." Priscilla sighed in frustration. "He's not well to do, and he's certainly not handsome. I don't know what she sees in him."

"Robert Gilmore's not *that* unattractive, in a rawboned sort of way. And according to my husband, he's a good student when he wants to be. He has a practical streak in him, Priscilla. There's at least a chance he'll make something of himself one of these days." Tamara laughed hollowly. "Unlike Allard Tyler, whom *my* daughter keeps throwing herself at."

Priscilla glanced over with a look of confusion. "Allard Tyler doesn't have to make something of himself. He already is something—the son of a shipyard owner."

"Yes, but Allard's the sort of romantic fool who would throw it all away to chase a dream. Do you know what he plans to do if we go to war against the Yankees?"

"No, I have no idea."

"He's going to resign from the Citadel to become a common sailor," Tamara said with a hint of venom in her voice. "Malachi wants to take him into the shipyard and give him a responsible position there, but Allard will have none of it. He wants to go to sea and fight the Yankees."

"Dear Lord! These men and their romantic notions! You'd never catch a woman doing something so impractical."

"Of course not." A smile curved Tamara's lips, but there was no humor in her eyes. "We're only impractical when it comes to our choice of men . . ."

The band had taken a short respite, but as they began to play again, Jacqueline summoned up her courage and said to General Beauregard, "Would you dance with me, General?"

"It would be my honor, young lady," he replied in his softly accented voice. This was perhaps a strategic mistake—if he danced with one of his female admirers, he would have to dance with all of them before the evening was over—but it was difficult, well nigh impossible, in fact, for any man with even a drop of the blood of France in his veins to refuse such a charming young mademoiselle as Jacqueline Lockhart. She even had a name as lovely as her face and figure. *Jacqueline . . .*

Robert's lips tightened in annoyance as he watched Beauregard and Jacqueline twirl across the floor. He was a lowly cadet, not even a graduating one, and Beauregard was a general, perhaps the most important figure in the new Confederate army. He certainly couldn't blame Jacqueline for wanting to dance with the man.

But he didn't have to like it, either.

It didn't help matters a moment later when Allard put a hand on his shoulder and said, "Lost your girl, I see."

Even though they were best friends, for a moment Robert wanted to plant a fist in the middle of Allard's smile. But he suppressed the impulse and said, "She's just trying to see to it that the general is properly welcomed to Charleston. And it's not like she's the only one, either."

"That's true enough," Allard said. "Most of the ladies seem quite taken with him. If I'm not mistaken, my mother is in the middle of that crowd."

It was true. Katherine Tyler was one of the ladies waiting to dance with the general.

"Do you think the women will ever fawn over us like that?" Robert mused.

"When we come back from the war, and you're a general, and I'm an admiral, and the Yankees have all been chased back up north where they belong, of course they will."

"I'll drink to that."

"Not here you won't," Allard pointed out. "There's no liquor in the punch."

Robert turned to him, quirked an eyebrow, and grinned. He pulled back the lapel of his uniform jacket just enough so that Allard caught the reflection off a silver flask tucked inside his friend's vest.

"We can do something about that," Robert said.

Allard's eyes widened. "You mean to spike the punch?" he hissed.

"I'm thinking about it."

"I'm not sure that's a good idea. If you're caught, you'll be drummed out of the Citadel."

"We're going to be resigning anyway, aren't we, as soon as the war breaks out?"

"But it might not," Allard said. "You've heard the rumors. Lincoln's secretary of war—what's his name? Seward?—is trying to work out some arrangement to end the stalemate. If the Yankees evacuate Sumter—"

"It'll never happen," Robert said confidently.

"But Lincoln sent that man Lamon down here to meet personally with the governor," Allard argued. "And Lamon led him to believe that the fort *will* be evacuated."

144

"And you'd believe the word of a Yankee? What about the rumors that Lincoln is about to dispatch a fleet to Charleston Harbor?"

Over the past three months there had been dozens of rumors, running the gamut from Northern capitulation and acceptance of the Confederacy all the way to an outright, full-fledged invasion by the Yankee army. In truth, no one really knew what was going to happen. One day war seemed imminent and the fire-eaters welcomed its beginning. The next it seemed there was still hope for a peaceful solution, and the more moderate elements—which were growing fewer in number all the time—welcomed those developments. But now, in the early days of April, the only thing truly certain in Charleston was uncertainty.

Recklessness pervaded Robert as he turned toward the long, cloth-covered table where the punch bowl sat. Allard gripped his arm as he moved toward it.

"Wait a minute," he said. "If you're going to do this, I'm going to be part of it, too. I'll distract Mrs. Wilkerson."

Allard referred to the large white-haired woman who stood near the punch bowl like a sentry. She had eyes like a hawk and could smell whiskey a hundred yards away, or so it seemed. She was related by marriage to one of the Citadel officers and was always present at dances and balls and parties.

"You're sure?" Robert said.

"Sure," Allard replied. "Move out."

With shoulders squared, the two cadets approached the table. They were almost on their objective when Diana suddenly appeared at Allard's side and took his arm.

"There you are," she said. "A girl leaves to powder her nose, and her escort up and disappears on her! How ungallant, sir." She laughed. "But you can make up for it by dancing with me."

Allard turned to her. "It'll be my pleasure, but there's one thing I have to do first—"

"Listen!" Diana said. "The band is playing 'Dixie'!" She tugged him toward the dance floor. "It's such a wonderful tune. Come on, Allard."

He looked helplessly at Robert, who smiled and said, "Go on."

"You'll wait for me?"

Diana said, "Wait for you to do what?"

"Nothing," Robert said. "It's all right, Allard. Go dance with your lovely lady."

Allard saw the devilry twinkling in his friend's eyes. Robert was going to go through with it on his own, and Allard felt sure that he would get caught. There was no stopping Robert, though, once he had his mind set on something . . .

Except on the rare occasion, such as now, when he was distracted by something—or someone—he cared even more about. Jacqueline appeared at his side, flushed from dancing, an excited smile on her face. She clutched his arm. "Did you see that? I danced with General Beauregard!"

"I saw," Robert told her with a nod. "The general is a very handsome man."

"He certainly is." Awareness suddenly dawned on Jacqueline's face. "Land's sake, you're jealous!"

"No, I'm not," Robert insisted.

"You are. You're jealous of General Beauregard." Jacqueline clutched his arm tighter. "Don't be silly, Robert. He may be a general, but he's not nearly as handsome as you. And he's *old*." She pulled on him. "Dance with me. Don't you just love 'Dixie'?"

"I do," he said, and with a sigh and a last glance at the punch bowl, he took her in his arms and began to dance with her.

Allard relaxed when he saw that and put his arms around Diana, and both young couples joined the others on the floor as the strains of the song that meant so much to these Southerners filled the ballroom.

# CHAPTER TWELVE

# Bombardment

B Y APRIL 9 THE talk of a Yankee fleet on its way to Charleston was no longer a rumor. Through information gathered by operatives in Washington and even from Northern newspaper stories, it was common knowledge that seven warships under the command of Capt. Gustavus V. Fox were en route to deliver supplies to the troops on Fort Sumter in direct defiance of Governor Pickens's edict that such a relief expedition not be allowed to enter the harbor. The hopes of those who wanted peace were dashed; the fears of those who believed war was the best, even the only, course of action were relieved.

With the city thrown into an uproar over this news, the board of visitors, the controlling authority over the Citadel, decided to cancel commencement exercises. Even though the ceremony did not take place, the cadets were given the customary several days' leave following graduation. Allard returned to his parents' house, and as over the Christmas holiday, Robert went with him instead of journeying to his family's farm inland. Given the situation, the cadets could be called back to duty at any time, on a moment's notice, and Robert didn't want to be caught far away from Charleston in case hostilities broke out.

But he found himself at loose ends in the Tyler house. Allard was spending as much time as he could with Diana, and Jacqueline had returned with her parents to Four Winds, outside the city. Cam was upstate at Columbia, of course, attending classes at the Arsenal. That left Robert to rattle around in the big house and try to find ways to pass the time.

Lucinda was there, too, of course. Robert found her in the parlor as he entered the room the day after the cancelled graduation. She was sitting on the divan, focused on some needlework, but he asked anyway, "What are you doing?"

"What does it look like?" she replied in surly tones without looking up at him.

"It looks like you're making a sampler."

"That's right. It's going to say 'Home Sweet Hell.' Do you think I ought to hang it here in the parlor when I'm done?"

"I think anywhere you are is going to be hell, Lucinda."

That made her glance up at him with hatred glittering in her icy blue eyes. "You despise me, don't you, Robert?"

"I might, if I wanted to waste the time and energy to give you that much thought."

"What have I ever done to make you feel that way? We barely know each other." She grimaced. "I'll bet Allard's been telling you all sorts of lies about me, hasn't he? He's a horrible little brat, and he always has been. You can't trust anything he says."

"He's my best friend," Robert said. "I think I'll believe him."

Lucinda looked down at her needlework again and shrugged. "Go ahead. I don't give a damn what you think of me."

"How ladylike of you to phrase it that way."

"I don't give a damn about being a lady, either." Abruptly, she set the needlework aside. "Have you got a cigar?"

The question took him by surprise. "What?"

"I asked if you have a cigar."

"No, I don't."

Her hand delved in the folds of her skirt. "Well, I do," she said as she brought out a tightly rolled cylinder of tobacco. "And I'm going to smoke it."

She took a lucifer from the pocket where the cigar had been hidden and scratched it into life on one of the fireplace stones. She put the cigar in her mouth, held the flame to the other end, and puffed until it was lit. She coughed delicately as she took the cigar out of her mouth. Smoke hung in the air in front of her face.

"Are you shocked?" she asked Robert.

"Nothing you do shocks me. You're liable to get in trouble with your parents, though."

Lucinda waved a hand through the coils of smoke, shredding them. "Father's at the shipyard and won't be home for hours. Mother's already been nipping at the sherry today, so she doesn't know and doesn't care what I do. *You're* not going to tell, are you, Robert?"

He hesitated only a second before he shrugged and said, "No, I won't tell. I've never been one to carry tales."

"I didn't think so." Lucinda held the cigar out to him. "Have a puff?"

Again he hesitated. Then he took the cigar from her. He had smoked a few cigars in his life, and this was a fine one. He inhaled deeply and blew the smoke out then handed the cigar back to Lucinda.

"Why don't we play cards?" she suggested. "We've both been left alone with nothing to do, so we might as well entertain ourselves. A few hands of whist might be enjoyable."

"Do you know how to play poker?"

She shook her head. "That's not a game for young ladies. But maybe you could teach me."

"I reckon I could do that. Got a deck around here?"

With the cigar in her mouth, Lucinda retrieved a deck of cards from a drawer in an expensive, ornately carved side table. She handed them to Robert, who drew up a wing chair so he could sit across from her and deal the cards on the low table in front of the divan.

They passed the cigar back and forth as Robert explained the basics of the game to her. Lucinda nodded as he talked but didn't seem to fully grasp what he was telling her. They played a few hands, with Lucinda losing each one.

"Aren't you supposed to bet in this game?" she asked.

"Yes, but that would hardly be fair, given your inexperience," Robert said.

"Don't patronize me," she snapped. "If you're supposed to bet, I think we should bet."

"All right. Do you have any money?"

"Well . . . no."

"What are you going to bet, then?"

"How about a kiss?"

That surprised him again. "You want to kiss me?"

She looked horrified. "Good Lord, no! That gives me a mighty good reason to win, doesn't it?"

"Wait a minute," he said. "If I win, you kiss me, is that it?"

"That's right."

"But if you win, what do I do? That is, assuming you don't want me to kiss you."

"Most definitely not. Do *you* have any money?"

"A little."

"That's it, then. I'll wager a kiss against, say, a nickel."

He frowned. "I think I'm getting the short end of this wager."

"Just deal the cards and we'll see what happens."

Robert dealt while she put the cigar out on the hearth and stashed what was left of it in her pocket. Lucinda looked confused as she stared at her cards. Finally she discarded three, but when Robert had given her three more cards, she didn't look any happier.

"Is this anything?" she asked as she laid down her hand.

He looked at the cards and shook his head. "I'm afraid not." He laid down his own. "But I have a pair of fours. That's not much, but it's enough to beat you."

"All right. Come here." She patted the divan cushion next to her. "Collect your winnings."

"That's all right," Robert said without getting up from his chair.

"No, I insist. I won't be known as someone who won't honor her bets."

"Ladies aren't supposed to wager," he pointed out.

"I told you I don't care about being a lady. Now get over here."

He wasn't going to argue with her. He moved to the divan, sitting close enough to her so that they could reach each other without getting too close. As he leaned toward her, she raised her hands and rested one on each side of his face. She pressed her mouth to his. The kiss was hard and cold and artless, and her mouth tasted a little like the cigar. "There. Do you want to play again?"

"I'm not sure."

She glared at him. "What, my kiss wasn't good enough? Give me another chance. I'll beat you this time."

"I doubt that, but . . . all right, we'll try it again."

"Make the stakes a dime on your side this time?"

"Fine."

Robert retreated to the wing chair and dealt the cards again. The result was the same. Lucinda actually managed to get two sevens this time, but Robert beat her with two pair, twos and sixes. Lucinda sighed in frustration and said, "All right, get over here."

"You really don't have to—"

"Don't argue with me, Cadet Gilmore."

"Yes ma'am," Robert said dryly as he moved back to the divan. Once again Lucinda gave him a mostly passionless kiss, but he thought her lips were a little softer and more pliant this time.

"Deal again," she ordered.

"I'm not sure there's any point in it."

"Deal again. If I lose this time, I'll give you a kiss you'll never forget. But just to make things fair . . . how much money do you have on you?"

"I don't know . . . Let me see . . ." He delved in his pockets. "Six bits."

"Bet all of it against the best kiss you'll ever have."

He couldn't help but laugh. "I doubt that."

Lucinda glared at him. "You think that prissy little Jacqueline Lockhart can kiss better than I can?"

151

"I know she can."

"You'll think differently when I get through with you. Now put your money down and deal the cards."

Robert smiled, shook his head, and dealt the cards.

A few minutes later, he was staring in amazement as Lucinda laid down her hand and said, "Straight flush. I believe that beats that measly full house of yours." She scooped up all of Robert's coins from the table. They disappeared somewhere into the folds of her dress as she got to her feet.

He lifted his head to look at her. "You tricked me."

"You made the bet," she said coldly. "You took your chances. When you lose, you pay the price."

She started to turn away. He stood up and reached out to grasp her arm, stopping her. "What would you have done if you had lost?" he demanded. "You couldn't have paid up."

She laughed. "You think not?"

With that, she was pressed against him, her arms around his neck, her open mouth clinging hotly to his. Her lips were sweet and urgent and her tongue slid boldly into his mouth. Her body molded itself to his. Even through the stiff, starched fabric of her gown and her undergarments, he felt her warm, exciting curves. Arousal thundered through him.

After a moment that seemed timeless, she broke the kiss, stepped back, and gave a defiant toss of her thick blonde hair. "What do you say now?" she demanded. "Still think the wager wasn't worth it?"

Slowly, trying to keep his hand from trembling, he raised it and wiped the back of it across his mouth. "I reckon I got what I paid for, all right," he said.

Her face went white, and her hand flashed up in a slap aimed at his face. But he caught her wrist before the blow could land. From a distance of no more than six inches, she glared into his face and hissed, "You're contemptible. You're nothing but a poor farm boy."

"And no matter how much money your family has, you'll never be anything but a cheap trollop," he grated back at her.

"Your brother didn't think so."

That shocked Robert enough to make him let go of her wrist. She didn't try again to slap him, though. She just lowered her hand and gave him a cold, evil smile.

"Cam?" he choked out.

"When you see Cam again, give him my best . . . No, wait. I've already done that. Several times."

"You . . . you . . ."

"Say it again and I'll tell my father you made advances toward me. He'll have you horsewhipped and drummed out of the Citadel. I know you're going to resign anyway, but if you're discharged first, that dishonor will follow you wherever you go."

"You wouldn't dare."

"Try me," she said, and he knew she meant it.

Again he wiped the back of his hand across his mouth. "Stay away from Cam."

"What I do is none of your business. You'd better just stay out of *my* way."

"Don't worry. I don't want to have anything more to do with you."

With a sniff of contempt, she turned and left the parlor. Robert stood there for a long moment, feeling like he had just had an encounter with something unclean. The idea that her tongue had been in his mouth made him want to spit. Either that or drink some of the fieriest whiskey he could find in hopes it would wash away any corruption she had left behind.

A soft step made him turn sharply. He relaxed a little when he saw it was only Ellie.

"Marse Robert, I know it ain't my place to be sayin' anythin', but you don't want to be messin' with Miss Lucinda. She . . . she ain't right in the head sometimes."

"Don't worry. I don't intend to have anything more to do with her."

"That's good, 'cause I heard what she told you, an' I know she wouldn't hesitate to do what she said. She'd ruin your life, suh, and then laugh about it." Ellie came a step closer. "I seen and I heard, though, an' if she'd tried that, I'd've told Marse Malachi what really happened. No matter what Miss Lucinda done to me, I'd've told the truth."

"That's fine," Robert said, "but Mr. Tyler wouldn't believe a slave over his own daughter, now would he?"

With that, Robert left the parlor, too, not looking back.

Which meant that he didn't see the hurt in Ellie's eyes at the harshness of his words.

ON APRIL 11 word arrived in Charleston that the fleet of Captain Fox's ships was approaching the South Carolina coast. General Beauregard's response was to send a pair of emissaries to Fort Sumter with a note for Major Anderson demanding that the fort be evacuated. Otherwise, Fort Sumter would be fired upon. Anderson expressed regrets but replied that he could not comply. But he asked if he would be notified before firing commenced, and Beauregard's messengers replied that he would.

That moment could not come soon enough to satisfy most of the people in Charleston. Guns were now trained on Fort Sumter from a variety of locations: the floating battery, the ironclad battery on Morris Island (so-called because of its thick armor plating), Fort Moultrie, Fort Johnson, Cummings Point, Castle Pinckney, White Point, and the Battery on the city's harbor wall itself. The citizens who still hoped for a peaceful solution remained in their homes for the most part. They were far outnumbered by those who were sick and tired of waiting. The fire-eaters—and by this time most of the Charlestonians could have been said to have partaken of that scorching dish—took to the streets to demonstrate their impatience. Editorials screamed from the pages of the city's newspapers, demanding a beginning to the conflict.

Meanwhile, Beauregard was in contact via telegraph with the Confederate government in Montgomery. During Anderson's conversation with Beauregard's emissaries, he had made the comment that he would be forced to surrender when his supplies ran out, which would be in a matter of days. After being informed of this, President Davis and his cabinet instructed Beauregard to press Anderson for a specific date and time of surrender. If they could receive this commitment from the major, hostilities might still be avoided. Beauregard's aide, Col. James Chesnut Jr. was rowed out to Sumter yet again to present this demand to Anderson.

The narrow window of opportunity soon closed. Major Anderson agreed to surrender and evacuate Fort Sumter—at noon on April 15. That was too late. The fleet of Federal ships would arrive by then. Though there were steamers patrolling the channel, and though dozens of Confederate guns commanded a field of fire on the approach to Fort Sumter, that was no guarantee some of the warships would not get through. If Anderson received even a single boatload of supplies, he might be able to hold out for days, if not weeks.

The Confederates could not afford to risk that. Early on the morning of April 12, while at Fort Sumter, Colonel Chesnut informed Major Anderson that shelling would commence in one hour. Then Chesnut and another officer, Capt. Stephen D. Lee, left the fort and were rowed the mile and a third to Fort Johnson, on James Island at the southern side of the harbor.

Most of Charleston was asleep as the minutes ticked by between 3:30 and 4:30 on that fateful morning. Allard Tyler and Robert Gilmore certainly were. But like nearly everyone else, they heard the heavy thump of a mortar at 4:30. Allard rolled out of his bed and sprang to the window, throwing back the curtains to peer out at the darkness. It was a foggy night, with no stars showing in the sky, but the lurid glare of a mortar round arching above the harbor was visible even through the fog. Allard guessed from the trajectory of the round that it had come from Fort Johnson. The shell burst high in the sky above Fort Sumter. A moment later, another boom sounded as a second mortar round was launched. This one wasn't a signal, as the first one had been. This one was aimed straight at the Yankee fort.

"It's begun," Allard whispered.

On Morris Island, at the battery manned by the Palmetto Guard, Edmund Ruffin yanked the lanyard that fired the friction trigger of one of the big guns in that armored battery. The elderly firebrand had asked for the honor of firing one of the first shots in the conflict, and that request had been granted. Ruffin's aim was good, too—the heavy ball soared over the water and slammed into the parapet of the besieged fort.

That was just the beginning. Batteries all around the harbor opened up, some right away, others gradually getting into the action over the next half-hour. But by five o'clock in the morning, the sky over Charleston Harbor was almost as bright as day, lit up by the constant flashing of the barrage. No one could tell exactly how much damage was being done to the fort, but it was obvious that the thick walls of masonry were taking quite a few hits. Smoke began to billow up from inside the walls, and the clouds took on an orange tint from the explosions.

Allard and Robert had a good view of the spectacular fireworks. They had hurried to the Citadel, and along with the other cadets who were still at the academy and those who had stayed in Charleston, they were dispatched to White Point, on the eastern side, near the tip of the peninsula where the city was situated. A battery of guns had been mounted there, in White Point Gardens, and it was the job of the cadets to man them.

Maj. Stafford Pinckston was in charge at the battery. "Stand to your guns but hold your fire," he told the cadets. "We've not yet received orders to join in the bombardment."

That was understandable, thought Allard, since these smaller guns did not have sufficient range to reach Fort Sumter. The fort was a good three miles away, and the largest gun they had was a 12-pounder. Still, they would be ready if the order came to fire.

In the meantime, they had a grand seat for the spectacle. All of Charleston was watching, in fact. The rooftops of the buildings were crowded with people, and every window above the first floors had faces peering out avidly. This was war, the long-rumored civil war, feared by some and anticipated by others. And it was beginning in Charleston's own backyard.

Allard and Robert stood watching the shells burst against and above the fort. Allard said to Stafford Pinckston, "Major, how long can the Yankees hold out against something like this?"

Pinckston just shook his head. "I don't know, lad. It's as if all the forces of heaven and hell are arrayed against them. They cannot stand for long."

Allard felt no sympathy for the Yankees. They had brought this on themselves. But as he felt the explosions of the guns cause the earth to tremble like thunder and watched the heavens flicker from the blasts as if from lightning, he found himself hoping for the sake of those trapped on that lonely fort that this deadly storm would soon come to an end.

# CHAPTER THIRTEEN

# Surrender and Aftermath

THIRTY-FOUR HOURS. That was how long the bombardment lasted, well into the day on April 13.

On the morning of April 12, after the sun rose and while the shelling was still at its height, the Yankees on Sumter attempted to mount a resistance. Plumes of fire and smoke gushed from the casemate gunports as the cannon began to roar. The guns mounted in barbette atop the parapet were not used, since any gun crews there would be exposed and unprotected.

Fort Moultrie and the floating battery to the north and the ironclad battery to the south were the closest targets, so it was in those places that the Federals concentrated their fire. There were no mortars inside Fort Sumter, so the Yankee gunners could not lob shells high into the air as the Confederates were doing. They had to settle for straight-on shots from their guns, and although their accuracy was good, the rounds did little damage. Several cannonballs struck the ironclad battery, but its armor plating did its job superbly. The balls simply bounced off. In the time since the Federals had abandoned Fort Moultrie in late December, the Confederates had strengthened its fortifications considerably, so the Yankee rounds that landed there were largely ineffective. With the exception of one horse on Morris Island that was killed by a projectile, there were no casualties on the Confederate side.

Later in the day a lookout inside Fort Sumter spotted several ships on the horizon. Cheers went up from the men inside the embattled fort. They were convinced that the ships they saw were the vanguard of Captain Fox's rescue fleet.

Indeed they were, but Fox halted his vessels well off the coast and didn't come any closer, unwilling to risk his ships in the firestorm that engulfed the entrance to Charleston Harbor. Assistance for the Yankees was maddeningly close but stayed just out of reach.

In Charleston it had become obvious that the guns inside Fort Sumter posed no threat to the city itself. Once again a festive atmosphere gripped the population. Thousands climbed to the rooftops and lined the harbor to cheer on the gunners who were pouring round after round into the fort. No holiday celebration could equal what went on in Charleston during that day. Even the coming of rain showers that night failed to dampen the spirits of the Charlestonians. The bombardment went on into the night as did the party.

The rain helped to control the fires that had been started inside the fort, but it had stopped by the next day. Confederate mortars lobbed hot shot into the fort. These rounds exploded as they landed and sent flames in all directions. It wasn't long before various parts of the fort were on fire again, and these blazes were too fierce to be extinguished. Despite that, the Yankees were still trying to put up a fight. They were running low on ammunition, but from time to time a round would come from the fort toward Moultrie or Cummings Point.

By the middle of the day the bombardment had been going on for more than thirty hours. Clouds of black and gray smoke billowed up from inside the fort. The Confederate gunners were exhausted and covered with grime from the powder smoke, but at least they were better off than their Northern counterparts. In the early afternoon, overcome by sympathy for the gallant, hopeless defenders, and with the natural Southern admiration for valor, several members of one of the gun crews ceased firing and climbed to the top of their battery instead. They yanked off their hats, waved them over their heads, and let out a cheer for the Federals.

The display spread. More and more of the big guns fell silent as the Confederate gunners climbed into the open and cheered and waved. From Moultrie to Cummings Point, from Fort Johnson to Castle Pinckney to the White Point Battery where Allard and Robert and the other cadets had watched the battle from the beginning, the South Carolinians paid tribute to their enemies. The guns of Fort Sumter fell silent, too, although whether it was in response to the Southerner's display or because they were out of ammunition, no one knew.

Unseen in the smoke rolling over the harbor, a Confederate colonel and former senator from Texas, Louis Wigfall, was rowing out to Sumter under a flag of truce. He entered the fort, scarcely noticed by the harried, exhausted troops, located Major Anderson, and formally asked for his surrender. Anderson hesitated only briefly before agreeing.

Fresh cheers went up from everyone on shore as the American flag over Fort Sumter, which had been knocked down once during the bombardment and then put up again, was slowly hauled down and replaced by a white flag. Allard and Robert and the other cadets whooped and pounded each other's backs, their weariness forgotten in the excitement. The ships that stood off the coast had not dared to come in, and the Federal troops who had illegally occupied Fort Sumter had been forced to surrender. The South Carolinians had struck a blow for freedom and for the right of the Confederate States of America to exist. Maybe now the damn Yankees would see that they meant business, they thought. The *Star of the West* incident hadn't done it, but no one could mistake what had happened here.

The time for politics was over; the time for war was now. The Yankees would regret rousing the sleeping giant that was the South. Maybe they had learned their lesson from the fall of Fort Sumter, but if they hadn't, that was fine, too. Southerners stood ready to defeat them again and again, for however long it took for the Yankees understand.

The Union, as it had once stood, was dead.

DIANA SAT in the swing on the porch of the Tyler mansion. She leaped up when she saw Allard and Robert coming and rushed down the walk toward them. With no thought of propriety she threw her arms around Allard and kissed him.

"Are you all right?" she asked as she stepped back to look at him. He seemed to be fine except for the lines of weariness on his face.

"I'm fine," he told her. "The Yankees did a little shooting, but not at us."

"We had a front-row seat for the festivities, though," Robert put in. "We could see nearly every round as it struck Sumter."

That was all the cadets had been doing for the past day and a half, watching the bombardment of that lonely fortress rock in the mouth of the harbor. The guns in White Point Gardens had been manned around the clock, although they hadn't been used at all in the attack. The cadets had caught snatches of sleep here and there, but not enough to keep them from being quite tired. Robert just wanted to go to his room, collapse on the bed, and get some real sleep; Allard, although just as worn out, was glad that Diana had waited here to welcome him home and wanted to spend a few minutes with her.

They wouldn't be spent in privacy, however. Malachi and Katherine Tyler came streaming out of the house when they heard their son's voice. Malachi embraced both young men and said, "So it's over, is it?" His face wore an excited expression. Despite his practical streak, he wasn't immune to passions that had been inflamed by months of posturing and hostility between North and South.

"It's over for now," Allard said. "Major Anderson has surrendered and agreed to evacuate the fort. The Yankees won't be gone from there until sometime tomorrow, but as long as they leave as they've agreed to, there won't be any more shelling."

"Good. Maybe that will be the end of it."

"I hope so," Katherine said. "All that shooting is a terrible thing. I hope no one was hurt too badly."

"I don't know about the Yankees, but I've heard it said that we didn't sustain any casualties, not even any wounded," Allard told them.

162

"Thank the Lord for that!" Katherine said.

Diana put a hand on Allard's arm. "Then my father's all right, too?"

"Certainly. Our battery wasn't even involved in the bombardment." Allard couldn't keep a hint of disappointment from creeping into his voice.

Malachi clapped a hand on his shoulder. "I'm sure you boys would have been ready if you'd been called on. Let's go inside. Cook's got some food ready for you—"

"If it's all the same to you, sir," Robert said, "I'd rather sleep than eat right now."

"Of course, whatever you'd like to do. How about you, Allard?"

Allard looked at Diana and realized that he could prolong his time with her if he sat down to a meal. "I could eat," he said.

"Come along then."

Allard held Diana's hand as they went inside. His parents led him to the dining room, and he sat down at the table and had some fried chicken and biscuits and apple pie. He actually was hungry, and his appetite grew even stronger as he began to eat. Despite his slender frame, he had always been able to pack away a considerable amount of food. As he ate, he told Diana and his parents about everything he had seen during the eventful past day and a half.

Robert went upstairs toward his room, but before he got there, the door to another room opened and Lucinda stepped into the hallway. "Home from the war?" she asked with a sneer.

"I'm sorry I didn't get my head blown off by a Yankee cannonball. I'm sure that would have pleased you a great deal."

"I never gave it that much thought," she said carelessly. "Now, if your brother had been out there, possibly being fired upon by the Yankees, I might have worried."

Robert's eyes narrowed. "Why are you so interested in Cam? He's three years younger than you. He's nothing but a kid."

"You don't know your brother very well if that's what you think. He's already more of a man than you'll ever be, Robert Gilmore."

Robert muttered a curse and started to move past her, not wanting this shrew to keep him from his rest any longer. Lucinda shifted her position so that she partially blocked his path, and his arm brushed across her breasts as he went past her.

"Does that give you any ideas," she said, "or are you too tired from playing war?"

"There wasn't any playing about it," he snapped. "It was the real thing."

"Did anybody die?"

"I don't know. Not on our side."

"It wasn't much of a battle, then, was it?"

In truth, it hadn't been. The clash had been too one-sided to call it a battle. If the Yankees had been able to put up a better fight, it might have been a different story.

Robert didn't answer the gibe. He trudged on toward his room, not looking back at Lucinda. He heard her laughing softly but wasn't sure what she found so amusing. Nothing good, he was certain of that. Anything Lucinda found funny would probably be tragic to a normal person.

After the door of Robert's room had closed behind him, the smile disappeared from Lucinda's face. She had just been trying to annoy him, to get some sort of reaction from him. Young men had hated her in the past, when she was finished toying with them, but all too often, what she sensed from Robert Gilmore was indifference. He didn't like her, that was plain enough, but really, he didn't even pay that much attention to her. That was what really stung.

But that certainly hadn't been the case with his brother. Cam had been eager for any scrap of affection she deigned to dole out to him. His devotion was doglike. *That* was the way young men were supposed to react to her, not with hostility and ennui.

As she turned away, she spotted one of the housemaids coming out of a nearby alcove. "You there!" Lucinda hissed. "What were you doing in there?"

"Jus' dustin', Miss Lucinda," the slave answered. "Jus' cleanin' like I'se 'sposed to."

"You're the girl called Ellie, aren't you?"

"Yes'm."

Lucinda's eyes narrowed. "You're always sneaking around whenever Robert's nearby. Are you sweet on him? Is that it? Have you forgotten that he's white and you're just a slave?"

"Lawsy, no, Miss Lucinda! I wouldn't never do that." Ellie cast her eyes toward the floor and added in a murmur, "*I* ain't the one who's sweet on Marse Robert."

Lucinda didn't know whether she was intended to hear that comment or not, but hear it she did, and it kindled anger inside her. As Ellie started to turn away, Lucinda grabbed her arm and hauled her around. "You insolent wench!" she cried as she brought her other hand up and slapped Ellie hard across the face.

The blow cracked sharply and jerked Ellie's head to the side. She didn't show any reaction, just stood there breathing hard and looking down at the floor until Lucinda let go of her arm. Then she muttered, "I'se sorry, missy," and hurried away down the hall.

She glanced back only once. Lucinda had already turned away, so she didn't see the hatred smoldering in Ellie's eyes.

THE WATERS of Charleston Harbor were thronged with boats the next day, as many of the citizens turned out to get a firsthand view of the evacuation of Fort Sumter. April 15 was a Sunday, and although the church bells rang and preachers gave thanks from their pulpits that the devil—in the person of the Yankees—had been driven from their midst, many of the pews were empty. People wanted to see for themselves as Satan tucked his tail between his legs and ran.

Inside the fort, Robert Anderson was making final arrangements for the evacuation. General Beauregard had stayed away from Sumter, not wanting to embarrass Anderson by seeming to supervise things personally. There were plenty of other officers on hand, however, and they brought with them sacks of mail intended for the Federals, mail that had gone undelivered during the siege. They brought several bottles of brandy as well. With the same sense of honor and civility that permeated the officer class of both sides, Federal and Confederate alike drank together, laughing and sharing stories of what the bombardment had been like from their perspective. Amazingly enough, considering all the shelling, no one inside the fort had been killed, and only a few men had suffered minor wounds. This undoubtedly made it easier for the erstwhile enemies to enjoy each other's company.

The terms of the surrender had not changed from Beauregard's initial offer several days earlier. The Yankees were allowed to retain their arms and personal possessions, and they would be able to fire their parapet guns in a salute to the American flag as it was lowered for the final time.

The Confederate steamer *Isabel* pulled up next to the fort that morning. When the Yankees were ready to leave, they would board the vessel and be ferried out to the ships of Captain Fox's fleet, which still waited a short distance offshore. Although that was supposed to take place at eleven o'clock that morning, there were delays—as there always are in moving any large group of men—and it was a couple of hours after midday before the Federal troops were ready to board. As they lined up, the parapet guns began to fire, one after the other, in their final salute.

It was then that the only death in Fort Sumter occurred, as the accidental ignition of a bag of powder caused an explosion that killed a member of a Yankee gunnery crew and wounded several others. Despite that, the other guns continued to fire, and not knowing about the tragedy, the Confederates all around the harbor cheered at each shot.

Caring for the wounded men caused yet another delay, so it was late in the afternoon before the evacuation was complete and all the Yankees were aboard the *Isabel*. Unfortunately, the tide had already gone out, and the steamer was stuck fast on the bottom of the harbor, unable to depart as scheduled. The plan had been for them to be well away from the fort before the Confederates occupied it, but that plan had to be scrapped. The Yankees had to swallow the bitter pill of watching their enemies swarm over the place they had so stubbornly defended.

There was no holding back the celebration in the harbor and in the city itself. Governor Pickens, General Beauregard, and Mayor Mc-Grath of Charleston were all on hand as members of the Palmetto Guard disembarked and marched into Fort Sumter to raise the South Carolina flag with its blue background and white palmetto tree, along with the Stars and Bars of the Confederate States of America. As the flags were pulled up the pole and came into view above the walls of the fort, Charleston exploded in celebration. Bells pealed, cannon boomed, and the thrilling sound of victory shouts welling from thousands of throats filled the air. Earlier in the afternoon, the Citadel cadets had marched in a dress parade for a vast throng of spectators, and their voices added to the uproar. Among them, Allard Tyler and Robert Gilmore both threw back their heads and gave the long, drawn-out cry that some would come to refer to as a Rebel Yell.

There was still danger of another sort of explosion. Small fires still burned inside Fort Sumter, and if the flames reached the powder magazine, even the severely depleted supply of powder would be enough to cause a tremendous blast. Members of the Palmetto Guard, along with fire companies from the city, spent all night and some of the next day extinguishing the fires and making sure they stayed out.

When the tide came in the next morning, the *Isabel* was finally able to get under way, steaming up the channel that would take her out of Charleston Harbor to the open sea where Captain Fox's fleet waited. Major Anderson stood at the railing as the boat went past Morris Island, and he saw the Confederates lined up on the beach there, their hats and caps taken off and held in their hands as they paid tribute to the defeated foe. There was gallantry aplenty on both sides in this conflict.

But whether that gallantry would produce a peaceful solution or more violence, no one could yet know on that sunny Monday morning in April.

# CHAPTER FOURTEEN

# Choices

"B Y GOD, I THOUGHT you would have come to your senses by now!" Malachi Tyler's fist slammed down on his desk as if to punctuate his angry words.

"I never said I had changed my mind," Allard said tightly as he stood in front of the desk and tried not to quail before his father's angry glare. The flush on Malachi's face extended well up to his mostly bald scalp.

He shook a finger at his son and said, "What you need is a swift kick in the rear. That might knock some sense into you, because it seems that's where your brain must be!"

"You can insult me all you want," Allard said. "It's not going to change my mind. My letter of resignation from the Citadel is already written and signed. All I have to do is present it to Major Stevens."

Malachi leaned back in his chair with an exasperated sigh. "It's not the resigning from the Citadel that bothers me, although it would certainly be all right with me if you wanted to stay there and finish your studies. You know damn well what I don't like is this foolish notion of joining the navy."

"The Confederate navy will need good sailors," Allard pointed out. "Right now they're short of vessels and men and everything else. I can make a difference there, Father. I'm convinced of it."

169

"You can make a difference helping me build boats for the Confederate navy! One common sailor more or less means nothing."

Deep down, Allard knew that his father was mostly right about that. In the long run, whatever he might accomplish by working at the Tyler Shipyard would mean more to the Confederacy than mending sails and swabbing decks or whatever other tasks he might be assigned on a ship.

But in all likelihood, working for his father would also mean sitting behind a desk most of the time, shuffling papers and adding up numbers and a myriad of other deadly boring chores.

"I'm sorry, Father," he said. "I'm a seagoing man, and there's nothing I can do about it."

"You're a damned idiot!"

The stalemate continued, as it had for the past month, ever since the bombardment of Fort Sumter and the Yankees' subsequent surrender.

The plan made by Allard and Robert had called for them to resign from the Citadel as soon as war broke out. The question was, had war really broken out, or was the attack on Fort Sumter to be the end of it? Politicians in both North and South, led by their respective presidents, Abraham Lincoln and Jefferson Davis, made speeches and issued statements that hinted a peaceful solution was still possible. On the other hand, on April 15, one day after Major Anderson's surrender, Lincoln had called for seventy-five thousand volunteers to take up arms for the Union for a period of three months. Yankees and Confederates alike regarded that, rightly so, as a sign that Lincoln was preparing for war.

Lincoln got his volunteers, but the surge in enlistments in the North was matched by the eagerness with which Southern men signed up to fight. Charleston was more crowded with soldiers than ever, and as before, it fell to the cadets of the Citadel to help with their training.

After considerable argument, Malachi had persuaded Allard not to withdraw immediately from the Citadel but to finish out the current academic term. There was no fighting yet; there would be time for

Allard to resign later if he chose to. And Robert had followed Allard's lead. Both young men had split time between their classes and their duties as instructors for the recruits pouring into the city.

General Beauregard was in charge of Charleston's defenses, and if war came, he intended to be ready. Fort Sumter was now fully garrisoned by Confederate troops who repaired the damage from the attack, completed the previously unfinished construction, and installed a full complement of guns. Yankee ships had set up a regular patrol outside the harbor, blockading it, and the Confederate navy was not strong enough to prevent them from doing that. But if the Union warships ever tried to steam into the harbor itself, they would find themselves facing a warm welcome indeed from the guns of Fort Sumter.

In addition, several older ships had been scuttled and sunk in the channels leading into the harbor, forming obstructions that would also make it difficult for Federal vessels to enter.

All these preparations did not mean that war was imminent. Both sides just wanted to be ready. With the Citadel's term over, though, Allard saw no point in waiting any longer to withdraw. As he saw it, he had fulfilled his promise to his father, and now he was ready to act on his earlier plan.

"Robert's not going to tarry," he said. "He's going to join the Hampton Legion."

Malachi grunted. "I know Wade Hampton. Damned foolish thing he's doing, if you ask me, using his own money to outfit such a big group."

Quite a few wealthy men from around the state had formed their own companies of volunteers, which they then intended to lead into battle if war came. Col. Wade Hampton, a successful planter and businessman, had put together an even larger force of infantry, cavalry, and artillery. Someone had dubbed it Hampton's Legion, and the name had stuck.

"I'm surprised Robert could get in," Malachi went on. "From what I've heard, young men from the finest families in the state are joining the legion."

Allard bristled. "There's nothing wrong with Robert's family, just because they don't have as much money as some others. Colonel Hampton is an old friend of Robert's father, in fact."

"That explains it, then," Malachi said offhandedly. "But no matter what Robert does, that doesn't change your situation a bit. You have two perfectly good options available to you. Either would be a productive and honorable course of action. Yet you insist on throwing them away." Malachi's eyes narrowed. "And I know why, too. Don't think I don't."

"I'm sure I don't know what you're talking about," Allard said stiffly.

"My father! You're still caught up in the whole romantic notion of being like my father. You think it'll be dashing and exciting to be a sailor and fight the Yankees. Well, you're wrong. I've been to sea enough to know that it's a hard, dirty, dangerous business. There's nothing glamorous about it."

"For you, perhaps, that's true."

Malachi slapped the desk this time instead of striking it with his fist. "Damn it, I know what I'm talking about! You read about Black Nick, and you think it'll be like some story from a book to live that way, but you're wrong. Dear Lord, I wish you'd never found out what sort of man he was!"

"I've always been glad that I did."

Malachi glowered and shook his head, his frustration and annoyance plain to see on his face. Abruptly, he said, "What does Diana say about all this?"

Allard tensed. He had been hoping that his father wouldn't bring up the subject of Diana. "She's accepted my decision," he said.

"You two love each other, don't you?" Malachi asked bluntly.

Allard felt his face warming in embarrassment. "Well, I . . . I hope that Diana feels about me the same way I feel about her . . . I think she does . . . We've declared our intentions toward each other . . ."

"Good God, quit nattering around about it! I hope you don't stumble all over yourself that way whenever you kiss her!"

172

What happened when he kissed Diana was just about the last thing Allard wanted to discuss with his father. But he didn't say anything, just stood there uncomfortably.

"If you went to work for me," Malachi went on, "you'd stay right here in Charleston, you'd be doing valuable work for the Confederacy, and you'd be able to see Diana all the time, instead of sailing off away from her for God knows how long. If you've got an ounce of red blood in your veins, boy, it seems to me like that would be enough right there to make you see that I'm right."

Allard summoned up his determination and said, "It's true that I don't want to be away from Diana. But everyone has to make sacrifices during a war. We've discussed this, and we're willing to wait for each other—"

Malachi made a slashing motion with his hand, cutting off Allard's words. "She says now that she's willing to wait, but what happens when you've been gone for six months or a year and some handsome beau starts paying court to her? Do you honestly think she won't consider succumbing to his advances?"

Against his will, Allard's hands clenched into fists, and he took a step toward the desk. "By God, sir, if you weren't my father, I'd . . . I'd . . ."

"What?" Malachi demanded. "Strike me for insulting the honor of your young lady?" He gave a curt laugh. "Being a Southern gentleman, I shouldn't say this, but the power of honor is often overrated, Allard. Most people, North and South, are weak. They live by their concept of honor as long as it's easy and convenient for them. When it's not, they do what they want, or what they think they need. If the temptation is strong enough, they give in to it." He paused and then added confidently, "You'll do it, too."

Allard shook his head stubbornly. "No, I won't. Just because you're that way, it doesn't mean I will be."

"It doesn't have anything to do with how I am. It has to do with being human."

Allard wanted to put his hands over his ears and shut out his father's cynical, disgraceful words. Malachi was wrong. Wrong about him, wrong about everything. Allard was sure of it.

"Go ahead and do what you want," Malachi said. "I'm tired of arguing with you. But you're going to break your mother's heart, and you're probably going to break the heart of that girl you claim to love. And in the end you'll wind up getting yourself killed for nothing."

"The cause of the South is *not* nothing," Allard said in a shaky whisper. "Some things are worth dying for."

Malachi took a cigar from the humidor on his desk and bit off the end. Clenching the cigar between his teeth, he said, "Some things are worth *living* for. I pray to God that someday you'll figure that out."

ROBERT SET his letter of resignation on Major Stevens's desk and stepped back. Without picking it up, the superintendent of the Citadel looked at it then nodded slowly.

"I'm not surprised by this, Cadet Gilmore," Stevens said. "Many of our young men are choosing this path."

"Yes sir," Robert said crisply. "I hope you know that it indicates no reflection on the Citadel or anyone involved with it, sir."

"I understand, Cadet." The major smiled wryly. "As I said, you're hardly the first to come knocking on my door with a letter such as this. May I ask what your plans are?"

"I'll be enlisting in the Hampton Legion, sir."

Stevens nodded. "I'm sure you'll be pleased with your choice. Colonel Hampton is a good man. Will you be joining his cavalry?"

"No sir. No horse. It'll be the infantry, I reckon."

"You realize that if you wait another year and then enlist, you'll go in as an officer? I'm not trying to change your mind, you understand, just making sure you're aware of the situation."

"Yes sir, I know. But if I wait another year . . ." Robert couldn't keep the emotion out of his voice. "If I wait another year, the war's liable to be over."

"Other than the capture of Fort Sumter and the blockade the Yankees have thrown up around the harbor, the war hasn't really started, has it?"

"Could be any day now, sir. Abe Lincoln's got the seventy-five thousand men he asked for and more. I reckon it won't be much longer before the Yankees come marching down here bold as brass."

"You could be right." Stevens finally reached out and picked up Robert's letter. "Very well, Cadet Gilmore. It is with regret but understanding that I accept your withdrawal from the South Carolina Military Academy." He stood up and extended his hand out. "And since you are no longer a cadet, it's as one gentleman to another that I wish you the very best of luck in your future endeavors, sir."

Robert's chest was tight with emotion, and his voice was choked a little as he shook hands with Major Stevens and said, "Thank you, sir. As a former student, I'll not bring disgrace on the name of this fine institution."

Stevens smiled. "It never entered my mind that you would, Robert."

THE MOOD was tense and strained around the dinner table in the Tyler mansion that evening. Robert had withdrawn from the Citadel that afternoon, Allard knew, but Allard's letter to Major Stevens was still in his room. At least Robert was sensitive enough not to bring up the subject, even though he was probably excited by the upcoming changes in his life and would have liked to talk about it with his best friend. Robert knew, though, about the trouble between Allard and Malachi and wisely kept silent for the most part.

Lucinda was not so considerate. She smiled across the table at Robert and said, "So I suppose you'll be leaving us soon, Robert. Going off to fight the Yankees."

"Oh, Lucinda, no war talk at the table, please," Katherine said quickly.

"I'll be enlisting in the Hampton Legion," Robert said to Lucinda. "Whether there'll be any fighting or not, I don't know." He looked at Katherine and added, "Beg your pardon, Mrs. Tyler, but I didn't bring it up, and I thought it would be rude not to answer Miss Lucinda."

"Lord knows you'd never want to be rude," Lucinda said.

"That's enough," Malachi snapped. He was generally more tolerant of Lucinda's behavior than he was of Allard's, but tonight he was still upset from the argument with Allard earlier in the day.

"Thank you, Malachi," Katherine said. "There's no reason we can't enjoy a nice, peaceful dinner—"

The bell rang.

"Who the devil—" Malachi muttered as he picked up his napkin from his lap and threw it on the table beside his plate. "Thomas! Are you getting that?"

"Yes suh," came Thomas's reply as he slowly made his way toward the front door. The bell rang again before he could get there. Everyone in the dining room heard the door open, but they were too far away to make out any voices.

A minute later, Thomas appeared in the entrance to the dining room. "Major Pinckston say it important that he see you, Marse Malachi."

Stafford Pinckston bustled past Thomas without waiting for permission, a breach of etiquette that showed how upset he was. Allard thought the major looked pale and shaken, and immediately he was afraid that something had happened to Diana.

"Malachi, I need to talk to you," Stafford said. "I'm sorry to interrupt your dinner, but it's important."

"Is it about the war?" Malachi asked as he got to his feet.

"What?" Stafford gave a little shake of his head, like a man trying to fight his way out of a daze. "No, it's nothing to do with the war. It's a . . . personal matter."

Again, Allard felt a surge of fear. Something had happened to Diana. He knew it. Even though he was aware that it was impolite, he stood up and asked, "Is Diana all right?"

Stafford gave him the same confused look he had given Malachi a moment earlier. "Diana's fine," he said. "Well, I suppose she's upset, of course—"

"Upset? What about?"

"Mind your manners, boy," Malachi growled. "Come into the study, Stafford, and we'll talk about whatever's bothering you. We were almost through with dinner anyway."

Allard wasn't sure where he found the courage, but he said, "I'm coming, too."

Malachi was about to snarl at him in anger, but Stafford said, "That's all right. Maybe Allard should hear this. You, too, Robert. You're both practically grown men, after all."

"Grown men?" Lucinda scoffed. "I'm sorry, Major, but they're hardly—Ow!"

His sister's sudden exclamation of pain made Allard look around. He saw Lucinda staring at their mother, an expression of utter shock on her face, and he realized to his great amusement that Katherine had just kicked her on the shin to shut her up.

Stafford Pinckston ignored all of that. He fretted and fidgeted as Malachi steered him into the study. Allard and Robert trailed behind. The glances that Malachi gave them made it plain as day he didn't want them involved in this, but Stafford had said it was all right and Malachi wasn't going to go against the wishes of a guest in his home.

When the four of them were in the study and the door was closed, Malachi said, "Stafford, you look like you could use a drink."

"Yes, I think I could. Something to steady my nerves."

Malachi poured a shot of whiskey on the sideboard and handed the glass to Stafford. The major emptied it like the whiskey was nothing more than water. It put a little color back in his face as he blew his breath out in a long sigh.

"Whatever's wrong," Malachi said, "you'd be better off just to say it, Stafford. Get it off your chest."

"You're right." Stafford took another deep breath. "Tamara has left me."

"What!" Malachi looked like he couldn't believe it. "You mean—"

"I mean she packed some of her clothes and her other belongings, and she left. She took a carriage and went back to her parents' home."

"What about Diana?" Allard ventured to ask. "Did she go with Mrs. Pinckston?"

"No, she didn't," Stafford replied, and despite the seriousness of the situation, Allard felt a surge of relief. Diana was still close by, instead of all the way on the other side of Charleston with her mother and grandparents. "This was all her mother's idea," Stafford went on. "Diana wanted no part of it."

"Well, that's good at least, I suppose," Malachi said. He looked distinctly uncomfortable now. He had braced himself for news of some sort of political or military crisis, and instead his friend had presented him with an affair of the heart, the sort of trouble that is intensely personal. The very sort of thing that Malachi Tyler wasn't the least bit comfortable dealing with.

Stafford held out his empty glass. "I think I could use another drink."

Malachi gave a little start as he realized he was still holding the whiskey bottle. "Of course," he said as he splashed more of the fiery liquor into the glass. "Maybe you should sit down, Stafford."

The major tossed back the second drink as quickly as he had the first one. Then he set the empty glass on Malachi's desk and sank down on an ottoman. His hands hung limply between his knees. His head was thrust forward on his burly shoulders. Allard thought he looked like a big, sad bulldog.

"This wasn't totally unexpected," he said. "There's been trouble between us for a long time. Tamara was never happy about having to live on my salary from the Citadel. When she married me, she believed that my family had more money than it did."

"Women are never happy with the amount of money we make," Malachi said. "If they had more than they could ever spend for the rest of their lives, they'd still be unhappy. That's just the way the female mind works. Trust me, Stafford. I know what I'm talking about."

Stafford didn't look convinced. "I thought things would get better when Diana was born. I thought we would have more children, and Tamara would be too busy to be unhappy. But that never happened, and then I had to go off to war in Mexico when Diana was still small, and when I came back I could tell that something in Tamara had changed while I was gone. Changed for good. Or for bad, I should say. But it never went away. I didn't want to believe it, but deep down I knew it was just a matter of time until . . . until something like this happened."

Malachi rested a hand on his shoulder. "I wouldn't worry too much about it. Women get angry, but they get over it. Give her a few days to calm down, and I'm sure she'll come back. She'll beg your forgiveness and promise that it'll never happen again."

"I wish that were true." Stafford shook his head. "I wish I could believe it. But I saw the look in her eyes when she left. She's gone for good."

"But she can't divorce you! It would be a terrible scandal."

"She doesn't want a divorce. She just doesn't want to be with me anymore."

Allard said, "There's no one else?"

Malachi swung around sharply. "Allard! Have you lost your mind? How dare you ask a question like that?"

Stafford lifted a hand and said, "No, it's all right, Malachi, really. I asked myself the same question, and then I asked Tamara. She swears that there's no one else. That's why she doesn't want to divorce me. There's no need. But she swears she'll never live with me again, either."

"I'm sorry, Major," Allard said.

"So am I, Major," Robert added, the first thing he had said since they'd come into the study.

Stafford nodded glumly. "Thanks, lads. I thought you might lend a sympathetic ear. And thank you, too, Malachi, for listening. I . . . I just had to talk to someone."

"Of course. No one can blame you for being thrown by all this."

The major took a deep breath, squared his shoulders, and said, "Well, in one respect, this makes things easier for me. I knew that Tamara would be upset about the decision I've reached."

"What decision is that?"

"I'm going to resign my teaching position and enlist in the army. I'm sure they can find a use for an old artillerist like me."

Allard and Robert exchanged a glance. Major Pinckston had had the same idea as them.

"Enlist?" Malachi said with a frown. "At your age?"

Stafford gave a humorless laugh. "Being a bit blunt, aren't you, Malachi?"

"I mean no offense—"

"None taken, not between old friends like us. You're right, of course. I'm a little old to be going off to war. But there are plenty of older men who are doing the same thing. I have years of experience with cannon. It would be a shame not to put it to good use, now that the South needs all the fighting men it can find."

"I'm sure you'd do a fine job, but you have responsibilities, Stafford. A job—"

"I can be replaced on the faculty without any great difficulty."

"And you have a family," Malachi went on. "A wife and a daughter—"

"A wife who has just walked out on me," Stafford reminded him. "But I'm glad you mentioned Diana. She's another reason I came over here this evening."

Allard's interest perked up again at the mention of Diana. He leaned forward and asked, "What does Diana have to do with this, Major?"

"Well, if I enlist and go off to fight, she won't be able to stay in the house alone. We have servants, of course, but it wouldn't be proper."

"No, certainly not," Malachi agreed. He hesitated then said, "Maybe she should stay with Tamara and her folks—"

"No," Stafford said emphatically. "She doesn't want to, and I don't want her to. That's why I have to ask you, Malachi . . ."

Allard's heart suddenly sped up, pounding heavily in his chest as he realized what the major was about to say.

"Could she stay with you and Katherine, Malachi?" Stafford asked. "I can't think of a better place for Diana than right here."

# CHAPTER FIFTEEN

# Departures and Arrivals

**W**ELL, THIS WAS A fine kettle of fish, thought Allard, although, in truth, he had never seen what was so fine about a kettle of fish to start with. All he really knew was that the developments of the past twelve hours had been very pleasant in some ways but had added unneeded complications to his life in others.

It was hard to believe that he was sitting in the parlor of his own house with the woman he loved sitting across from him . . . and she would be here not only every day but every night, too. Diana Pinckston lived here now. She had moved into the Tyler mansion this morning, bringing several trunks and carpetbags with her. The servants had unloaded the luggage from Major Pinckston's carriage and taken it upstairs to the room that would belong to Diana for the foreseeable future. Now, with the exception of Lucinda, the family was sitting in the parlor with their houseguest, and a somewhat uncomfortable silence had settled over the room.

Diana attempted to break it by saying, "Mr. and Mrs. Tyler, I have to tell you again how much I appreciate this—"

"Why, don't think a thing in the world about it, dear," Katherine broke in. "Land's sakes, we're glad to have you stay with us. Aren't we, Malachi?"

Her husband grunted but summoned up the graciousness to say,

"Of course we are. You're welcome in our home for as long as you need to stay, Diana. But for her own sake, I haven't given up hope that your mother will come to her senses—"

"Malachi!"

"There's no point in dancing around the subject, Katherine," Malachi said. "Tamara Pinckston did a very foolish thing by leaving Stafford. He's a good man."

"He is," Diana agreed. "And I think my mother knows that. She's just not happy with him."

"Oh, fiddle," Katherine said. "If everyone had to be happy all the time, nobody would ever get anything done. No offense, my dear."

Diana smiled. "None taken, Mrs. Tyler. I know what you mean. You were always friendly to my mother and tried to help her any way you could."

"Of course I did. That's one reason I don't mind taking you in now. This difficult time will be easier for everyone concerned if your mother and father both know that you have a place to stay. A place to call home, if that's what you want."

"Right now," Diana said, "that's exactly what I want."

She looked at Allard, and the warmth that passed between them as their eyes met set his pulse to racing and his heart to pounding. How could he leave now, *with Diana living under the same roof as he?*

On the other hand, maybe it would be a good idea for him to follow his original plan. He wasn't sure if he could withstand the temptation of having her so close to him all the time. Of knowing, in the darkness of the night, that she was only a few yards away, right down the hall . . .

His father had told him that he would give in to temptation if it was strong enough, and Allard had taken that assumption as an affront to his sense of honor. But maybe Malachi had been right. The flesh was weak, no doubt about that. His sure as hell was.

With a clumping of boots, Robert came down the stairs. His cadet uniform was carefully folded and packed away in a small trunk with some of his other belongings. He was going to send the trunk back to the Gilmore farm. Where he was going, he would be traveling lightly until he got there.

Robert wore high-topped black boots, brown whipcord trousers, a cotton shirt, a black-silk cravat, a tan jacket, and a brown planter's hat. Around his waist was strapped a cartridge belt, and in his holster was a new .36-caliber Remington-Beals navy revolver. He had bought it the day before, along with the new clothes, using the last of the money his family had scraped up and sent with him when he came to the Citadel. He had been extremely frugal all year, instinctively saving as much of the money as he could. Now he knew why.

"Oh, my," Katherine said when Robert strode into the parlor. "You look like a . . . a gambler or some such, Robert. And a dangerous one, at that."

"Thank you, Mrs. Tyler," Robert said with a faint smile.

Allard stood up and grasped his friend's upper arm. "You don't look like a cadet anymore, that's certain." He became more solemn. "Do you really have to go today?"

"No point in waitin'." Robert's hill-country drawl was more pronounced now that he was no longer trying to keep it under control. "If things keep goin' like they are, there's Yankees gonna need killin' soon."

Katherine fluttered her hands. "Don't talk about killing, Robert. I pray to the Good Lord every night that it won't come to that." She wiped away a tear that had welled up in her eye. "I pray that He'll watch over you, too. This year you've become almost like another son to me."

Robert took his hat off, bent, and kissed her cheek. "Thank you, Mrs. Tyler. You've all been like a second family to me. You don't know how much it means to me, knowin' that y'all will be prayin' for me."

Malachi stood and extended his hand. As Robert took it, the patriarch said, "Take care of yourself, son. I'm sure you'll do just fine, and you'll make us all proud of you."

"Thank you, sir."

He turned to Diana next, who put her arms around him and hugged him. "Be careful," she told him quietly.

"Don't worry about me," he told her. "I'll be fine."

That just left Allard. The two friends embraced, slapping each other's back one last time. "You'll see to it that the things I packed are sent to my family?"

"Of course."

"And don't do anything too foolish."

"Of course not. You're a big enough fool for the both of us."

Robert grinned, stepped back a little, and punched Allard on the arm. "That's right. And don't you forget it."

"You're going to the depot?" Malachi asked.

"Yes sir. The legion is forming for training up close to Columbia. I'll catch up to them and enlist there."

"What about Cam?" Allard asked.

Robert shrugged. "His term's over at the Arsenal, so I reckon he's headed home by now. There's a letter for him in my trunk, along with letters for everybody else in the family."

"He's not going to be happy that he didn't get to say good-bye to you in person."

"It can't be helped." Robert looked around the parlor. "Well, I reckon that's it. I'd better get goin' if I don't want to miss my train. So long, everybody."

A chorus of good-byes followed him out of the room. Allard would have come with him, but Robert motioned him back. "Better just to let me go," he said quietly.

Allard nodded in understanding and remained in the parlor. Robert prided himself on controlling his emotions. He didn't want any of them to see how choked up he really was at this moment.

But Allard knew.

In the foyer, Robert had his hand on the knob of the front door when a voice said quietly but urgently behind him, "Marse Robert?"

He paused and looked back, saw the housemaid Ellie standing there, her eyes big and shining with tears.

"You goin' off to the war, Marse Robert?"

"I'm joining the Hampton Legion," he said. "I reckon if there really is a war, I'll be part of it."

"You take care o' yourself," Ellie said as she came a step closer. "Don't you let none o' them damn Yankees shoot you."

He laughed. "I'll do my best, Ellie, I can promise you that."

"I got to thank you, Marse Robert. You was always nicer to me than anybody else in this house. The Tylers, they good people, but they don't never forget who's a slave and who ain't. But you, Marse Robert, you treated me like I was . . . like I was reg'lar folks or somethin'."

Robert frowned. "I don't believe in mistreatin' anybody. No point in it."

"That 'cause you a good man, the best man I ever knowed . . ."

Suddenly, she stepped close to him, reached up, put a hand behind his neck, and came up on her toes to press her mouth to his. Robert was so taken by surprise that he couldn't move, couldn't pull away. Ellie's lips were warm and sweet.

Then he stiffened, and she stepped back abruptly, as if the enormity of what she was doing had just occurred to her. She lifted a hand and pressed it to her mouth. "Lord God Almighty, Marse Robert, I . . . I'se sorry. I don't know what come over me." She backed away, a horrified look on her face. "Please don't tell nobody. I don't want a whippin'—"

"There won't be any whipping," Robert told her. "Some things . . . well, they just weren't meant to be, but that doesn't mean they're all bad, or that they deserve punishment."

"No suh," she whispered. "They ain't all bad."

She had backed away now so that there was a short distance between them. It looked as if the two of them had never been any closer than that. Robert turned away and reached for the doorknob again, turning it, opening the door, and stepping out onto the verandah . . .

A rush of footsteps sounded behind him.

He turned, halfway expecting to see Ellie running toward him, but instead it was Lucinda Tyler. She had come downstairs, charged past Ellie, and now she threw herself into Robert's arms. In self-defense if nothing else, he had to take hold of her. She reached up, twined her arms around his neck, and pulled his head to hers. Her mouth found his in a hard, passionate kiss that left him shaken. Her body trembled as he began trying to push her away gently.

She pulled back and hissed, "Damn you, Robert Gilmore! Damn you to hell!"

Then she kissed him again, despite the fact that he didn't respond to her.

When that one was over, she said, "Don't you dare go off and get yourself killed, you bastard."

"What a touching sentiment," he said, narrow-eyed.

"You know good and well what I mean."

"Maybe I do."

"You know, all right. You know." She put her hands against his chest and gave him a push as she stepped back. "Go on, now. Get out of here."

"All right. Good-bye, Lucinda."

She stood there as he turned away, went down the steps from the verandah, and along the drive toward the street. Her hands were clenched into fists so tight that the nails dug into her palms. Robert didn't look back.

Lucinda watched until he was out of sight.

Then she turned back to the house. Her steps were a little un-steady as she went inside. She walked past one of the maids, who had been there when Lucinda hurried through the foyer after Robert. She glanced at the girl, recognized Ellie, and said, "You again. What are you doing here, and why are you smirking?"

"Ain't smirkin', Miss Lucinda. I gots to get to work."

"That's right, you do. Go on with you."

Ellie smiled as she turned away, hiding the expression so that Lu-cinda wouldn't see it. It wasn't a smile of victory—this was one con-test she knew she could never win. But there was a certain satisfaction just in the playing, and in the knowing that for a moment Robert Gilmore had been just as close to her as he was to that blonde bitch.

Maybe even closer.

DIANA WAS in the gardens behind the house when Allard found her that evening after dinner. The magnolias were blooming, and their sweet scent filled the moonlit air. Diana's red hair was dark in the silvery illumination. The moonglow struck highlights and gave her an ethereal beauty that took away Allard's breath. For a moment he was so overcome with emotion that he couldn't speak.

When he finally found his voice again, he said, "I . . . I thought I saw you come out here."

"Your mother has the most beautiful gardens," Diana said. "I could spend hours out here, just looking at all the flowers and smelling their fragrance."

"I feel pretty much the same way about you."

She laughed. "You're comparing me to a bunch of plants?"

"If you *were* a plant, you'd be the prettiest one out here."

"That's sweet, Allard. A bit silly, but sweet."

"Yes, you've described me quite well. Silly but sweet."

She stepped closer to him and gave him a quick kiss on the lips, touching his arm as she did so, but that was the only contact between them. Allard longed to take her in his arms, but Diana didn't seem to want that right now. In fact, she turned away and started strolling along one of the paths through the garden. Allard fell in step beside her.

"I'm going to miss Robert," she said. "He was a good friend."

"He still is. Nothing is going to change."

"It won't? You don't think the war will change him?"

"He'll still be Robert."

"My mother always said that my father changed when he went off to the war in Mexico. She said he was different when he came back."

Allard hesitated. The previous evening, Stafford Pinckston had said that his wife changed while he was away in Mexico. Obviously, the feeling had gone both ways. Allard wasn't sure, though, if Diana needed to know that. While Diana made no secret of the fact that she was angry with her mother for leaving her father, she had to still love Tamara. Allard wanted to be careful not to say anything that would come back to haunt him later.

"I wouldn't know about that," he said, "but I do know that Robert will always be Robert, no matter what."

Diana stopped on the path, and he did likewise. She turned to face him in the dappled moonlight and said, "What about you, Allard? Will you still be the same when you come back? *If* you come back?"

He put his hands on her shoulders and said, "There's no doubt about that. And of course I'll be the same. I'll love you just as much then as I do now."

"I wish—" Diana stopped and turned her head to look away.

Allard tightened his grip on her shoulders and leaned closer to her. "Diana, we've talked about this," he said. He didn't want to argue with her, didn't even really want to talk about it. But maybe they had to. It was too big to ignore, just as if a circus elephant had tromped across Katherine Tyler's flower beds. "Sometimes, there are things that a man just has to do—"

"I know that! Truly, Allard, I do. I know that my father feels he has to serve the Confederacy, and Robert has to, and you have to as well. But there are other things you could do, other ways to serve that don't involve such danger . . ."

Allard felt a chill go through him at her words and the implication they carried. In a low voice, he said, "My father's been talking to you, hasn't he?"

"Mr. Tyler just wants what's best for you, for me . . . for us."

He let go of her and turned away, shaking his head. "That's not what he wants. He just wants to force me into going along with his wishes. He believes that he knows what's best for everyone, and he'll do whatever he has to in order to make them comply."

"I'm sure that's not true. He just said that it seemed more reasonable for you to stay here in Charleston so that you can help him at the shipyard. The Confederate navy is going to need all the ships he can build, and you can be part of that, Allard."

"He had no right . . ." Allard drew the back of a shaking hand across his mouth. "He shouldn't have talked to you. He shouldn't have interfered. He had no right." And he turned and started toward the house.

Diana caught at his sleeve. "Allard, wait! Don't go in there now, while you're so upset."

He pulled away, saying, "No, this has to be settled. He has to understand that he can't make my decisions for me, and he can't trick you into doing his dirty work for him, either!"

"Allard—!" Diana hurried after him. She had no trouble keeping up, since her legs were almost as long as his. She started to grab hold of his arm again but hesitated, unsure of just how much she ought to mix into this. She was a guest in the Tyler house, after all, and even though she loved Allard, she knew he wouldn't want her interfering between him and his father. But she didn't want to see him get hurt, either, and she was afraid that was what was going to happen.

As they neared the open French doors that led from the house into the gardens, the sound of upset voices floated out into the night. Allard paused in surprise. Was there an argument going on in there, and if so, between whom?

The thing of it was, although one of the voices in particular sounded disturbed, it didn't seem all that angry. And it was familiar, too, but not one that Allard heard every day. Suddenly, he realized who the voice belonged to.

At the same instant, Diana clutched his arm and said, "Is that—"

"Cam!" Allard said.

His own emotional turmoil momentarily forgotten, he hurried toward the house with Diana at his side. They went in through the French doors, and the voices led them through the dining room to the hallway in the center of the house.

Cam Gilmore stood there in his cadet's uniform, his campaign cap clutched in one hand. His face was a mixture of confusion and anger. Malachi and Katherine faced him.

"I . . . I don't understand," Cam was saying. "He just up and *left?*"

"He was going up to Columbia to enlist in the Hampton Legion," Malachi explained. "He took the train today, in fact. You boys must have passed each other while one of you was on a siding somewhere."

Cam noticed Allard and Diana and addressed his next question to them. "How could he do that? We were supposed to go back to the farm together!"

Allard shook his head. "I'm sorry, Cam. Robert didn't say anything about that. He thought you had probably gone home already. He wrote you a letter—"

"A letter! My own brother abandons me, and he writes me a letter?"

Katherine said, "Oh, dear, you're not abandoned, Cam. You can still go back home, or you can stay here for a few days if you want to."

Malachi shot her a narrow-eyed look, and Allard knew what his father was thinking. The Tyler family had already taken in one possibly permanent houseguest in Diana; Malachi wasn't that fond of the idea of extending their hospitality to Cam as well.

But the offer was already made, and Malachi wasn't the sort of man to go back on something like that. He said grudgingly, "That's right, Cam. You can stay here . . . for a day or two. Until you can make arrangements to go home."

"This is terrible," Cam said in a half-moan as he twisted his cap in his hands. "I thought I'd surprise Robert and then we'd go home together." He looked at Allard again. "Where's his letter?"

Allard grimaced. "Well, it's, uh, on its way to the farm. It was in a trunk with some of Robert's things and letters to the rest of the family, and I took it to the train station this afternoon and shipped it, like he asked me to. I'm sorry, Cam. But you can read the letter when you get home."

"I suppose that's what I'll have to do," Cam said glumly.

Feeling sorry for him, Katherine took his arm and said, "Why don't you come in the parlor and sit down? You must be tired after that train ride. Are you hungry? I can have the cook fix you something to eat."

Cam perked up a bit at the mention of food. "I *am* a little hungry," he said. "I suppose it wouldn't do any harm for me to eat something."

Malachi slapped him on the shoulder. "Of course it won't do any harm! A full stomach is the best thing in the world for what ails you."

Allard hadn't forgotten why he had been angry with his father. That anger came back now as Malachi and Katherine took Cam into the parlor. Katherine bustled back out almost right away, intent on finding the cook and seeing to it that Cam had a good meal. Allard started into the parlor, intent again on having a showdown with his father.

But the front door bell rang. Thomas appeared from wherever he had been and went slowly toward the door while Malachi stepped out of the parlor and muttered, "Now who the devil can *that* be? All these comings and goings are enough to drive a man mad!"

Allard was mad, all right, but not insane. He stepped toward his father, not caring who was at the door.

Thomas opened it, and a deep, booming voice said, "I'm lookin' for Malachi Tyler."

Malachi stiffened, evidently recognizing the voice.

"Father—" Allard began.

Malachi ignored him, stepping past Allard and striding toward the door. Allard turned to glare after him, angrier than ever now. Malachi had had no right to draw Diana into the disagreement between them, and now he had brushed off his own son when Allard wanted to talk to him about it. Well, he couldn't get away with that. Allard stalked down the hallway after him, and Diana hurried after Allard.

Thomas had stepped aside to admit the visitor, a tall man, broad-shouldered and powerful looking despite a certain gauntness about his face. He had long, gray-streaked dark hair that fell to his shoulders and a close-cropped beard with the same salt-and-pepper coloring.

His face was brown and weathered from long exposure to the sun and wind, and his eyes were deep-set behind a pair of spectacles. He wore a cheap black suit, and although his shirt collar was buttoned up, he didn't have a tie around his neck. A sailor's cap was in his left hand. Judging from the gray in his hair and the lines on his face, he was in his fifties at least, if not older.

The visitor looked down the hall, saw Malachi coming toward him, and a grin stretched across his rugged face. "By the Great Horn Spoon!" he said. "Malachi? Is that you? Ain't seen you in years, but I reckon I'd know you anywhere, even without your hair! Damn my eyes, it's good to see you, son—"

Malachi never slowed his brisk walk toward the visitor. He just drew back his arm, cocked his fist, and slammed it into the taller man's jaw as hard as he could.

# CHAPTER SIXTEEN

# Barnaby Yorke

LLARD STOPPED IN HIS tracks, utterly flabbergasted by what he had just seen. Despite all the threats of violence that had spewed from Malachi's lips over the years, Allard had never seen his father actually strike anyone.

Until now.

The stranger was thrown back against the jamb of the still-open front door by the force of the punch. He dropped his cap and caught the jamb to keep from falling. As the man straightened, Allard wondered if he was going to throw a punch in return. The stranger was taller and heavier than Malachi and had obviously lived a more active life. Malachi had had the element of surprise on his side; that was how he had been able to land that blow. But he would be no match for the other man in a real fight. If a brawl broke out, Allard would have to help his father.

The problem with that was that he didn't know if even the two of them would be able to handle this tough-looking, rangy visitor . . .

Instead of striking back, though, the man just smiled ruefully, raised his hand, and rubbed his jaw where Malachi had hit him. "That was a good punch," he said. "I didn't expect it from you. Reckon I hadn't ought to be surprised, though. You're Black Nick's boy, after all."

The man was obviously no stranger to Malachi, who said, "You're not welcome in this house, Yorke."

"Seems like I might've had somethin' to do with this house bein' built," the man called Yorke said. "After all, 'twas your father's first mate I was on the *Carolina Belle,* back when he was makin' his fortune."

"You mean when he was a bloody-handed pirate," Malachi shot back. "And leave my father out of this! He's dead and gone, and he no longer has anything to do with me and my family!"

"Not to contradict a man in his own home, but you're wrong about that, laddie. Dead or not, Black Nick will always be a part of your life."

Allard didn't know what flabbergasted him more: seeing his grandfather's old shipmate standing there in the flesh or hearing his father called "laddie."

"You're Nick's son, whether you like it or not," Yorke went on. "And you always will be."

"What are you doing here?" Malachi asked tightly.

Yorke didn't answer. Instead he looked over Malachi's shoulder, his eyes widening a little in surprise. "Allard?" he asked. "Is that you, boy?"

Allard nodded. "That's right."

Still ignoring Malachi, Yorke stepped past him and came to Allard, holding out a hand. When Allard grasped it, Yorke pulled him into a hug, enfolding him in long, powerful arms and slapped him on the back so hard it threatened to knock his breath out.

After a moment, Yorke stepped back and rested his hands on Allard's shoulders. Allard tried not to gasp for air after the bear hug.

"I knew about you, but I never saw you before. I'd say you're the spittin' image of your grandpa, but that would be stretchin' things a mite," Yorke said with a big grin. "Damn me for a landlubber, though, if I don't see some o' Nick's devilry in your eyes. You've got the Tyler blood in your veins, that's for sure."

"Really?" Allard said, impressed that one of Black Nick's old comrades-in-arms would say such a thing about him.

"No doubt about it!" Yorke turned toward Diana. "And who's this? Not a granddaughter, surely."

"No, not at all," Allard said hastily. "This is Miss Diana Pinckston." He started to perform an introduction, saying, "Diana, this is—" only to stop short when he realized that he didn't know Yorke's name or, really, anything about him other than what he had just heard. He had been unaware of the man's existence until minutes earlier.

"Barnaby Yorke," the older man said. He caught hold of Diana's hand, bent over it, and kissed it. "'Tis a heathen European custom, to be sure, but from time to time even they get somethin' right. I'm pleased to meet you, Miss Diana Pinckston with hair like the sun settin' over the sea."

She was flustered but pleased by his attention. "Hello, Mr. Yorke," she managed to say. "I'm glad to meet you."

"The pleasure is all mine, lass—Katherine!" Yorke practically bellowed the name as Allard's mother stepped out of the parlor to see what was going on and he caught sight of her. He added, "Excuse me, Miss Diana," as he practically lunged at Katherine, wrapped his arms around her, and lifted her off the floor. She cried out in mingled surprise and excitement.

"Barnaby?" she said. "Barnaby, is it really you?"

"Aye, none other! Gimme a kiss, lassie!"

"By God!" Malachi exploded. "I'll not stand for this!" He started down the hall as Yorke planted a hard kiss on Katherine's mouth.

Allard's head was spinning again. Seeing this grizzled old sea dog kiss his mother like she was some beautiful young Southern belle was even more astounding than the way Yorke had talked to Malachi.

Yorke lowered Katherine's feet to the floor and beamed down at her. She was smiling, too, and a little breathless, and her face glowed warm and pink. "You're as beautiful as ever, darlin'," he told her. He turned his head as he heard footsteps coming toward him and lifted a hand to point his finger at the furious Malachi. "One free punch is all you get, laddie."

His voice held a hard edge that made Malachi stop. With his fists clenched, Malachi said, "You have no right to be here. You have no right to come in . . . disrupt my household . . . assault my wife—"

"Oh, don't carry on so, Malachi," Katherine said. "You know that Barnaby was Nick's best friend. He's always welcome here. Why, considering how many times they saved each other's lives, you might not even be here if it wasn't for him!"

"That's not true," Malachi said stiffly. "I was born before they even knew each other."

"Aye, but if I hadn't blowed that English dog overboard before he could slip his saber through your pa's guts on that stormy day off Cape Hatteras, you'd have been an orphan at an early age, Malachi," Yorke said.

Malachi still looked like he wanted to throw a punch, but he restrained the impulse. Instead, he said, "You still haven't told us what you're doing here."

"Why, I came to talk business with you, lad."

"Business?" Malachi repeated, shocked. "What business could I possibly have with you?"

"The same as I've always had with your family . . . war business."

Cam came out of the parlor at that moment, looking confused. "Somebody was supposed to get me something to eat," he said. He came over to Allard and Diana, frowned at Yorke, and added, "Who's that?"

"An old friend of my grandfather's," Allard explained. "Evidently he was the first mate on my grandfather's ship."

"The pirate ship?" Cam asked excitedly.

"Privateer," Yorke said sharply. "We were never buccaneers. We sailed under the flag of the United States, not the Jolly Roger." He turned back to Malachi. "Now we need to talk, lad."

"Since you're already here, I suppose we might as well," Malachi said grudgingly. "Come into the study—and try to keep your hands off my wife while you're about it."

Yorke leered at Katherine and said, "I'll try, lad, but it's powerful difficult to do." Katherine laughed.

Malachi and Yorke went down the hall and disappeared into the study. Once they were gone, Allard said, "Mother, that . . . that was just about the most amazing thing I've ever seen."

Katherine smiled. "Yes, Barnaby Yorke is something of a force of nature, isn't he? He sweeps in like a sea squall. But he's really a harmless old dear."

"He didn't kiss you like he was all that harmless," Allard pointed out.

"Wait a minute," Cam said. "That old man kissed your mother, Allard?"

"You boys hush," Katherine said, blushing now. "Barnaby and I are old friends, that's all. I knew him when I was just a girl."

Yes, but knew him how well? Allard found himself wondering, and then he shoved that line of thought completely out of his head, not wanting to ponder the question for even a second longer.

"I HOPE you don't expect me to offer you a cigar or something to drink," Malachi said as he sat down behind his desk and curtly motioned Barnaby Yorke into the chair in front of it.

"I *am* a mite thirsty . . ." Yorke waved a hand. "But never mind about that. Time enough for socializin' later, after we've settled things between us."

"There's nothing to settle."

"That's where you're wrong. I expect you know a couple o' fellas named Stephen Mallory and Raphael Semmes."

Malachi stiffened. "Of course I know them. Mallory is the secretary of the Confederate navy, and Semmes was the captain of the *Somers* and head of the Lighthouse Service."

"Rafe Semmes is in New Orleans right now, seein' to it that a passenger steamer called the *Habana* is turned into a warship. When he gets through rebuildin' it, he's goin' to christen it the *Sumter* and go after the Yankees with it. I visited him down there and offered him my services, seein' as I've got experience along those lines, you might say."

"Indeed," Malachi said dryly.

"Semmes had other ideas, though," Yorke went on. "He knew I'd captained quite a few ships o' my own in the years since I sailed with Black Nick—"

Malachi winced. "I really wish you'd stop saying that name."

"I don't have to say it." Yorke shrugged. "Whether I call him by that name or not, we both know what your pa was like."

"Yes. We certainly do." With a sigh, Malachi said, "Go on."

"All right. Semmes told me to go to Richmond and see Mallory. He gave me a letter of introduction."

Virginia had seceded from the Union on April 17, a few days after the surrender of Fort Sumter. Since then it had been decided that the capital of the Confederacy would be moved from Montgomery, Alabama, to Richmond, Virginia. That transfer of power was going on at the present. Malachi knew that Secretary of the Navy Mallory was already in Richmond. The Gosport Navy Yard, in nearby Norfolk, was the largest naval installation in the country, and it had been abandoned by the Federals in late April. Before the Yankees left, they put the buildings in the yard and many of the ships to the torch, unwilling to let the Confederates seize them. Despite those efforts, the damage had not been all that great. Many of the yard's facilities were salvageable, as were some of the ships that had been scuttled or partially burned. The Confederates had also seized twelve hundred cannon and nearly three thousand barrels of gunpowder when they took over Norfolk. As a man who made his living from ships, Malachi had been glad to hear that the Yankees had failed to destroy all the vessels there.

"When I got in to see Mallory," Yorke continued, "he sent me to talk to a man named Hawkins. I believe you're acquainted with him, too."

"I know him," Malachi said flatly.

"Then somethin' happened that makes you realize what a small ol' world this really is." Yorke smiled. "Hawkins had the idea that I ought to come and see a fella in Charleston by the name o' Malachi Tyler." He threw back his head and laughed. "I didn't tell him that I've knowed you since you were nothin' more than a little sprout, Malachi."

"Get on with it," Malachi growled. "Why did Hawkins send you to me?"

"So you could give me a ship." Yorke reached inside his coat and brought out a folded paper. He opened it, slapped it down on the desk, and said, "There's the letter of marque and reprisal, with Jefferson Davis's own signature on it, with your name as owner and mine as master. All we have to do is fill in the name o' the ship, and we'll be ready to start strikin' the fear o' God into them Yankees."

Shocked, Malachi couldn't do anything for a moment except stare at the document on his desk. As Yorke had said, it was a letter of marque and reprisal, the same sort of authorization used by privateers during the War of 1812 to justify their strikes against British shipping. The names of Malachi Tyler and Barnaby Yorke were printed prominently on the paper.

"This . . . this is insane!" he finally burst out when he could form words again. "I'm not a privateer! I build ships! I don't sail them!"

Yorke tapped a long, somewhat gnarled finger on the letter of marque. "That's why I'm down as master. I'd buy the damned vessel from you, Malachi, if I had the money to do it. But I don't, so that's why you've got to be listed on the letter, too."

"What vessel?"

Yorke smiled and shrugged his broad shoulders. "That'll be up to you. I trust your judgment, laddie. Pick me out a good ship, and I'll use it to raise hell with the Federals."

Malachi leaned back in his chair and shook his head. "This is all too much. When Hawkins came to see me, I agreed to build ships for the Confederate navy at a fair, reasonable price. I didn't say anything about giving one away to an old pirate!"

"There you go again with that pirate talk," Yorke said, his eyes narrowing. "Seems to me that if I can refrain from talkin' about Black Nick, you could stop callin' me a pirate."

"As you said yourself, certain things are true no matter what words we use." Malachi shoved the document back across the desk toward Yorke. "I won't do it. I won't have anything to do with this harebrained scheme."

"There's nothin' harebrained about it," Yorke insisted. "Hawkins told me they've gotten several thousand applications for letters of marque already. Why, right here in Charleston, the schooner *Savannah* is bein' refitted and turned into a privateer. So's the *America*."

Malachi frowned in surprise. He had heard about the *Savannah*, but the fact that the *America* was going to be used as a privateer was news to him. Everyone connected to the shipbuilding industry knew about the speedy yacht *America*, which had won the first International Cup Race between the Americans and the British a decade earlier in 1851.

"There's plenty o' others, too," Yorke went on. "It's just common sense. Until there's a real navy to fight the Yankees, we got to harry 'em any way we can, and the best way to do that is with privateers."

Malachi rubbed at his chin and said slowly, "I don't know . . ." The old man's words made sense, but Malachi's dislike for Yorke and all the bad memories the man dredged up made him reluctant to accept the argument.

After a moment, Yorke said, "Hawkins told me that if you needed more convincin', I was to give you this." He took another paper from inside his coat. This one was folded and closed with wax, and pressed into that wax was the seal of the Confederate States of America.

Malachi hesitated before taking it. He turned it over in his hands a couple of times before he picked up a letter opener from his desk and broke the wax seal. When he unfolded the letter, the first thing he saw was the signature scrawled at the bottom: Jefferson F. Davis.

"I have letters from Secretary Mallory and Captain Semmes, too," Yorke said with a faint smile, "but I figured I'd go ahead and break out the big guns first."

Malachi didn't say anything. He read the letter, which was an appeal to his patriotism and a declaration that President Davis would regard as a personal favor any efforts Malachi could make toward helping the Confederacy attain ascendancy on the high seas over the Yankees. Finally, he placed the letter on the desk and said, "How can I refuse this?"

"That's sorta what I was thinkin', too. Remember, though, we ain't askin' you to make a big sacrifice, Malachi. You'll come out ahead in the long run. Most o' the prizes we take will go to the Confederacy, but there'll be shares for you and me and the men who sail with me, too."

Malachi was tempted to point out that Yorke was verging on talk of piracy again, but he refrained. Instead, he said, "I suppose you'll want to go down to the yards and look over the ships."

"I reckon 'twould be best. Between us, we'll pick the best o' the lot for our purposes."

"All right, then." Malachi stood up, and so did Yorke. "You understand, of course, that I'm doing this against my better judgment, and only because I'm loyal to the Confederacy."

"As am I."

"I'm not so sure about that," Malachi said bluntly. "You've spent, what, the past forty years sailing all over the world?"

Yorke grinned. "Aye, I've sailed all seven seas and put in to port in just about every spot on the globe."

"So why do you feel any connection to the Confederacy? I'd think that if anything you'd consider yourself a citizen of the world."

"I was born in Mobile, Alabama. Ain't surprisin' that I ran away to sea at an early age, since I fell in love with boats the first time I seen 'em in Mobile Bay, but the South's my home port and always will be."

Malachi shrugged. "Whatever you say. I don't really care. Just bring my ship back safely to me when you're through with it."

"I'll do my damnedest, laddie, but I expect the Yankees will have a little somethin' to say about that."

Malachi grunted and opened the study door. As he ushered Yorke down the hall toward the front of the house, he said, "I suppose you're staying at some tavern or rooming house here in town?"

"Well, I ain't really settled on a place yet . . ." Yorke began, just as

Katherine came out of the dining room, where Cam sat at the table, eating the late supper the cook had prepared. Allard and Diana sat with him, although they weren't eating.

"A place to stay, you mean?" Katherine said.

Yorke nodded and said, "Aye." If he saw the horrified expression that suddenly appeared on Malachi's face, he gave no sign of it.

"Well, you don't have to worry about that. We have plenty of room here, don't we, Malachi?"

"Katherine . . . we've already taken in Diana, and we're letting Cam stay here for the time being . . ."

"So, you see, Barnaby, what does one more guest matter?" Katherine said.

Allard got up from the table and joined the little group in the hall, saying, "Yes, Captain Yorke, please stay. I'd love to talk to you and hear all the stories about my grandfather and his days fighting the British."

"Oh, aye, there are plenty of yarns about ol' Black Nick, and every one of 'em is excitin'." Yorke glanced at Malachi. "Beggin' your pardon, lad. I didn't mean to bring up that name again."

"Don't worry about that," Katherine said. She slipped her arm through Yorke's. "Have you had supper yet?"

"As a matter o' fact, I haven't. I was on the train from Columbia down here—"

"So was I," Cam said from the table, his mouth half-full. "I didn't see you."

"There were quite a few people on that train," Yorke pointed out. "The South is a busy place these days."

"It certainly is," Katherine agreed. "Come on in here and sit yourself down, Barnaby. I'll tell the cook to bring out more food."

"Thank you kindly, Katie."

She laughed happily. "Land's sake, nobody's called me that for such a long time. Sit down, sit down."

Allard took the chair next to Yorke and said, "Tell me everything you can remember about my grandfather."

From the doorway Malachi watched as his wife and son fussed over the old reprobate, and as he saw the admiration glowing in Allard's eyes, a feeling of horror spread through him like the slow advance of ice across a pond on a freezing day. Barnaby Yorke had come to Charleston to ask him for a ship . . . but now the sickening realization had dawned on Malachi Tyler that before it was over, Yorke might take his son away, too.

# PART FOUR

I hear the great drums pounding
And the small drums steady whirring
And every blow of the great convulsive drums
Strikes me through and through.

       —*Walt Whitman,*
           *"Dirge for Two Veterans"*

# CHAPTER SEVENTEEN

# Four Winds

HE RAILROAD LINE RAN north from Charleston to Florence then turned west to Columbia. Robert Gilmore got off the train when it stopped at the Mount Holly station, about twenty miles north of Charleston. He hadn't told anyone in the Tyler household that he was stopping there, not even Allard. Another train would come through the little town that evening, and Robert intended to be on it, with his trip delayed for only a short time.

That is, if everything worked out as he planned. Where affairs of the heart were concerned, a fella could never be completely sure about that.

His mind had been in a dizzy whirl during the short trip from Charleston to Mount Holly. It wasn't enough that the housemaid Ellie had been audacious enough to kiss him, breaking the most stringent taboo in the South. No, Lucinda Tyler had had to come along and further complicate things by kissing him, too. What was he to make of both those events?

Even though the Gilmore family owned no slaves and never had, Robert had been around other farms and plantations where slaves did most of the work. He was an observant young man, and he wasn't naive enough to think that nothing ever went on between the white masters and the slave girls. He had seen enough light-colored slaves and slaves with red hair or blue eyes to know that their owners, or some other owner, had fathered them. It was a common practice. Hell, Robert thought, even Malachi Tyler had urged Allard to take one of the housemaids to bed, just so Allard could achieve his manhood.

Robert wondered suddenly about Ellie. Had Allard ever . . . ?

No, almost certainly not. Allard was too much in love with Diana Pinckston, and besides, if Malachi wanted Allard to do something, chances were Allard would refuse just to spite his father.

So despite the abhorrent face that Southern society placed on such things, Robert knew it was only a facade. He could take Ellie, or any other darky gal like her, to bed, and nobody would care.

But for Ellie to approach him, for her to kiss him as she had done, like there was some sort of genuine affection involved—*that* was unsettling. It was almost unheard of. It disturbed Robert deeply.

But the business with Lucinda was equally disturbing. She hated him. He would have bet money on that. She had barely said a civil word to him in all the time he had known her. And yet she had seemed just as drawn to him, against her will, maybe, as Ellie was. Somehow he aroused such passion in her that she couldn't control it.

That was insane, and totally different than the situation with Cam. Whatever was between Lucinda and Cam was rooted in pure lust. Knowing about it bothered Robert, but there was nothing he could do to put a stop to it, at least not now. This war with the Yankees had come along and overwhelmed personal concerns. All he had been able to do was write to Cam and warn him about Lucinda, urging him to be cautious in his dealings with her. He wouldn't go quite so far as to say that she was evil . . . but given the chance, she would hurt Cam. Robert was sure of it.

Which still didn't answer the puzzling question of why she had acted toward *him* as she had. During that first encounter, when he had supposedly been teaching her how to play poker—a game she was obviously familiar with—he had thought she was just teasing him, playing with him like a cat would with a mouse. Now, after her impulsive farewell kiss, he wasn't so sure.

That was just his luck, he thought wryly as he disembarked from the railroad car onto the platform at the Mount Holly depot, to be kissed by two attractive young women when all he really wanted to do was be with another young woman, the one he actually loved.

He approached the ticket window and asked the clerk inside, "Is there some place around here I can borrow a horse?"

"Livery stable just down the block will be glad to rent one to you, young fella," the pudgy, balding clerk in sleeve gaiters and eyeshade said. "Don't know of anybody who'd give you the borrow of one, though."

Robert nodded. "Thanks," he said then added, "By the way, can you tell me how to get to the Lockhart plantation?"

"Four Winds? You ain't from around here, are you, son? Ever'-body in these parts knows where Four Winds is."

It was true. Robert had never visited the Lockhart plantation before. Every time he had seen Jacqueline, it had been in Charleston. She had said many times that she wanted him to visit her at her home, but between his classes at the Citadel and her mother's opposition to the relationship between them, that visit had never come about.

"Just tell me how to find the place," he said curtly, thinking that having to pay to rent a mount would just about clean him out.

"Now, don't get testy," the clerk said. "That's the trouble with folks today, especially you young ones. It's always hurry, hurry, hurry. Shoot, folks down here are gettin' to be as bad as the Yankees about hurryin' ever'thing up."

With an effort, Robert hung on to his temper. "Four Winds?" he prodded the clerk. "How do I get there?"

The man leaned forward through the open ticket window and pointed. "You see that road right over there?" He indicated a road that led west from the depot.

"I see it," Robert said.

The clerk shook his head. "Well, you don't want to take that road. It won't take you anywhere close to the Lockhart place."

The man had to be doing this to punish him for being impatient,

Robert thought. Well, two could play that game. He folded his arms and nodded, saying deliberately, "All right, I won't take that road."

"Good." The clerk pointed again, this time to a road that ran southwest out of the little settlement. "That's the road you want to take, right there."

"And once I'm on that road, how many miles do I go?"

"That depends. Headin' for Four Winds, you said?"

"That's right."

"Well, then, you go about five miles down that road. You'll come to another road that crosses it at an angle and runs almost due north and south. You want to take the left-hand turn—"

"That would be south," Robert said. He couldn't help it.

The clerk nodded and looked a little annoyed at being interrupted. "South it is. You follow *that* road another mile, and you'll see the lane that leads to Four Winds. You can't miss it. There's a sign there, nailed to a tree, unless some wild young scallywag out on a lark has torn it down since I been along there."

"I think I can find it," Robert said. "Much obliged for your help."

"Oh, 'twas my pleasure, my pleasure. Good day to you, young fella."

Robert left the depot and walked toward the livery barn. No one was in front when he got there, but he heard the ringing of a hammer on an anvil out back. The double doors both front and back of the barn were wide open, so he went along the hard-packed dirt aisle between the rows of stalls and out the rear of the big building.

Sure enough, there was a little blacksmith shop back there, where a massively muscled black man was hammering out a pair of horseshoes. He wore a pair of canvas trousers and a thick leather apron. His arms were bare, and as Robert approached he saw the marks on the dark skin where flying sparks had burned it, apparently hundreds of times over the years.

The smithy lifted his head to look at Robert. Then he set his hammer aside and asked, "Somethin' I can do for you, mister?"

"I need a horse."

"Lookin' to buy?"

"No, I just need a saddle mount for a short time."

The black man nodded. "Reckon I can he'p you. Gots several fo' rent."

"*You* do?" Robert asked pointedly.

"Yes suh. I'se a freedman, an' this here place is half mine. Name of Tobias."

"I'm Robert Gilmore."

"Pleased to make yo' acquaintance, Mr. Gilmore." Tobias started to walk into the barn with Robert. "Whereabouts you headed?"

"Out to Four Winds."

Tobias stopped short and turned to look at him. "That a fact? I used to live there."

"Really?"

"Yes suh." Tobias's head bobbed up and down in a nod. "'Twas Mist' Everett Lockhart that done manumitted me an' give me this liv'ry stable to run. Some o' the other plantation owners 'round here give him a mighty lot of grief over it, on account o' they don't never like to see a freedman make anythin' out of hisself, but Mist' Everett, he don't care what they say. Told me the place was half mine and he wouldn't interfere in the runnin' of it as long as I was doin' a good job. Proud to say that I have been, goin' on three years now."

Robert hadn't known that Everett Lockhart owned a livery stable in Mount Holly. The man had business interests all over the state in addition to his plantation, though, including in Charleston. If not for that fact, Robert might never have met Jacqueline.

Curious, Robert asked, "How did Mr. Lockhart come to free you?"

"Well, suh, he was grateful to me, I reckon. He has a daughter, a mighty pretty girl called Miss Jacqueline."

Robert nodded. "Go on."

"Miss Jacqueline, she likes to ride hosses, an' when she was younger, she wouldn't listen to nobody tried to tell her what to do."

That sounded just about right. Jacqueline still didn't like being told what to do.

"Mist' Everett, he gets this bad hoss in a deal, but he don't know just how bad it really is," Tobias went on. "He tell Miss Jacqueline she can't ride that hoss—"

"Which was a mistake," Robert guessed.

"Yes suh, it was! That just made Miss Jacqueline want to ride it more, so she snuck into the stable and figgered she'd take that ol' devil hoss for a jaunt. I done all the blacksmithin' on Four Winds, so I was close by. Thank the Good Lord for that, 'cause I was able to get there mighty quicklike when Miss Jacqueline let out a scream."

"What happened?" Robert asked, caught up in the story.

"That bad hoss, he had Miss Jacqueline cornered in one o' the stalls and was reared up an' flailin' his hooves at her. Reckon he might've kicked her to pieces if'n I hadn't got there in time to stop him."

"How did you do that?"

Tobias grinned again and said, "Grabbed him 'round the neck an' rassled him down to the ground. Miss Jacqueline run out whilst she had the chance, and I let go an' scurried right after her. I knew I couldn't hold that hoss very long that way."

Robert let out a low whistle. "No, I don't reckon anybody could. Not many men could pull a horse down like that to start with."

"No suh, I reckon not." Tobias went on, "We better find you a hoss to ride. If'n you don't mind me askin', why yo' goin' out to Four Winds?"

"It just so happens I'm going to see Miss Jacqueline."

Tobias looked at him intently again. "You be the Robert Miss Jacqueline talks about all the time?"

It was Robert's turn to grin. "I hope I'm the only one she talks about."

"Lawd, when you tol' me yo' name, suh, it never occurred to me you might be Miss Jacqueline's young fella. I'm gonna give you the best hoss I gots to ride, an' it ain't gonna cost you a penny."

Robert felt a surge of relief. "That's mighty nice of you, Tobias. I'd insist on payin' you if I wasn't, well, a mite short on funds."

214

"An' I'd tell you to keep yo' money. Any friend o' Miss Jacqueline's is a friend o' mine."

Tobias went into one of the stalls and led out a tall chestnut gelding with three white stockings. It was a fine-looking horse, and Robert nodded in approval.

"Reckon you'll need a saddle an' tack."

"That's right. I appreciate you fixin' me up this way, Tobias."

"Don't think nothin' of it, suh."

"You know," Robert said, "the ticket agent at the depot knew I was headed for Four Winds, and he sent me down here to get a horse. Surely he knew about your connection with the Lockhart family, but he never said a word about it."

Tobias snorted. "That'd be ol' Mr. Branchley. He a prickly ol' cuss, won't tell folks nothin' unless they ask him just right, an' the right way to ask him might be different today from what it was yesterday."

Robert laughed and said, "That's the impression of him I got, too. Maybe I'd better tell you the directions he gave me, so I can be sure they're right."

He repeated what the ticket agent had told him, and Tobias nodded. "You just follow along like that, and you won't have no trouble findin' the place." He was finished saddling the chestnut, so he handed the reins to Robert. "You be comin' back today, suh?"

"Yes, I have to. I've got to catch the evening train and get on up to Columbia. I'm on my way to join the Hampton Legion."

Tobias's smile disappeared. "You goin' off to the war, Mist' Robert?"

"If there *is* a war. No one seems to know for sure what's going to happen, one way or the other."

"Oh, there be a war, all right," Tobias said solemnly. "Folks ain't gonna give up their prop'ty without a fight. Only way to stop it is for them Yankees to back down, and I don't think that's gonna happen."

"Neither do I," Robert agreed. "That's why I had to stop here on my way and see Jacqueline again. I couldn't leave without telling her good-bye."

Tobias's eyes narrowed. "You gonna make that little gal cry. I don't know if'n I wanna give you that hoss or not."

"You wouldn't keep us from saying our farewells, Tobias." Robert felt a surge of desperation. "You can't."

"Nah, I reckon I can't," Tobias said with a shrug of his broad shoulders. "You go on out there . . . but you be as gentle with Miss Jacqueline as you can, hear?"

"I intend to."

Robert swung up into the saddle. As he turned the chestnut toward the barn's entrance, Tobias added, "Seems like I remember Miss Jacqueline sayin' that her mama don't like you much."

"That's a fair statement. An understatement, in fact."

"Well, then, here's what you do. When you turn off the road onto the lane leadin' up to the house, there another little path that goes off to the right. You follow it instead, an' it'll take you aroun' the place, past the quarters an' the blacksmith shop an' the granary, and you'll come to a spot behind the plantation house where there's a pretty lil' pond with some trees around it. Most days, Miss Jacqueline goes out there an' sits by herself for a while of an afternoon. You talk to her there, there's at least a chance Miss Priscilla won't even know you's on the place."

Robert nodded. On an impulse, he held his hand out and said, "Thanks for the advice, Tobias, as well as for the loan of the horse."

The burly blacksmith hesitated for a second then took Robert's hand. This had been quite a day—kissed by a slave in Charleston and now shaking hands with a freedman in Mount Holly. A man should always try to experience new things, Robert thought wryly.

Tobias released Robert's hand and shook his head. "I wish you was carryin' better news to Miss Jacqueline," he said heavily.

"So do I, Tobias," Robert said. "So do I."

THE RIDE to Four Winds took Robert a little less than an hour. As he had been told by both the train agent and Tobias, the plantation wasn't hard to find. When he reached the lane that led directly to the big house, he reined in and studied his surroundings for a minute.

Cotton fields stretched out as far as the eye could see on both sides of the lane and on the other side of the main road as well. At this time of year the cotton plants were up but had not flowered yet, forming a low, leafy green carpet on the ground. Field hands with hoes worked among the rows, digging out weeds that might steal nutrients from the cotton plants. Robert looked around but didn't see any overseers. One of the field hands probably performed that task in return for some extra privileges.

On the far side of the fields, a number of magnolia trees grew, surrounding the plantation house itself. Even at a distance, it was an impressive structure, three stories tall with large white columns out front that supported the roof over the verandah. Shrubs and beds full of brightly colored flowers stood out against the whitewashed walls of the mansion. It was a beautiful place, and looking at it, Robert could understand how a beautiful girl like Jacqueline, growing up here with doting parents and slaves to wait on her hand and foot, could turn out to be rather spoiled and headstrong. That didn't make him love her any less.

He lifted the reins and clucked to his horse, which started up the lane at a walk. He had gone only a short distance when he came to the smaller path Tobias had mentioned. He followed it between a couple of cotton fields. The path curved and began to follow a small creek lined with gnarled oak trees that dripped with Spanish moss. To Robert's left, perhaps a hundred yards away, were some of the plantation's outbuildings. He heard a hammer striking an anvil and knew he was passing the blacksmith shop where Tobias had been working when Jacqueline had her dangerous encounter with the horse.

Thank goodness Tobias had been close by that day. Robert couldn't begin to conceive of the world without Jacqueline Lockhart.

The creek and the path that followed it continued to curve. Robert caught glimpses of the back of the plantation house now, although the magnolias grew thicker behind it and screened most of it from view.

But likewise, the trees formed a barrier between the house and the pretty little pond into which the stream suddenly widened. A rock dam, four feet high and perhaps a dozen feet long, had been built to form the pond. Water flowed over its top and cascaded down over the rocks. A green, grassy, gentle slope surrounded the pond. A gazebo had been built on the slope, and there, shaded by the roof of the gazebo, Jacqueline sat in a wicker chair, looking beautiful in a white dress.

Robert reined in sharply. She hadn't seen him, and if she heard the approaching hoofbeats, she paid no attention to them. She looked out over the smooth surface of the pond, which was mottled with shade from the surrounding trees. Her right profile was turned toward Robert, and he thought she was heartbreakingly lovely. He heeled the horse into motion again, sending the animal walking forward slowly, but still, Jacqueline didn't turn her head and look at him. When he was within twenty feet of her, he thought that surely she was aware of his presence by now. She continued gazing out over the pond.

"Jacqueline," he said softly.

Finally, she turned her head toward him, and he saw the streaks on her face that the tears had left as they rolled down her cheeks. She had known he was there, he realized. She had known all along. She just hadn't wanted to admit it. Because if she admitted it, then she would also have to admit that she knew *why* he was there.

As he stepped down from the saddle, she rose from the chair and took a step toward the edge of the gazebo.

"Robert," she murmured as she lifted a hand.

He came toward her, bounded up the steps into the gazebo, and took her into his arms, drawing her close in his embrace. Her head tilted back, and his mouth came down on hers. Her lips clung to his with a fierce urgency as their arms tightened around each other. Robert wished they could stay there like that forever, molded to each other, so close that nothing could come between them. Not the disapproval of her mother, or the fact that his family didn't have as much money as hers, or the damned, senseless war that the Yankees were about to foist on the entire nation in their stubbornness and arrogance . . .

But the moment couldn't last, of course. Such moments never could. Jacqueline drew back with fresh tears coursing down her cheeks. "You've come to say it, haven't you?" she whispered. "You've come to say good-bye."

"I don't have any choice, Jacqueline."

"The first time you ever come to my home, and you come to break my heart." She clenched one hand into a small fist and struck him on the chest. "And don't lie to me! You have a choice! Of course you have a choice. You don't have to go and fight. You don't even own any slaves!"

"It's not about that, no matter what the abolitionists say," he insisted stiffly. "Would you have me stand by and do nothing while our homeland is invaded by barbarians, just like Rome was invaded by the Goths and the Vandals?"

"Damn the Citadel! You learned too much history there . . ."

She leaned against him, sobbing, and there was nothing he could do except hold her and wish that she understood.

Finally, her sobs died away, leaving him with a wet shirt front. She lifted her head and smiled weakly at him. "Well, if we're to say good-bye, we should do it properly. There's a shed over there, on the other side of the pond. We can go there. I've known for a long time that you would come sooner or later, so I put a blanket there to be ready."

Robert stared at her. "You mean . . ."

Her fingers clutched his arms and dug into his flesh through his jacket and shirt. "If you think you're going to leave without making love to me, Robert Gilmore," she whispered fiercely, "you're sadly mistaken!"

# CHAPTER EIGHTEEN

# Farewells

ROBERT HAD NEVER DREAMED that such a thing was possible. He had dreamed of making love to Jacqueline, of course, ever since the first time he had held her in his arms and kissed her. The passion she aroused in him cried out to be expressed physically. But before that could ever come to pass, there would have to be a long courtship and an elaborate wedding. Then and only then would the two of them be able to be together as man and woman, husband and wife. With a girl like Jacqueline Lockhart, that was a foregone conclusion.

Evidently, he had been wrong.

She took his hand and led him around the pond, through some trees to the shed she had mentioned. A few shovels and hoes were leaned in a corner. The slaves whose job it was to tend to the carefully manicured lawns and gardens kept the tools here, but according to Jacqueline, they wouldn't be needing them today.

"All the yard work was taken care of a couple of days ago," she explained to Robert as she closed the door of the shed, leaving them in the shadows of its interior. "No one will disturb us."

"You're sure?" His heart slugged heavily in his chest, and he felt lightheaded. Some of that was excitement, to be sure, but some was caused by worry, too. Lord knew what would happen if they were discovered.

"I'm certain. I've been thinking about this day for a long time, Robert." She stepped closer to him, and even in the gloom of the shed, she seemed radiant. She put her arms around his neck, and the delicate scent she wore made him even dizzier. "It would have been nice if things were different," she murmured, "but they're not. We have to take the chances the world gives us."

"It seems like those are the sort of things *I* should be telling *you*."

"I know better than that," she said. "I know you'd never act in what you considered a dishonorable fashion. You wouldn't try to seduce me into doing anything that we shouldn't." An impish smile curved her full lips. "Women are more practical than men, Robert. That's why we have to do most of the seducing, whether men know it or not. If we sat around and waited for you to get around to it, nothing would ever happen."

That might be true in love, Robert thought, but not in war. Men always got around to making war sooner or later—usually sooner.

He shoved those thoughts out of his head. He had no room in his brain for musing on war at this moment. All of his thoughts were focused on this beautiful, slender woman in his arms . . .

Getting a girl undressed was a lot more complicated than he would have thought it would be. There were all sorts of buttons and snaps and stays and hooks to be undone. He felt like cursing in frustration and embarrassment every time his fingers fumbled at their task. Jacqueline had to think he was the clumsiest fool ever. But each time her soft, cool fingers were there to help him, and she murmured gentle words of encouragement that eased his worries. She leaned close to him, kissed his neck and the line of his jaw, clasped his hands in hers and lifted them to press her lips to them. He had no idea how long it took to divest her of her garments, but it was a glorious, intimate time, and a part of him would have been happy if it had never come to an end.

But of course it did, and when she was naked, he let his eyes play over her fair-skinned loveliness. Her dark hair, loosened from the grip of its pins and combs, tumbled around her head and down her back.

She pressed herself against him, sleek and surprisingly strong, and after they kissed for another long moment, she stepped back and lowered herself to the ground, stretching out on the thick blanket she had spread there earlier.

Getting his own clothes off proved to be a lot easier—and quicker—for Robert.

Then he was beside her, wrapping her in his arms, pausing only when she whispered, "Robert . . . be careful . . . I . . . I've never . . ."

"It's all right," he told her. "Neither have I."

FOR TWO people who hadn't really known what they were doing, things had gone surprisingly well, he told himself later. At least he hoped they had. Since he didn't have any frame of reference, he couldn't be certain. But Jacqueline had seemed to enjoy herself, and he knew that he had never before experienced anything even half as wonderful.

Being in love with each other probably had something to do with how well it had gone, he reasoned.

It wasn't until afterward, when they were getting dressed, that Jacqueline began to cry again.

All Robert could do was take her in his arms and try to comfort her. He said, "We shouldn't have—"

That was as far as she allowed him to get. "Of course we should have! It was wonderful, Robert, absolutely wonderful. The only thing wrong is that you're going off to get yourself killed in that stupid war, and we'll never have the chance to do it again."

"I'm not goin' to get killed—"

Again she interrupted him. "You can't be certain of that. I know it's awful of me to even say such a thing, but it's true! This may be the last time we ever see each other."

"The future isn't guaranteed to anyone," he pointed out. "No one knows what it will bring. We can plan for it, but when you come right down to cases, folks have to live for today, because that's all we've got, Jacqueline."

"I know . . ." She trembled in his embrace. "I know."

Finally she stepped back, squared her shoulders, and wiped away her tears. "At least you'll have a good memory to carry with you," she went on. "I hope it will be a good memory."

"My God!" he said as he rested his hands on her shoulders. "How can you say that? Good memory? This has been the most amazing day of my entire life!"

She smiled. "All we did was make love, Robert. Millions of people all over the world do the same thing every day."

He shook his head and said, "Not like that. That was special. There's never been anything like it before."

Jacqueline laughed. "Now you're just being silly . . . and I love you for it."

"I love you," he said, and again they found themselves in each other's arms, their lips clinging together tenderly.

Something began nagging at Robert's mind, and when they broke the kiss at last and stepped apart, he hauled out his pocket watch. "Five o'clock," he murmured.

"Do you have to leave?" The words seemed to catch in Jacqueline's throat as she asked the question.

"Soon. The next train comes through Mount Holly at seven. I checked the schedule before I rode out here."

"Where did you get the horse?"

He grinned. "From a fella at the livery stable named Tobias. A freedman."

"Tobias!" A smile lit up Jacqueline's face. "He saved my life once."

"I know. He told me about it." Robert chuckled. "Said something about you bein' a headstrong little imp who got mixed up with a bad horse you shouldn't have."

"That's not *exactly* the way it was . . ." She stopped and laughed and shook her head. "Well, actually, I suppose that *is* the way it was. But shame on Tobias for being so forthright about it."

"I'm just glad he was here to help you. If he hadn't been, you and I might not ever have met."

She stepped closer to him again, a sultry look in her eyes. "And if we hadn't met, we couldn't have done what we just did."

Robert might have said more, or he might have kissed her again, but at that moment, the sound of voices came faintly to their ears from somewhere outside the shed. Jacqueline's head came up as her eyes widened in alarm. "That sounds like my father!" she said.

Robert tensed. Everett Lockhart was an intelligent man. If he found them together like this in the shed, with a blanket spread on the ground, he would immediately draw the correct conclusion. And then, even though Mr. Lockhart liked him, Robert knew there would be hell to pay.

The horse he had borrowed from Tobias was tied to the railing around the gazebo, he recalled. There was no way Mr. Lockhart could miss seeing the animal if he walked by there.

Fear thundered along Robert's veins, and it was almost as potent a feeling as the passion he had experienced a short time earlier. Yet he was also consumed by helplessness; it was too late, and there was nothing he could do to prevent discovery. The voices were even closer now.

Jacqueline clutched his arm. "That's my father and George Jenks, one of the overseers. There's a path that goes past the back of this shed and on out to the fields. If they don't stop here—and they don't have any reason to—and if they don't see your horse, then maybe . . . maybe they won't find us."

It was a faint hope, but the only one that Robert had to cling to. He took Jacqueline's hand and held it tightly as they stood side by side, waiting. The tension seemed to thicken the air inside the shed and make it hard to breathe.

Robert could even hear the footsteps of the two men now, and suddenly he was seized by an irrational urge to rush out of the shed and confront them. What he and Jacqueline had done was wrong, of course, but the love they felt for each other ought to excuse it. He was acting like a craven coward, he told himself, when what he ought to be doing was stand up for himself and for Jacqueline. This sneaking around and hiding was something Cam would do!

That thought shamed Robert even more, and he went so far as to take a step toward the closed door of the shed before Jacqueline's fingers tightened on his hand and she breathed into his ear, "What are you doing?"

"We shouldn't be hiding," he whispered back, a fierce edge in his voice. "Our love is noble and good. We should go out there and tell your father what happened."

Her hand clenched even tighter on his. "*Have you lost your mind?* You wonderful, romantic fool! Trust me, Robert. Confronting my father would be the absolutely worst thing you could do right now!"

Under the circumstances, he supposed he had to defer to her wishes. After all, she knew her father better than he did. And, as she had pointed out earlier, women were more practical creatures than men.

The footsteps faded, and then the voices did likewise. Robert closed his eyes and heaved a sigh of relief.

"Let's get out of here while we have the chance," Jacqueline said.

She cracked the door open an inch and peered out, just to be sure no one was nearby, then stepped outside and motioned for Robert to follow her. He closed the door behind him, and they walked quickly around the pond and back to the gazebo, where they sat down side by side in the wicker chairs. Robert's pulse was still pounding hard in his head, and it was several minutes before it began to settle down.

"I suppose you'll have to be leaving soon," Jacqueline said. Her voice was calm, and when he looked at her, he saw that a brave mask had settled over her face.

"That's right. I have plenty of time to ride back to town before the train rolls through, but I wouldn't want to take a chance on missing it."

"No," she said, "you shouldn't take a chance. You'll be doing enough of that soon enough."

"Jacqueline—"

She lifted a hand to stop him. "No, that's all right. I'm sorry, Robert. I know that nothing we feel will ever change the world. It lumbers along on its violent path, paying no heed to love or loss. People are like ants crushed under the wagon wheels of time and events."

That seemed like a rather bleak way to look at life. Robert said, "We still have hope."

Jacqueline's lips curved in a faint smile. "Hope and memories. Two sides of the same coin. The only currency we have to spend."

He reached across the space between the chairs and took her hand.

"Mr. Gilmore," a cool, unfriendly voice said behind them.

Both Robert and Jacqueline jumped a little, unable to control the reaction. Robert stood up and turned to see Jacqueline's mother standing there on the green grass. Priscilla Lockhart was as beautiful as ever. Not quite as lovely as her daughter, maybe, but mighty close. The expression in her eyes as she looked at Robert reminded him of a hawk about to swoop down out of the sky and snatch up an unsuspecting mouse.

"Mother!" Jacqueline said, her voice cracking a little from the strain. "Mother, Robert's here. He came to visit me."

"I can see that," she murmured. "Mr. Gilmore, how are you?"

"Why, I'm, uh, just fine, Mrs. Lockhart," he managed to say as he stood up, faced her, and took off his hat. "And how are you?" He thought he sounded fairly normal.

"I'm wondering what you're really doing here," Priscilla said bluntly.

"Mother! I told you Robert came to visit me." Jacqueline's chin lifted in the customary gesture of defiance he knew so well. "If you don't believe me—"

"Oh, I believe you," Priscilla broke in. "He wouldn't come all this way to see any of the rest of us, now would he?"

It bothered him the way she spoke of him as if he weren't standing right there. "I came to tell Jacqueline good-bye," he said.

For the first time, Priscilla looked pleased by something she had heard. "You're not going to see her anymore?"

"I didn't say that. But I won't be seeing her for a while because I'm on my way up to Columbia to enlist in the Hampton Legion."

"You're going off to war?" Priscilla said.

"That's right."

"How noble of you." Without her having to say it, he could almost hear the rest of her thought: *Now, if you would just be so accommodating as to get yourself killed so that you can't bother my daughter anymore . . .*

"There's nothing noble about it. I'm just doing my duty. If the Yankees invade our home, we'll be there to stop them."

"Well, if you've said your good-byes, don't let us keep you," Priscilla said. "Are you riding that horse all the way to Columbia or will you be catching a train?"

"A train. The one that comes through Mount Holly this evening."

"You should hurry, then. You don't want to miss it."

Robert relaxed a little. Obviously, Priscilla had no idea what had happened earlier in the shed. If she had known that her precious daughter had been befouled by a young man with the poor judgment to have less money than the Lockhart family, she would have been screaming her head off and calling for her husband to bring the shotgun. Robert could see her summoning a preacher and having a hasty wedding ceremony carried out—before instructing her husband to blow the interloper's head off and make Jacqueline a proper widow.

All he had to do was finish his farewell to Jacqueline and head back to Mount Holly. It would have been nice to have some privacy to do that, but Priscilla didn't look like she was planning to budge. Since he didn't have any choice, he stepped over to the chair where Jacqueline sat and reached down to take hold of both of her hands.

"I *will* be back," he said quietly. "You have my word on that, and I keep my promises."

"I pray that you're right, Robert. I'll pray for you every day."

"And I'll pray for you. We'll be together in that way while I'm gone, until I return and we can be truly together again."

He saw worry flare in her eyes for a second, and he thought he

228

might have gone too far with that last comment. If Priscilla interpreted that to mean what it really did . . .

But Priscilla, wonder of wonders, seemed not to be paying any attention to them anymore. Instead, she was gazing out over the pond. She might be unwilling to leave them alone, but at least she wasn't glaring at them in disapproval of their love. Robert leaned closer to Jacqueline and brushed his lips across hers. The kiss was brief, but it was soft and sweet, and he would take it with him and carry the memory of it inside him forever.

Then he straightened, clapped his hat on his head, and knew there was nothing left to say. They had said it all. In their words . . . and in other ways.

"Good-bye, Mrs. Lockhart," he said as he stepped down from the gazebo and reached for the horse's reins to untie them.

"Good-bye, Mr. Gilmore."

"I hope you'll pass along my best wishes to Mr. Lockhart and tell him good-bye for me as well."

"Of course. As you wish."

He swung into the saddle, not daring to look at Jacqueline. Instead he lifted a hand to the brim of his hat, nodded to Priscilla, and pulled the horse's head around. Pressure from his heels sent the animal loping along the path that circled the plantation house and led back to the road.

He glanced behind him only once, and as pain gnawed on his heart at the sight of Jacqueline still sitting there, so small and alone, he wished he hadn't.

"You don't fool me, you know."

Jacqueline looked at her mother as fresh fear welled up inside her. "What do you mean?" she made herself ask.

"I know what you did," Priscilla said coldly. "You took that boy out there to the shed and gave yourself to him."

Jacqueline gasped. She knew that she shouldn't, since doing so was practically an admission of guilt, but she couldn't help it.

Still, she had to try to convince her mother that she was wrong. "That's insane," she declared. "You know I would never do such a thing, Mother."

"On the contrary, I know that you're foolish enough to do exactly that. You're young, and your blood is hot, and your head is full of romantic notions." Priscilla laughed. "You thought that if you let him do what he wanted, he wouldn't leave you. You thought he'd forget about going off to war. But he didn't, did he? He rode away, just as he would have if you hadn't sacrificed your virtue to him."

Jacqueline wanted to scream at her mother, wanted to say that it hadn't been Robert's idea to make love, but hers. She knew, though, that Priscilla would never believe her. She wanted to blame everything on Robert, and nothing would convince her otherwise.

Besides, Jacqueline was hurting too much right now to argue. Robert was gone, and she might never see him again.

"You're probably worried about what your father's going to say, aren't you?" Priscilla went on. "Well, there's no need. I'm not going to tell him."

"Why not, if you're so convinced you're right?" Jacqueline knew it was foolish to goad her mother that way, but she was too sad and upset and angry to keep quiet.

"Because it wouldn't do any good. What's done is done. Besides, with everything that's going on, Everett doesn't need anything else to worry him."

Jacqueline felt a little surge of relief. Priscilla sounded like she was telling the truth about not exposing the secret to her husband. It was bad enough that she knew. Jacqueline could live with that, though, as long as her father didn't know.

"You'd better hope that you're not with child," Priscilla added. "Everett may be a bit dense at times, bless his heart, but even he will notice if his daughter's belly swells up and she drops a sucker like some darky wench."

230

"Mother!" Jacqueline exclaimed, astounded at her mother's crudeness. And terrified at the same time that Priscilla might be right. Unbidden, Jacqueline's hand strayed to her belly and pressed against it. So flat and taut right now, but as time passed . . . was it possible?

Of course it was possible. And even as fear that it might be true coursed through her, something else touched the back of Jacqueline's consciousness and eased her terror just a bit.

If it was true . . . if the unthinkable happened . . . if Robert never returned from the war, at least she would have a part of him still with her. She would have not only her memories of this day to cherish but also a child, a son or a daughter that she and Robert had come together to create . . .

"Come along inside," Priscilla said. "This time of day, the mosquitoes will be out any minute now."

# CHAPTER NINETEEN

# The Hampton Legion

**R**OBERT MADE IT BACK to the Mount Holly depot before the northbound train arrived, although he took out his watch and looked at it worriedly several times during the ride into the settlement. Tobias was inside the livery stable when he rode in. The burly freedman had a pitchfork in his hands and was tossing fresh straw into one of the stalls.

"You find Four Winds all right?" Tobias asked with a grin.

"Yes, I did." Robert dismounted and handed the reins to him. "Thank you for all your help."

Tobias's smile went away. "Did you make Miss Jacqueline cry?"

"I'm afraid I did. To tell the truth, I shed a few tears myself."

Tobias sighed. "Well, sayin' good-bye ain't never easy, I reckon. I recollect when I was a boy, my daddy got sold away from the plantation where we lived. My mama, she 'bout cried her eyes out for nigh on to a month after he was gone. She never seen him again, o' course."

Discomfort stirred inside Robert. It was just such stories that made him glad the Gilmore family didn't own slaves. As much as he liked Everett Lockhart, he had no doubt the man would break up a slave family like that if he thought it was a good business decision.

"Well, I've got to get on down to the depot," he said to change the subject.

Tobias wouldn't be diverted quite so easily, though. He said, "Miss Jacqueline, she was all right when you done left out there?"

Robert nodded. "Yes, she was fine. Sad, of course, but she'll get over that."

"I ain't so sure. I reckon she'll miss you until you come back to her, Mist' Robert. If you go to fightin' them Yankees, you be mighty careful. Keep yo' head down as much as you can."

"You have my word on that, Tobias."

With that, Robert left the livery barn and walked toward the train station. He checked his watch again along the way and saw that the time lacked a quarter-hour of being seven o'clock. When he got there, he saw that the ticket window was closed. Old Mr. Branchley must have gone home for supper. According to the information chalked on the board next to the window, though, the northbound train was on schedule.

Sure enough, a short time later Robert heard the shrill sound in the distance of a locomotive steam whistle. A few minutes after that, a faint rumbling came through the rails themselves, and that grew into the thunder of the engine as it approached.

When the train rolled in and stopped, Robert boarded one of the passenger cars and looked for a seat. The train was crowded. In times of upheaval such as this, folks seemed to travel more. Somebody was always going somewhere.

He was surprised when he heard his name called. Turning around, he saw that he had just passed a seat where a thickly built man in uniform sat with a carpetbag beside him. Major Stafford Pinckston lifted a hand in greeting and said, "Cadet Gilmore, what are you doing here?" Before Robert could answer, Pinckston went on, "Sorry, you're not a cadet anymore. I know that. I'm just a creature of habit, I suppose."

"It's all right, Major," Robert told him. "I was proud to be a Citadel cadet, and I certainly don't mind being recognized as one."

Pinckston moved the carpetbag, placing it on his lap. "Sit down, sit down," he invited. "I'm not sure you're going to find a seat anywhere else on this train."

"I was about to come to the same conclusion." Robert sat down beside the major.

"You're bound for Columbia, I expect, same as me."

"Yes sir. I'll be enlisting in the Hampton Legion when I get there."

"As will I. I've already been in touch with Colonel Hampton, in fact, and I'll be retaining my rank as a major."

Robert nodded. "That's fine news, sir. You deserve it."

"Well, I have experience, and if there's one thing the army is in need of at the moment, it's experienced officers. Luckily, there's no shortage of eager volunteers such as yourself." Major Pinckston paused for a second then went on, "Say, I have an idea. You have a considerable amount of training yourself, Robert, and I know from your classes at the Citadel that you're quite familiar with the practical uses of artillery. I expect to be given command of an artillery unit. Perhaps there would be a place for you on my staff."

The idea was an intriguing one. Though Robert had only limited experience with the big guns, including his time at the battery on Morris Island that had fired on the *Star of the West,* he enjoyed the science of artillery, figuring elevations, trajectories, windage, and things such as that. He had expected that he would wind up as a private in the infantry, no different than thousands of other raw recruits. Here was a chance to do something better and maybe more meaningful.

"Thank you, sir. It would be an honor."

"Such a thing might not be possible, you understand," Pinckston said. "But I'll do my best to see that it comes about. Stay with me when we get to Columbia. We'll see Colonel Hampton together."

"Yes sir."

It had been quite a day, Robert reflected again as the rocking and clattering of the train began to lull him into a half-doze. Images swam though his memory—the faces of the housemaid Ellie, Lucinda Tyler, Tobias and old Mr. Branchley, Priscilla Lockhart, Major Pinckston . . . and above all, Jacqueline. The woman he loved, the woman who had changed his life forever. The woman whose love had given him something to live for, as if he had needed a reason.

War with the Yankees was inevitable. He had no doubt in his mind about that. But as he fell into an uneasy slumber, he prayed that it would be a short war, so that soon he would be back in Jacqueline's arms once again.

COL. WADE HAMPTON was actually Wade Hampton III. His grandfather, the first of that name, had been a distinguished officer in both the Revolutionary War and the War of 1812. By the time of his death in 1835, he owned three thousand slaves and was known far and wide as the wealthiest planter in the entire nation.

The family home near Columbia was called Millwood, and while Wade Hampton II was the head of the family, the estate became the center of political and polite society in South Carolina. The library at Millwood boasted more than ten thousand volumes, making it one of the largest private libraries in the country. Politicians, educators, philosophers, and military leaders all came to the Hampton plantation to visit. Wade Hampton III, who would grow up to found Hampton's Legion, came to manhood in these vital, cultured surroundings, rubbing shoulders with the rich and famous and powerful. It came as no surprise to anyone when the quick-witted young gentleman was able to graduate from South Carolina College in Columbia at the age of eighteen.

However, he was more than just a successful scholar. He was also an avid hunter and fisherman and physically powerful enough so that on more than one occasion, armed only with a knife, he was able to kill a bear. He was an expert rider as well.

Although he had studied law in college and after graduation, he didn't take up the practice but rather concentrated instead on the business empire established by his father and grandfather. The Hampton holdings stretched all the way into Mississippi, and at a young age, Wade was managing them adroitly, making them even more successful.

Naturally enough, having grown up around politicians, Wade's interests eventually turned in that direction, and he was elected to the South Carolina General Assembly in 1852. The emotionally divisive issues of slavery and secession were beginning to be debated in the assembly, the newspapers, and elsewhere. Hampton had already reached the conclusion that slavery, as it was practiced in the South, was becoming economically unfeasible and would have to come to an end sooner or later. Left alone, he believed the practice would die a natural death within a decade or two. Therefore, he was no fire-eater and made speeches against secession, arguing that it would unnecessarily cause a bitter division within the country, a schism that might ultimately result in war.

He was right about that, of course, but his efforts in the General Assembly could do nothing to halt the runaway train of secessionism. Despite his personal feelings, Hampton was a loyal son of South Carolina, and once secession was a fact, he resigned from the assembly and went home to Millwood. It was his intention to enlist as a private in the hastily organizing Confederate army, but Governor Pickens wouldn't hear of that. He had a colonel's commission waiting for Hampton.

Once it was official, Hampton threw himself into his newfound profession of soldiering. He had the wherewithal, and after a meeting with Jefferson Davis, he had the sanction of the government to create his own legion. Loans secured by the vast Hampton holdings would feed, clothe, and equip several regiments of infantry as well as smaller units of cavalry and artillery. The combination of branches of service led to the designation of legion. Hampton planned that, when the time came, the legion would go into battle with its founder and benefactor in command. Even though he had no military training, Wade Hampton had been a smashing success at everything else he had ever attempted. There was no reason to think that war would be any different.

ROBERT HAD been to Millwood before; his father, Arthur Gilmore, had been friends with Colonel Hampton years earlier, when they had both attended South Carolina College. Arthur Gilmore had been there only a short time and had never graduated due to his family's lack of funds to complete his education, but the bond of friendship formed between the two young men had lasted anyway.

The surrounding plantation seemed to have been transformed since the last time Robert was there. Instead of producing cotton and tobacco and corn and rice, the sprawling fields now apparently grew soldiers. There were tents and marching men everywhere. As Robert and Major Pinckston drove up in the buggy that the major had rented in Columbia after riding the train all night, they passed several companies of sharply uniformed troops drilling smartly under the command of their officers. They also saw cavalrymen going through mock charges, yelling and waving sabers that glittered in the sunlight.

"Where are the cannon?" Pinckston asked as he handled the buggy horse's reins and looked around the makeshift encampment. "They have to be here somewhere."

"I'm sure they are," Robert said. "A legion can't fight a war without artillery."

"That's right. Even the ancient armies had their catapults. Well, I'm sure we'll find them in time. Right now we'll look for Colonel Hampton and let him know that we're at his service."

Pinckston drove up to the great house itself. A slave met them and took hold of the horse's harness. The major stepped down from the buggy and asked, "Is Colonel Hampton inside?"

"Yes suh, he talkin' to some o' his officers."

Pinckston and Robert went onto the wide verandah of the beautiful house, where the major grasped the bell pull and tugged it. An elderly slave, who reminded Robert of Thomas, the butler at the Tyler house, answered the summons and opened the door.

"Major Stafford Pinckston to see Colonel Wade Hampton," Pinckston announced himself. He didn't identify Robert.

Before the servant could respond, a tall, balding, officious man in uniform came up behind him, brushed him aside, and saluted. "I'm Lieutenant Forsythe, Major, Colonel Hampton's aide. Can I help you?"

"I've come to offer my services to the colonel," Pinckston said stiffly and properly as he returned the lieutenant's salute. "I'm Major Stafford Pinckston, formerly professor of mathematics and artillery at the South Carolina Military Academy at Charleston."

"The Citadel, eh, Major?"

"That is correct."

"I'm positive the colonel would like to speak to you." Forsythe glanced at Robert. "And who's this?"

Pinckston took care of the introduction, saying, "Mr. Robert Gilmore, also formerly of the Citadel."

Forsythe frowned slightly. "No offense, Mr. Gilmore, but you hardly appear old enough to have been an instructor like Major Pinckston."

"That's because I had the honor of being a cadet, sir," Robert said.

"How old are you?"

"Eighteen, sir."

Major Pinckston put in, "I thought that perhaps Robert could serve with me, since I know he's well-versed in artillery."

"That will be up to Colonel Hampton," Forsythe said. "Come along, both of you."

He led the way along a luxuriously furnished hall to the great library of Millwood, where Hampton and several other officers stood around a table spread with maps. The colonel was a handsome, vigorous man, just under six feet tall, with a full head of thick, dark hair and an impressive, sweeping mustache that merged with bushy side whiskers. When Lieutenant Forsythe dryly announced, "A couple of new recruits, Colonel," Hampton turned toward them with a smile spread across his face.

"Robert Gilmore!" the colonel boomed as he stepped forward and extended his hand. "It's good to see you again, lad. How's that old scoundrel Arthur doing?"

"Just fine, Colonel," Robert replied as the two shook hands. "I haven't spoken with him lately, but I'm sure, if I had, he would have sent his kindest regards."

"A good man, your father," Hampton said.

Robert glanced at the lieutenant. Forsythe looked surprised by the warmth and effusiveness of the colonel's greeting. Robert tried not to smile.

Hampton turned to Stafford Pinckston. "Major, it's good to see you again, too. It's been a while."

"Yes, it has."

"Your letter said that you wish to join our effort?"

"With your permission, Colonel."

Hampton's expression turned serious. "I wish this time had never come, but now that it has, the Confederacy needs all the good men it can muster. As I indicated to you in my letter, you'll be commissioned a major of artillery in the Hampton Legion as soon as you're sworn in."

"Thank you, sir."

Hampton turned back to Robert. "Now what are we going to do with you?"

"I'm at your disposal, Colonel," Robert said.

Pinckston interjected, "I thought perhaps Mr. Gilmore could serve on my staff—"

Hampton shook his head, cutting off Pinckston's suggestion. "I'm sorry, Major," he said. "I know Robert has an excellent grounding in the use of artillery if he was a student in your classes, but I also know from his father's letters that the young man excelled in all his classes at the Citadel. We're very much in need of men with formal military training to take charge of preparing our soldiers for battle." The colonel turned to Robert and went on, "I'm told that the Citadel cadets did most of the training and drilling of the militia in Charleston over the past few months. Is that true?"

Robert couldn't very well lie to the man, even though he saw his opportunity of serving with Major Pinckston slipping away. "Yes sir."

"You have personal experience in such things?"

"Yes sir. I was in charge of drilling one of the militia companies."

Hampton ran his fingers through his thick beard. "You're aware that graduates of the Citadel are being commissioned as officers in the Confederate army?"

"I am, sir . . . but I'm not a graduate. I had one more year to go when I withdrew from the academy."

Hampton waved that off. "A young man who has completed two years at the Citadel is experienced enough for a commission, to my way of thinking. Especially when I happen to know he's a very competent young man. Welcome to the Hampton Legion, Lieutenant Gilmore."

Robert couldn't help but glance at Forsythe. Just like that, he was the same rank as the aide. Forsythe frowned.

"Captain Connelly of Company E, Third Infantry, is in need of a second-in-command," Hampton went on. "I think you'll fill that position very nicely, Lieutenant."

Robert had no choice but to nod and say, "Yes sir." He had been prepared to enlist as a private and fight in the infantry if need be; he had come to serve wherever South Carolina and the Confederacy needed him the most. He had to admit to himself, though, that he was excited to have been appointed a junior officer so quickly.

Hampton gestured to Forsythe. "Take care of the enlistment papers for these two gentlemen, Lieutenant."

"Right away, sir," Forsythe answered.

The colonel clapped a hand on Robert's shoulder, and his voice eased from its official crispness and held a trace of warmth as he said, "It's good to have you with us, son. I know you'll make your father proud."

"I hope so, sir."

Hampton stepped back to the table and motioned to Pinckston. "Join us, Major," he invited. "We were just studying these maps of the Washington area. If the Yankees invade the Confederacy—or perhaps I should say *when* the Yankees invade the Confederacy, since it seems inevitable—their army may well start from the District of Columbia, since that's where they're assembling. We were trying to figure out the likely routes they'll take from there . . ."

DESPITE HIS training at the Citadel and his experience in drilling troops around Charleston, the next six weeks were like nothing Robert had ever known before. Day after day, sometimes in drenching rain, sometimes in blazing sun, as summer arrived in South Carolina and brought with it oppressive humidity and clouds of voracious mosquitoes, Robert worked from before dawn to after dusk, helping Capt. Jeremiah Connelly mold the men of Company E, Second Infantry, Hampton's Legion, into actual soldiers.

They marched. Endlessly, they marched. They went through close-order drill. They had target practice with the squirrel guns they brought with them and the Enfield rifles imported from England and provided by Colonel Hampton. Yelling at the top of their lungs, they charged across fields that had not been planted in cotton this year, attacking imaginary enemies. They routed rank after rank of pretend Yankees. Bayonets ripped into dummies stuffed with corn husks. Officers studied *Hardee's Tactics*, the standard infantry manual written by William J. Hardee, now a general in the Confederate army, and they tried to pass along what they learned to their men. Robert had something of an advantage there, because he had read *Hardee's Tactics* while at the Citadel and absorbed its lessons.

The recruits memorized drum and bugle calls and learned that most of the decisions concerning their daily life had now been taken out of their hands. They rose at a certain time, ate in a certain order, went where they were told to go, and did what they were told to do. Colonel Hampton might not have been regular army, but he and his officers, right down to the most junior lieutenants like Robert, ran the legion in a crisp, professional manner. Uniforms, weapons, and other supplies were well cared for, and if they were not, the soldier responsible would regret it. The vast encampment spread across the Hampton plantation was kept clean and orderly as well. It took a great deal of hard work from everyone involved, but by early July 1861, by any standard of judgment, the Hampton Legion was a real army. Small by military standards, perhaps, less than a thousand men, but they were well trained, well disciplined, and ready to fight.

As they had for months now, rumors of impending war continued to swirl. Lincoln's call for seventy-five thousand volunteers had been answered and then some. More than a hundred thousand Federal soldiers were assembled in and around Washington, D.C., according to newspaper accounts.

Already, there had been a few skirmishes between Northern and Southern forces. A Yankee officer, Col. Elmer Ellsworth, had been killed in late May when his regiment of Zouaves had crossed the Potomac River to Alexandria, Virginia, to occupy the city in a protective move to make it easier for the Federals to defend their capital in case of an attack. At a place called Big Bethel, also in Virginia, a Union force had blundered into a Confederate camp, resulting in a melee that could hardly be called a battle. But men were killed on both sides, and they were just as dead as if two mighty armies had engaged in a well-planned conflict.

Despite the blood that had been spilled, neither side expected the real fighting to last long once it began. Southern newspapers circulated freely through the camp at Millwood Plantation, and their editorials proclaimed in fiery rhetoric that the Confederates would crush the Union army so quickly and so decisively that Lincoln would have no choice but to give up and agree that secession and the formation of the Confederacy were legal and just. As Robert read those remarks, he wondered if the Northern newspapers were saying pretty much the same thing, only turned around so that the Yankees would emerge triumphant in short order. He reckoned it was pretty likely they were.

Newspapers weren't the only things he read, of course. He received letters from home and from Allard, who was still in Charleston. Robert was a little surprised that Allard hadn't yet joined the Confederate navy, but his friend's letters soon explained why that wasn't the case. Allard had fallen in with an old friend of his grandfather's, Capt. Barnaby Yorke, and he was helping Yorke outfit a ship from the Tyler Shipyard to be used as a privateer against the Yankees. A grin spread across Robert's face as he read that. He could imagine how thrilled Allard must be to have old Black Nick's first mate around. Allard had idolized his grandfather for years. And as happy as Allard probably was, Robert suspected that Allard's father was equally unhappy.

Allard didn't say anything about Lucinda, and of course he didn't mention Ellie. It would never occur to him to pass along news of one of the family's slaves. Robert wondered about both of them, but they were far away now, and it might be a long time before he saw either of them again. It wasn't difficult to push any worries about them out of his mind.

The subject of Lucinda cropped up again, though, in Cam's letters. Before returning home, Cam had spent a week in Charleston after finishing his term at the Arsenal. And from the sound of Cam's letters, he and Lucinda had grown even closer during that time. Cam was angry that Robert had left without saying good-bye to him in person; the fact that they had crossed paths, Robert departing Charleston as Cam had been arriving, just made things worse. So, naturally, Cam had responded by dropping veiled hints about how close he and Lucinda had become.

If Cam wanted to ruin his life by getting involved with a witch like that, it was his decision to make, Robert told himself. Cam was almost grown. Still, the situation bothered Robert. He felt as if he had failed his younger brother in some way. He was supposed to look after Cam, and here he had allowed Lucinda to get her hooks into him. All he could do was hope that someday Cam would come to his senses, Robert thought with a sigh every time he folded one of his brother's letters and placed it in the small trunk where he stored his personal items.

Most important, of course, he received letters from Jacqueline, and they were the most precious to him. For the first two weeks after he had joined the Hampton Legion, no letters from her had arrived, and Robert had tortured himself by trying to figure out why she hadn't written. Several terrible scenarios played out in his mind: Her parents had discovered what they had done in the shed and had forbidden her to write to him. They had discovered the secret and disowned her, sending her away in shame and scandal. She had decided that she didn't love him after all, didn't want to wait for him, and would have nothing more to do with him.

All those possibilities struck fear into his heart, and he wished there was some way he could leave the camp and return to Four Winds for a short time, just long enough to be sure that Jacqueline was all right and still loved him. But of course he couldn't do that. He had too many duties keeping him busy eighteen hours a day. Lord knew when he would have a chance to visit her again.

At moments like that, he almost wished the Yankees would just invade so they could get this damned war over with.

One more possibility began to occupy his mind. What if that wonderful afternoon in the shed had left Jacqueline with child? It was certainly possible. The idea that he might be a father was both exhilarating and terrifying. A pregnancy would be the ruination of Jacqueline, of course, and for that reason he hoped it wouldn't turn out to be true.

But at the same time, the idea that the two of them had come together to create a child . . . that tightened Robert's chest and made his eyes sting and filled him with a warm glow. The timing wasn't right, certainly, but someday . . . someday . . .

Then letters from her began to arrive, and there was nothing about them to indicate that anything was wrong. They were full of professions of her love for him, and they didn't mention any sort of trouble between her and her parents. Things were all right after all. It had just taken her a while to get started writing to him. Now she promised that he could look forward to regular letters from her. Robert felt a huge weight lifted from his shoulders.

He had just placed Jacqueline's most recent letter in his trunk when Captain Connelly came into the tent they shared. The captain was a tall, broad-shouldered man with a close-cropped, gray-shot beard. Before joining the Hampton Legion he had been a journalist, working for one of the Columbia newspapers. Robert liked him. Connelly pushed his men hard, but he wasn't brutal about it like some officers tended to be at times.

Now Connelly took off his hat, wiped sweat off the inside of the band, and said, "Colonel Hampton has called a meeting of officers tonight, Lieutenant."

Robert straightened from where he had crouched in front of his trunk and asked, "Do you know what it's about, sir?"

"Not officially, no." His attitude became less formal as he said, "I can make a guess, though. I have friends who work on some of the Northern newspapers, and they tell me that old Abe's under a lot of pressure to do something. He's got this big army sitting in Washington, and so far he hasn't had them do a blasted thing."

"So your friends think the Yankees are going to move against us?"

"The Confederate Congress is due to convene in Richmond next month. I wouldn't be surprised if the Yankees intend to march to Richmond and stop that from happening."

"If they try that . . ." Robert began.

"If they try that," Connelly said grimly, "we'll be sitting there, right smack-dab in their way, ready to spank them and send them back where they came from."

# CHAPTER TWENTY

## The Ghost

I N CHARLESTON IT WAS difficult for Allard Tyler not to question his luck. Things had worked out so well for him that he had begun to worry lately that the pendulum might shift the other way.

Instead of being forced to say good-bye to Diana, as he would have if he had carried out his original plan to enlist in the Confederate navy, he was still here in the old, gracious city, living in the same house as the beautiful young woman he loved and working with a man he greatly admired, Capt. Barnaby Yorke. He was a lucky young man indeed.

And a sailor had to have luck on his side. Yorke had told him that more than once.

"'Twas a fogbank that saved us when a damned Redcoat frigate was right behind us," Yorke had said when he was spinning yarns for a raptly attentive Allard. "To this day, I don't know where it came from. It wasn't there and then suddenly it was. We sailed into it and give that frigate the slip neat as you please. Ol' Neptune was really lookin' out for Nick and me and all the rest o' our crew that day."

"The god of the sea," Allard murmured.

"Aye. And another name for sailor's luck. That's your best friend when you're on the waves, laddie. Better remember that."

Allard would. He knew, though, that a sailor couldn't always count on good fortune. It was a capricious thing, like the sea itself, and could desert a man when he needed it the most. So it paid to work hard and be prepared for any emergency. That was another lesson taught to him by Barnaby Yorke.

The day after Yorke's arrival in Charleston, the old sea dog and Malachi Tyler had gone to the shipyard to look over the vessels under construction there, especially the ones nearing completion. Allard had tagged along with them, ignoring his father's glares of disapproval. Malachi stopped short of ordering Allard home, although he certainly looked like he wanted to.

Once in the shipyard, Yorke's eye had been caught right away by the sleek lines of a two-masted schooner. The ship was both sail- and steam-powered, with a smokestack rising from its engine between the two fore-and-aft-rigged masts.

"Who built the engine?" Yorke inquired, nodding at the schooner.

"Langford and Hughes of Liverpool," Malachi answered.

Yorke nodded in approval. "A fine company. They do good work."

"Indeed they do," Malachi said stiffly. Allard could tell that his father didn't like the way Yorke was looking at the schooner.

"She seems built for speed, too," Yorke went on. "Good clean lines, and if I'm not mistaken, you could rig some extra sail on her."

"I had in mind selling her to one of the passenger lines as a clipper ship," Malachi explained. He shrugged. "Now, with the war . . ."

"People will still need to sail from one place to another." Yorke rubbed his close-cropped beard for a moment before continuing, "But I think we can put that beauty to even better use."

"Don't you want to even look at the other ships?"

"Oh, aye. We'll look at them all. But I'm thinkin' it's doubtful we'll find a better one than this pretty lady right here, Malachi."

The two men, with Allard trailing after them, spent the rest of the morning studying the other vessels in the shipyard. Yorke seemed tempted by a few of them, but always shook his head when he glanced back at the schooner. In the end, the first ship he had seen was the one he chose.

"We'll need guns mounted fore and aft," he said. "Eighteen pounders, I think."

"Where am I supposed to get those?" Malachi asked. "I never built pirate—I mean, warships. I never built warships before."

Yorke said, "Leave that to me. I know some lads who ought to be able to put their hands on a couple o' big guns."

"I'm sure you do," Malachi muttered under his breath. Allard didn't know if Yorke heard the comment or not. If he did, he gave no sign of it. Allard heard it, though, and wished his father didn't despise the old sea captain so much.

Malachi estimated that about a month's worth of work remained to be done on the schooner before she was ready for her maiden voyage. "You'll not be mindin' if I spend most o' my time down here watchin' your men put the finishin' touches on her, will you?" Yorke asked.

Allard could tell that his father *did* mind, but Malachi just nodded and said, "That'll be fine." At moments such as this, Allard thought, Malachi probably forced himself to remember the letter from the president. If he hadn't been a loyal Southerner, he never would have gone along with all of Yorke's requests.

Allard wondered what would happen when he told his father that he intended to become a member of Captain Yorke's crew.

In the meantime, Malachi and Katherine both seemed happy that Allard had evidently given up the idea of joining the navy. Malachi might suspect that Allard had something else up his sleeve, but if he did, he kept quiet about it.

There were other things going on in the Tyler household, of course. Yorke was staying there, and he flirted so shamelessly with Katherine that it made even Allard a little uncomfortable, despite his fondness for the old sea captain. Katherine seemed to enjoy the attention, though. She had a glow about her, and Allard thought she was staying away from the port and the sherry and the madeira. Certainly, there was nothing going on between them other than harmless flirting—at least Allard fervently hoped that was the case—but that was enough by itself to put a glare on his father's face and an angry flush on the back of Malachi's neck whenever he witnessed it. It wasn't bad enough that Yorke was a constant reminder of what Malachi considered his father's illicit, unsavory past. No, Yorke had to put a smile on the face of Malachi's wife and a lilt in her laughter that hadn't been there for a very long time.

Then there was Cam Gilmore. Cam had accepted the invitation to stay with the Tylers not so much because of the surprise of his brother's enlistment in the Hampton Legion but because Lucinda was there. Allard was convinced of that. Lucinda had continued her usual ambivalent behavior toward Cam, teasing him playfully at times, treating him with disdain at others. And although Allard hadn't witnessed it for himself and couldn't prove it, he was convinced that his sister and Cam carried on in a scandalous manner whenever they had a chance.

He didn't say anything about that when he wrote to Robert, figuring that his friend didn't need the extra worries. Besides, Robert was smart enough, he had probably figured out already what was going on.

Over and above all the distractions, though, Allard spent more time thinking about Diana than anything else. It was wonderful seeing her at every meal, hearing her voice early in the morning and late at night, looking at her when she wasn't aware that he was watching her, studying the smooth curve of her cheek or the way her thick red hair draped over her shoulders or the graceful way her hand reached out to touch something. He loved her, loved everything about her, and there were times when he thought he would be a fool to ever leave her.

Then he remembered the war that was surely coming and the patriotism that stirred in his chest and the way the water seemed to call to him whenever he looked out over the harbor and thought about the vast, beguiling sea beyond . . .

Everyone had to make choices, of course, but sometimes, Allard thought, those choices were just too blasted *hard.*

HE PAUSED as he walked by the arched entrance into the parlor. Diana sat alone in there. Allard didn't see any sign of his mother or sister, and he knew his father was at the shipyard. Nor were any of the servants around at the moment.

Just Diana, sitting on a divan, a book in her hands, looking so beautiful she made his heart pound.

Allard believed in seizing opportunities whenever and wherever they presented themselves. There was no way of knowing when they might come around again.

He entered the parlor.

Diana glanced up at him, and a smile played over her face. Allard might have said that the expression made her even more desirable, but of course, that was impossible.

"What are you doing here in the middle of the day?" she asked. "I would have thought that you'd be down at the shipyard with your father or Captain Yorke."

"I decided to stay home for a while after lunch," he said. "I wasn't feeling very well."

A look of concern appeared on her face as she sat forward slightly. "Are you all right?"

He waved a hand and said, "I'm fine. Probably just a touch too much sun this morning. I was clambering all over the schooner with Cap'n Yorke."

"Cap'n Yorke," Diana repeated, smiling again. "You sound like a sailor, Allard."

"That's exactly what I intend to be—one of these days."

They hadn't really discussed his postponed plans. He hadn't come right out and told her that he intended to sail with Yorke when the privateer left Charleston. Both of them had deliberately ignored the subject, content to enjoy the other's company and the respite from fate.

Diana set the book aside and patted the divan next to her. "Before you sail away, you old sea dog, sit with me for a while."

Grinning with contentment, Allard settled himself on the soft cushions of the divan. His right thigh was pressed firmly against

Diana's left, and he felt the warmth of her flesh through their clothing. When he leaned toward her, she closed her eyes, tipped her head back just slightly, and parted her lips a little. Allard pressed his lips to hers.

As always, her mouth was warm and sweet, and the taste of it set off tremors of passion that shivered all through him. He slid his right arm around her shoulders and drew her closer. Without thinking about what he was doing, he rested his left hand on her knee for a moment and then slid it upward. Although sometimes it was hard to tell, what with all the stiff petticoats underneath her dress, he knew her leg was in there somewhere. He kneaded what he hoped was the pliant flesh of her inner thigh.

Over the months since they had declared their love, he had grown bolder in his caresses. He had still never touched her body except through her clothing, but she had given him increasingly free rein to explore its curves. Allard longed for her to touch him as well, but so far she hadn't, and he would never dream of forcing her to do such a thing. Their mounting desire would be indulged at her pace, not his. That was the gentlemanly way to proceed.

But sometimes, he thought as he kissed her, it was all he could do not to—

He suppressed the image in his head before it had a chance to become dangerously explicit. There was nothing wrong with just kissing. It was mighty enjoyable, in fact, he told himself.

When she reached down and took hold of his hand, he expected her to remove it and place it back on his own. Instead she lifted it, pressed his palm hard against the small, firm globe of her right breast, and opened her lips wider. Instinctively, his tongue slid between them, and she met it with a thrust of her tongue as she moved his hand in a circular motion.

Allard felt almost as shocked as if lightning had struck him. This was the boldest Diana had ever behaved with him. The slight awkwardness of her movements told him she had never done this before. Neither had he, of course, but he hoped that wasn't *too* apparent. A man was supposed to have some worldly experience. For a second he thought that maybe it would have been better if he *had* taken Ellie or one of the other maids to his bed, as his father had urged, just so he wouldn't be a total novice at this.

No, he decided abruptly as the softness of Diana's breast filled his hand and her tongue darted hotly and wetly into his mouth, some experiences were better shared for the first time, fumbling or not, and this was one of them.

Diana's fingers dug hard into his muscles of his neck. With her other hand, she reached to the bosom of her dress and pulled it down. Allard cracked an eye open and tried to look in that direction without breaking the kiss. Was it possible that . . . Yes! She had bared her left breast, letting the creamy flesh pop out of her dress so that he could see the pale pink nipple that crowned it. He slid his hand over and cupped it. His thumb found the nipple and rubbed it into hardness. Diana made a low moaning sound in her throat.

Well, this was certainly the most shameless, wanton thing he had ever done. He knew it wasn't proper, the way they were carrying on.

He also knew that he couldn't stop now. Nothing short of an earthquake or a hurricane or some other natural disaster could make him cease what he was doing.

That—or the slamming of a door.

"Allard!" Barnaby Yorke called from the foyer. "Allard, are you here, lad?"

Allard sprang away from Diana. He landed a couple of feet away at the far end of the divan as Diana yanked up the neckline of her dress and straightened it. She picked up her book and laid it open in her lap. Other than a faint flush on the upper part of her chest and her rapid breathing, she looked perfectly normal, not at all like Allard had just been pawing her like she was some sort of harbor-front trollop.

He glanced down at himself. Luckily, all his clothing was in order. There was no evidence—well, almost no evidence—and that was quickly going away . . .

What had they been thinking? Why had they been so foolish as to carry on that way in the parlor in the middle of the afternoon? From now on they were going to have to be very careful not to get carried away. They couldn't afford to give in to their emotions like that.

Yorke stepped into the parlor entrance. "There you are."

"Hello, Captain Yorke," Diana said with a bright smile. "I was just reading some poems to Allard. Would you care to sit down and listen?"

"Ah . . . no, Miss. but I appreciate the offer. Sea chanteys are about the only poems an old salt like me really has an appreciation for. And I'm afraid Allard doesn't have time to listen anymore, either. I've got to steal the poor boy away from you."

Allard felt a touch of alarm at Yorke's words. "What's wrong, Cap'n?"

"Wrong? Nobody said anything was wrong. But I need you to come back to the shipyard with me, Allard. Big doin's goin' on. Mighty big doin's."

"But it's not some sort of trouble?"

"No, lad," Yorke answered with a trace of exasperation in his voice. "Now, are you comin' or not?"

Allard glanced at Diana and sighed, torn between staying with the girl he loved or going to the shipyard with the man he admired so much.

Diana resolved his dilemma, bless her heart, by saying, "Go on with the captain, Allard. You and I can always . . . read poetry . . . again some other time."

He hoped Yorke didn't see the blush that suddenly made his ears warm. "Yes, of course," he said. "It was very enjoyable, Diana. You read beautifully."

She smiled and patted his hand. He stood and walked over to join the captain. "Hoist your sails, lad," Yorke urged as he turned toward the door.

Before they could leave, Katherine appeared in the hallway. She said with obvious pleasure, "I thought I heard your voice, Barnaby."

He swept off his cap. "I'd love to stay and talk with you, Katie, but the lad and I have urgent business at the shipyard."

A concerned expression appeared on Katherine's face. "Is everything all right? There's not something wrong with Malachi, I hope."

"Oh, no. That husband o' yours is fit as a fiddle. And there's no problem in the yard. Just somethin' that we got to take care of."

"Well, all right. Land's sake, the way you men rush around, always busy with something. You'll be here for supper, won't you?"

"Aye, should be done before then, no doubt." Yorke clapped his hat back on his head and took hold of Allard's arm. "Come on, mate."

As they went down the walk to the street, Allard said, "You're sure there's nothing wrong?"

"Just wait and see, lad. Wait and see."

They walked quickly through the streets of Charleston toward the harbor. When they reached the shipyard, just above the Battery, Allard saw the workers gathered around the schooner, which was a thing of beauty with its clean lines and fresh paint and neatly furled sails. The clerks from the office were on the dock as well, and so was Malachi Tyler, Allard noted in some surprise. Ever since Captain Yorke had taken over the supervision of the ship's outfitting, Malachi had steered clear of it for the most part.

"Here's the lad, Malachi," Yorke announced as he and Allard walked up. "I reckon we're ready now."

"Yes, I suppose we are." Malachi held out a square of folded cloth. "You'll want to do the honors."

Yorke took the cloth, which Allard recognized as a folded flag. He turned and extended the flag toward Allard. "No, I think that's a job for your son and Nicholas Tyler's grandson."

Malachi's mouth tightened a little at the mention of his father, but at least Yorke hadn't referred to him as Black Nick this time.

Allard frowned at the flag in Yorke's hands. "What is this?"

"We're ready to raise the Confederate flag and give this fine vessel a name." Yorke smiled. "Got any ideas along those lines? I thought you might want to call her the *Diana*."

Allard was tempted to agree. But there was only one Diana, and as beautiful as this ship was, she couldn't hold a candle to the real thing.

"She's your ship, Cap'n. You should be the one to name her."

"Well . . . I suppose I can do that. But only if you'll run up the flag."

Allard took the cloth from Yorke's strong, gnarled fingers. "All right. Shall we go on board?"

Side by side they started up the gangplank, but then Yorke stopped and looked back. "Come with us, Malachi," he said.

Malachi waved a hand and shook his head. "This is your vessel—"

"The letter of marque is in both our names," Yorke pointed out.

"You've supervised all the work."

"She never would have been built without you."

Allard thought that as stubborn as his father and the captain were, they might stand there and argue about it all day. Hoping that he could swing the balance, he said, "Come on, Father. It's time you set foot on the deck of a ship again, at least for a few minutes."

Malachi glowered at him for a second, but then his expression eased a bit. "You may be right, Allard," he said. He took hold of the rope next to the gangplank and started up, looking a little apprehensive as he glanced down at the water lapping against the dock pilings. Some men would always be landlubbers at heart.

The three men went to the rear mast, where the flag halyard was attached. Allard unfurled the Stars and Bars of the Confederacy and attached it to the line.

"We'll get a South Carolina flag, too," Malachi said. "This ship will sail under the palmetto tree."

"Aye, that's just what we need," Yorke agreed. "Haul away, Allard."

With his hands on the line, Allard hesitated. "The name, Cap'n. This ship needs her name."

Yorke nodded slowly. In an unusually solemn tone, he said, "We'll call her the *Ghost,* because I plan to sail her past those damned Yankee blockaders without them ever seein' her."

"The *Ghost* it is," Malachi said, and Allard pulled on the line, raising the Confederate banner on the halyard until it reached the top of the mast. The offshore wind caught it and snapped it out, so that it flew proudly over the schooner. Cheers went up from the workmen on the dock. They pounded their callused, tar-stained hands together in fervent applause.

The three men stepped back and looked up at the flag flying atop the mast. "I reckon this means you're just about ready to sail," Malachi said without taking his eyes off the Stars and Bars.

"Aye," Yorke agreed. "As soon as I finish puttin' together my crew, we'll be ready to head out and make life miserable for any Yankee merchantman on the water." He lowered his gaze from the flag and looked over at Allard. "I'll be needin' a good third mate to come along and learn the ropes o' command."

Before Allard could respond to the offer he had been expecting, Malachi said, "I was afraid you were going to say that. Jeff Davis asked me to do everything I can for you, Yorke, and I've given you this ship. But there's nothing that says I have to give you my son as well."

Yorke regarded him coolly. The stirring emotions that all three of them had felt moments earlier had vanished. "The lad's of age," Yorke said. "Seems to me it's his decision."

"He's still my son," Malachi said stubbornly. "I have a say—"

"Wait a minute, both of you," Allard broke in, unwilling to stand there in silence while the two of them wrangled over him. "I'm sorry, Father, but it *is* my decision . . . and I choose to go with Cap'n Yorke."

"Allard, don't be a fool."

"I'm not," Allard insisted. "You were willing to let me join the navy—"

"Not really. I always hoped you'd come to your senses before I had to put my foot down."

"It's too late for that," Allard said. "And this is better, Father. You'll see. It may be months before the navy amounts to anything. You know as well as I do how much trouble Secretary Mallory is having putting his hands on seaworthy ships. This is a chance to strike at the Yankees *now*, instead of waiting. And since we'll be coming back to Charleston between voyages—" He glanced at Yorke. "We will be coming back, won't we?"

"Aye, lad. Got to bring in all the prizes we'll be takin'."

Allard nodded. "Since we'll be coming back here, I'll be home a lot more often than if I was posted to a navy vessel somewhere. And if I don't want to make one of the voyages, I won't have to."

"What you're saying makes sense," Malachi admitted grudgingly, "except for one thing."

"What's that?" Allard wanted to know.

"You'll still be a damned pirate!" Malachi held up a hand to silence Yorke as the captain opened his mouth to protest. "I know, you're going to say you're a privateer. I don't care."

"You can't keep me from going," Allard said.

"We'll see about that." Malachi turned and stalked over to the gangplank. Allard could tell that he wanted to stride angrily down it but was too nervous to try it. He held the rope tightly again and slowly made his way to the dock without looking back.

"Your father's a difficult man, lad," Yorke said with a sigh. "There are times when I have a hard time believin' that he's Black Nick's boy. But he's got Nick's stubbornness, that's for damned sure, even if he didn't inherit any of the other qualities."

"He can't stop me from going," Allard said again.

"No, maybe not, but are you sure you want to burn that many bridges? I'll understand if you decide that you can't—"

"No!" Allard cut in. "I'm going. I'll be ready to sail whenever you say, Cap'n." An image of Diana appeared in his head then, and he felt an odd fluttering in the pit of his stomach. "There are a few things I have to do first . . . a few decisions that have to be made . . . but I'll be ready when the *Ghost* sails out of Charleston Harbor."

# CHAPTER TWENTY-ONE

# Out to Sea

Allard could feel the tension in the air like a physical thing when he entered the Tyler mansion later that afternoon. Thomas greeted him at the door. The old slave regarded Allard glumly, shook his head, and sighed.

"What's wrong?" Allard asked.

"I reckon you know what's wrong, Marse Allard," Thomas said. "Your mama, she's up in her room cryin'. Miss Diana, she done shed a few tears, too. An' your pa's 'bout mad enough to chew nails."

"It's not my fault," Allard said. "I don't see why they can't understand!"

"'Cause they love you, boy. Can't *you* see *that?*"

Allard felt a flash of anger. An old darky butler had no right to talk to him like that, with disapproval so evident in his voice.

But as quick as that thought went through his head, he banished it. He had known Thomas all his life and knew that the old man loved him. That gave Thomas the right to speak his mind.

"I didn't mean to make everyone upset. There are just some things that I have to do."

"Ever'body have to do somethin'. Best to give plenty o' thought to what it is."

Allard nodded and went down the hall, pausing to look back over his shoulder and ask, "Do you know where Diana is?"

"No, I don't. Reckon you'll have to find her for yo'self. I don't want no part of it."

Again Allard was irritated by Thomas's attitude, but he shoved the irritation away. He went into the parlor, hoping to find Diana there. However, the room was empty.

As he turned back toward the hall, his mother appeared in the doorway. "I thought I heard you come in," she said. She was composed, but her eyes were red, evidence of what Thomas had said about her crying. "Malachi tells me that you're going to sail with Barnaby."

"I thought you'd be pleased, Mother. You like Cap'n Yorke, and this is much better than my joining the navy—"

"You'll be risking your life! How do you expect me to react when my only son is going to run away and become a pirate?"

"We won't be pirates! We'll be privateers!"

Katherine came closer and said, "Stop it, Allard. You're not a fool. Barnaby Yorke can argue about the name all he wants, but that doesn't change the facts. He plans to attack and capture or sink Yankee ships, and that makes him a pirate. If you sail with him, you'll be one, too."

The fact that Yorke had a government commission to carry out his raiding still seemed like an important distinction to Allard, but he knew it was pointless to argue about that. The real issue was much different.

"You just don't want me to leave," he said. "You're afraid something will happen to me."

"Well, of course I am! What mother wouldn't be?"

"Thousands of mothers have watched their sons go off to war in the past few months," Allard pointed out, "in the North and the South, both. I know it's hard for you, Mother, but why should it be any different for us? Why shouldn't I do my part for the cause?"

Katherine's face contorted suddenly, and fresh tears sprang from her eyes. "Because you're my baby!" she wailed. She stepped forward and threw her arms around him.

Allard didn't know what to do. He stood there without moving for a moment and then awkwardly began to pat his mother's back as she sobbed against his chest.

Several minutes went by. Gradually, Katherine's sobs died away into sniffles. Finally, she was able to lift her head and dab at her eyes with a lacy handkerchief she took from a pocket of her gown.

"I'm sorry, Allard," she said in a voice still thick with emotion. "I know it's not fair of me to put you in this position. I just can't help it. I love you so much, and I don't want anything to happen to you."

"I know," he told her gently. "But like I said, Mother, it's the same all over. When your country is threatened, you have to do something about it. You can't just stand by and wait for the enemy to come in and take over."

"No. No, I don't suppose you can." Katherine took a deep breath. "I don't like it, but I won't stop you from doing what you have to do."

"What about Father?"

Katherine summoned up a smile and fluttered a hand. "Don't you worry about your father! I can handle him." She paused and then went on, "And don't get the wrong idea about me and Barnaby Yorke, Allard. Anything that was between us was over a long time ago, and it didn't really mean anything to start with."

"You don't have to explain, Mother."

"I just don't want you to think that because there was a time when Barnaby and I—"

"No, I mean you *really* don't have to explain, Mother," Allard said hastily, not wanting her to say any more than she already had. "That's none of my business."

Katherine laughed. "No, I suppose it's not. I do enjoy the attention that Barnaby pays to me. He's an old flatterer, and every woman needs a little of that every now and then. More than I usually get from your father, Lord knows! . . . Anyway, I know and trust Barnaby. He's a good captain, and if you can do everything he says, you'll stand a better chance of coming back to me, to all of us, alive. Promise me that you will."

"Of course I'll follow his orders. He's the captain of the *Ghost*, and I'll just be the third mate."

"The *Ghost?* Is that the name of the new ship?"

"That's right." Allard smiled. "The cap'n says it's because the Yankee blockaders will never see her."

"Well, I pray that he's right! When are you sailing?"

Allard became serious again. "Tomorrow night. Cap'n Yorke said we'll just go out a short distance and come back, just to prove that the *Ghost* is seaworthy and see how she handles. But even doing that, we may run into the Yankees."

Katherine squeezed his arm. "I'll be praying for you the whole time you're gone."

"I would hope so. We need all the help we can get, divine and otherwise." Allard squared his shoulders, knowing that he couldn't put off the main thing he needed to do. "Do you know where Diana is?"

"Up in her room, I think." Katherine's forehead creased in a frown of concern as she said, "I think she heard your father ranting about what you're planning to do. So she knows you're leaving."

"It won't be for long," Allard said. "She'll have to understand."

He hoped that would prove to be the case.

"OF COURSE you have to go, Allard. I know that. You've talked of little else for months now. I was resigned to your joining the navy when that was your plan, and I regarded the extra time you spent here after Captain Yorke came as a gift, an unexpected blessing. Now the time has come. I know it and accept it."

Allard couldn't help but stare at Diana as she spoke. Her lips were curved slightly in a faint smile. She was saying exactly what he wanted to hear. He had hoped that she would be this reasonable, but he hadn't really expected it.

"The only other thing I want to add," she went on as they stood together in the second floor hallway, next to a window that overlooked a spreading magnolia tree, "is . . . you bastard, how can you leave me this way?"

Her smile vanished and she covered her face with her hands as she began to cry, leaving Allard stunned by this sudden reversal.

After a moment he managed to find his voice. "Diana, I . . . I don't know what to say."

She lowered her hands and said, "Tell me that you're not going to leave."

"But . . . but you know I have to!"

"Why?"

"Because I have to do what I can for the Confederacy—"

"Don't lie to me, Allard," she cut in, her voice cold and hard. "You can help the Confederacy by staying here and working with your father. You just want to run off to sea and have adventures with Captain Yorke!"

Allard put his hands on her shoulders. She flinched a little, but she didn't try to pull away from him. "That's not true," he said then stopped short. He loved this woman, so he owed her the truth. He owed himself the truth. "Or maybe it is, at least to an extent," he said thickly. "For years, ever since I was a little boy, I've wanted to be out there on the water, sailing the seas like my grandfather did. I can't help it, Diana. It's a dream that's been a part of me for such a long time."

"Did your dream include a war?"

To be honest, it hadn't. When he thought of such things, it had been more vague and undefined, a boy's longing for glory and excitement, with no real thought given to the dangers that might be involved.

Now he was no longer a boy, but those early dreams had never gone away completely. They blended now with the situation as it really was. His nation was faced with a war, a possible invasion, and like all able-bodied Southern men, Allard wanted to do his part to oppose the Yankees. In his case, though, he had a chance to combine that patriotism and devotion to duty with his childhood ambitions. He knew that maybe he was being a little selfish, but not really. No more so than the thousands of other young Southerners, like Robert, who had already marched off to confront the enemy.

Without answering the question, he said, "Diana, you have to understand. This is the best for all of us. I won't be gone long. A few days, maybe a week . . ."

"Long enough to get yourself killed."

He lifted his hands, pressed his fingertips to his temples for a moment as he closed his eyes. When he opened them again he said, "If this is the way you feel, why did you say those other things? Why did you act like you understood?"

"Because I love you, Allard. I tried to tell you what you wanted to hear." A sad smile touched her lips. "But in the end, I couldn't. I just couldn't. My head understands, but my heart . . . my heart just can't."

He sighed and stared out the window at the branches of the magnolia tree with their green leaves and sweet white blossoms. "I don't know what to do or what to say," he said without looking at her.

"I wish I could help you, Allard. I really do. But I can't change the way I feel."

"Neither can I."

She turned toward the door. "Just go," she said. "You're leaving tomorrow. Just go, and don't try to see me between now and then. We'll talk again . . . when you get back."

"You mean . . . this is good-bye?"

"For now."

The flatly spoken words pierced him. He wanted to lunge after her, grab her, and turn her around so that he could hold her and kiss her and somehow make everything all right. But he knew he couldn't do that. She might not resist him, but it wouldn't change anything between them. The specter of his choice would still loom there, a barrier that couldn't be breached.

So he let her go, and he tried to tell himself that she would feel differently about things once she had settled down and gotten used to the idea. She would see that it wasn't really that bad. He would be gone from Charleston for a few weeks at a time, maybe a month now and then, but he would still be around a great deal, too. Once they settled into a routine of sorts, things would be fine.

But despite all his attempts to convince himself of that, when he looked at the closed door of her room, a band seemed to tighten around his chest, and he knew the ache he felt was the pain of something lost, perhaps for all time.

THE NEXT day could not have dawned more beautiful. The arching vault of blue sky above Charleston was dotted here and there with puffy white clouds, and there was a bit of a breeze to relieve what would become a hot June day before it was over. From where he stood in his room, Allard could see the Citadel to his left and the rest of Charleston to his right, all the way to the Battery and the blue waters of the harbor beyond.

The beauty of the day and the anticipation he felt about what that night would bring were almost enough to make him forget that he hadn't seen Diana since the previous afternoon. She had not come down for dinner and had refused the tray that Katherine had had Ellie take up to her. When Allard left his room, he glanced toward the closed door of her room and wondered if she had relented and gone downstairs for breakfast or if she intended to be true to her vow not to see him again before he left.

To his disappointment, he saw that she wasn't in the dining room with the rest of the family as he came into the room. His mother and father were seated at opposite ends of the table, and Lucinda sat on one side, picking listlessly at the food on her plate. She was pale and looked a little sick. Ever since Cam had left Charleston and returned to the Gilmore farm, Lucinda had spent most of her time brooding in her room. Since they had never gotten along well anyway, Allard didn't particularly mind her behavior. As he looked at her now, though, he felt a small pang of worry. She was his sister, after all, and he didn't want her to be ill.

Lucinda perked up a little at the sight of her brother, but only because his presence gave her the opportunity to say, "I hear that you're going to sail away tonight and become a pirate, Allard."

"The *Ghost* is sailing tonight, yes," he said, too weary of the whole thing to argue the issue of piracy versus privateering.

"The *Ghost* is a fitting name for that ship, since everyone on her will probably be killed by the Yankees."

"Lucinda!" Katherine said, horrified. "How can you say such a thing?"

Lucinda shrugged. "I'm just trying to be realistic, Mother. What chance will one little schooner have against the whole Union navy?"

"We're not going to fight the whole Union navy," Allard pointed out as he sat down. "That's why Cap'n Yorke wanted a fast ship. We'll be able to pick the battles we want and avoid the ones we don't."

"You mean you'll be able to run away with your tail between your legs if the odds are against you," Lucinda said.

Allard's jaw tightened in anger. Lucinda knew quite well how to rub him the wrong way. She had years of experience, after all.

"Choosing your battles isn't running away."

Lucinda shrugged. "Call it what you will."

Malachi spoke up for the first time since his son had entered the dining room. "You're determined to go through with this?"

Allard nodded decisively. "Yes sir."

Malachi pushed his chair back and stood up. "Come into my study then, when you've finished with your breakfast." He strode out of the room.

Allard didn't know what to make of that. He hoped his father hadn't come up with some plan to force him to stay.

Lucinda left the table next, looking queasy again. Allard ate the food placed in front of him, but in his worry about Diana and his excitement over the upcoming voyage on the *Ghost*, he didn't really taste much. He became aware that his mother was watching him.

"What's wrong, Mother?"

"I'm just trying to memorize everything about you, Allard. You'd think after eighteen years I'd know my own son's face by heart, but I see things there I don't think I've ever noticed before." She hesitated then went on, "I hate to say it, but you really do remind me of your grandfather in some ways."

That made Allard feel better. To be told that he reminded someone of the famous Black Nick Tyler was quite a compliment.

Then his mother added, "He could be the most stubborn, infuriating man on the face of the earth, too."

Allard burst out laughing, unable to contain it, and Katherine joined him. It was going to be all right, Allard told himself. There would be rough patches, to be sure, but things were going to be all right as long as he had faith and trusted in sailor's luck.

"Have you seen Diana since yesterday afternoon?" he asked when he had finished eating.

Katherine shook her head. "No, but I'm sure she's all right. She's just upset right now. She'll get over it."

Allard hoped that was true.

He stood up from the table. "I guess I'd better see what Father wants. I hope he's not planning to tie me up or lock me in my room to keep me from going."

"Oh, I'm sure he's not. If I thought that would do any good, I'd try it myself."

Allard smiled and went around the table to kiss his mother before he left for the study.

When he stepped into that room a few moments later, he found his father sitting at the desk. A closed polished wooden case lay in front of him. Allard had never seen it before.

"What do you want, Father?"

Malachi frowned darkly. "Since I seem to be unable to talk you out of this madness, I suppose the least I can do is see to it that you're well equipped for it." He pushed the wooden case toward Allard. "Here."

"You're giving me a present?" Allard asked incredulously.

"Just open it," Malachi snapped.

Allard turned the small brass catch and lifted the lid. Inside the case, nestled in hollows on a bed of dark blue velvet, were a pistol and a knife. Both weapons gleamed in the light of the study window.

"My God," Allard breathed. He couldn't recall ever seeing anything that looked so beautiful and so deadly at the same time.

"That's the newest model Colt Navy," Malachi said. "Thirty-six caliber, six shots. It was manufactured at Colonel Colt's British factory, though, not the one in Connecticut. It came in on one of the last ships from England before the Yankees threw up their infernal blockade."

Allard touched the weapon's gleaming cylinder then switched his attention to the heavy, wickedly curving blade of the knife. "What about this?"

"A Bowie knife," Malachi said. "I thought about getting you a cutlass, but I thought you might be able to handle this better."

"It's a little big and heavy for work on ship, isn't it?" Allard asked, hoping that he didn't sound ungrateful.

"It's not for work," Malachi replied, a harsh edge coming into his voice. "It's like the gun. It's for protecting yourself. It's for killing."

A chill crept along Allard's veins. "You mean—"

"If you sail with Barnaby Yorke, sooner or later you'll find yourself in danger." Malachi practically spat the words. "Either you'll be attacking another ship, or you'll be under attack. There'll be boarding parties and combat at close quarters." He reached out and closed the case, and the sharp slap of the lid falling made Allard jump a little. "That's what these are for, to help keep you alive and see to it that the son of a bitch you're fighting dies instead."

Allard couldn't say anything. He knew his father was right, but he didn't want to think about such things right now. He wanted to think about the majesty of the waves and the way the salty wind would blow through his hair as the *Ghost* raced over the sea . . .

"You don't know how your grandfather died, do you?" Malachi asked abruptly as he leaned back in his chair.

"I . . . No, not really. I know he got sick . . . I assumed he was just old . . ."

"He was less than fifty years old," Malachi said. "Your mother and

I were already married, and Lucinda was a mere babe. You wouldn't come along for a couple of years yet. Your grandfather was always at sea, captaining merchantmen for the most part. He came home from time to time. I never really saw him that much while I was growing up. But I saw my mother gradually pining away for her husband until, I'm convinced, sheer loneliness killed her."

Allard had never heard his father talk so plainly about the past. By nature, Malachi Tyler was a closemouthed man. But now that he was being expansive for a change, he seemed to be drifting away from what he had started to say. Allard hesitated to interrupt, but he said, "You were going to tell me about my grandfather, not my grandmother."

"You never knew either one of them. Let me tell this in my own way."

Allard felt there was a good chance he wouldn't like the point of this story, whenever his father got around to it. "Sorry," he said.

"Whenever your grandfather came to visit, he usually had Barnaby Yorke with him. They always sailed together, during the war and afterward. It was during one of those visits, while I was courting your mother, that she met Yorke and . . ." Malachi's right hand clenched into a fist and thumped lightly on the lid of the case containing the revolver and the Bowie knife. "Never mind," he said curtly. "That has nothing to do with anything. It was on another visit, a later one . . . the last time I saw your grandfather . . . when I could tell something was wrong. He wasn't well. I asked him about it and he didn't want to tell me, but finally he admitted that he was a sick man. During the war a shell burst near him during a battle at sea and a piece of it hit him . . ." Malachi touched his own belly lightly, just above the waist. "He survived the wound, and once he had recovered, he always claimed that he was fine. But a piece of that shell was still inside him. It stayed there for the next thirty years, festering, until finally it got so bad he couldn't eat anymore. The corruption was consuming him from the inside out."

Allard swallowed hard. A wave of sickness touched him, and he supposed he felt about like Lucinda had looked earlier.

"When he was here that last time and told me about it," Malachi went on, "I tried to convince him to see a doctor, but he wouldn't do it. Said it was too late, and that the last thing he wanted to do was to die in bed. I might have tried to argue with him some more, but I never got the chance. He left, headed back to sea, and took Barnaby Yorke with him."

"Did he . . . did he die at sea?" Allard managed to ask.

Malachi nodded. "Died at sea, buried at sea. I suppose that's what he wanted. But what really killed him, even though it took thirty years to do it, was that battle wound. He died that day. He just didn't know it then."

Allard looked down at the floor and blinked away a warmth in his eyes that threatened to turn into tears. Something was wrong with what his father had just said, and after a moment, Allard knew what it was. He lifted his head and said, "You have it backward, Father."

Malachi frowned. "What are you talking about?"

"Maybe he didn't die during that battle because he loved the sea and loved life too much to let it go. Maybe that love gave him thirty years he wouldn't have had otherwise."

Malachi leaned forward and slapped the desk. "Damn it, no! You can't cheat fate—"

"Maybe you can fool it for a while, though," Allard said. He reached forward and picked up the wooden case, tucking it under his arm. "Thank you for the gifts. I hope I don't need them, but if I do, I'll use them to the best of my ability."

"Allard—"

"I have to go now. I expect the cap'n's already on board. There's still plenty to do before we sail tonight."

"Allard—" Malachi said again.

But Allard had already turned and was striding out of the room, not looking back.

HE SPENT the day on board the *Ghost,* helping Yorke as he checked out everything and made sure the ship was ready to sail. Yorke had put together a crew of twenty men and four officers, including himself and Allard. Allard had been around sailors quite a bit in his life, but the obvious toughness of these seasoned, veteran sea dogs made him feel a bit ill-qualified to be in command of them. He would do his best, though, and by watching Captain Yorke closely, he thought he could learn how an officer was supposed to conduct himself at sea. Besides, he knew quite a bit about sailing. He'd had a small sloop of his own when he was a boy and had taken it out into the harbor frequently.

Hard work kept his mind off the argument with Diana and the unsettling story his father had told him that morning. He was grateful for that, even though there were times he wanted to ask Yorke for more details about his grandfather's death. He didn't figure that Yorke needed that distraction right now, though, so he didn't say anything about it.

Late in the afternoon, Yorke put a hand on his shoulder and said, "Go home and eat a good supper, lad, then say good-bye to your folks and that gal o' yours. We'll be sailin' afore the moon rises."

Allard just nodded. He didn't explain that he might not get to say good-bye to Diana.

The mood at home was somber. Allard could tell that his mother was fighting not to cry at the dinner table. Lucinda looked pale and drawn. Malachi wore his habitual frown. None of them said much during the meal.

"What about Diana?" Allard asked when he was finished.

"I saw her earlier," Katherine said. "You don't have to worry about her, Allard. She'll be fine. She just . . . doesn't want to see you."

He nodded numbly, disappointed that Diana hadn't changed her mind. He knew there was nothing he could do to make her feel differently toward him, short of changing his plans. And he wasn't going to do that.

He placed his hands on the table and slowly levered himself to his feet. "I have to go," he said.

"I know," Katherine said. "Be careful, Allard. Please be careful."

He summoned up a smile. "It'll only be a few days."

Malachi took a cigar from his vest pocket and put it unlit in his mouth. "Tell Yorke to bring that ship back safe and sound," he grated around the cylinder of tobacco.

Allard nodded. "I will."

To his relief, Malachi stood up and extended a hand. "Do your duty," he said gruffly. "Obey orders. Don't shirk."

"Yes sir," Allard said as he clasped his father's hand. It seemed odd to be shaking hands this way with his own father, but it felt good, too.

Katherine and Lucinda stood up and came around the table to hug him. Allard expected that from his mother, but Lucinda surprised him. "Take care of yourself," she told him quietly, sounding like she meant it. He looked at her and saw something in her eyes, some pain that she was keeping to herself.

"Lucinda . . . ?"

She gave him another quick hug. "Just go."

Then Katherine embraced him. Allard was glad she wasn't crying. "Oh, fiddle," she said. "I'm not going to carry on. I'm not. It's not like I'm the first mother who's had to say good-bye to her son."

"I'll be back," he told her with a smile. "You can count on it."

"Of course you will be." She gave him another quick, hard hug, then forced herself to let him go.

Allard left the dining room and walked to the front door of the mansion. All the gear he was going to take with him was already on board the *Ghost*. His family came into the hallway behind him, and he paused at the door for one last look at them. His glance flicked to the staircase, hoping to see Diana descending it.

But she wasn't there. The stairs were empty.

He smiled as best he could, lifted a hand in farewell. Then he stepped out into the early evening and walked toward the street. He listened for the sound of the door opening behind him, the rapid patter of footsteps as she hurried to catch up to him. He was ready to turn and sweep her into his arms and kiss her as she told him that all was forgiven, that she understood, that she would be there waiting for him when he returned from the sea . . .

Charleston was a large, busy town. There were plenty of sounds in the soft air, even at this hour.

But the ones Allard longed to hear were not among them. Instead he heard only his own steps on the paving. The only remaining farewell was the raucous cry of a seagull as it winged overhead.

CAPT. BARNABY YORKE stood at the top of the gangplank. "I was hopin' we wouldn't have to sail without you, lad," he said as Allard hurried onto the ship.

"No sir, Cap'n, I'm here and ready to go."

"So are all the other members of the crew. We'll be castin' off in a few minutes." Yorke glanced at the sky, which had faded through blue and purple and gray almost to black. Pinpricks of stars were beginning to be visible. "The moon won't be up until we're out o' the harbor and well off the coast. Those Yankees won't catch even a glimpse of us."

Allard nodded eagerly. His departure had been an emotional strain, but he could feel himself beginning to put that turmoil behind him and get caught up in the excitement of sailing.

They would use the engine to get out of the harbor and over the bar, then raise the sails when they were in the open water. Yorke headed for the bridge with Allard trailing him. Once there, Yorke called down through the speaking tube to the engine room and ordered the engines back a quarter. The first mate ordered the crew to cast off. The mooring lines were unhooked from the dock and thrown aboard, followed by the sailors who had loosed them. Allard felt his breath coming faster as the *Ghost* moved away from the long wharf that jutted into the harbor from the Tyler Shipyard. No longer was the ship fastened to the land. Now there were no more tethers holding her. She was in the grip of the waters on which she sailed.

Yorke had a helmsman he trusted, but he had the wheel himself at this moment, spinning it to turn the rudder and send the ship into a graceful turn that pointed her outbound. "Ahead a half," he said to Allard, and it took Allard a second to realize that he was supposed to relay the command to the engine room. He grabbed the speaking tube and did so. The deck under his feet shivered just a little as the engine took hold and sent the ship surging forward.

Out from the land, out and around, past the Battery, past Shute's Folly Island where the lights of Castle Pinckney burned. Out Folly Island Channel and past the big sandbar known as the Middle Ground, onto Rebellion Road between Fort Sumter to starboard and Sullivan's Island and Fort Moultrie to port. Then a swing hard to starboard to avoid Drunken Dick Breaks and get into the main channel, the same channel that the *Star of the West* had attempted to follow on its ill-fated attempt to reach Fort Sumter. That day back in January seemed far, far in the past to Allard now. Fort Sumter had fallen, Robert had left Charleston, and now Allard was going, too, setting out on a voyage that would take him . . . where?

He didn't know. All he knew was that Captain Yorke had just called out, "Raise the sails!" So Allard turned and bellowed, "Raise sails!" And with a fluttering and snapping, the canvas was lifted and caught the wind. As the sails filled, the rumble of the engine died, leaving the only sounds in the night the hiss of water against the hull and the groan of ropes and the seductive whisper of wind against fabric, the music that sailors had listened to for thousands of years, the music of the sea and its vastness and the courage of the men who dared to venture out upon it.

All rivers run into the sea, the Scriptures said, and likewise in the end the sea called its wayward children home.

Tonight Allard Tyler was answering that call, and as the *Ghost* cut through the waves, the lights of Charleston faded in the distance, unseen because Allard never looked back.

# CHAPTER TWENTY-TWO

# Clash by Night

THE *GHOST* SHOWED NO running lights. No lantern burned any-where on her. The sails had been dyed gray, and when Allard asked why they weren't black, to make them even less visible, Captain Yorke had explained that despite what one might think, black sails—and a black ship, for that matter—were more visible at night because they stood out against the radiance of the stars reflected off the surface of the water.

"Even on a completely overcast night," Yorke said, "some o' the glow comes through. And on a clear night, it's a lot brighter out on the water than you'd expect. Nothin' gets spotted faster'n somethin' dark movin' against a lighter background."

Allard supposed the captain knew what he was talking about. Yorke was the one with decades of experience at such things. In addi-tion to serving with Black Nick Tyler during the War of 1812, Yorke had dropped a few hints that he had done quite a bit of smuggling since then. No one Allard had ever met was more qualified for the job of taking a ship stealthily past the Yankees.

Now, as the *Ghost* followed the main ship channel when it made a sharp bend to the east, Allard was glad to have Yorke in command. His presence gave them all their best chance of coming back alive.

With the engines still, the ship sailed in relative silence. Allard stiffened as he heard a familiar sound drifting over the water from somewhere off to port. In a half-whisper, he said, "Cap'n, I hear something."

"Aye, lad. Damn my eyes if that ain't a steamer's engine. One o' them Yankee blockaders, unless I miss my guess."

Allard felt his heart begin to beat faster and harder. "Can you tell how far away it is?"

"Far enough," Yorke said easily. "We're makin' good headway. We'll be well past before they come steamin' through here."

Yorke's confidence made Allard relax. The captain knew what he was doing. But a few minutes later, with the sound of the engines still audible to port, Allard heard another steady-beating rumble to starboard. He saw Yorke stand a little straighter and heard him mutter, "Damn, I didn't think there would be two so close together."

"Is that another ship, Cap'n?"

"Aye." Yorke took a collapsible spyglass from his coat pocket and lifted the tube to his right eye. He peered through the lens for a long moment. "Hard to tell, but I think it's a Union side-wheeler, probably a frigate. It's ahead of us and quarterin' in to cut us off, although probably by accident. I ain't convinced the Yankees even know we're here yet."

"But they will," Allard said.

Yorke shrugged. "We ain't easy to spot. They'll have to be almost on top of us. Could be we'll still slip by without them noticin'." He paused then went on, "Just in case we don't, find Mr. Curwood and tell him to have men standin' by the guns."

"Aye, Cap'n," Allard said. He hurried from the bridge and located the first mate on the main deck. "Mr. Curwood, the cap'n says to have men standing by the guns."

Curwood, a burly sailor who had served as first mate to Yorke on other ships in the past, nodded and said, "Already done, Mr. Tyler. I heard those Yankees, too. Tell the cap'n we'll give 'em a hot reception if they come to call."

"Aye." Allard started to turn away but hesitated. "You know, I have some experience with eighteen-pounders, Mr. Curwood. I've fired them before, if my services are ever needed in that area."

"I'll keep that in mind. For now, I think the cap'n wants you with him."

Allard nodded and went back to the bridge. "The guns are manned, Cap'n," he reported.

Yorke grunted. "Good. Here's hopin' we don't have to use 'em. I wasn't plannin' on a fight our first night out. If the Yankees want one, though, we'll damn sure give it to 'em."

Allard waited in tense silence as the ship continued gliding smoothly through the water. The engine sounds from port had faded somewhat, indicating that Yorke had been right about the *Ghost* crossing the path of that vessel before it could intercept them. The side-wheeler to starboard was a different matter, though. Its engines were louder now, and Allard could see its lights. He estimated that the ship was about a mile away, angling toward the *Ghost*.

Yorke turned the wheel over to the regular helmsman and ordered a change in course that would take them a bit more to port. "Don't want to turn too much," he said to Allard, "because that would take us across their beam and make us easier to spot. We're a smaller target as long as we're sort of goin' toward them. Don't want to sail right at them, though."

"No, I don't think that would be a good idea," Allard said.

Yorke studied the ship through the spyglass again. "Definitely a side-wheel frigate. Probably carries ten or twelve guns."

"And we have two," Allard said.

"Aye, but we're faster. Her top speed is around eight knots, and we can do ten or eleven, maybe even a bit more with both the engine and the sails."

"So we can outrun them?"

"If we had turned around and headed straight back to Charleston when we first heard the engines, I reckon we could have. I didn't much feel like doin' that. But now we're in range o' their guns, and it's mighty damned hard to outrun a cannonball."

Allard felt his stomach clench in fear. He had known logically that they might come under fire, of course. But knowing that something *might* happen was completely different from experiencing it firsthand. He took a couple of deep breaths to calm himself. He didn't want to embarrass himself on his very first voyage by giving in to panic.

The *Ghost* hadn't slackened speed. In fact, the wind had picked up a bit, so she was going a little faster now. "Another two degrees to port," Yorke said quietly to the helmsman.

As the ship swung slightly in the course correction, Allard moved to the railing around the open bridge and gripped it with both hands, leaning forward to peer intently at the lights of the approaching ship. No more than a quarter of a mile separated the *Ghost* from the Yankee frigate now. This was a good test of how difficult it was to spot the privateer vessel at night.

The other ship's engines sounded very loud, beating and throbbing as they drove the frigate through the water. Allard's hands tightened on the rail. He could hear the splashing of the paddle wheels mounted on the frigate's sides. The gap between the vessels narrowed to no more than three hundred yards. Even with the naked eye, Allard saw men moving on the deck of the Yankee ship whenever they crossed in front of one of the lanterns. Didn't they have lookouts over there? How could they have missed seeing the schooner?

Then Allard realized with a shock that the lights of the Union ship were beginning to fall behind them. Their courses hadn't quite crossed, and the *Ghost* was now past the Yankee and pulling away from her. He took another deep breath, but his racing pulse didn't slow. It had been too close a call for that. He would need a little while to get over it.

"All ahead full," Yorke said.

He had to say it again before Allard realized that the captain was talking to him. Springing to the speaking tube, Allard grasped it and said into the mouthpiece, "All ahead full!" The deck shivered underneath him as the engine once again came to life. He felt the *Ghost* pick up speed as its propeller bit into the water and sent it surging ahead.

Yorke turned his head and called, "Mr. Curwood! Bid the Yankees a fond farewell with our rear gun!"

"You're going to fire at them?" Allard asked in surprise. "But we slipped past them, just like you said we would!"

"Aye, and now we're goin' to rub their Yankee noses in it!"

Allard wasn't going to question Yorke's decision, but it seemed rather foolish to him to announce their presence to the Yankees when they were on the verge of slipping away undetected. As Yorke had said, though, they were faster by several knots than the frigate. It wouldn't take them long to pull out of range.

A moment later, the cannon mounted at the rear of the ship roared as it sent an eighteen-pound ball whistling through the night air toward the Yankee frigate. Yorke turned so that he could keep his spyglass fixed on the enemy ship. After a couple of seconds, he thrust a fist into the air and called, "A hit! The ball struck her amidships. That'll wake up those damned Yankees!"

It still seemed to Allard that waking up the Yankees was just about the last thing they wanted to do. It was done now, though, and as the *Ghost* poured on the speed, crimson fire bloomed in the distance as the frigate fired a round then another. Allard held his breath, waiting to hear the scream of the cannonballs cutting through the air toward them. Both shots fell well short, though, sending little geysers of water into the air as they struck the surface a good fifty yards astern of the schooner.

Yorke chuckled. "Clean misses. I expect they'll try again, though."

They did, firing two more rounds a moment later. One of the balls fell short again, but the second splashed into the ocean a short distance to starboard. They were getting the range.

"Don't worry," Yorke said to Allard. "We're pullin' away from them. They had to make a turn to come after us, and that gave us even more of a lead. Another minute or two and they won't have a chance in hell o' hittin' us."

That was all well and good, but first they had to survive that minute or two. Allard watched wide-eyed as the Yankee ship fired two more rounds. Both fell short again as the *Ghost* continued to increase the distance between her and the Federal vessel.

"You can breathe easy now, lad," Yorke said. "They may chase us for a while, but there's no way they'll catch us."

Allard wanted to believe that, but he knew there was no way he would breathe easily again until the Yankee ship was no longer in sight.

By the time the moon rose, that was the case. The Yankees had given up the pursuit and no doubt returned to their regular patrol. The blockade had been fairly ineffective so far, and now Allard knew why. The Yankees didn't have enough ships, and they were spread too thin.

If they ever put together a large enough navy, though . . . it wouldn't be so easy. Then the South would be in for real trouble.

It was up to the privateers to see that that didn't happen.

BY THE next morning Allard's fear had gone away and his confidence had returned. He had to admit that Captain Yorke had been right all the way down the line. The Yankees hadn't spotted them, and once Yorke had thumbed his nose at them by firing the shot, the Yankees hadn't been able to catch them, either.

It was a gloriously golden morning at sea. Allard had been out this far before, but not often. As he stood at the rail, peering over the waves, Yorke came up beside him and asked, "How are you feelin', lad? Any seasickness?"

Allard shook his head. "Not a bit. It's never taken me very long to get my sea legs."

Yorke clapped a hand on his shoulder and laughed. "That's because you're a born sailor, just like your grandpa was, God rest his blackhearted soul!"

"Was he really that bad?" Allard asked as he turned his head to look at Yorke. "Did he deserve the name Black Nick?"

"The British sure as hell thought so when he was sinkin' their ships. They gave him the name. I got to say, though, Nick always seemed to like it." Yorke looked out over the waves but seemed to be gazing back through the years rather than into the Atlantic distance. "But if you're askin' was he a bad man . . . no, he wasn't. Not at all. He could be hell in a fight, but he had his quieter moments, too, and he loved his family and his friends. You'd never find a better comrade."

"Then why did my father hate him?" Allard asked bluntly.

Yorke rubbed at his bristly beard for a moment before replying. "That's a mite hard to say. Truth to tell, I don't know your pa all that well. Never have really understood the man. But I suspect it has somethin' to do with Sarah."

"My grandmother?"

Yorke nodded. "Aye. She died fairly young, and Nick was gone when it happened. Could be that Malachi blamed him for her passin'. Still blames him, for that matter."

"I think that's true," Allard said, remembering some of the things his father had said to him. "He told me that his mother died from loneliness because my grandfather was always gone."

Yorke frowned at him. "No offense to your pa, but that ain't right. Sarah understood Nick Tyler better'n anyone else alive. She knew the sea was in his blood, knew that he'd wither up and die if he had to spend the rest o' his days on land. She's the one who always urged him to go back out. I know it's true, lad, because I seen it with my own eyes and heard it with my own ears."

"I suppose it must have seemed different to my father."

"Maybe . . . but that don't mean Malachi's version o' the truth is right and mine ain't."

"No, I suppose it doesn't." Allard started to ask Yorke something about his mother, but then he decided he didn't want to know. Katherine had come perilously close to telling him details he didn't want to hear, and it would be foolish to invite them now from Yorke. Instead he said, "My father told me a couple of days ago how my grandfather died. I had never known about that before."

To Allard's surprise, Yorke threw back his head and laughed. It seemed a totally inappropriate reaction. Yorke's words came as another surprise as he said, "So Malachi told you about Black Nick and the Malay pirates, eh?"

Allard stared at him and said, "What? Malay pirates? No, my father told me about the fragment from an exploding British shell that lodged in my grandfather's belly and how it finally killed him."

Grinning, Yorke shook his head. "Oh, but that ain't the whole story, not by a long shot. You want to hear the rest of it?"

Did he really have to ask? Allard nodded his head eagerly.

"Well, 'twas like this," Yorke began. "We were in the South China Sea on a fast little clipper called the *Lady Grigsby's Arse*—never mind why it was called that, it don't have anythin' to do with this story—and we were runnin' a load o' tobbo from Bintulu up the coast o' Siam to Bangkok. I don't reckon you've ever heard o' the notorious tobbo shops o' Siam?"

Allard could only shake his head, caught up as he was in Yorke's colorful tale.

"Well, they're known from one end o' the Orient to the other, and sailors know to stay away from 'em unless they want certain bodily appendages to shrivel up and drop off, if you know what I mean."

Allard nodded as a shiver went through him at the very thought.

"Anyway, there was this Malay pirate chieftain named Phu Dan, and him and Nick had had some ruckuses before. Phu Dan swore that the next time Nick sailed into the South China Sea would be the last time. Nick never was one to back down from trouble, and by that time he knew he didn't have much longer to live."

"Because of the shell fragment in his belly," Allard said.

Yorke nodded. "That's right. His lovely Sarah was gone, and he'd been home to say good-bye for the last time to Malachi and Katie, your folks. You weren't born yet, you was still just a gleam in your pa's eye." He added under his breath, "Although I don't reckon Malachi's eye ever really gleamed all that much."

Allard didn't want to hear about that. He said, "What about Phu Dan and the pirates?"

"Nick knew that Phu Dan was likely waitin' for him somewhere off the coast o' Siam. Just because his time was about up didn't mean that was the case for the rest o' his crew, so when we stopped in Bintulu to take on that load o' tobbo, he told us all to get off. He said he was sailin' to Bangkok by his own self." Yorke shook his head. "Well, that was a crazy idea, o' course, and me and the rest o' the crew told him so. A man alone couldn't handle a ship like the *Lady Grigsby's Arse*. Anyway, the rest of us didn't like Phu Dan any better'n Nick did, so we told him we were comin' along and he might as well get used to the idea."

"So you left—where was it—Bintulu and headed for Siam?"

"Aye. We cut across the South China Sea and then hugged the coast, and for the first week we didn't see anything of ol' Phu Dan. But then, early one mornin' just as the sun came up, here he comes, slippin' out of a cove in a junk full o' bloodthirsty cutthroats. They sailed right at us, and the cannons began to roar."

An almost wistful note came into Yorke's voice as he went on, "Oh, it was a hell of a fight, lad. Cannonballs flyin' through the air and clouds o' powder smoke rollin' over the water and all the time them Malays was screamin' and yellin' at the tops o' their lungs. Black Nick didn't try to run. He pointed that ship straight at Phu Dan's junk, and in the end it was Phu Dan who swung away so that we came alongside like we was takin' the fight to them. They boarded us and we boarded them, and it was hand to hand, man against man, all over both ships. The Malays were armed with old blunderbusses, so our guns were better, but there were more o' them and they had cutlasses and these wicked curved knives called krises. We were puttin' up a good fight, but chances are that in the end they would've overrun us and slaughtered every last one of us . . . if not for the ace that Black Nick had up his sleeve. Or on his back, I reckon I should say."

"What was it?" Allard asked eagerly.

"None of us knew about it ahead of time . . . If we had, we might've tried to talk him out of it . . . But Nick had himself a keg o' black powder with some straps fastened to it. He buckled that keg onto his back, reached around behind him to get hold of the fuse, and lit it."

Allard's eyes widened.

"That's right, lad," Yorke said. "He cut that fuse so it'd take a few minutes to burn all the way up. After it was lit, he snatched up his saber and started cuttin' his way to the rail of our ship. When he got there he jumped across to Phu Dan's junk. He had already spotted Phu Dan on the bridge o' that vessel, so he started for him, hackin' and slashin' at any o' those Malays who got in his way. Truth of it is, when they seen that keg o' powder and that burnin' fuse, most of 'em got out of Nick's way as fast as they could. They didn't want to be any-where close to him when it went off."

"That . . . that's crazy!" Allard said. "He had to know he couldn't survive such a thing."

"He wasn't goin' to survive anyway," Yorke said softly. "I'd been in his cabin that mornin', just before the lookout spotted Phu Dan's junk, and I saw him throwin' up blood. He didn't have hardly any time left, and he knew it."

"Even so—"

"Nick knew what he wanted to do," Yorke said, his voice firm. "He wanted to die with a sword in his hand and the deck of a ship under his feet. If he could take some of his enemies with him, so much the better. So he charged ol' Phu Dan with that keg o' powder on his back. When Phu Dan saw him comin', he grabbed up an old blunderbuss pistol and blasted Nick, but Nick just grinned and kept on acomin'. No pistol ball was goin' to stop him. Phu Dan whipped out his cutlass, and those blades flew faster'n any you ever saw, with sparks goin' every-where and the sound of 'em ringin' together like the tollin' of a grand set o' bells."

Yorke took a deep breath. "In the end, Nick was too good a swordsman for Phu Dan. He buried two feet o' fine Toledo steel in that blackhearted pirate's guts . . . and then he threw his arms around Phu Dan and hugged him just as that keg o' powder went off. Blew 'em both to bits, and blasted a big chunk out o' Phu Dan's junk, too. It went down in a hurry, and we finished off all the pirates who didn't go down with the ship."

Allard stared at Yorke for a long moment without speaking. He had never heard such a gruesome, lurid story. And he had enjoyed every minute of it.

Finally, he said, "So my grandfather was . . . blown up?"

"Aye."

"He wasn't . . . buried at sea?"

"Well, in a manner o' speakin', he was. He wound up in the South China Sea, that's for damned sure."

Allard hesitated then asked, "Does my father know about this?"

Yorke shook his head. "I never told him the details, just that Nick had died at sea, like he wanted. And that was the truth o' the matter as far as I was concerned."

"What happened to the . . . tobbo, was it?"

Yorke grinned and said, "We delivered the cargo to Bangkok and sold it, just like Nick would have wanted us to." He took out his pipe and added, "I think Nick would've approved o' me spendin' part o' my share on them three Siamese joyhouse girls that night, too."

With that, Yorke strolled off down the deck, smiling nostalgically. Allard watched him go, and he suddenly wondered if there had been a lick of truth in that bizarre yarn. It was entirely possible that Nicholas Tyler had finally died from that old injury he had sustained, that there had never been a Malay pirate called Phu Dan. The notorious tobbo shops of Siam might not even exist.

But Allard found himself hoping that they did exist and hoping that his grandfather had indeed met his destiny in such a spectacular fashion. Allard decided that he was going to tell himself he believed the story. Because even if it wasn't true, he thought . . . it ought to be.

THE *GHOST* sailed a good distance out into the Atlantic that day, relying on the wind instead of her engine, before coming about late in the afternoon and heading back toward the South Carolina coast. Captain Yorke planned to sail back into Charleston Harbor about an hour before dawn, when the night would be its darkest.

Allard felt good about the way the day had gone, but he knew Yorke was a little disappointed because they hadn't sighted any more Yankee vessels. If they had, Yorke probably would have attacked them.

As they came about, Yorke pointed off to the southeast and said, "Two or three days' good sailin' that way are the Bahamas. The British own those islands, and Nassau will be a good place for us to put in for supplies when we're at sea. The Confederacy has plenty of friends there, I'm bettin'." Yorke grinned. "Some o' the prettiest ladies you'll ever see are in Nassau, too."

Allard nodded, looking forward to that—even though he intended to be faithful to Diana, of course, no matter how pretty the women were in Nassau. He had heard about the beautiful islands of the Bahamas and thought it would be enjoyable to visit there.

Yorke was pleased with the way the *Ghost* had performed during this initial voyage. He had noticed a few little things that needed attention when they got back to Charleston, but overall he pronounced the ship ready for her privateer career.

The trip had been tiring, too. Allard had caught a bit of sleep in one of the cabins, but most of the time he had been too excited to doze off. The human body could only be pushed so far, though, and as night fell he found himself yawning prodigiously and shaking his head to try to keep himself awake.

Yorke clapped a hand on his shoulder. "Why don't you go below and get some sleep, lad? I reckon we can do without you on the bridge for a while."

"I might miss something exciting," Allard replied honestly.

Yorke laughed. "If it's excitin' enough, you'll get woke up. The roar o' cannons has a way o' doin' that. Most fellas can't sleep through a commotion like that . . . although I've known a few who could!"

"All right," Allard said as he stifled another yawn. "But if you need me, Cap'n, please don't hesitate to send for me."

"Oh, I won't," Yorke said dryly. "You can be sure o' that."

Allard went down to the small cabin he shared with Hendryx, the second mate, and stretched out on one of the bunks. He was asleep almost immediately, falling into a deep slumber that remained unhaunted by dreams . . . except for a few fleeting images of Diana Pinckston. Allard missed her and hoped that things would be better between them when he got back to Charleston.

If he had been awake, though, he wouldn't have held out much hope that such would be the case.

He slept soundly, and he had no idea what time it was when a hand suddenly gripped his shoulder and shook it roughly. "Get on deck!" a voice hissed. Allard bolted up out of sleep, and it took him a few seconds to get used to being awake before he recognized the voice as Hendryx's.

"What's wrong?" he asked as he stood up from the narrow bunk.

"The Yankees were waiting for us!"

Allard bit back a curse. He knew what had happened. That brief fight that the *Ghost* had had with the Federal frigate the night before had alerted the Yankees to their existence. The captain of the blockader must have figured there was at least a chance the ship would try to return to Charleston, so he had been especially watchful. That was just a guess, but it made sense.

Grabbing his cap, Allard jammed it on his head and ran out of the cabin behind Hendryx. The two young men hustled up the steep companionway that led to the main deck. As they came out on deck, Allard saw that the sky was utterly black except for a few stars. That told him there was a patchy, incomplete overcast. The sea all around was a dark gray. He could barely see as he blundered his way to the bridge.

"Third Mate Tyler reporting, Cap'n," he said breathlessly as he came up behind the tall, erect figure of Barnaby Yorke.

"Sorry to have to wake you," Yorke said, "but I reckoned you'd want to be in on this fight."

"Yes sir! I appreciate that. Where are the Yankees, Cap'n?"

Yorke lifted an arm and pointed. "Out there."

Allard couldn't really see what he was pointing at. "Have you spotted them?" he asked.

"I don't have to spot them. My gut tells me where they are."

Allard wondered for an instant if there were really any Yankees nearby, or if Yorke's senses were simply playing tricks on him.

Then flame ripped through the night a few hundred yards away as several big guns opened up, and Allard knew that Yorke's instincts hadn't played him false.

None of the balls struck the *Ghost*. Some of them passed harmlessly overhead while others splashed into the water off to port. The Yankees didn't have the range yet. But by firing the first shots, they had revealed their position, and Yorke called to the first mate, "Fire at will, Mr. Curwood!"

"Aye, sir!" the reply came back from the bow gun.

Surely Yorke didn't intend to fight it out with the frigate, Allard told himself. They were outgunned by a factor of at least five to one. The next moment, though, the 18-pounder blasted away, and then Allard heard wood splintering under the impact of the ball.

"Hard a-port!" Yorke called to the helmsman as soon as the shot was off. The *Ghost* turned so sharply that the deck leaned under Allard's feet for a few seconds. He had to grab a stanchion to brace himself as Yorke bellowed, "Hard starboard!" and the schooner went back the other way as the helmsman spun the wheel.

As agile as the *Ghost* was, however, those maneuvers could be done only so fast. The guns on the Federal frigate slammed out another round of shells, and one of them tore through the railing amidships. The damage was minor, but it showed that the fire from the Yankee vessel was becoming more accurate.

The bow gun roared again, and by now the two vessels were close enough so that Allard thought he actually *saw* the impact. Pieces of wood flew into the air. Yorke said excitedly, "We hit their starboard paddle! Look at 'em slue around!"

With the starboard paddle disabled but the port one still turning until the Yankee captain could order the engines shut down, the frigate began a sharp turn to starboard. That put them broadside to the *Ghost*. "Hurry, lads, hurry," Yorke said quietly, and Allard knew he was talking to the gun crew. They had to take advantage of a moment of utter confusion on the frigate.

Flame lanced out from the cannon again, lighting the night for an instant. Again Allard heard the splintering sound of the heavy ball tearing through wood.

"Fire rockets!" Yorke shouted.

One of the crew members touched off the fuses of a couple of rockets. They arced toward the frigate, burning fiercely as they flew through the air, and the light they cast revealed the gaping hole in the side of the Yankee vessel.

"We holed her at the waterline!" Yorke said. "Hard a-port! Rear gun ready!"

As the *Ghost* began to swing around, more shots came from the damaged frigate. One of the balls came close enough that Allard heard the wind-rip of its passage. He was too excited to be scared, even though he knew that death had just come within a few feet of him. He waited to see what would happen next.

"Fire!" Yorke called to the rear gunners, and the 18-pounder mounted on the stern belched flame. "All ahead!" Yorke shouted, and Allard quickly relayed the order through the speaking tube.

The shot from the rear gun struck the axle on which the port paddle turned, disabling it as well. The Yankee frigate was now dead in the water as far as its steam power was concerned. It still had its sails, of course, but they wouldn't allow the frustrated captain to catch up to the Confederate phantom that had just outdueled him. Besides, the Yankees were probably busy trying to keep their ship afloat, since it had to be taking on water through the hole left by that cannonball.

"By God, that was good shootin'!" Yorke shook a fist in the air toward the battered Federal vessel. "You'll think twice before layin' another trap for Barnaby Yorke, you Yankee bastards!"

Quickly, they left the damaged frigate behind. Yorke ordered two more rockets launched, and by their light he studied the Union ship through his spyglass as they pulled away from it.

"They're abandonin' ship!" he said delightedly. "I reckon she's goin' down. Would have been nice to take her as a prize, but I'll settle for sinkin' her."

"We won our first fight, Cap'n," Allard said.

Yorke nodded. "O' course we did. What did you expect? Before we're through, Yankee captains from Florida to Maine will curse this beautiful *Ghost* and her crew of good old Southern boys!"

# PART FIVE

A reckless and unprincipled tyrant
has invaded your soil.

—*Gen. P. G. T. Beauregard, to the
citizens of Virginia, June 1, 1861*

# CHAPTER TWENTY-THREE

# A Creek in Virginia

B EFORE THE MEETING OF the officers of the Hampton Legion at Millwood, Robert sought out Maj. Stafford Pinckston. He had seen Pinckston only infrequently during the crowded weeks of training, but now that it appeared the legion would soon be going into battle, he wanted to talk to his old instructor again.

He found Pinckston on the verandah of the great house, talking to several artillery officers. Politely, Robert waited until the conversation was over then saluted and addressed his former instructor. "Major."

Pinckston returned the salute. "Lieutenant." Then he dropped the military formality for a moment and embraced Robert. "How are you, son?"

"Fine, sir. And you?"

"Never better! Getting the smell of powder in my nose again was the best thing I could have done. Teaching the theories of artillery usage to intelligent young men such as yourself has its rewards, of course, but they can't compare to the real thing."

"No sir, I suppose not," Robert said with a faint smile. He wasn't sure if Pinckston was being completely honest with him. He knew how badly the major had taken it when his wife left him, and that still had to be bothering him. But it was true that Pinckston was probably better off here with plenty to occupy him than he would have been if he had remained in Charleston, brooding over the failure of his marriage. Robert added, "What do you hear from Diana these days?"

A frown creased Pinckston's forehead. "No offense intended, Robert, but that friend of yours is a jackass."

"You mean Allard?"

"Who else? He's determined to run off and become a pirate, no matter how much pain that causes my daughter."

Robert knew about the *Ghost* and Barnaby Yorke from Allard's letters. He knew as well that there was considerable tension these days between Allard and Diana. But he felt he had to defend his friend from Pinckston's comment.

"He's just trying to do his part, like you and me," Robert pointed out. "It seems to me that sailing with Captain Yorke is better than joining the navy, as Allard originally intended."

"Maybe," Pinckston said, but he didn't sound convinced. "All I know is that he's made Diana unhappy."

Robert thought about his relationship with Jacqueline Lockhart and how they had been forced to say good-bye for God knows how long. He wondered suddenly if Allard had gotten the same sort of farewell from Diana that he had gotten from Jacqueline . . .

Quickly, Robert shoved that thought aside. Such things were none of his business, and it wasn't gentlemanly to even speculate about them. Instead, he said, "If this war is over as soon as everyone seems to think it will be, I'm sure Allard and Diana will be able to patch things up."

Pinckston nodded. "I certainly hope that's the case. The Yankees don't have the stomach for fighting, to say nothing of the skills. I don't see how they can hope to wage a successful war against us. An engagement or two, a couple of resounding defeats, and the politicians in Washington will be screaming for Lincoln to make peace. With any luck we'll have a treaty recognizing the Confederacy by the end of summer."

That seemed optimistic to Robert—but why not be optimistic? Dwelling on the possibility of failure never did anyone any good.

Lieutenant Forsythe stepped onto the verandah to call the officers into the house. Colonel Hampton was ready to address the commanders of his legion.

They gathered in the ballroom, Robert saying a friendly good-bye to Pinckston and rejoining Captain Connelly. Hampton moved to the front of the room, a heavy brass scabbard slapping lightly against his leg as he did so. Instead of the fairly light, curved saber carried by most officers, Hampton carried a straight, double-edged sword that was nearly four feet long. He had the strength to wield the heavy weapon in battle, too.

Hampton was a bit pale and drawn-looking, the result of a recent illness. "Gentlemen," he greeted his officers, "I want to say first that all of you have done sterling service in the cause of the Confederacy. I've inspected the men of the legion and found them to be, without exception, well trained and ready for battle. Morale is high, and I know we're all eager to engage the foe even while we continue to hope that such conflict will prove unnecessary."

Hampton paused and shook his head as a solemn expression came over his bearded face. "Unfortunately, with every communication that comes from Richmond, it becomes more and more obvious that the Yankees are unbending and will allow no compromise. I'm told that an army of thirty-five thousand men, under the command of General Irvin McDowell, has gathered in and around Washington and stands ready to march into Virginia, with their ultimate goal being the capture of Richmond."

Angry murmurs came from the crowd of officers. Though the Federal offensive was aimed at Virginia, not their home of South Carolina, they felt a strong kinship for their fellow Confederate state and the people of the Old Dominion. If the Yankees invaded Virginia, it would be almost as bad as if they had set out to plunder the Palmetto State.

Colonel Hampton raised his hands for silence. "General Beauregard, the hero of Fort Sumter, has been placed in overall command of our forces that are even now gathering in northern Virginia to confront the aggressors. God willing, gentlemen, we will be able to take part in that defense of our land and our liberty. I've secured the use of a train to carry us to Richmond. Some companies will depart tomorrow. Others to follow at intervals." Hampton called out the particular units that would leave the next day, including Company E of the Third Infantry. "Have your men ready to board first thing in the morning," he told those company commanders.

Captain Connelly and the other commanders snapped to attention and saluted. Hampton's orders were simple; there was no need for questions. After the colonel dismissed them, they returned to their units.

Robert didn't get a chance to speak to Major Pinckston again. As he and Captain Connelly strode back toward the field where Company E was camped, Connelly smacked a fist into his palm and said, "This has been a long time coming, Lieutenant. A long time."

"Yes sir. You don't think there's any chance the Yankees will back down when they see our forces arrayed against them?"

Connelly shook his head. "No, the abolitionists have eaten just as much fire as the secessionists down here. They're too proud to give an inch. And we can't, of course, because we have right on our side. No, Robert, forces have been put in motion now that can't be stopped."

Robert knew the captain was right. And he knew as well that once he had carried out whatever orders Connelly gave him regarding the preparation for Company E's move in the morning, he needed to write a few letters . . . to his parents and Cam, to Allard, and especially to Jacqueline . . . just in case.

MORNING WILL see us on the move, as we board train cars and head north to Virginia to join the rest of our gallant army in defense of our homeland. I remain confident that the coming conflict will be minor, little more than a skirmish, and that our side will emerge victorious. When you hear people talking about what happens or read stories concerning the battle in the newspapers, don't worry, dear heart, because I shall be fine. I know that *no harm can befall me because your love forms a shield around me and will protect me from all misfortune. I carry your beauty and your graciousness with me at all times, in my memory, in my hopes, in my heart and soul. I love you, Jacqueline, and I pray to God that this conflict is such that I will be able to see you soon . . .*

*Promise me, Cam, that you'll remain at the Citadel once the next term begins and don't harbor any foolish notions of withdrawing and enlisting in the regular army. I know that by waiting you'll probably miss the fight, but it can't be helped. Ma and Pa don't need more than one son in this ruckus at a time. It would be too hard on them to lose both of us. Of course, I'm pretty damned sure nothing is going to happen to me. I may not even get to do more than smell a little powder smoke before it's all over. But just in case, I know you'll honor my request, because you're my brother, and I trust you . . .*

*All say that it won't be much of a fight, and I reckon that's probably true. Major Pinckston says the Yankees don't really have the stomach for this fight, and I believe him. So, once it's all over, you can give up this privateering business and get back to Charleston—and Diana. Who knows, maybe both you and I will wind up back at the Citadel, finishing up there like we planned. I sort of hope so, although after these past few months, the idea of sitting in a classroom again and listening to some professor lecture doesn't hold a lot of appeal. Getting out and tasting real life will do that to you, I reckon. Anyway, Allard, good luck to you, and I know when you get this you'll wish me luck in return. Maybe we'll both get our chance to kill us some Yankees and maybe we won't . . .*

APPROXIMATELY HALF of the Hampton Legion's infantry companies, more than three hundred men, marched into Columbia at dawn the next morning. The rest of the infantry, along with the cavalry and artillery, would follow later, as transportation became available.

Although Robert didn't see Major Pinckston before Company E left Millwood, he suspected his old professor was champing at the bit to get to Virginia.

Robert looked at the smartly uniformed soldiers lining the platform of the depot and felt a surge of pride that he was one of them. His own uniform of gray trousers and long gray coat was spotless and neatly kept. The crown of his gray campaign cap with its stiff black bill was pushed down a little, the way most officers wore theirs. The brass buttons on the coat and the buckle of the wide belt around his waist gleamed from repeated polishing, as did the black boots he wore. A leather scabbard hung at his side, suspended from a strap that ran over his right shoulder and across his chest. The saber he carried was honed to a keen edge. Attached to the belt around his waist was a flapped holster and revolver. The saber and revolver, like the rest of his uniform, had been furnished by the Hampton Legion. The only things Robert had been required to furnish were courage and a fighting spirit, and he hoped he had plenty of both.

Locomotives pulling strings of passenger cars began to roll into the station. A cheer went up from the assembled troops. They knew that the trains would carry them through North Carolina and Virginia to Richmond. The men eagerly boarded the cars. Robert found himself in the rear seat of a car that held most of Company E. With a slight jolt and a clashing of metal against metal, the train got under way. Robert settled back to relax and enjoy the trip, which would take a couple of days.

They traveled from Columbia northeastward all day, into North Carolina, to Raleigh and beyond, the border between North Carolina and Virginia falling behind during the night. Men slept, cramped and uncomfortable in their seats. Then another long day passed as the trains rolled on, finally through Petersburg and into Richmond in the dusk. There they were greeted by cheering crowds.

Life in Charleston had prepared Robert for the glittering metropolis that was Richmond, capital of the Confederacy. The citizens were eager to welcome the soldiers pouring in, especially the cultured, well-to-do members of the Hampton Legion. The troops pitched their tents on the grounds of an estate known as Rocketts to wait for the rest of the legion to arrive and to see what the Yankees were going to do, but officers were invited to stay in the finest homes in the city. Robert and his captain made their bivouac in a gracious mansion on a tree-shaded street. The residence, which belonged to an elderly couple named Sherrington, reminded Robert very much of the Tyler house in Charleston.

Although the Yankee threat loomed maddeningly near in Washington, they didn't seem to be in any hurry to launch their rumored assault on the Confederacy. Several days passed as more units of the legion arrived in Richmond. When Colonel Hampton himself reached the capital city, he lost no time in instituting a series of drills and marches to keep a sharp fighting edge on his men. This seemed like a good idea to Robert. Already, just in the short time the legion had been in Richmond, there had been numerous balls and parties to occupy the men and officers and distract them from the task that might soon be facing them.

The few times Robert saw Hampton during this time, he sensed the colonel's impatience. General Beauregard and thousands of troops were already at Manassas Junction, northwest of Richmond on the Orange and Alexandria Railroad. During one officers meeting that Robert attended, called when news arrived that the Yankee army had finally left Washington, Hampton said, "My understanding is that the general intends to set up a defensive line along the southern bank of a creek near the town of Manassas Junction. The Yankees' first objective will no doubt be the capture of the railroad junction, and General Beauregard's plan is to prevent them from doing so and perhaps force them to retreat back to Washington." Hampton was obviously eager to join Beauregard, but he could not get the legion moving until he received orders to do so.

Those orders finally arrived late in the day on July 19. Members of the legion hastily converged on Richmond's train station. When Robert got there, one of the first people he saw was Maj. Stafford

Pinckston, whose beefy face was flushed even darker than usual with anger.

"They're not taking the artillery!" Pinckston burst out before Robert could ask him what was wrong. "They say they don't have any train cars capable of carrying the guns, or the cavalry's horses, for that matter!"

"The infantry is going, isn't it?"

Pinckston nodded. "Of course. You'd better find your company and get aboard, Robert." He added bitterly, "Or else you're liable to miss the fighting like I'm going to!"

"I'm sorry, Major. I'm sure you'll get into the next battle."

Pinckston snorted in disdain, "There probably won't be another battle. If the Yankees have even one good fight in them, I'll be surprised!"

Robert left the major on the platform and boarded the train with his company. There were maddening delays as cars were switched from one line to another, but finally the train pulled out, headed up the Virginia Central Railroad to its junction with the Orange and Alexandria, south of the little town of Culpeper Court House. Manassas Junction, Robert remembered from the maps he had studied, was the next major settlement to the north, beyond Culpeper. The Manassas Gap Railroad came in from the west and intersected the Orange and Alexandria there, and it was that junction of rail lines that made it an appealing target to the Yankees. If they controlled it, they would also control the flow of men and munitions into the Shenandoah Valley to the west. Ultimately, of course, their goal was to continue southward and march right into Richmond.

That would never happen. Not while a single drop of blood remained in the veins of even one Southern man.

Anyone who expected a speedy trip from Richmond to Manassas was due to be as bitterly disappointed as Major Pinckston had been at being left behind. The trains were heavily loaded, and the engines were too small for their task. The top speed they were able to attain was barely faster than the pace of a marching man. As the hours stretched out, and it seemed they had hardly left Richmond behind them, the men grew bored and tired. Robert told himself to relax.

That proved to be difficult, though. His heart was beating rapidly, and he couldn't seem to slow it down. That was just anticipation, he told himself. He was eager to get to where they were going and to face the Yankees at last. He didn't want to think that some of the reaction could be caused by fear.

And yet, deep inside, he knew that despite the confident words he had written in his letters to his loved ones when he left Columbia, he *was* afraid. Sure, there was a good chance the Yankees would turn tail and run once they faced the opening volleys from Confederate guns. But what if they didn't? The Yankees were supposed to have thirty-five thousand men, maybe even forty thousand. That was a damned big army, maybe the biggest that had ever been assembled on this continent. And from what Robert had heard, the Confederates pouring into northern Virginia totaled only fifteen thousand. If more than fifty thousand armed men came together and were determined to fight . . .

Well, it wouldn't take much for that to turn into one hell of a battle, Robert reasoned. Anything could happen. Anything. Especially when one side so outnumbered the other.

He wasn't the only one thinking such thoughts. The laughter and boasting that had been common as the trains pulled out of the station gradually died away as they crept northward. Men either talked among themselves in low voices, or else they sat in silence, with intent expressions on their faces, the solemnity of which mirrored their thoughts. Occasionally someone would laugh, or the talking would get a little louder for a few minutes. Every now and then a man would let out a raucous yell and brag about how many Yankees he was going to kill. But to Robert those outbursts sounded strangely like the whistling of a little boy on his way past a graveyard.

A man couldn't go into battle without thinking at least a little of his own mortality. It just wasn't humanly possible. Nobody wanted to dwell on the possibility of dying, but it couldn't be escaped completely, either. Once Robert accepted that, he began to feel a little better.

Men dozed sitting up during that long night. Morning came, and Robert was sure they would reach Manassas before the day was over. But the straining engines seemed to be moving even slower now, and when another night fell, the legion was still on its way to the battle-field. More than one man loudly expressed his displeasure at the delay, proclaiming that the Yankees would be whipped before they ever got where they were going.

Finally, in the gray dawn of July 21, a Sunday morning that was growing hot already, despite the early hour, the trains pulled into the station at Manassas Junction and shuddered to a halt. Quickly, the men disembarked. Orders came for the legion to assemble in a field behind a mansion called Portici, which belonged to a family named Lewis and was serving as General Beauregard's command post. Once there, the South Carolinians were to fall out and prepare their breakfast.

*Breakfast?* Robert thought when he heard those orders. They had spent a day and two long nights getting here on that infernal train, and now they were supposed to cook breakfast and wait some more?

He saw one of the locals loitering near the depot, an old man with a long white beard who was watching the soldiers get off the train with the avidity the elderly often displayed when they watched the activities of the young. "Do you know where the Yankees are or what they're doing?" Robert asked the old-timer.

The man waved a gnarled hand toward the northwest. "From what I hear, they's squattin' up there on the other side o' Bull Run, just like Beauregard's squattin' on this side. You ask me, I don't think they's gonna do anythin' except sit there and glare at each other."

Robert doubted that was the way things would turn out, but he was glad at least that the battle hadn't been going on the whole time the legion was stuck on those slow-moving trains. It would have been mighty frustrating to get here and find that the battle and the war were all over.

The infantry marched north, out of Manassas Junction, and found Portici on a rise overlooking the twisting line of woods that marked the course of Bull Run, about a mile distant. They spread out across the field behind the mansion, and smoke soon spiraled into the sky from dozens of cooking fires. Bacon sizzled in a multitude of pans. Robert saw Colonel Hampton ride up, dismount, and go into the mansion along with his second in command, Lt. Col. B. J. Johnson, to confer with General Beauregard.

Hampton and Johnson didn't stay inside the mansion for very long. When they came out, Hampton snatched his horse's reins from his aide, spoke hurriedly to Johnson, then swung up into the saddle. As Hampton moved off briskly, Johnson passed along orders to his subordinates. The word spread quickly: the legion was moving out, heading for the Warrenton Turnpike and the stone bridge on which the road crossed the steep-sided stream. There they would reinforce the commands of Gen. Barnard E. Bee and Col. Francis S. Bartow, who were trying desperately to turn back a Federal flanking movement.

Robert folded some bacon in a piece of bread, and between hastily chewed mouthfuls he issued orders to Company E. A short time later they were marching toward the winding creek where the Confederate army was making its stand. As Robert strode beside his men, he heard the rumble of artillery and the rattle of small-arms fire in the distance. He looked up at the head of the column, where Colonel Hampton rode proudly, leading his men in person.

The battle had been joined, and soon the Hampton Legion would at long last have its chance to strike a blow against tyranny, against aggression, against the Northern invaders who wanted to destroy a way of life and grind the South into the dust. Robert's head was clear, and the fear he had felt on the journey was gone. There was no time for it now.

Destiny was waiting, and he was eager to embrace it.

# CHAPTER TWENTY-FOUR

# To Make a Stand

A S THE SOUND OF firing grew louder, the legionnaires started up a long, gradually sloping hill. At the top of the hill stood a two-story farmhouse with a green roof, its whitewashed walls gleaming brightly in the morning sun. A shed with the same sort of white walls and green roof stood off to a side, and several good-sized trees shaded parts of the house. It would have been a peaceful scene if not for the sound of gunfire and the clouds of powder smoke that rolled in the sky on the far side of the hill.

Robert felt his heart thudding. He drew his saber as the men advanced, then thought better of that, sheathed the blade, and drew his pistol. Again, uncertainty assailed him. An officer should have his saber in hand, he thought, so that he could use it to signal to his troops as he gave them orders. But he wanted to be able to shoot at the Yankees when he spotted them, so he used his left hand to awkwardly pull the saber out of its scabbard again. Now he had a weapon in each hand.

Connelly was nearby, and Robert heard the captain suddenly exclaim, "What the hell! Who are those men?"

Robert saw men pouring over the top of the hill on both sides of the farmhouse. They streamed down the hill, running for all they were worth. For a second he thought they were the Yankee army, because he saw blue uniforms among them. Then he remembered the warning they had been given that some Confederates wore blue instead of gray or butternut. In fact, both sides in this conflict were something of a rainbow when it came to the uniforms, because each militia unit, each volunteer company, had its own differently styled and differently colored uniforms. Robert saw enough soldiers wearing gray to realize that the running men belonged to the Southern forces.

And from the looks of it, they were in full retreat. Their withdrawal might even be called a rout.

Robert's spirits fell as he realized his countrymen were running from the foe. After hearing for months about how one Confederate was worth twelve Federals in a fight . . . after hearing the scornful laughter and the bold declarations that the Yankees had no stomach for fighting and would give up at the first sign of resistance . . . it came as a shock to see Confederates running for their lives.

These fleeing men had to come from General Bee's and Colonel Bartow's commands. They had failed to hold against the Union flanking maneuver.

Things would be different now, though. The Hampton Legion was here. The well-disciplined South Carolinians marched on, paying no heed to the reckless flight of those passing them by. The enemy was up ahead, over that hill, so that was where the legion was going.

They topped the rise, and Robert looked into chaos and sudden death. The far side of the hill dropped down to the turnpike, a small bridge over a branch that ran into Bull Run, and the stone bridge over the larger creek. The ground down there was covered with men, most of them in blue uniforms but some in the colorful red and blue of Zouave companies. As the Yankees surged toward the crest, giving chase to the Confederates who had fled, Robert looked around and realized that he and the rest of the legion infantry were alone, a bare six hundred men against thousands.

None of the legion broke and ran, though. Instead, following the orders of their officers, they formed a line just below the top of the hill. Colonel Hampton rode back and forth, bellowing commands, as did Lieutenant Colonel Johnson. The soldiers brought their rifles to their shoulders, and a volley ripped out, tearing into the approaching blue line.

The Yankees were so close that Robert opened fire with his pistol. As he pulled back the hammer and squeezed the trigger and felt the gun buck against his palm, he thought that never before had he shot at another human being. He had never tried to take the life of another person.

But that was why they were here, he reminded himself, and the Yankees sure as hell weren't being shy about trying to kill him. The Northerners returned the Confederate volley, sending a storm of lead whistling around the valiant South Carolinians. Once, as a foolish youngster, Robert had chunked a rock at a hornet's nest. He had hit it, too, and a second later the air around him swarmed with angry, vicious insects. That was what it sounded like now as Yankee bullets ripped all around him.

Robert forced himself to remain calm. He wanted to throw himself to the ground so he would be a smaller target, but he stayed on his feet. He fired his pistol again and saw a Yankee soldier about twenty yards away go over backward, blood splashing from his head. Robert couldn't be sure if his shot had hit the man or if one of the other thousands of bullets flying through the air had killed him. He felt certain in his own mind, though, that he was responsible for that man's death.

Luckily, maybe, he didn't have time to think about it. There were plenty of other Yankees coming up the hill, and they were intent on killing him. He emptied his pistol, stuck his saber in the ground at his feet, and reloaded. From the corner of his eye he saw Captain Connelly running toward him. Connelly stumbled suddenly, dropped his saber, and lifted both hands to his throat. They couldn't stop the flow of blood, though, where a bullet had ripped away his throat. He stumbled again as momentum carried him forward, and then he pitched to the ground and lay on his face, writhing a few seconds before he grew still.

Robert snapped the pistol closed and raised it again, already growing numb from the carnage surrounding him and the deafening roar of cannons and rifles and pistols. He stood there, trying to pick his targets as all around him men were shot and blown to pieces and run through with bayonets. One burly Yankee rushed straight at him, powder-grimed face contorted as the man screamed incoherently. The Yankee lowered his rifle, aiming his bayonet at Robert's belly. Robert shot him in the face, blowing him backward and off his feet while he was still a dozen feet away.

Colonel Hampton himself rode by, staying in the thick of the fight despite his rank. He was not the sort of man to direct a battle from the rear. Robert saw the colonel's horse suddenly lurch and go down. Hampton kicked his feet free and vaulted out of the saddle, rolling in the dust of the battlefield as he landed. He was down for only a moment, though, before he pushed himself back to his feet, picked up a rifle someone had dropped, and drew a bead on a Yankee officer. Robert saw the man go spinning off his feet as Hampton fired.

Then the colonel turned and waved toward the top of the hill. "Fall back!" he roared over the crash of battle. "Maintain your ranks, but fall back!"

The legion began an orderly withdrawal. Staying bunched together, they continued to reload and fire as they moved to the top of the hill and then beyond. Robert saw other troops moving up to form a line. He didn't recognize their battle flags but thought they might be Virginians.

The legion halted in a small hollow on the side of the hill as a defensive line fell into place around them. Robert tried to catch his breath and reload his pistol. He realized to his horror that he didn't have his saber. It was probably still standing where he had driven its point in the ground. He bit back a moan of dismay. To lose his saber in his first battle—!

Well, at least he hadn't lost his life . . . yet.

Hampton walked by during a lull in the firing and paused to grip Robert's shoulder. "I'm told Captain Connelly is dead."

"Yes sir," Robert choked out. His throat was sore from breathing powder smoke.

"Company E is yours, then, Lieutenant—what there is left of it."
Hampton's face was grim. He was taking no glory in this battle. It was
a job of work to him, a job he intended to do to the best of his ability.

Robert nodded in acceptance of the added responsibility. "Yes sir.
Are we going to hold here?"

"That's right. We've been joined by General Jackson and his men,
and General Bee is attempting to form up his command again. We'll
not retreat again, Lieutenant. When we leave here, we'll be advancing."

Robert couldn't help but grin, even though he was scared and
exhausted. Fighting the Yankees was tiring work. Obviously, somebody had forgotten to tell them that they were supposed to turn tail
and run.

A glance at the sky told Robert that the sun was slightly past its
zenith. It was afternoon already. The battle had lasted for several
hours with him hardly being aware of the passage of time.

The brief respite was over. The firing intensified. This time, however, the Hampton Legion was not fighting on its own. Gen. Thomas
J. Jackson's brigade had moved up and formed a solid line stretching
for several hundred yards along the crest of the hill. The Union advance had been stopped dead in its tracks, thanks in large part to the
stubborn stand made by the South Carolinians. Now the legionnaires,
in company with Jackson's Virginians, had caught their breath and
were ready to take the fight to the Yankees once more.

It wasn't a simple affair, however. Union artillery had been moved
up so that it was able to pound the Confederate line. The whistling of
shot and the thump of exploding shells made a ghastly racket as they
blended with the moans and cries of wounded men. A Confederate
cavalry charge drove off the infantrymen providing protection for that
Yankee battery, and the Southerners surged forward toward the big
guns. They were successful in capturing the artillery, but they held the
cannon only a short time before a counterattack drove them back to
the defensive line atop the hill.

Back and forth the advantage went as the scorching afternoon
wore on. Robert wasn't sure he would ever be able to hear properly

again, and he was certain his nose and throat and lungs would burn forevermore from the smoke. He limped, not from a bullet wound but rather from a bruise he suffered when a stray round hit a rock and sent it flying through the air to strike his right thigh like a hammer blow. He knew he was lucky that none of the bullets had actually touched him. Scores of men hadn't been so fortunate.

At last, the entire Confederate line attacked as one, advancing down the hill toward the Yankees. The Hampton Legion, with the colonel himself in the lead, drove straight toward the artillery battery that had been the focus of much of the combat that afternoon. As Robert moved forward in a stumbling run with the rest of Company E, he sensed that this was the end, that the outcome of the battle would turn on this fateful charge.

He opened his mouth and hoarsely joined in the yell that came from the throats of hundreds of men. They went down the hill, firing and shouting and killing. Colonel Hampton fell, wounded, a bloody streak on his head. The legion never slowed. The standard bearer tumbled off his feet, a bullet through his body. Robert saw the flag go down and started toward it, intending to pick it up and carry it forward. A man on horseback got there before him, reaching down to lift the Palmetto flag high. Robert saw to his shock that the man was P. G. T. Beauregard himself, the commander of the army. Beauregard urged his horse toward the cannons, and the South Carolinians followed. A moment later they overran the position, cutting down some of the gunners and sending the others fleeing for their lives.

Those Yankee gunners weren't the only ones running. Finally, the Union line broke. Shattered, actually. Men dropped their weapons and fled frantically, not daring to look back at the howling hordes giving chase. Finally, the prediction of the fire-eaters came true. The Yankees gave up and headed for home as fast as their legs would carry them.

All it had taken was hours longer and scores, maybe even hundreds, of lives more than any Southerner had thought it would. All it had taken was gallons of blood spilled on the banks of the meandering creek called Bull Run and the hills that surrounded it . . .

THE ROUT of the Yankees lasted the rest of the afternoon, with some stubborn Confederates harassing Union stragglers almost to the outskirts of Washington itself. Robert heard that some of the well-to-do residents of the Federal capital had journeyed to the battlefield that morning in buggies and fancy carriages, bringing picnic lunches and making a social occasion of the battle. He wasn't sure what they had expected to see—a lot of soldiers marching around, a few shots exchanged, then a polite surrender on the part of the upstart Confederates, maybe. It hadn't worked out that way. Those arrogant nabobs had found themselves caught in the middle of the chaotic retreat. The Great Skedaddle, some Southerners were already calling it. Although Robert didn't wish any harm to the foolish Washingtonians, he hoped some of them had been so scared they'd had to change their drawers when they were safely back on the other side of the Potomac River.

It came as a great relief to the legion that Colonel Hampton's head wound wasn't serious, just a bullet graze. And considering the hellish fight they had gone through, their losses were comparatively light: fifteen men killed during the battle, a handful more wounded so seriously that they probably wouldn't make it, and a hundred or so with lesser wounds. Only two men were missing, and one of them was probably a soldier who had broken under the strain of the fighting and run off. Several men had witnessed that incident. The other missing man had likely been taken prisoner by the Yankees, or else he was dead and his body hadn't been found yet.

One of the men killed was Lt. Col. B. J. Johnson, Hampton's top subordinate. And Capt. Jeremiah Connelly, of course, leaving Robert in command of Company E. He expected Hampton to appoint a higher-ranking officer to take over the company, but after the legion had withdrawn to the field behind Portici, Lieutenant Forsythe, the colonel's aide, sought out Robert and told him, "You're to continue in command of this company, Lieutenant."

"For the time being, you mean?" Robert asked.

"Permanently. The colonel was impressed with your actions and leadership during the battle."

Robert could tell from the look on Forsythe's face that the aide didn't particularly like delivering this news. Forsythe didn't care much for him, Robert knew. That attitude dated from the first day Robert and Major Pinckston had arrived at Millwood. He seemed jealous and resentful of the personal attention Hampton paid to Robert as the son of an old college friend.

As for Robert, he didn't care one way or the other what Forsythe thought of him. He was much more concerned with the idea that he would be in charge of Company E. That was a big responsibility. He was confident he was up to the task, but it was still a bit daunting.

He wasn't sure what he had done during the battle that had caught Hampton's eye, either. The whole day was sort of a blur in his memory, but all he could remember doing was standing there and firing at the Yankees and calling encouragement to the rest of the men. He hadn't had to make any tactical decisions or anything like that.

But what he had done was enough. After Forsythe left, Robert looked out over the men resting on the ground or huddling over cooking fires. They were filthy and exhausted, their faces darkened by powder smoke. Some had bloody rags tied as bandages around arms or legs or heads. But nearly all of them were grinning. Maybe it hadn't been as easy as everyone had thought it would be, but they had come up against the enemy in their first real test, and they had emerged victorious. It was a damn sure thing that the Yankees in their camps in and around Washington weren't grinning tonight. They had taken quite a licking, and they would be a long time living it down.

Even though it had been a hard fight, maybe this was exactly what was needed, Robert told himself. Maybe now there was no doubt on the part of the Yankees about the Confederates' determination to claim their rights. Maybe this struggle near Manassas Junction, along the banks of Bull Run, would be the first—and last—real battle of the war.

A short time later a brief commotion drew Robert's attention to

Colonel Hampton's tent, where a man on horseback had ridden up, accompanied by someone in a buggy. As the rider dismounted, Robert saw his face in the light of a lantern and recognized General Beauregard. A man climbed out of the buggy and stood next to Beauregard for a moment, and a shiver of surprise went through Robert as he realized this man was Jefferson F. Davis, president of the Confederacy. Davis and Beauregard went into Hampton's tent and stayed for quite a while. Robert had no way of knowing what they were discussing in there, of course, but he hoped that Davis and Beauregard were commending Hampton for the part he and his men had played in the battle. The colonel certainly deserved whatever compliments the Confederate leaders gave him.

The Lewis mansion was being used as a field hospital, and when Robert noticed a tall, dark-haired captain in the blue uniform of the Thirty-third Virginia helping a wounded sergeant inside, it prompted him to think that he was going to need a good company sergeant if he was going to be in charge. He would mull that over and try to settle on someone, but he figured he had a little time. The Yankees wouldn't be coming back down here any time soon, not after what had happened today. The legion would have a chance to rest and recuperate, to lick their wounds and catch up on eating and sleeping. They would need to take full advantage of whatever respite the Yankees gave them.

Because if reason didn't prevail, if this wasn't the end of the war, then sooner or later those Northerners would come marching along the road again, intent on trampling the rights of the Southerners who should have been their brethren.

When and if that happened, the Hampton Legion would stand ready to defend the liberty and honor of the Confederacy, to the last man if necessary.

Meanwhile, Robert limped back to his tent to hunt up a piece of paper. He wanted to write to Jacqueline and let her know that he was all right. Just as he had told her it would, her love had shielded him from the storm of Yankee lead.

That was as good an explanation as any.

# CHAPTER TWENTY-FIVE

# Decisions

**T**HE FAMILY WAS JUST sitting down to breakfast when Allard and Barnaby Yorke reached the Tyler house. Allard rang the bell, and he could just imagine his father sitting at the table in the dining room, glaring and demanding to know, "Who the hell is it at this time of the morning?"

Thomas opened the door a few moments later. The elderly butler's eyes lit up at the sight of the two men on the doorstep. "Marse Allard!" he said warmly. "An' Cap'n Yorke. Come on in this house, the two o' you."

Allard and Yorke were both tired from the voyage, but there was a spring in their step as they entered the foyer. As they went toward the dining room, Malachi stepped out and saw them. Allard caught the relief that flashed in his father's eyes for an instant before Malachi was able to force his usual stoic expression back onto his face.

"So you're back, are you?" he said. "You didn't manage to get that ship sunk out from under you, I hope. I have a lot of money invested in it, you know."

"No, the only ship that was sunk was a Yankee side-wheel frigate, not far outside the mouth of Charleston Harbor," Yorke said. His tone was nonchalant, as if such things happened every day.

Malachi gaped at them in surprise. "You sank a Yankee ship?" he finally managed to say.

"We would have preferred to take her as a prize," Allard said, "but we didn't get a chance to do that."

At the sound of voices, Katherine had gotten up from the table and come to the entrance of the dining room. Now she saw Allard and Yorke and exclaimed happily. Hurrying forward, she threw her arms around Allard and hugged him. "Land's sake, are you all right?" she asked breathlessly. "I heard somebody say something about a ship sinking!"

"Not to worry, Katie," Yorke said. "It was the Yankee that went to the bottom, not us."

"Was the *Ghost* damaged in the fight?" Malachi wanted to know.

"One little piece o' railin' carried away by a cannonball," Yorke replied. "Other than that, she came through without a scratch."

Katherine stepped back and gripped Allard's arms, a look of horror on her face. "The Yankees shot *cannonballs* at you?"

"We knew they were liable to, Mother," he said. "It's nothing to worry about."

"Nothing to worry about? Nothing to worry about? You'll think it's nothing to worry about when they start shooting cannons at somebody you love!"

Allard had no answer for that. Besides, he was looking down the hallway toward the dining room, where Diana had just stepped out hesitantly. The look on her face was a mixture of fear, happiness, and longing. Allard couldn't stop himself. He stepped past his parents and went quickly toward her. She didn't try to run away, but when he took her in his arms, she didn't return his embrace and stood there stiffly.

Allard was so glad to see her and to hold her again that for a moment he didn't notice her reaction—or lack of one. Then he realized what was going on and drew back slightly, resting his hands on her shoulders.

"Diana, I'm back," he said as he looked into her lovely green eyes from only a few inches away. "Don't you care?"

"Of course I care," she said, but her voice was level, betraying no emotion. "I'm happy to see that you weren't hurt on your trip, Allard."

She didn't sound all that happy, Allard thought. In fact, she didn't sound like she felt much of anything. The coolness of her answer sent chills through him.

He looked past her into the dining room and saw that the table was set for only three. There was no sign of his sister, Lucinda. He wasn't surprised. Lucinda had never been one to spend a great deal of time with the rest of the family. And he had other things to worry about now, most notably the way Diana was treating him.

"I was hoping that by the time I got back, you wouldn't be angry with me anymore."

"You weren't gone very long," Diana pointed out. "Anyway, I'm not angry with you, Allard. Didn't I say that I'm glad to see you're all right?"

"Yes, but you're not glad to see *me*. Anybody could tell that."

Yorke came up behind Allard before Diana could respond to his charge. The captain tapped him on the shoulder and said, "Sinkin' Yankee ships is hungry work, and I'd like to have a mite o' breakfast. How about continuin' this discussion later so's we can get somethin' to eat?"

The gaze that Allard fixed on Diana was as cool and as carefully controlled as the way she had been looking at him. He said, "I'm not sure there's any discussion to continue. Diana has made herself clear." He stepped around her and entered the dining room. "I'm hungry, too, Cap'n. Mother, is there enough food for all of us?"

"Of course there is!" Katherine said as she followed Allard and Yorke into the dining room. Diana moved aside to make it easier. Katherine bustled around, calling for servants to set two more places at the table and bring more food from the kitchen.

Out in the hallway, Malachi said quietly to Diana, "My son is an obstinate young ass. And a fool to boot."

A sad smile touched Diana's lips. "Thank you, Mr. Tyler. I know you're trying to make me feel better. But Allard is what he is, and I'm beginning to think that there's nothing any of us can do to change him."

Malachi began, "A swift, well-placed kick—"

"Wouldn't do a bit of good," Diana said.

Malachi sighed. "No, I don't suppose it would." He shook his head slowly. "For better or worse, I reckon he's a man now, making his own decisions . . . but that doesn't mean he's still not a damned fool."

DIANA WENT upstairs, her mind in a dizzy whirl. At her first sight of Allard, her heart had given a spirited leap as relief flooded through her. It had taken quite an effort of willpower not to reveal her true feelings. But she was still angry at him, despite what she said, and she didn't want him knowing how much she had missed him and worried about him. He would be insufferable if he knew that. And such knowledge would give him the upper hand in their argument, and she couldn't allow that.

Although it would have been easier, she supposed, at least in the short run, to give in and let Allard do what he wanted, supporting him every step of the way whether she agreed with him or not. The problem was that she had too much pride to do that. She couldn't pretend that she liked the idea of his sailing off with Captain Yorke to do battle with the Yankees.

As she started along the second-floor hallway toward the guest room she was using, she felt a twinge of guilt. The last letter she had gotten from her father, he had told her that the Hampton Legion would be going from Columbia up to Richmond to prepare for a possible battle with the Union army massing in Washington. Since then the news had reached Charleston that the Yankees had indeed left Washington, crossed the Potomac, and marched into northern Virginia. It was a foregone conclusion that within a few days North and South would clash for the first time in a major engagement. For all Diana knew, her father might be in the middle of that fight, commanding an artillery battery as it bombarded the Yankees and taking heavy fire in return. It was even possible that he would be wounded or—

She didn't let herself think about that other alternative, but it stayed in the back of her head anyway, along with a question. She loved her father very much, yet it had never occurred to her to try to keep him from joining the Hampton Legion. Why was she willing for her father to go off and risk his life in battle without resenting him for it or being angry with him, but she couldn't bring herself to afford Allard Tyler that same consideration?

The answer, of course, was simple. She loved her father, yes, but she was in love with Allard. She wanted to spend the rest of her life with him. She wanted to bear his children, raise them with him, grow old at his side. Her father, as callous as it might sound, had lived a great deal of his life already. She and Allard were young, just starting out on what could be a long, joyous future together . . .

Despite that, she worried that she wasn't being fair to him. As Mr. Tyler had said, Allard made his own decisions now.

An odd sound from the room she passed intruded into her melancholy thoughts. Something was wrong in there, Diana thought as she paused. That was Lucinda's room. The sound came again, the unmistakable retching of someone who was sick as a dog.

Frowning, Diana tapped lightly on the door. "Lucinda?" she called. "Lucinda, are you all right?" She knew it was a foolish question as soon as she asked it. Of course Lucinda wasn't all right. If she was, she wouldn't be in there throwing up.

Diana reached down and tried the doorknob. It turned without difficulty. She eased the door open, wrinkling her nose at the smell that came from inside the room. She thought about closing the door and backing away, but the Tylers had been good to her, letting her live here with them while her father was off with the Hampton Legion and her mother was sitting in her own parents' house, brooding and feeling sorry for herself. If she could do something to help Lucinda, she felt she ought to at least make the attempt.

She stepped into the room and swung the door closed behind her. Lucinda lay sprawled across the four-poster bed, her head hanging above the porcelain chamber pot she clutched tightly in her hands. Her nightgown was twisted and soaked with sweat, and her hair fell in lank tendrils around her head. Her body convulsed as she began to vomit again. Diana didn't ask any more questions. She just stepped forward and gathered up Lucinda's hair, holding it out of the way.

Lucinda had been growing more and more sickly over the past few weeks, Diana recalled. She ate hardly anything these days, and she usually looked rather green around the gills, as Diana's father would have phrased it, especially in the mornings. That thought went through Diana's head now, and her eyes suddenly widened as she realized what could be causing Lucinda's illness.

Proper young ladies weren't supposed to know anything about such indelicate matters, of course, but Diana did. All the young ladies of her acquaintance did, too. Young ladies always knew more than their fathers and beaus and other men thought they did.

Lucinda's spasms eased and finally ceased. Diana saw her grip on the chamber pot slipping and reached down to grab it before she could drop it. She set it carefully on the floor and then helped Lucinda crawl back onto the bed. Lucinda's head flopped back against the pillows, her face pale and covered with beads of sweat.

There was a rag and a basin of water on the dressing table. Diana dipped the rag in the water, squeezed it out, and went back to the bed to wipe the wet cloth over Lucinda's face. The cool dampness seemed to make her feel a little better. Her harsh, rapid breathing eased a bit.

"Lucinda," Diana said with a quiet urgency in her voice. "Lucinda, can you hear me?"

Lucinda's eyelids fluttered open. She stared blearily up at Diana. "Wh . . . what do you want?" she asked, then closed her eyes again and moaned.

Diana leaned closer, ignoring the sour smell that came from the older girl. "Lucinda, listen to me. Are you . . . are you with child?"

Lucinda opened her eyes again and struggled to focus on Diana.

"N-no!" she said after a moment. "Of . . . of course not! I'm not even . . . married . . ."

Grimly, Diana said, "We both know that you don't have to be married to be . . . that way. And I know that . . . well, I know that you and Cam—"

With surprising speed and strength, Lucinda reached up and grasped Diana's arm. "Don't say it!" she hissed. "It's not true! It's not!"

"Lucinda, Allard told me—"

"Allard!" Lucinda laughed weakly but scornfully. "My brother . . . is an idiot . . . He doesn't know anything."

"He knows what you and Cam were doing every chance you got while Cam was staying here," Diana snapped, irritated by Lucinda's denials. "And while he was here during the Christmas holiday, too."

Lucinda's fingers tightened on Diana's arm. "You won't . . . you won't tell anybody . . . my parents . . ."

Diana pried Lucinda's hand off of her, and she was none too gentle about it, either. "If your parents don't know about your behavior, it's not my place to tell them," she said. "But it's not going to do you any good to pretend that things aren't the way they are. You're going to have a baby, and they have to know about it sooner or later."

Stubbornly, Lucinda shook her head, and the motion made her groan again. "I . . . I can't tell them. My father would . . . disown me."

Knowing how tolerant Malachi had always been of his daughter's behavior, Diana doubted that and said as much. "You have to let them help you," she went on. "You can go away somewhere. You can tell everyone that you married some boy who . . . who went off to the war. That way when you come back with a baby—"

"Not going to be any . . . baby," Lucinda grated out. She pushed herself up on an elbow and seemed to draw strength from somewhere inside. "You really think I'd give birth to Cam Gilmore's idiot bastard?"

"You don't have any choice."

"The hell I don't. I've heard the slaves talk. There are old darky women who can . . . take care of things like this. I'll just get one of them to help me."

Diana couldn't help it. She straightened and took a step back from the bed as horror coursed through her. "You . . . you can't mean that!" she gasped.

"Oh, but I do. And you're going to help me."

Diana shook her head. "I couldn't. I just couldn't."

"Grow up," Lucinda snarled at her. "Things like this go on, and people just have to live with them. It can't be helped. Now . . . go find Ellie for me. I don't like the little black bitch, but she always seems to know what's going on in this house. I don't think this will come as any surprise to her."

Diana wanted to refuse to do even that much to help Lucinda with what she wanted to do—but if she turned the matter over to Ellie, then it wouldn't be her responsibility anymore. Maybe that was the cowardly way out, but Diana didn't feel very brave right now.

"All right," she said. "You just try to rest and get some of your strength back. I'll get Ellie."

"Hurry, before I . . . back out."

Diana left the room, thankful that none of the other members of the household happened to be passing by in the hall. She went back downstairs and avoided the dining room. She heard Allard and Captain Yorke still talking in there, and Katherine laughed at something Yorke said. She hoped Malachi was still at the table, too.

Circling around, she came to the kitchen, and sure enough, Ellie was in there, talking to the cook. Both women fell silent and glanced somewhat resentfully at Diana as she came up to them.

"Ellie, Miss Lucinda needs to see you up in her room, right away."

The housemaid nodded and walked toward the door of the kitchen, not moving any too quickly. As unpleasant as Lucinda usually was, Diana supposed she couldn't blame the girl for dragging her feet a little. But the sense of urgency she felt prompted her to say, "Please hurry."

Ellie frowned, but she moved a little faster. Diana wondered if she should come along or stay away from Lucinda's room entirely.

Curiosity and concern for Lucinda made her follow Ellie up the back stairs. A few moments later, Ellie knocked on Lucinda's door and called, "Miss Lucinda? You wanted to see me?"

Diana reached past her, grasped the knob, and turned it. Ellie's eyebrows raised in surprise. "Go on in," Diana said.

Lucinda had pulled herself into a half-seated position, Diana saw, and had several pillows propped behind her. There was still no color in her face and she looked almost as haggard as she had when Diana left to fetch Ellie. The maid regarded her mistress coolly and said, "Miss Lucinda, you sick again? You want I should fetch somethin' for you? Some sort o' tonic or potion, maybe?"

"What I want is for you to help me get rid of this damned baby inside me," Lucinda snarled.

Again, Diana felt a little faint, but Ellie didn't seem surprised by Lucinda's callous demand. Slowly, Ellie shook her head and said, "I wouldn't know nothin' about things like that, Miss Lucinda."

"Don't lie to me. You're bound to know some mammy who can take care of it. Tonight, when my parents are asleep, you find her and bring her here. And if you tell anybody about this, I'll whip you myself until all the black hide's flayed off your back!"

Ellie endured the harsh words without any change of expression on her face. She said, "You're tellin' me that you're in the family way, Miss Lucinda?"

For a second Diana thought that Lucinda was going to come up out of the bed and attack Ellie physically. Instead, Lucinda gasped, "My God! Are you feeble-minded? Are you going to help me or not?"

For a long moment Ellie made no response, but finally she said, "I might know somebody . . ."

"I can make your life here easier, you know," Lucinda said, "or I can make it pure hell on earth. It's up to you."

Ellie nodded, although she still appeared reluctant. "I'll fetch Aunt Susie. Maybe she can help you, maybe she can't. Up to her. I really don't know."

Lucinda sagged back against the pillows propped behind her. "All right. But it's got to be a secret." She looked from Ellie to Diana and back again. "Nobody says anything to anybody else. Do you both understand?"

Diana nodded, and deliberately thickening her accent, Ellie said, "Sho', I understand. I may be just a dumb darky, but I know you don't want your folks to know about this. Marse Malachi, he'd go up in the hills an' kill that Cam boy."

Lucinda closed her eyes and sighed. "Does *everybody* know about that?"

Diana said, "If you're going to carry on so, you might want to learn to be a little quieter about it."

Lucinda grimaced. "Get out," she hissed. "Both of you."

"All right," Diana said, "but I'm done with this. It's between you and . . . and this Aunt Susie. I don't want to know anything more about it."

"Fine. Just go." Diana started to turn toward the door, and Lucinda added quietly, "Thank you."

That expression of gratitude surprised Diana so much she had to glance back. Lucinda had managed to look haughty and imperious despite being sick, but in this instant she just looked tired and scared, and for a second, Diana's heart went out to her again.

But then she got over it, and with a curt nod she stepped out of the room, taking Ellie with her.

In the hallway, after the door was closed, Ellie said, "That Miss Lucinda, she a hard one to help."

Thinking about Allard—and about herself and the dilemma that gripped her—Diana nodded and said, "Yes, most people are."

AFTER BREAKFAST, Allard went up to his room and slept like a stone most of the day, catching up on the sleep he had missed the past two nights at sea. It would be different on longer voyages, he knew. He had been too excited to sleep most of the time on the *Ghost*'s maiden voyage.

He had dozed off thinking of Diana, and when he woke up late that afternoon, her face was the first image he saw in his mind's eye. He got dressed and went downstairs, eager to see if her attitude toward him had softened any.

He couldn't find her right away, but he came across his father and Barnaby Yorke in Malachi's study, talking together in a surprisingly civil way. They were discussing the *Ghost* and the things that Yorke wanted done to the ship while she was in port this time. Allard supposed that was why his father was getting along with Yorke for a change. Malachi truly loved ships, at least their construction and maintenance. It was just sailing them he didn't care for.

"Have either of you seen Diana?" he asked when they looked up at him.

Yorke shook his head, and Malachi said, "Not since breakfast." He paused then added, "You're a damned fool, you know."

Allard wasn't shocked. He had heard that sentiment from his father on numerous occasions in the past. He asked, "Why do you say that this time?"

"Because that girl loves you," Malachi replied bluntly. "And you're going to throw it away on some foolish boy's notion of adventure and glory."

"I'm fighting for the Confederacy—" Allard began.

"No, you're not," Malachi cut in disdainfully. "You're just trying to live up to what you consider to be your grandfather's legacy, probably fueled by a bunch of lies from this old reprobate." He gestured toward Yorke.

The captain just grinned at him. "If you want to offend me, Malachi, you'll have to try harder than that. I've been called a lot worse than an old reprobate."

Allard held up his hands to stop both of them. "I appreciate the advice, Father," he said, even though he really didn't. "I'm looking for Diana, though, and if you haven't seen her—"

"I haven't," Malachi said.

"Neither have I," Yorke put in.

"That's fine." Still holding his hands up toward them, Allard backed out of the study.

He almost bumped into Ellie, who was passing by along the hall. She said quickly, "Beg pardon, Marse Allard," as if she were the one at fault.

"Have you seen Miss Diana?" he asked her.

Something flickered in Ellie's eyes, but Allard couldn't tell what it was. Worry, maybe. She said, "No sir, I ain't. You want me to find her for you?"

Allard shook his head. "No, that's all right. But if you do happen to see her, tell her that I'm looking for her, will you?"

"I sure will."

He went on to the kitchen, cadged a late afternoon snack of bread and butter from the cook, and was sitting at the big butcher-block table when his mother came in. Katherine looked unusually solemn. Allard started to say, "Mother, have you seen—"

"She's in the parlor."

Allard came to his feet. "Good," he said around the last of the bread and butter. "I want to talk to her."

Katherine reached out and put a hand on his arm. "Allard, wait."

He paused impatiently. "What is it?"

"Diana has come to a decision," Katherine said. "She's leaving."

Allard jerked back in surprise and stared at her. "Leaving?" he repeated. "Where's she going?"

"To stay with her mother. Tamara is sending a carriage for her, and it ought to be here any minute. Diana wanted to say good-bye to you before she left, though."

Allard frowned as he struggled to wrap his mind around this shocking, unwelcome news. "But she *can't* leave!" he said. "She . . . she doesn't want to stay with her mother. She's angry with Mrs. Pinckston for leaving the major!"

"I expect she still is. But she'd rather be there than . . . than . . ."

Allard stiffened. "Than here where I am. Is that it?"

"Oh, Allard." Katherine reached up and patted his cheek as if he

326

were a small boy who had just scraped his knee. "It's just too painful for Diana to stay here and watch you come and go, never knowing if you're going to return safely."

"It's only been one trip!"

"But there'll be more," Katherine said quietly. "We both know that. I . . . I know how persuasive Barnaby Yorke can be."

Allard pressed his fingertips to his temples, but it didn't help the crazy spinning whirl in which his brain found itself. Thickly, he asked, "You mean I have to choose . . . between Diana and the country?"

"Everyone has choices and decisions to make, Allard. Diana has made hers. She's not asking anything of you, except a chance to tell her good-bye before she goes."

"All right!" Anger welled up inside him. He lowered his hands and made a slashing motion with the right one. "If that's the way she wants it, that's fine."

He started to turn away, but his mother stopped him again. "Allard, don't burn any bridges," Katherine cautioned. "No one knows how long this war will last. I'll swan, a month from now, things may be completely different!"

"I hope so. But for now, I don't want to cause Diana any more pain." He took a deep breath. "I won't say anything to hurt her."

Katherine patted his arm. "That's good. Go to her now, before it's too late."

He hurried from the kitchen and a moment later found himself standing in the door to the parlor, looking at Diana as she stood there in a dark green outfit with a hat of the same shade on her red hair.

"Allard," she said. She took a deep breath and squared her shoulders. "Allard, I'm going to—"

"I know. My mother told me."

"I'm sorry. I just think this . . . this will be better for both of us. You won't have to worry about me—"

"I'll always worry about you," he broke in. "I love you."

A sad smile touched her lips. "I love you, too. And I worry about you. That's why I have to leave."

"It won't be any easier, you know. Nothing will really change."

"Maybe not." Her chin lifted a little. "But at least I won't have to watch you leave to go off and risk your life."

"Like your own father is doing." He could tell from the way she flinched slightly that the shot had gone home, and he regretted it in a way. It was too late to call back the words now, though.

"That's different."

"Not really."

"Yes, it is," she said firmly. "And if you stop and think about it, you'll understand."

"Right now . . ." He sighed. "Right now, I don't know if I understand anything anymore."

"Then you know how I feel." She started toward the door. "I have to go."

He held out a hand toward her. "Diana . . ."

"Please, Allard. Don't try to stop me, and . . . and don't touch me. Please."

He moved aside, although it felt like his feet were mired in lead. "This is really the way you want things to be?"

"This is the way they *have* to be."

Allard opened his mouth but then closed it again as he realized there was nothing he could say or do to sway her from her decision. Nothing except give up the dream that he'd had for so long, for even more years than he'd had the dream of loving her.

She walked stiffly past him, and he whispered, "Good-bye, Diana."

"Good-bye, Allard," she said without looking around at him.

He stood there until she was gone, and then he went over to the windows and looked out at the shrubs and magnolia trees that surrounded the house. Through the open windows, he heard the clopping of hoofbeats and the turning of wheels. They stopped for a few minutes and then started again, and he knew the sounds came from the carriage that had arrived to fetch Diana and her things across Charleston to her grandparents' house. As the sounds faded away, he felt like something was dying inside him and hardening into stone.

Things couldn't end like this. They just couldn't.

IN THE carriage, Diana leaned back against the seat and tried to fight down the feeling of sickness. Already she missed Allard so badly she could barely stand it. Regret tormented her. Had she made the right decision? More important, had she made a decision she would be able to live with?

Had she been fair to Allard? She had cared for him ever since they were children?

Their country was at war. Sacrifices had to be made. In her head, she knew that. In her heart . . .

There was the matter of her pride, too. She had made her stand. She couldn't back down from it. When you know you're right, plant your feet and don't budge, her father had taught her.

But how to know when you were right and when you were just being stubbornly foolish?

The second thoughts continued to assail her as the carriage rolled through the streets. She was so caught up in the painful doubts she didn't hear the hoofbeats at first, didn't notice the horse drawing alongside the carriage until a fist pounded on the door and a familiar voice shouted, "Diana! Diana, stop! I love you!"

Her head jerked toward the window, and she saw his face, anxiously peering in at her. Without thinking, she called for the driver to stop the carriage.

As the vehicle halted, Allard swung down from the saddle and jerked the carriage door open. He practically lunged inside. Diana found herself in his arms, held tightly, and their mouths joined in a kiss both sweet and desperate.

"Allard!" she gasped when they moved apart. "You . . . you came after me."

"Of course I did," he said. "I realized I couldn't let things end like that. Diana, I . . . I want to marry you."

Her heart leaped. Though they knew they loved each other, they hadn't talked about marriage. Until now. "You're sure?"

"Of course I'm sure! Diana, please . . . be my wife."

She was about to nod, about to utter the words that would banish all the trouble between them, but then she thought of everything that had happened, everything they had said. And she hesitated.

He saw it in her eyes and asked, "What's wrong?"

"You were going to sea with Captain Yorke. Have you changed your mind?" And she could tell by the look on his face that he hadn't.

Allard said, "I've given my word, Diana. One more voyage. That would give you time to get ready for the wedding, and when I get back, we'll be married, and I . . . I'll work at the shipyard with my father after that."

So another decision was facing her: say good-bye to him one more time in the hope that, after that, she would never have to bid him farewell again . . . or stick to her guns, as her father might say. Compromise or force him to bend to her will?

But if she forced him to comply with her wishes, he would no longer be the man she loved. On the other hand, compromise would mean that he would be risking his life yet again.

As if reading her mind, he leaned closer to her and rested his fingertips on her cheek. Looking into her eyes, he said, "There will always be risks, Diana. As long as we live, we take chances. But as long as I live, I want to take my chances with you."

For a long moment she didn't say anything. Then she whispered, "Yes, Allard."

A hopeful expression brightened his face. "You mean . . . ?"

"Yes, I'll marry you. When you get back from this voyage, I will marry you."

He grinned broadly and kissed her again. She returned it with all her heart. Yet in the back of her mind lingered a tiny, nagging worry. She forced it away.

In the end, the heart usually triumphs over the head . . . and that was the way it should be.

ELLIE MOVED along the dimly lit upstairs hallway, her slipper-shod feet making no noise on the carpet runner. The hour was very late, and the Tyler house was fast asleep.

Well, mostly. Miss Lucinda was still awake, but the tonic Aunt Susie had given her a short time earlier would soon make her sleep. It had been a rough hour, there in Miss Lucinda's room, after Ellie had snuck Aunt Susie into the mansion through the kitchen and up the rear stairs. The old woman was good at what she did, though, and had helped plenty of gals in the past who didn't want to birth no sucker planted in them by one of the masters. She had given Miss Lucinda a leather strap to clamp between her teeth so that she wouldn't yell out, and in a while it had been over. Aunt Susie had taken away all the evidence with her. Now all Miss Lucinda had to do was rest in bed a few days—and nobody would think anything of that because she'd hardly left her bed for the past few weeks anyway—and she would be her old self again. Her old, bossy, demanding, arrogant, aggravating self. Served her right, everything that had happened, Ellie told herself, and then she right quick asked the Lord's forgiveness for being so judgmental and having such an unkind thought. She didn't like Miss Lucinda Tyler, not hardly, but she didn't want to wish pain on anybody, either.

Ellie hoped this whole experience had drummed some sense into Miss Lucinda's head. Seemed doubtful somehow, though.

At least Miss Diana was back in the house, after leaving for a short time that afternoon. Marse Allard, bless his heart, had finally come to his senses and gone after her, asked her to marry him. They had worked it out so that Marse Allard would go on one more privateering voyage with that Cap'n Yorke, then come back to marry Miss Diana. Marse Malachi was mighty happy about that, and so was Mistress Katherine. It was good to know that sometimes things worked out like they were supposed to.

All Marse Allard had to do was get through one more voyage . . .

# CHAPTER TWENTY-SIX

# Dawn at Sea

THE SECOND VOYAGE OF the *Ghost* was even more successful than the first. A few days into it, she had sunk a pair of Yankee cutters in one afternoon. It had been a frantic battle, full of smoke and noise and fury. Allard had been thrown off his feet by the concussion of a bursting shell, and he had seen a crewman struck by a cannonball and killed. That gruesome sight had wiped away any vestige of the romantic notion that privateering was all glory and adventure. There might be moments like that, but for the most part, it was hard, grim, bloody work.

Despite the danger, though, and the way he missed Diana, Allard had to admit that he was enjoying himself. Slender to begin with, he had lost a little weight. His muscles were stronger, like bundles of wire under skin that was becoming deeply tanned. He stopped shaving, and although his beard grew out patchily at first, it soon filled in. His hair was longer, falling around his ears almost to his shoulders. He carried the gun and knife his father had given him tucked behind his belt, although he hadn't had to use either weapon yet in close combat. The fights in which the *Ghost* had engaged so far had all been settled at longer range.

Allard wasn't sure how long Captain Yorke intended to stay at sea. They had enough provisions and water to last another week or more.

In addition to the two Union ships they had sunk, they had also encountered three merchantmen. Two of those vessels had been so heavily damaged in the fighting that they couldn't be salvaged, so Yorke had his men load as much of the cargo on board the *Ghost* as possible and then let the ships go down. The other one was on its way back to Charleston. The captain had the scent of blood and powder smoke and victory in his nose, and he didn't want to turn back just yet.

Allard knew, as well, that Yorke was reluctant to lose him as third mate. The captain had accepted his decision easily enough, had in fact pumped his hand and given Diana a hug and a kiss when they announced their plans to be married. But Allard had seen the disappointment in Yorke's eyes. He was a seagoing man and couldn't fully understand how a woman could be more important than being on the endless waves.

Allard would miss life on the Ghost, too. But some things were more important, and his and Diana's happiness was one of them.

The schooner was gliding off the east coast of Florida, near a chain of tiny islands Captain Yorke called Bimini. The Yankees still held Fort Pickens, around on the other side of the peninsula near Pensacola, and Yorke had the idea that by lurking in this area, they might get themselves a Union supply ship on its way around Key West. So far that hadn't happened, but Yorke assured Allard it was just a matter of time.

Allard had turned in a few hours earlier to snatch a little sleep. It seemed he had barely closed his eyes when he was jerked out of his slumber by the clanging alarm bell. He bolted out of his bunk, grabbed his cap, and charged topside.

Dawn had just broken over the Atlantic, showering the waves with scintillating bands of gold and orange and red. Allard rubbed knuckles in gritty eyes as he hurried toward the bridge, unable at this moment to appreciate the beauty of the new day. He found Yorke standing beside the helmsman, squinting through his spyglass. When Yorke became aware that Allard had come up, he turned and pressed the glass into the younger man's hands.

"Take a look, lad. I told you we'd find one of those Yankee sons o' bitches."

Allard peered through the glass in the direction the captain was pointing. It took him a moment to focus on the ship that had caused such excitement on the *Ghost*. From the location of the other vessel, Allard thought it had just emerged from behind one of the little islands.

"Look how low in the water that sloop is," Yorke said. "She's carryin' a heavy cargo. Her holds are full."

Allard picked out the American flag flying over the other ship. "She must be bound for Fort Pickens."

"Aye. Her cap'n probably thought to slip through those islands in hopes of throwin' off any privateers lurkin' around these waters. Then he'd make a run for the coast, around Key West, and up to Pickens. 'Twas his bad luck to run into us, though."

Allard handed the spyglass back to Yorke. "We're going to take her?"

"Damn right we are. Hard starboard! All ahead full!"

The *Ghost* swung around and headed east on a course to intersect the Yankee sloop. The wind was favorable to Yorke's maneuver. The sails popped and swelled as they filled with air, and the propeller churned the water as the ship surged forward. Allard kept an eye on the enemy vessel. They were closing in quickly on her, cutting toward an opening between two of the low, tree-dotted islands.

"Cap'n," the helmsman suddenly said, "I've been through these waters before. Ain't there a sandbar betwixt them two islands?"

Yorke nodded. "Aye, but the tide's high enough and our draft shallow enough we can get over it. That's the only way we'll be able to catch that sloop."

Allard frowned and wanted to ask if Yorke was sure, but he held back. Yorke was the captain of this vessel, and a mate didn't challenge the captain's authority that way. If he said they could make it, then by God they could make it!

The *Ghost* surged ahead. Yorke ordered the gun crews to load the

18-pounders and stand by the guns. Allard leaned forward at the railing, able now to see the yellowish stretch of water that marked the sandbar between two of the islands. He frowned worriedly. The *Ghost* only had about twelve feet of draft, but that might be too much. It didn't look to him like there was twelve feet of water above that bar.

But it was too late to turn back now, though. The *Ghost* plowed over the sandbar. Allard felt as much as heard the faint scraping as the hull dragged over the sand. For a heart-stopping moment, he thought they were going to hang there, but the wind and steam power pushed them on through, and the ship leaped ahead like an unchained animal.

Yorke laughed. "Told you we'd make it, didn't I, boy?"

"Yes sir, you did!" Allard answered, equally enthusiastic. Now there was nothing standing between them and the rich prize in front of them. It would require a fight to claim it, of course, but Allard was confident of victory.

In his excitement, he barely heard the distant boom, but he heard the huge splash and felt the sting of the water as it sprayed across the deck. Although he was stunned by what had just happened, his brain was functioning well enough for him to realize that the splash had been caused by a cannonball striking the water dangerously close to the *Ghost*.

"Yankees!" the lookout bellowed from his nest in the rigging. "Yankee ship off the port bow!"

Allard twisted his head in that direction and saw a Union frigate steaming straight toward them. He knew without thinking that the Yankee ship must have laid back behind the island while the cargo sloop sailed on. The sloop was the bait, and the *Ghost* had taken it and charged right into the trap.

"Hard a-port!" Yorke shouted. "Cut the engines!"

The helmsman spun the wheel desperately as a gun boomed once again on the Yankee frigate. The bow of the *Ghost* began to turn; that movement was all that saved the ship. The shot missed by mere feet, slamming into the water and throwing another geyser into the sky.

"Show 'em our teeth!"

The crew on the forward gun fired the 18-pounder in response to Yorke's bellowed order. The ball went too high, over the deck of the Yankee frigate, but it was close enough to send their gunners diving for cover. That gave the Confederate ship a momentary respite. The gunners began reloading.

Allard wished there was something he could do other than stand and watch and be ready to follow any orders Yorke might give him. He tried to calm his rattled nerves. They had been in a tighter spot than this when they battled those two Yankee cutters, he told himself. They had emerged victorious then, and they would do so now.

But the cargo sloop was armed, too, and she opened fire, sending a round whistling past the stern. Yorke sent men running to the rear gun. The *Ghost* was caught in a crossfire. And there was nothing they could do now except fight their way out.

The surroundings worked against them, too. If they tried to make a run for it back the way they had come, the sandbar might block them. The ship had barely cleared it the first time; there was no way of knowing if she would do so again. The two islands also hemmed them in to a certain extent. There wasn't much room to maneuver.

"Tricked me," Yorke muttered bitterly over the roar of the cannons as the ships traded rounds. "And I waltzed right into it like a damned little boy out on a pond in his first rowboat!"

"The only reason they tried this is because they're already afraid of you and the *Ghost,* Cap'n!" Allard said.

That seemed to mollify Yorke a little. He jerked his head in a savage nod and said, "Let's show 'em that they've grabbed a wildcat by the tail. All ahead full!"

Allard relayed the order, and the engines throbbed again. The Yankee frigate was still steaming toward them, and as the *Ghost* began to pick up speed once more, the gap between the two ships closed quickly.

The sudden splintering of timbers and a heavy jolt that ran through the whole ship made Allard glance back over his shoulder. He saw to his horror that a cannonball had smashed into the deck behind the bridge and penetrated the ship, doing God knows how much damage. This was the hardest hit that the *Ghost* had suffered. He hoped it wasn't enough to sink her.

Both guns were still blasting as fast as their crews could load and fire. An exclamation from Yorke made Allard jerk his head toward the bow again. He saw that a shot from their forward gun had struck the foremast on the frigate and blown it in half. The sails rigged on it were down, causing confusion on the deck of the Yankee vessel.

"I wish I had a keg o' powder," Yorke said. "I'd set a fuse and jump on their deck, just like ol' Black Nick!"

"There's a big difference, Cap'n," Allard said. "You're not dying, and that's not a junk full of Malay pirates!"

Yorke nodded grimly. "We may have to ram them. Get ready for a hand-to-hand fight, lad."

Allard swallowed hard and touched the butt of the pistol tucked in his belt. He could fight if it came down to it. At least, he thought he could.

The two ships continued surging toward one another. The frigate carried at least a dozen more guns than the *Ghost,* but they had to be fired through gunports on the sides of the ship. As long as Yorke sent the *Ghost* straight at the Yankee vessel, that extra firepower couldn't come into play. It was a duel now, forward gun against forward gun, and more important, the iron nerves and steel will of Barnaby Yorke against the Yankee captain's.

The 18-pounder and the forward gun on the frigate roared and belched smoke and flame at practically the same instant. Allard had no time to react before there was a huge crash right in front of him. As he was thrown backward, something stabbed his leg like a knife going into the flesh. He opened his mouth to shriek in pain, but before any sound could come out, he was slammed down on his back so hard that all the air was knocked out of his lungs. Stunned and unable to think, he rolled onto his side and lay there gasping for breath, his leg on fire.

Gradually his senses began to function again. There was a grinding crash and a heavy jolt. Allard pushed himself onto an elbow and lifted his head, peering blearily around him. His hair had fallen in his eyes, so he couldn't see very well. Somehow he managed to raise his other hand and push it back.

He was stunned mentally rather than physically as he saw that the last Yankee shot had struck the bridge itself. There was no sign of the helmsman, and Allard had the sickening feeling that the round had carried him away. The wheel was gone, too.

Yorke lay a few feet away with the rubble of the shattered deck around him. Blood covered his face, but he was moving a little so Allard knew he wasn't dead. Relief went through Allard at that realization. But there was no telling how badly Yorke was hurt, and angry shouts and blasts of small-arms' fire hammered home the fact that they were still in danger. Allard pushed himself into a sitting position.

He saw that the *Ghost* lay alongside the frigate. The Yankee vessel had a huge hole in its port bow, and the sight of the damage told Allard that the *Ghost* had rammed it. She hadn't been able to turn aside after that shot ruined her bridge, and the Yankee skipper had waited too late in issuing his orders. The frigate hadn't been able to avoid the collision.

And from the looks of it, the Yankee ship had taken the worst of the damage, maybe even enough to sink it. But that didn't mean the frigate's crew was giving up. A Union boarding party had boarded the *Ghost*, and fighting raged along the deck of the schooner.

Allard reached to his belt to see if the Colt was still there. His fingers closed around the walnut grips. Rolling onto his belly, he braced the gun with both hands, drew back the hammer with a thumb, and set his sights on a big Yankee sailor running toward the wrecked bridge with a rifle in his hands. Allard pressed the trigger.

The revolver roared and bucked in his hands. The Yankee sailor went backward off his feet as the bullet drove into his chest. Allard cocked the Colt again and drew a bead on a Yankee about to plunge his bayonet into one of the *Ghost*'s crewmen. Allard's shot tore through the man's body and spun him to the deck.

He fired three more times and dropped two more Yankee sailors. Then a bullet smashed into the deck beside him and splinters stung his face. He rolled a couple of times and saw a sailor at the railing of the frigate aiming a rifle at him. Allard knew there was just one round left in the Colt. He fired it by instinct, not really aiming, and felt sick as he saw splinters fly off the railing and knew he had missed. All that Yankee had to do now was pull the trigger, and Allard would be a dead man . . .

Another shot exploded close by Allard's head, making him flinch and close his eyes. When he opened them a second later, he saw the Yankee rifleman double over, drop his weapon, and pitch to the deck of the frigate. A strong hand clamped onto Allard's shoulder, and Captain Barnaby Yorke shouted, "Up, lad, up! We've got a battle to win!"

Yorke held a smoking pistol in his other hand. Allard pushed himself up and with Yorke's help made it to his feet. Pain shot through his leg once more as the limb tried to buckle under him. Yorke's steadying hand kept him upright. He looked down and experienced a moment of panic when he saw the growing bloodstain on the leg of his trousers. A jagged piece of wood about an inch wide and three or four inches long stuck out of his leg. Allard knew the rest of the fragment was buried in his flesh.

"Leave it there for now!" Yorke said. "Get to the rear gun! That sloop's closin' in on us, and the rest o' the crew's got their hands full!"

Allard nodded understanding. Yorke's face was bloody from a long gash on his forehead, but other than that he didn't seem to be hurt. The captain was still in command, which meant they still had a chance.

"I'm headin' for the engine room!" Yorke went. He slapped Allard on the shoulder. "Get to that gun!"

Gritting his teeth against the pain, Allard hobbled along the deck. It was littered with debris and puddles of blood and sprawled bodies. Smoke hung thick in the air. Allard wondered fleetingly why the Yankees hadn't been able to overwhelm them by now. The frigate carried a considerably larger crew than the schooner and should have been able to muster a large enough boarding party to have overrun the Confederates. The fact that they hadn't must mean that there was so much damage aboard the Yankee vessel, most of the crew was occupied in trying to keep the vessel afloat.

That offered a glimmer of hope. Allard felt the deck shiver under his feet as the engines throbbed. If Yorke could pull away from the frigate . . . and if they could keep the sloop from sinking them . . . they might have a chance to get out of this trap alive.

A blue-clad sailor suddenly loomed out of the smoke in front of him. The man pointed a rifle at him and shouted, "Throw down that gun!"

Allard realized he was still holding the empty Colt. He dropped it to the deck at his feet. The Yankee grinned and lunged at him with a bayonet. Allard realized that the man had bluffed him. The Yankee's rifle was empty, too, but now he had the upper hand and intended to gut the young Confederate.

Twisting desperately, Allard felt the tip of the bayonet rake along his side, leaving behind a line of fiery agony. With his left hand he grabbed the barrel of the rifle and wrenched at it. At the same time he plucked the Bowie knife from behind his belt and drove it at the Yankee's throat. The blade went in cleanly. Blood spurted hotly over Allard's hand as the man's eyes widened in pain and horror. Allard shoved the dying Yankee aside, ripping the knife free as he did so.

After that, no one else got in his way as he stumbled toward the rear gun. He saw that one crewman was still on his feet there, trying to single-handedly reload the gun. Allard lurched up, shouted, "I'll help you!" and grabbed a bag of powder as the crewman finished swabbing the barrel.

Allard glanced at the approaching sloop as he and the crewman finished loading the cannon. The sloop's bow gun fired, and the ball hit the *Ghost* somewhere amidships. Allard wasn't sure where or how bad the damage was. He knew, though, that the elevation was all wrong on the 18-pounder. As he tried to remember everything Major Pinckston had taught him at the Citadel, he began cranking down the barrel of the big gun. There was no time now for anything but an educated guess . . .

He grabbed the lanyard and tugged it, igniting the friction trigger. The roar of the cannon was deafening, striking his unprotected ears like double fists. He cried out in pain. The world went silent around him, but only for a few seconds. Then the cacophony of battle ebbed back into existence. Smoke stung his eyes and made it hard to see. When he blinked them clear, he saw the hole in the sloop's bow, right at the waterline. The sloop began to turn away, abandoning its attack.

Allard let out an exultant whoop, but as he turned his head toward where the bridge had been, he saw smoke coming from somewhere inside the *Ghost*. There was a fire down below, and unless it was extinguished quickly, the ship was doomed. He became aware that he could no longer feel the throbbing of the engines. One of the Yankee rounds must have knocked them out and started the fire.

And the last time Allard saw him, Captain Yorke had been headed to the engine room.

Allard hobbled toward the gaping hole in the deck, shouting, "Cap'n! Cap'n!" He looked around and didn't see any more of the Yankee boarding party except the ones who lay on the deck either dead or badly wounded. He saw heads bobbing in the water and realized the few survivors had jumped overboard to get back to their ship. A hundred yards or so now separated the *Ghost* from the frigate, which seemed to be as dead in the water as the schooner was. All three vessels that had engaged in this battle were in grave danger of sinking.

Yorke clambered out of the hole onto the deck before Allard could get there. His face was mostly black from smoke now, although crimson still showed through here and there. Wracked with coughing, he pushed himself shakily to his feet. He and Allard caught hold of each other, each of them bracing himself on the other man.

"Fire's . . . under control," Yorke gasped, "and we ain't holed . . . below the waterline." A weary grin stretched across his face. "They ain't sunk us yet, lad!"

"The sloop's retreating," Allard reported. "And the frigate's not going anywhere except the bottom!"

"Aye, we blasted the hell out of 'em! You drove off the sloop?"

Allard nodded. "A fortunate shot."

"A sailor makes his own good fortune." Yorke straightened and looked around, tilting his head back to gaze upward at the *Ghost's* sails. The canvas was a little tattered in places from small-arms' fire, but the masts were intact and the wind still pushed the schooner along. That was what was carrying them steadily away from the frigate, which had begun to heel over a little in the water.

Yorke pointed at the frigate and went on, "Another half-hour and she'll be gone under. The sloop's runnin', Lord knows where. Maybe she'll still try to limp around to Fort Pickens."

"Are we going after her?" Allard asked.

Yorke laughed. "It's temptin', ain't it? But even though I said a sailor makes his own luck, it ain't wise to fly in the face of fate, neither. This gallant lady of ours needs a hell of a lot o' patchin' up before she's ready for another fight. We'll let our sails carry us to the Bahamas. We can make port there, rest up, and put the *Ghost* back into shape." He placed a hand on Allard's shoulder. "Come, lad. We've got to rig up a makeshift helm if we don't want to just drift. And one more thing—"

He reached down and jerked the piece of wood out of Allard's leg.

Yorke did it so quickly Allard didn't know what was coming. He felt the pain, though, and it doubled him over so that he would have fallen if the captain hadn't grabbed his arm and held him up. Yorke held out the big splinter in his other hand. Three inches at the end were daubed with Allard's blood, showing that it had been embedded that far in his leg. More blood gouted thickly from the wound.

"Reckon we better tie that up, first thing," Yorke said. "Wouldn't want you bleedin' to death before you get a chance to see how pretty the gals are in Nassau!"

Allard didn't want to bleed to death, but not for the pretty girls in Nassau. There was only one pretty girl he was interested in.

She was in Charleston, and her name was Diana.

# One Summer Night

ROBERT WAS SITTING ON a three-legged stool in front of his tent, composing a letter to Jacqueline, when footsteps sounded nearby. He looked up to see Maj. Stafford Pinckston approaching. Robert came to his feet to salute, but Pinckston waved him back down.

"No formalities between us tonight, lad," Pinckston said. "I've come to stay good-bye."

Robert's eyes widened in surprise. "Good-bye, sir? You're going home?"

"No, I've just come from a meeting with Colonel Hampton. It's been decided that the organization of the legion is too unwieldy. Our artillery is being transferred to the regular artillery, and likewise the cavalry. From now on, the Hampton Legion will be strictly infantry." Pinckston smiled. "I hear that you've done well as the commander of your own company since Manassas."

"Thank you, sir," Robert said mechanically, not really registering the compliment. He didn't know what to make of the major's news. While it was true that they hadn't gone into action together, Robert had taken some comfort in knowing that at least his old professor and mentor was close by. That likely wouldn't be the case any longer.

But in war, soldiers went where they were told to go and did what they were told to do. Robert knew that all he and Major Pinckston could do was to wish each other luck and follow their orders.

"I have one other bit of news," Pinckston went on. "Happier news, I hope."

"What's that, sir?"

"I've received a letter from Diana. She and Allard Tyler are going to be married."

Robert caught his breath. "That . . . that's wonderful," he said. "But I thought Allard had gone to sea with that privateer . . ."

"For one final voyage, Diana tells me. Then he's going to marry her and work with Malachi at the shipyard."

"Well, I wish them all the luck and happiness in the world." Robert couldn't help but wonder if the marriage had been Allard's idea. His friend had been adamant about going to sea . . . but things changed, especially where romance was concerned.

And that thought made him wonder . . . would things ever change between him and Jacqueline? What if the war kept them apart for too long? Could their love last?

Or would this great conflict be the death of it?

JACQUELINE SAT in the gazebo, letting the warm night breeze caress her. If she closed her eyes, she could almost imagine that it was Robert's arms enfolding her in a soft embrace.

She sighed and reached down to lightly touch her belly. There was no baby there, no little piece of Robert that she could carry around with her from now on. Enough time had passed since his leave-taking that she was sure of that. And ever since she had known for certain, she had been unsure how she felt about it. Relief and disappointment had mingled within her. There would be no scandal, but somehow Jacqueline felt as if she had lost something. But how could a person lose something she never had?

Love was the most incredibly complicated thing in the world, more complicated than politics and wars and all the other things that people considered so important. But none of it meant anything without love. None of it . . .

She reached into the pocket of her dress, pulled out the letter she had already read a hundred times. Robert had survived the first battle, and now he was a company commander. Jacqueline couldn't bring herself to be happy about that. It meant that he would be out in front, leading others into battle, risking his life more than ever.

Risking her life, too, because without one, there would never be the other.

At least one person in her life was happy. Diana had Allard, and they would be married soon. Jacqueline had happily agreed to be the maid of honor. She looked forward to it, yet dreaded it at the same time. It would be nice to see her friends united like that, but the ceremony would also be a reminder that she and Robert could never be together until this war was over.

"Jacqueline." Her mother's voice sounded behind her. "It's late. You should come in the house now. Besides, it doesn't do any good to sit out here and brood over that boy."

"No," Jacqueline said as she got to her feet and slipped Robert's letter back into her pocket. "It doesn't do any good at all."

CAM DREW back his arm and let fly with the small handful of pebbles. They clattered against the second-floor window of Melody Harper's bedroom. The Harper farm was next to the Gilmore place, and Cam and Melody were old friends, having grown up together. Really good friends since that day in the hayloft a couple of years earlier when Melody had pulled her dress up.

Cam had sneaked over here all summer, meeting Melody on the sly. She liked what they were doing as much as he did, and since Cam would be going off to Charleston to attend the Citadel in the fall, they did it as often as they could while they had the chance.

Of course, once he got back to Charleston, he would have to visit Lucinda Tyler. It wouldn't be as easy this time. Since Robert wasn't staying at the Tyler house anymore, Cam wouldn't have a good excuse for being there. But he would find a way. He had been thinking about Lucinda a lot lately . . . when he wasn't thinking about Robert and how his older brother was off fighting the damned Yankees while he was still stuck here at home.

Bedding an old pal like Melody was fun, of course, but Cam was convinced that fighting the Yankees would be even better.

The window went up, and Melody called down in a half-whisper, "Cam? Is that you?"

"Who else?" he asked then regretted his bravado. With a girl like Melody, he probably didn't want to know the answer to that question.

*The wedding, of course!* The thought suddenly came to him as Melody started to climb out of her window. Surely he would be invited to Allard Tyler and Diana Pinckston's wedding. And that would naturally give him a chance to see Lucinda again. No doubt the wedding might work to his advantage.

Cam pondered the possibilities so much that he almost didn't hear the trouble approaching until it was too late.

Old Granville Harper, Melody's father, stepped around the corner of the house and called out, "Who's there? Damn it, who's sneakin' around my place?"

Melody gasped and started hurriedly back up the trellis toward her window. Cam crouched lower in the bushes, but that just made the branches rustle together. A second later he heard the twin metallic clicks as Harper cocked the shotgun he held.

Cam dived deeper into the shrubbery as the first barrel blasted. Buckshot tore through the bushes, luckily missing him. He was already moving at a dead run as he burst out of the greenery and took off into the night. The shotgun boomed again as Harper shouted curses. Cam ducked his head instinctively and kept running.

And even then, he found that he couldn't get Lucinda's image out of his mind . . .

"WHAT ARE you doing out here?"

Diana turned sharply, startled by the sudden question. She turned in the garden behind the Tyler house and saw moonlight shine on blonde hair. Lucinda. Her future sister-in-law, she reminded herself.

"Never mind," Lucinda went on. "I know what you're doing. You're mooning over that stupid brother of mine, wishing he was here."

"He's going to be my husband," Diana said. "Of course I wish he was here."

"Don't be too sure about that."

Diana frowned. She knew she shouldn't let Lucinda get under her skin, but sometimes it was difficult to ignore her. Some people would have been changed by the unpleasant experience Lucinda had gone through several weeks earlier . . . but not her. The whole thing seemed to have rolled right off her back. She was as hard and brittle as ever.

"What do you mean?"

"I mean I know Allard," Lucinda said. "You can't depend on him, Diana. Something will catch his fancy, some new adventure, and he'll forget all about his promises to marry you and give up the sea."

"That's not true. We swore to each other—"

Lucinda laughed with more than a touch of scorn in her voice. "I know. You swore to love each other forever and to be together always. Do you really believe that? Are you really that naive? Men always say things like that, but they never mean them."

"Allard did," Diana insisted. She didn't know why she was arguing with Lucinda. It couldn't serve any good purpose.

"Well, when you're alone again and realize that it was all just a lie, you remember that I told you. I suppose I care about Allard—he's my brother, after all—but in the end he's still just a man."

Lucinda turned and walked toward the house, and as Diana watched her go, she didn't know whether to hate her—or pity her. Lucinda thought she knew the truth, but she was wrong.

In the end, Diana thought, love was stronger than this war, stronger than the distance that separated her and Allard, stronger than any obstacles that might arise between them. Time would tell the story.

Time and the tides that would carry Allard Tyler back to her.